WINDS OF DEATH

WINDS OF DEATH

WAR OF THE ALLIANCE

4

TARA GRAYCE

WINDS OF DEATH

Published by Sword & Cross Publishing

Grand Rapids, MI

Cover by Deranged Doctor Designs

Map by Md Shah Alam on Fiverr

Fort Defense Map by Zs Graphics on Fiverr

This book is a work of fiction. All characters, events, and settings are the product of the author's over-active imagination. Any resemblance to any person, living or dead, events, or settings is purely coincidental or used fictitiously.

To God, my King and Father. Soli Deo Gloria

LCCN: 2025913032

ISBN: 978-1-943442-64-5

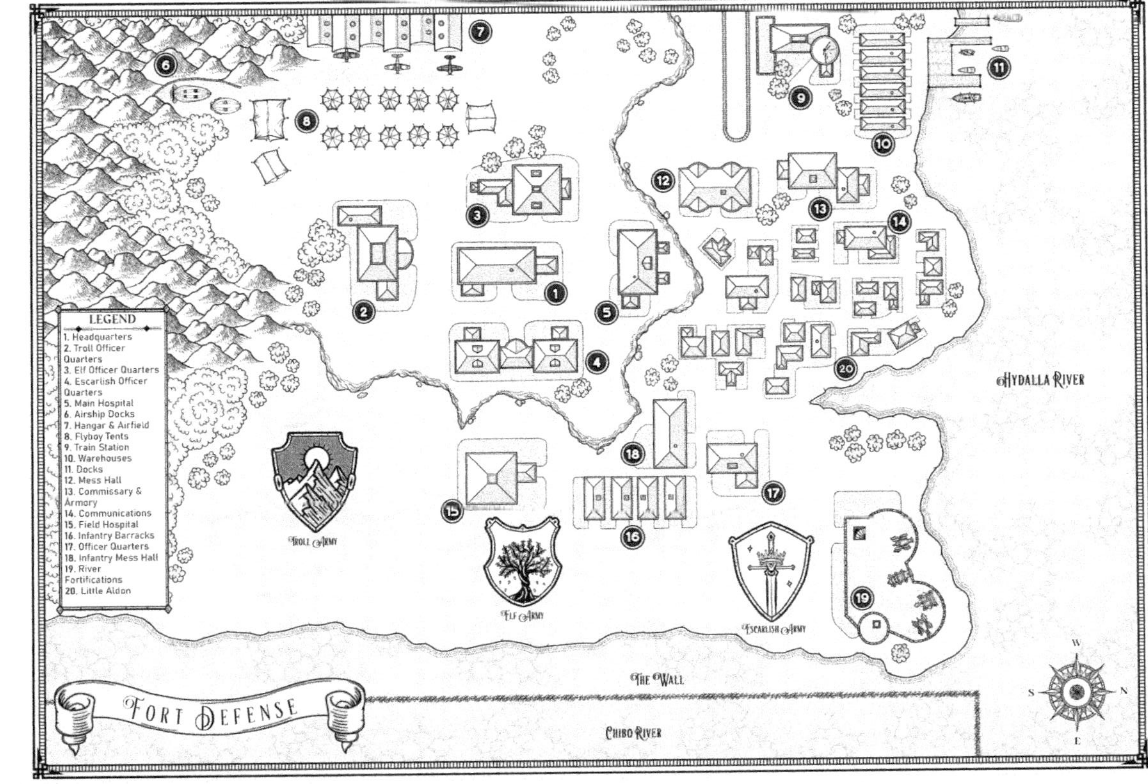

FORT DEFENSE
LEGEND
1. Headquarters
2. Troll Officer Quarters
3. Elf Officer Quarters
4. Escarlish Officer Quarters
5. Main Hospital
6. Airship Docks
7. Hangar & Airfield
8. Flyboy Tents
9. Train Station
10. Warehouses
11. Docks
12. Mess Hall
13. Commissary & Armory
14. Communications
15. Field Hospital
16. Infantry Barracks
17. Officer Quarters
18. Infantry Mess Hall
19. River Fortifications
20. Little Aldon
TROLL ARMY
ELF ARMY
ESCARLISH ARMY
HYDALLA RIVER
THE WALL
CHIBO RIVER

DWARVEN MOUNTAINS
MT. DETMUK
AFRISTANI PLAINS
Milnissi River
WESTE
TERMI

KOSTARIA
OSMANA
TINENRESH
DAR GORANTH
DROGENVROSH ISLAND
URIX DOR ISLAND
BRENZUK ISLAND
PEACE BRIDGE
Gulmorth River
TARENHIEL
LETHOREL
ESTYRA
NINTHALOR
PERSATRA AERODROME
SYLMARE
BRIDGETOWN
FORT LINDER
FORT DEFENSE
CHIBO RIVER
Hydalla River
PINE RIVER
AYRE
WINDERION LAKE
TREEHAVEN
ALDON
FORT CHARIBERT
WHITEHURST MOUNTAINS
LANDRI
DANORBIC OCEAN
ESCARLAND
MONGAVARIAN EMPIRE
Frogg's Hollow
GROYRIA
RN RAIL
NAL
N
W
E
S
THE WORLD OF THE
ALLIANCE KINGDOMS

Capt. Fieran Laesornysh lay strapped to a stretcher as the train rattled its way across the Escarlish countryside.

All around him, men moaned and cried out. Stretchers were attached to the walls of the train car in stacks three high. He couldn't see how far to each side of him the stretchers ran, but they must fill the train car from one side to the other. Or nearly so. A few of the spaces across the way from him were empty.

But Pip sat on the floor at his side, holding his hand. Throughout the whole trip as he slept and woke and slept again, she'd been there.

Fieran tried his best to keep his grip on her hand gentle, despite the ache spreading through him. It wasn't up to pain level, much less intense agony just yet, but it would get there before too long. Especially with all this jostling.

But the dangers of morphine use were better understood now than they had been years ago. The elven healers would do their best to make sure he didn't become addicted, but he'd rather he didn't rely on it more than necessary.

A nurse halted next to Fieran's tier, checking on the two men on stretchers above him. Both of them seemed to still be unconscious so the nurse moved on to Fieran. She checked his pulse. "How is your pain?"

"Manageable." Fieran squashed the temptation to let his magic flood through his veins. As much as his magic might fortify him, it would also burn through the last of the morphine and healing magic all the faster. Not to mention make it that much harder for the elf healer in Aldon to banish the pain.

The nurse pressed her mouth into a tight line as she jotted a note on a clipboard. "Then if you can manage, we are almost to Aldon. It would be best to wait on any more medication until an elven healer has seen you."

As he'd suspected.

Fieran nodded, doing his best not to wince as he breathed through the growing pain.

The nurse turned to Pip. "Miss, since we're nearing Aldon, I'm going to have to ask you to step back into the passenger car. You'll be disembarking separately from the wounded."

Pip nodded and gave Fieran's hand a squeeze. "I'll stop at the hospital when I can."

Then she was pulling her fingers free and pushing to her feet. She gave him one last pat on the shoulder before she disappeared from his view, her footsteps echoing on the wooden floor of the train car.

He shouldn't feel such a sense of loss. He'd see her again. He wasn't sure when, but he would.

Yet it was hard to let her go after holding her hand so tightly for the past few hours. Far harder with so much still unresolved between them. They hadn't had a moment alone since he'd crashed to continue their interrupted conversation.

And that interrupted kiss.

A stab of guilt joined the pain flaring through him. After everything that had happened, how could he dwell on thoughts of kissing? Merrik had lost his leg because of Fieran's mistakes.

If Fieran's propeller hadn't broken, then he wouldn't have crashed. Then Merrik wouldn't have crashed.

After all that, how dare Fieran think about romance?

He wrapped the fingers of his good hand around the pair of swords that lay next to him on the stretcher. A poor substitute for the warmth of her hand but better than nothing.

The train shuddered, giving a whistle as it came into the station.

A few of the others woke at the noise and the change in motion, filling the train car with even more noise as they asked the nurses for water, cried out in pain, or asked where they were and what was going on.

Once the train settled into a halt, men and women wearing basic green coveralls climbed onto the train and began unhooking stretchers from the wall before carrying them out onto the platform.

Fieran could do nothing but tap his fingers as he waited his turn. He wasn't used to being this helpless. Right now, he couldn't walk off this train. He couldn't even lift his legs, splinted as they both were all the way to his waist to keep his broken bones from shifting. One of his arms was pinned in a splint as well, leaving him with one limb he could move.

At least he had all four limbs. Unlike Merrik.

That sourness churned in his stomach again, and he had to restrain his magic from leaping to his fingertips.

Two of the volunteers finally reached him, jostling him as

they unhooked his stretcher from the brackets on the wall. They carried him down the aisle of the train car, then worked their way out the small door set in the side that was barely wider than the stretcher.

As he was carried onto the platform, he had to squint at the sunlight slanting through the glass arching over the station. The noise of incoming and departing trains reverberated through the space, punctuated with the hubbub of bustling people, talking and laughing as they went.

The volunteers set Fieran's stretcher down in the row they were creating along the platform before they left to retrieve the next man.

To one side, the brick wall of the station showed a large clock with its hands pointing at the late afternoon hour. On the other side, military police guarded a temporary barrier that divided this part of the station from the rest of it, even from the front part of the train where the few civilians and able-bodied military personnel on leave were disembarking.

A woman dressed in a white shirt and the tan bicycle bloomers that were all the rage in Escarland, her long red hair in a braid down her back, moved between the various men and women on stretchers. She paused by each wounded man, crouching in a lady-like fashion as she spoke to them, smiling as she did. The men lit up, their injuries temporarily forgotten in the warmth of meeting their princess.

Mama. Fieran released a breath. Perhaps it was silly—childish—to feel better knowing his mama was there, but he did.

As she stood, she turned, and her gaze landed on Fieran. For one heartbeat, her smile vanished into a look of utter devastation as she swayed backward.

Then she blinked, and the smile returned to her face, so

bright and natural even Fieran couldn't tell how much was genuine and how much was her mask.

In that moment, he understood his mama's strength. She might not fight on the front lines like Dacha, despite having the ability to wield his magic. But she had a core of iron to face the consequences of war with a smile.

She took the time to speak to a few more of the wounded before she reached Fieran. As she lowered herself into that graceful, princess crouch, her smile widened, her tone light. "I knew one of you would return home to me on a stretcher. I just expected it would be your dacha."

Fieran smiled in return, his voice as light as hers, despite the pain aching in his limbs and the choking lump filling his throat. "You know how accident-prone I am."

"Makes me wonder why you chose such an accident-prone part of the army." Mama shook her head, her smile never wavering. Her gaze dropped to the swords beside him, a twist almost like bemusement curving her smile, before she flagged down a pair of the volunteers. "Take this one to my truck, please. The front seat."

"Yes, Your Highness." The volunteers bowed before they bent to pick up his stretcher.

Mama stood as he was picked up, giving his shoulder one last pat before she moved on to the next injured man.

Fieran was carried out of a pair of wooden double doors guarded by more MPs, the noise of the train station changing to the noise of the bustling city of Aldon.

Outside along the back alley, various trucks waited in a line. Some were the green, army-style vehicles. Others were farm trucks with open beds that had temporary canvas coverings rigged over them. Still more were delivery trucks like the familiar AMPC truck, which waited third in line. Perhaps these vehicles had been pressed into service, or their drivers had volunteered their use for transporting the wounded.

At the truck with the AMPC logo emblazoned on the side, the volunteer at Fieran's head opened the double doors and set Fieran down on the floor of the cargo bed. The other volunteer shoved at Fieran's feet, and he and his stretcher slid over the wooden floor.

Where the stretcher normally would have hit the end of the cargo compartment, he instead was shoved through a hatch now connecting the rear cargo space with the front cab.

Usually, this cab had a passenger seat as well as a small bench seat in the back where Fieran and his siblings had often crammed.

Now, the passenger seat and the bench seat had been removed, and the stretcher rested on a board that had been bolted to the seat brackets to keep the stretcher flat.

Fieran found himself lying on his back with his head near the dashboard. His feet were sticking somewhere into the cargo area at the rear. Others would likely be loaded into the back with the stretchers set on brackets bolted to the wall, much like the train.

He was left alone for a while, and he closed his eyes to somewhat rest while he listened to the sounds of bustle and the occasional louder noises as someone was loaded into the back by his feet. The truck's windows were open, letting in the occasional breath of a breeze along with a few buzzing flies. At least this alley was shaded by the surrounding buildings so that it wasn't as hot as it could have been.

The driver's door opened, and Fieran opened his eyes as Mama climbed into the truck and settled into the seat. She sent a smile at him as she flipped the switches, then depressed a lever, cranking the engine on. "Comfortable?"

Not really. The bruises on his back and shoulders ached against the board beneath him, and his bones throbbed with each vibration the engine sent through the vehicle. His pain would only get worse once the truck set off across the cobbled roads that wound through the city.

But he matched Mama's smile and gave a shrug. "Comfortable enough."

"I'll have you at the hospital soon. They have the route cleared for us so we won't have to fight traffic." Mama pressed the clutch and worked the gear shift as she eased the truck forward.

Since he couldn't see what was happening outside the truck, Fieran could only guess that the line of vehicles had begun moving, setting off on the route to the main hospital in Aldon.

Mama worked the pedals, the gear shift, and the steering wheel smoothly as she guided the large vehicle out of the small alley and into what must have been another narrow, cobbled road that hadn't been designed for a truck like this.

"Do you volunteer to drive the wounded to the hospital often?" Fieran gestured at the cab. These weren't the modifications one would make for a single trip.

"It's a way to help out, and the AMPC had a vehicle we could volunteer." Mama shrugged as she peered at the mirrors and spun the large wheel to turn the truck down another road. "It's something I can do to help the war effort."

War effort. Fieran had been on military bases since the war began. Despite the letters he'd received, he still hadn't anticipated the changes that the war would make at home.

"Where are Ellie and Tryndar?" As much as he missed his younger siblings, he wasn't sure he was ready to see them just yet. He'd rather be a little more healed—and in a little less pain—when he saw them.

"With your Aunt Jalissa at Buckmore Cottage." Mama worked the gear shift, and the truck slowed to a crawl. "Ellie has been coming with me to visit those in the hospital—only some of the wards. Not the more serious ones. But I haven't brought Tryndar."

She didn't have to explain why. Beyond the fact that Tryndar was still very young, he was also sensitive.

"Normally they hang out with Louise at the AMPC. She has been staying there rather than commuting back to Treehaven each day. It's safer, and she's on hand to protect Aldon from bombing." Mama said this so matter-of-factly, as if bombing were a normal thing, even here in Aldon. "But Louise is meeting your mechanic friend at the train. She'll be staying at the AMPC as well."

Fieran eyed Mama. Did she know Pip was more than just a friend? Mama wasn't looking at him as she concentrated on guiding the truck slowly forward through an alley so narrow that Fieran could see the brick walls on either side through the windows.

Yet there was an undercurrent to Mama's voice, as if she was trying to be too casual. And surely she had to suspect something, if Dacha did. Especially if Dacha was the one who had gone through all the trouble of orchestrating Pip being sent to Aldon. Dacha didn't keep such things a secret from Mama.

But Fieran couldn't be sure. Mama was too good at hiding behind her smile.

Not that he minded if what he felt for Pip remained unacknowledged in this conversation. He had too much to discuss with Pip before he discussed any of it with his mama.

"I'm glad. Louise will help her settle in." Fieran worked to keep his own tone neutral. Just discussing a colleague, a friend. Nothing more. He clamped his mouth shut before he babbled something else about Pip. Like how much she would enjoy working at the AMPC. It would probably feel like a dream come true, even for a few weeks on temporary assignment.

But if Fieran started talking about Pip, there was no way he'd be able to hide the depth of his feelings for her.

The brick walls on either side disappeared, and Mama turned the truck one last time. She applied the brakes and the truck eased to a stop.

Mama smiled and half-turned in the seat to face him. "I have to make a second trip, but I'll come see you once I'm finished."

Fieran nodded, a sense of relief filling him. Getting settled into the hospital bed probably wasn't going to be pleasant. There were some things he would rather his mama did not witness.

Her smile grew a hint mischievous, a twinkle in her green eyes. "I know you're probably too old for this, but..." She leaned over and pressed a light kiss to his forehead.

"Mama..." His protest was more teasing than anything else. Perhaps it was that childishness brought on by pain and helplessness, but he rather hoped his mama's kiss made everything better as it always had when he'd been a child.

"All better?" Her smile still had that faintly teasing tilt, even if there was something to the look in her eyes. As if she wished he was still a child with a child's injuries that could be kissed away so easily.

"All better." He forced the words and the smile, even as he gritted his teeth against the pain gaining in intensity with every moment.

An orderly strode up to Mama's window, cleared his throat, and held up a clipboard. "Your Highness?"

"Yes. Let's get them unloaded." Mama turned away from Fieran, her expression instantly smoothing into her practiced princess smile, as she opened her door and stepped down to the road.

After only a short wait, Fieran was carried into the hospital and taken by lift to the second floor. There, he was set on one of the metal-framed beds that lined the walls. Several nurses descended, cheerfully seeing to his needs and getting him wrestled into a fresh hospital gown. By the time the whole ordeal was over, whatever pain medication and healing magic had been in his system had thoroughly vanished. He might just cry and beg for relief—he might even take another one of his mama's kisses to see if that would help—as he tried to breathe through it.

"Prince Fieran Laesornysh. Why am I not surprised to find you in my hospital ward?" The deep, dry tone rang from beside the bed.

Fieran peeled his eyes open, trying to smile with his jaw tightly clenched. "Healer Nylian. Good to see you."

Even better if the elf healer hurried up and used his magic.

Nylian, a tall elf healer with brown hair and a long, straight nose, eyed Fieran before he placed a hand on Fieran's forehead. The healer's gaze went distant as his healing magic sank into Fieran.

Fieran didn't have to work as hard to keep his magic in check as Nylian's healing magic washed through him. Perhaps his magic recognized Nylian's, given how often Fieran had been healed by Nylian while growing up.

As Nylian's magic swept through him, the pain receded, and Fieran could finally take in a deep breath once again.

His exhaustion pressed even deeper into him, an ache behind his eyes and at his temples that the healing magic didn't touch.

Nylian gave one last *hmm* before he withdrew his hand. "Given your injuries, you are in remarkably good condition. Although, I should not be surprised. The magic of the ancient kings seems to grant its wielders an incredible resilience."

Fieran let his eyes fall closed. That seemed like something rather important, but he was far too tired to question Nylian now. If Nylian said anything else, he didn't hear it as he slipped into sleep.

TWO

Clutching her bag, Pip joined the handful of other civilians and on-leave military personnel as they stepped off the train onto the platform in Aldon.

A glass ceiling arched overhead, supported by steel girders while brick walls rose on all sides. Several brick platforms ran along the train tracks while raised walkways allowed train passengers to move between the platforms. King's Central Station was the main train hub in Aldon, and one Pip was rather familiar with from her time at Hanford University.

On this particular platform, the closest to the station building, the end of the train was cordoned off by MPs. Pip stood on her tiptoes, but she couldn't see past the wall of men to spot if Fieran had been unloaded yet.

With a deep breath, Pip halted and stared at the bustle. Where was she supposed to go from here? Her orders had been rather vague. She was on temporary reassignment to the AMPC—the Alliance Magical Power Company. But what did that mean? Was she supposed to report in there? Or to a local military post before being sent there? Where would she be staying?

"Are you Pippak Detmuk-Inawenys?" A tall young woman with silver-blonde hair and striking light blue eyes strode from the crowd. There was something familiar about the shape of her face, the color of her hair.

"Yes?" Pip gripped her bag tighter, not sure why that came out a question rather than a statement. She shouldn't feel this off-kilter here in Aldon, not after she'd spent several years here studying at university.

But yet again, she found herself in an all-new situation, unsure of exactly what her purpose here might be.

"I'm Louise Laesornysh. It's a pleasure to meet you." The young woman stuck out her hand, a warm smile breaking onto her face.

And then Pip saw it. The silver-blonde hair and light blue eyes Louise had inherited from her dacha, Prince Farrendel Laesornysh. The smile that was so reminiscent of Fieran's, though Louise's had a little more serenity than Fieran's grin. The pointed ears that showed Louise's elven ancestry.

"Call me Pip." Pip took Louise's hand and shook it, trying to pretend her heart wasn't hammering. A year ago, she would have been intimidated enough, meeting one of Prince Farrendel's and Princess Essie's daughters. But now she was meeting one of Fieran's sisters, and that made this moment all the more important. Louise wouldn't know it, but Pip certainly did. Worse, Fieran wasn't even here to smooth the way.

Worse still, Pip wasn't sure where she stood with Fieran. She'd distracted him right at a critical moment, just as he'd feared, and it had caused Fieran to crash and cost Merrik his leg. Granted, she and Fieran had done a pretty thorough job of distracting each other. She wasn't all to blame.

But she certainly felt like she was to blame. Would Fieran feel the same way, once all the healing magic and drugs wore off?

That left her off-balance not just with Fieran but with his whole family.

"I'm afraid I didn't take the roadster—conserving magical power cells and all that—so we'll be taking the Underground." Louise turned and led the way through the crowded station, headed for a set of stairs leading downward. "Is your bag heavy? We can take turns carrying it."

"Not that heavy." Pip heaved the bag a little higher. She'd left most of her tools with Mak, trusting that he would see that they were sent to her if she didn't end up back at Fort Defense after this temporary reassignment. She'd taken her favorite wrench, of course, along with her clothes and other miscellaneous items.

"All right. Just let me know if you need a break." Louise looked over her shoulder and shot Pip a smile before she shoved her way into the throng of people headed down the stairs for the Underground.

Pip dove after her, trying to keep up as the taller young woman navigated the crowd with far too much ease.

Louise had already taken the time to purchase tickets for both of them so they hopped on the next train headed in the right direction. The train was already packed, so the two of them stood in the aisle. Louise held on to one of the leather straps hanging from overhead while Pip gripped a pole and braced her feet.

The underground train began moving, the tug pulling against Pip. Air whooshed past her face, then everything steadied and they were clacking through the nearly dark tunnels, lights flashing past the windows, and the overhead lights almost too bright. Louise swayed gracefully with the train's movement, all tall elven grace.

As they came to a station, the train slowed, a rush of air coming from the back of the train, before it halted. It was a familiar sensation, both from taking the trains that wound underground through the dwarven mountains and from Pip's time here in Aldon while at university. The Underground had been expanded and improved in the years since she'd last been in Aldon, but many of the main stops and stations were familiar.

Pip and Louise took the Underground for two more stops before they got off and switched to another train. They took this train for three stops before hopping off. After navigating through the underground station, they climbed up the stairs and out onto a sunlit, brick-paved square surrounded by tall buildings, also built of brick.

Louise led the way down the street. At the end, they were confronted with a high brick wall with an iron gate set in the road before them. The wall had a faint blue tint, and Pip could sense the subdued but waiting crackle of Prince Farrendel's magic in the stones before her. The tops of huge buildings were visible over the wall, iron walks connecting them, while the hum of machinery filled the air and vibrated through the cobblestones beneath Pip's boots.

Louise showed her badge to the guards at the gate, then gestured to Pip. "This is Pippak Detmuk-Inawenys. She's an expected guest."

One of the guards consulted a list, nodded, and allowed them to pass.

Pip tried not to gape as she strolled between the large warehouses and factories that made up the AMPC complex. So much activity and bustle. So much magic of many kinds radiating from various buildings.

A part of her wanted to clap her hands and squeal like a little girl. This was everything she had dreamed of growing up, and time hadn't dimmed the wonder of the melding of mechanics and magic going on in this place.

She had visited before during her time at Hanford University. Yet she'd been so overwhelmed back then and so nervous about possibly catching a glimpse of Prince Farrendel Laesornysh that she hadn't been able to truly take it in.

Now she'd met Prince Farrendel, and she knew she wasn't going to accidentally run into him here. She'd grown, thanks to the army forcing her to take charge more than she ever had before.

As they passed each building, Louise pointed to each of them. "There's where the empty magical power cells are made. Here's where the filled ones are stored before they're distributed. That building over there refurbishes used magical power cells before they are filled again. This building is where engines and other mechanics from various non-AMPC companies are tested before they are certified as compatible with the magical power cells. It's also where we fill the power cells."

Pip gazed around, trying to absorb it all, but there was too much bustle.

As they neared another building, a large troll man in overalls approached them. "Louise, can I get your signature for the next batch of magical power cells to be shipped out?"

"Sure." Louise took the clipboard from him, scrawled her name on the bottom of a page, and handed it back. Then she gestured from Pip to the troll. "Pip, this is Voron. He's in charge of overseeing the day-to-day operations here at the AMPC. Voron, this is Pippak Detmuk-Inawenys. She's going to be working here at the AMPC for the next little bit."

"Nice to meet you, Pippak." Voron gave her a wide smile and tipped his head to her. "I'm sure I'll be seeing you around."

"Likely. She's going to be living with me here in the AMPC." Louise turned from Voron to Pip. "Voron, his wife Rikze, and their two girls also live here in the AMPC complex. Rikze is my Aunt Vriska's younger sister."

That answered the question of where she would be staying. Pip smiled and returned Voron's nod. "I didn't have the pleasure of actually speaking with the general, but I saw her and General Julien Ardon a couple of times while at Dar Goranth and Fort Defense."

She'd heard that the famous troll general had led the reinforcements who rescued Fieran, but she hadn't seen that for herself. She'd been busy rescuing Merrik and defending headquarters at that point.

Voron tipped his head to Pip again. "Rikze will be happy to help if you need anything. Good to have you here."

With that, he moved off, the clipboard tucked under one arm.

Louise pointed to the building ahead of them. "This is the main building where we will be working." She pushed open one of the double doors and led the way inside.

Pip followed before letting the door swing shut behind her.

This building didn't have the bustle she'd heard from inside the other buildings. Here the cavernous space had a few random piles of junk along the sides. The center held what seemed to be scattered work stations where everything from some type of engine to a half-assembled biplane rested.

Louise strode between the work stations before she halted by a contraption so strange that even Pip wasn't sure what it might be for.

Two men worked on the machine, goggles over their eyes and wearing nearly identical long vests with multiple pockets. One had darker, sandy-blond hair while the other's was a lighter blond. The man with the lighter blond hair was slightly taller and appeared younger, but both of them had a slim build.

"Do you think we need to adjust the transducer?" The young man with the lighter hair spoke as Pip and Louise approached, but he seemed to be speaking to the other man instead of them. Neither man so much as glanced up.

"Hmm. Possibly."

"Uncle Lance, Bennett. Our guest is here." Louise raised her voice, as if the two men were hard of hearing.

The one with the darker hair flapped a hand at her. "Good. Good."

Louise sighed and shook her head. She pointed at the man with the slightly darker hair. "Pip, that's my Uncle Lance. And this is his and Aunt Illyna's oldest, Bennett. Proper introductions will have to wait until they are less wrapped up in a project."

"I can see that." Pip switched her bag to her other hand. It wasn't that heavy, but it would be nice to set it down.

"Sorry, I'll hurry this up. But cutting through this building is the shortest way to the apartments." Louise led the way farther into the building, and she halted by the half-assembled biplane. "Here's one of the things I'm hoping you can help with. We've been trying to figure out how to stop bullets from hitting the propeller." Louise's expression turned grim, her voice going a bit rough. "As you can imagine, we're even more motivated now."

Pip nodded, flexing the fingers of her free hand. A broken propeller had sent Fieran plummeting from the sky. "I'll help in any way I can. Especially with this."

"We've reconstructed the interrupter gear the Mongavarians have been using." Louise pointed to a mechanism of gears and wires in the engine compartment. "But it's glitchy. It works, but not reliably. Production has started on this model, but I think between all of us, we can come up with something better."

"Anything is better than nothing." Pip tried to push the thoughts of Fieran falling from the sky out of her mind.

"Yes." Louise blinked as she turned away, that cheery note returning to her voice as she pointed to the far wall, where several gigantic spools of braided cable wires rested. "And we were hoping you would also find time to infuse those with your magic so that more shields like the one you created for Dar Goranth can be built around other places. Contrary to what that first impression might lead you to believe, Uncle Lance has been begging Uncle Julien to reassign you here for months. It wasn't until now that Uncle Julien agreed."

So was it Fieran's Uncle Julien who had seen to it that she'd been sent here? On the long train ride during the few minutes he'd been awake, Fieran had shared with her some of his suspicions that his dacha had been behind her new assignment. Perhaps all three of them—his dacha and uncles—had colluded to get her here. At least it was beneficial for the war effort.

Still, it was daunting, realizing just how easily his family could move people about on a whim. Fieran's family had *power*.

"Easy enough." Shaking off her thoughts, Pip studied the spools, noting the big track in the ceiling for moving them. She'd have to rig up something to wind one spool to another one as she infused the wire with her magic. If Louise and the others didn't mind her making herself at home.

Louise grinned, the expression so reminiscent of Fieran's that it hurt deep inside Pip's chest. "I think you're going to fit in nicely here at the AMPC. Let's wrap up your tour and show you where you'll be staying."

They exited the large warehouse into what must have been an alley between it and the next building. But now it had a glass roof while the space had lovely metal tables and chairs scattered within, separated by planters bursting with vibrant blooms and small bushes.

"This is where many of us who work in the inventing room take our lunches. You're welcome to eat here as well." Louise gestured around them, then back at the warehouse they'd just left. "We were just in what was the original building. This other one is mostly storage and contains Aunt Illyna's workspace. There's a garden on the roof that you're welcome to visit during breaks, especially if you're the type who needs a lot of green and growing things around."

"No. Half-dwarf and all that." Pip shrugged, resting a hand on one of the metal tables as she and Louise strode past. "Given my magic, the metal calls to me more than plants."

"That makes sense." Louise shot her a grin as she opened a door set in the end of the alley.

This door led into a small courtyard with the outer wall surrounding the AMPC on one side, the wall of another building to the other side, and a small apartment building ahead of them.

Louise led the way inside the door on the right, then climbed the stairs to the second floor. "And here we are. Home away from home for both of us. I wish we could give you your own space, but all the units are claimed now that I've moved in for the duration of the war. But my unit has two bedrooms."

"I've had to share ever since I joined the mechanics auxiliary, so just having my own bedroom is a luxury now." Pip strode inside the neat space. A few miscellaneous items rested on a bench near the door while a table with two chairs sat in a small kitchen area. Several doors led off from the main area, presumably the two bedrooms and a washroom.

Louise shut the door behind them before she stepped past Pip into the main area of the space. She halted near the table, resting her hands on the back of one of the chairs as if she wasn't sure what else to do with them. "I'm planning on visiting Fieran tomorrow morning. If you'd like to come."

"Of course." Pip bit her lip. Had her agreement sounded too eager?

Then again, did she have to wait for Louise and go tomorrow morning? Why not brave Aldon and visit tonight? Unless the hospital had visiting hours she didn't know about.

"I'd rather go tonight, but Mama cautioned that we should give him some space to rest before everyone descends on him." Louise shifted, her voice going rough.

That made far too much sense. Pip's heart squeezed, but she let go of any thoughts of rushing to the hospital that night. Fieran would be busy resting, and no doubt the elf healers here would want to accomplish the next stage of healing, which would wipe him out further.

Besides, Pip wasn't family. She wasn't officially his girlfriend. They might not even let her see him, depending on how strict the hospital was about visitors.

As hard as waiting until tomorrow was on Pip, it had to be harder on Louise. She hadn't seen Fieran in months. Not since he'd left to join the army. Pip, at least, had seen Fieran since his crash and reassured herself that he was all right. Louise hadn't.

Pip set down her bag and walked to the other side of the table from Louise. If she and Fieran had actually been courting, she might have dared to give Louise a hug as she would a sister. Not that Pip had a whole lot of experience with sisters. All she had was a big brother.

"Fieran is going to be all right." Pip held Louise's gaze, trying to put as much reassurance into her voice as she could. "Yes, he was hurt pretty badly. But he's going to be fine."

"I know." Louise dropped her gaze, shifting as if she wanted to turn away, her voice even more rough. "But hearing about Fieran's injuries and then Merrik's…it's just hard when I can't even hug him."

Perhaps this was the moment when Pip should hug Louise. But she didn't know her well enough for that yet.

"Then let's get our mind off our worries tonight." Pip managed a smile. "I've been stuck on army bases with mostly guys for the past several months. I'd enjoy a girls' night."

"I'd like that." The smile returned to Louise's face, though not all of the worry faded from her eyes. "There's a bakery just a short walk down the street. With the sugar rationing, I'm not sure what they'll have left at this time of night, but we can see what we can get. Then we can come back here, make tea, coffee, hot chocolate, or whatever you prefer, and chat."

"Sounds good." After the long train ride, Pip was up for a short stroll through the neighborhood. Hopefully it would relieve the last of her restless energy and worries for Fieran.

And there was just something about Louise that made Pip relax. Louise wasn't family, and Pip didn't know if she ever would be. But she would be a fast friend before the night was out.

THREE

Pip trotted at Louise's heels as they followed the orderly up the hospital's stairs to the second floor. She tried to pretend she wasn't fidgeting, her stomach churning. How would Fieran react to seeing her? Would he be more awake than he had been when she'd last seen him?

Once they reached the second floor, the orderly led them down the aisle between the beds lined up on either side of the room. Most had their curtains drawn, but Pip caught glimpses of men still sleeping.

Perhaps Fieran would still be asleep. After all, she and Louise were coming rather early to squeeze the visit in before heading back to the AMPC to start work for the day.

The orderly halted in the middle of the room by a bed still hidden behind curtains and gestured to it. "This one."

Pip froze in the aisle. Well, Fieran was still asleep. They'd come all this way, and she wouldn't even get to see him.

Instead of turning to leave, Louise marched to the end of the curtain and gripped it, though she didn't fling it open right away. "Fieran, you had better be awake and decent."

"Louise?" Fieran's voice came from behind the curtain, rather more awake and alert than Pip would have expected. "Yeah. Come on in."

Louise shoved the curtain aside and stepped closer to the bed, leaving Pip little choice but to follow.

When Pip peeked around the curtain, Louise was bending over, giving Fieran a hug as he lay on the bed. "I'm glad you're all right."

Pip hesitated again. Perhaps this had been a bad idea. Was she intruding on what should be a family moment?

"Good to see you too, Weezer." Fieran grinned at his sister as she pulled back and gave him a light swat on the arm. Likely because of the use of her nickname.

Then Fieran's gaze swung past Louise to focus on Pip. For a moment, his grin dropped, and he reached for the blanket with one hand while trying to shove himself more upright with the elbow of the arm encased in a splint. "Pip. Uh, hello. I..."

Pip crept closer, trying to work up a smile. "You seem to be feeling better."

"Yeah." Fieran stopped trying to push himself upright and instead ran a hand over his hair, as if to smooth it. Not that the gesture did much good. His red hair stuck up in all directions and was especially flattened and sticking at odd angles in the back, likely from lying down for so long.

He wore a hospital gown, and he seemed determined to keep the thin hospital blanket pulled all the way up his chest.

All three of them lapsed into silence. Louise edged toward the chair set beside the bed, then glanced at Pip as if wondering if she should offer the chair to her instead. It was the only one. If both of them were to sit, one of them would have to sit on the edge of Fieran's bed.

Louise was currently closest to the chair, and Pip would have to edge awkwardly around her to take it.

Besides, this was Fieran. Pip had held his hand most of the train ride from Fort Defense. She'd braved the awkwardness of facing his dacha to see him after he crashed. She'd whispered with Fieran during moving pictures and fixed aeroplanes with him. If Louise hadn't been there—if things hadn't been so unsettled between them—Pip wouldn't have thought more than twice about sitting on the edge of his bed.

Before Louise could offer the chair, Pip boosted herself onto the edge of Fieran's bed next to his legs. The metal framed hospital bed sat high enough that her feet didn't touch the floor anymore once she was settled.

Something in Fieran's expression eased, and not just because his grin finally returned. He relaxed against his pillow again. "Have you settled in at the AMPC?"

Louise glanced between the two of them before she sank onto the chair, as if putting the pieces together of just how she'd ended up the third wheel on this visit.

"Somewhat. It was overwhelming yesterday. But I'm eager to get to work today." Pip forced herself to look away from Fieran to include Louise in the conversation. "Louise has been making me feel welcome."

Louise smiled back, though something searching remained in her expression. "I think you'll fit in great at the AMPC."

"Yeah, Pip is amazing." Fieran held her gaze for a moment before he blinked and looked away. "I mean, her magic is amazing."

Pip's face felt hot, and she stared down at her hands in her lap. Was Fieran still hopped up on drugs and healing magic? How much could she really trust anything he said at the moment, no matter how lucid he looked?

With the squeak of a wheeled cart, a nurse pushed aside a curtain. "Pardon me. I have breakfast for Capt. Laesornysh." The nurse picked up one of the trays from her cart and bustled past Pip and Louise to set the tray on the table beside Fieran. "Will you need help eating?"

"No." Fieran's ears turned red, and he struggled to sit up. He couldn't quite bend at the waist, and the nurse hurried to plump the pillows behind him to hold him somewhat upright.

Pip slid off the bed and glanced at Louise. "I think we should be going."

If she'd been there alone with Fieran—if their relationship had been more than it currently was—then Pip might have stayed. Perhaps she would have taken over the nurse's job and helped Fieran eat his breakfast.

But they weren't at that point, and right now, Fieran would find it more embarrassing than anything. The best thing they could do was gracefully bow out and let him retain some of his dignity.

Louise rose to her feet and stepped out of the nurse's way. "Yes. We don't want to be late on Pip's first day."

"I'm glad you came." Fieran glanced between them, not reaching for his food just yet. Perhaps it was her imagination, but his gaze lingered longer on Pip than on Louise, as if he, too, was aching with all the words that needed to be said.

"We'll come again as soon as we can." Louise gave Fieran one last hug.

Pip forced herself to turn away and follow Louise around the curtain into the aisle of the hospital ward, all while trying to pretend that visit hadn't been more than a little disappointing.

Pip sat on a table with her back to the brick wall. While she and Louise had been visiting the hospital, a work crew had rigged two spools of the large cables so that one spool would wind onto another spool. The machinery to turn the spools was fueled by a magical power cell and controlled by a foot pedal.

She pressed the foot pedal with her right foot, easing the cable forward beneath her hands. As she did so, she rested her fingers on the cable and infused it with her magic bit by bit.

The magic and repetitive motion was soothing after the emotional turmoil of the morning. She desperately needed to *talk* with Fieran. But she couldn't while he was in the public ward of the hospital with so many people around.

When would she have a chance? If she wanted to visit the hospital alone, she'd have to tell Louise…and Louise was bound to have questions. If Pip waited until Fieran was discharged, he would be sent home and constantly surrounded by his family.

It seemed the only way she'd get a chance to talk to him alone would be to admit to his family that they were something more than just friends. And that seemed far too presumptuous when Fieran would likely break up with her the moment they had a chance to talk.

Pip blinked, shook herself, and shoved those thoughts away. Her magic flared through her, and she poured the excess of magic and emotion into the cable.

This was so frustrating. If she could only resolve things between her and Fieran one way or the other, she could finally stop obsessing over it. Being stuck in this limbo was worse than just hashing it out.

"Pip?"

Pip started, and her foot pressed harder on the pedal. The

machine whined as it tried to ramp up the speed on the spool containing the heavy wire. She hurriedly relaxed her foot before she burnt out the mechanics of the machinery. "Yes?"

Louise stepped around one of the other spools of cable that waited for Pip to infuse with her magic. "Do you have a moment? I'd appreciate a fresh pair of eyes."

"Sure." Pip stood, awkwardly stepped over the cable, and hopped from the table to the floor. Any chance to get out of her own head was more than welcome.

After they'd returned from the hospital, both of them had shrugged into sets of brown coveralls over their clothes, with Pip rolling up the sleeves and pant legs of hers. The rolls made her wrists and ankles bulky, but she could manage. Pip had tied back her hair, but Louise had left hers long and flowing around her shoulders, as if daring grease to get into her elven hair.

They rounded the spools, both empty and full, and approached the half-assembled aeroplane. It perched directly on its belly on the ground so that Louise and the other inventor—the young man Bennett Marion—could work on the engine compartment without having to stand on a ladder. The wings were also missing, making it easy to reach the cockpit.

Bennett glanced up at their footsteps. A broad, open smile lit his face as he scrambled to his feet. He stuck out a hand to Pip. "You must be the new girl. I'm Bennett Marion."

Louise huffed and rolled her eyes. "You met her yesterday."

"I did?" His grin dropping, Bennett glanced at Louise, his hand still remaining in the space between him and Pip.

"Yes." Louise shook her head, as if she was resisting another eyeroll.

Bennett winced and shrugged as he turned back to Pip. "Uh, sorry. I honestly don't remember."

"I know what it's like to be so wrapped up in a project that you don't pay attention to anything else." Pip shook his hand firmly. "I'm Pippak Detmuk-Inawenys, but you can call me Pip."

Bennett's grin returned as he withdrew his hand. "Good to meet you again, Pip."

Pip nodded and strode closer to the aeroplane. "So, your mechanical problem."

"As I mentioned yesterday, we're trying to improve the rudimentary interrupter gear we reconstructed from the pieces we were sent from Mongavarian aeroplane wreckage." Louise pointed as she halted next to the open engine compartment. "We've rigged this particular gun so that the trigger is on the control column. All the newest aeroplanes are rolling out of the factory with this new firing mechanism. So the problem is that we need to synchronize the spinning of the engine with the firing mechanism."

"I'm assuming you've tried out various gear configurations?" Pip peered into the engine compartment, taking in the configuration of gears and connecting rods that Louise and Bennett had rigged.

"Yes. One gear. Two gears. Several gears in lots of sizes." Louise sighed and poked at one of the gears. "It's just... fiddly. Just when we think we have it figured out, the gears bind up or one engine spins faster than another engine or a different type of aeroplane has a different sized engine compartment which throws our calculations off."

Of course. Any variation in engine size, propeller type,

distance from the engine to the gun would change how the mechanism functioned.

"There are a lot of moving parts with this." Pip reached into the engine compartment to turn the gears, letting a little of her magic flow into her fingers to study the inner workings. "And it needs to be simple enough for the army mechanics to maintain and replace. Hardy enough to take a beating in battle."

"And the army really wants it to be universal for all aeroplane models and engine types." Louise's sigh was more frustrated than annoyed as she nudged a discarded gear on the floor with her boot. "It's no wonder the Mongavarian version is somewhat unreliable."

As Louise and Bennett started a brisk discussion of gears and engines, Pip relaxed further. This was where she was most at home, among gears, grease, wires, and metal. For a while, at least, she could set aside all thoughts of Fieran and romance.

FOUR

Fieran blinked at the ceiling above his bed, pulling himself from the haze of the light doze he'd fallen into after all the work of eating breakfast. Who knew the simple chore of eating could be so tiring?

With his curtain drawn mostly around his bed, he couldn't see much of the rest of the ward. Which was a bother. It left him with nothing interesting to look at, only a white ceiling overhead and an off-white curtain around him.

Worse, his mind seemed to be actually clearing. It hadn't been so bad, just lying there on and off sleeping when he'd been too drugged to care. But now his brain was functioning enough to get bored.

Footsteps sounded outside the curtain before Nylian strolled into Fieran's view, his mouth tugged into his resting frown. "Fieran. I see you are awake."

Fieran struggled to sit more upright, winced at the pain throbbing through him at that much movement, and flopped back onto his pillow. "Feeling more awake than I have in a while."

"Not a surprise. The last of the morphine is fully out of your system." Nylian rested a hand on Fieran's forehead.

Healing magic sank into Fieran, so familiar that Fieran's magic only stirred slightly before he tamped it down.

Fieran tried to breathe evenly and not squirm as he waited for Nylian to finish. For some reason, he always got the urge to talk when healers were examining him like this, even though the healer was too deeply concentrating to even pay attention to a conversation.

Finally, Nylian pulled his hand away. "You are healing well, but I will call one of the other healers to perform your next, more thorough healing."

Nylian started to turn away, but Fieran held a hand out to him. "Wait. Before you go, I have a question. What did you mean yesterday? When you said I was more resilient because of the magic of the ancient kings?"

Turning back to him, Nylian stared down at him a moment, as if formulating his response. His dour expression was more suited to delivering bad news than good. Yet that was Nylian. He always looked like he was about to tell someone they were dying.

Then the elf healer sat in the chair next to Fieran's bed, still holding Fieran's gaze. "I healed your dacha after he suffered extensive injuries. And yet he took down an entire fortress while still so grievously wounded. Even another elf would have succumbed."

"Dacha survived because of his heart bond with my mama. And because of Aunt Melantha's healing magic." While Fieran's parents hadn't told him all the specifics, he knew that much of the events that had left his dacha with many of his scars.

"Both of those things certainly played key roles in his survival. He was mortally wounded and would have died without the elishina." Nylian gave a slow nod. "And Queen Melantha's magic certainly assisted in sustaining him. Yet I would still argue that no other elf would have been able to be so sustained, even with the queen's powerful healing magic. Your dacha's extra resilience to survive such torture made saving him through the elishina and healing magic even possible. And then there is you."

"Me?" Fieran gestured at himself. "I didn't do anything so story-worthy. I just fell from the sky."

He'd distracted Pip. He'd raced into battle without thought. And Merrik…

No. Fieran shoved the thoughts aside. He couldn't think about all of that. Not yet. Not here in a large hospital ward.

"Exactly. You fell from the sky and sustained injuries that should have been fatal." Nylian studied Fieran, one finger tapping his chin as if taking in a medical experiment. "Even if another elf could have survived that fall, they likely would have gone into shock or died long before rescue could have reached them."

"Dacha told me to flood myself with my magic. It sustained me, I guess? Kept me alive." Fieran still wasn't sure why or how that worked. Nor did he really want to think too deeply about how Dacha discovered such a thing.

Nylian nodded, as if that just confirmed his hypothesis. "Your body endured a level of brutal punishment under which even other elves would perish and yet also took to healing afterwards in such a way that you will suffer no ill effects from the experience. Your dacha is the same way."

"We were born to be warriors." Down to their very bones and blood, it seemed. Fieran clenched his fists in the blankets as the weight of it sank into him.

"Yes." Nylian tipped his head. "Considering the nature of your magic, it is likely necessary for your bodies to have an extra resilience in order to wield such a magic. Otherwise your own magic would destroy you."

"Maybe." Fieran rolled the thought over. "Is that what happened to my great-grandfather Ellarin? He died of a disease of the magic."

"No. He inherited the disease that killed him from his mother. While it affected the magic of the ancient kings, which he inherited from his father's line, it was not inherent to that magic." Nylian's gaze went slightly distant, as if in deep thought. "Although I was born after the late King Ellarin died, I suspect that he would, in fact, prove my point rather than disprove it. He lived a remarkably long time for someone with that disease and took to Taranath's healing rather well."

Fieran blew out a breath as he tried to take it all in. He'd charged arrogantly into battle, thinking himself invincible, because of his magic. Ironic to discuss how hard to kill his magic made him while he was lying here in a hospital bed, knowing just how not-invincible he truly was.

Sure, his magic might make him extra resilient. He hadn't died this time because of it.

But he could still crash. He could still bleed. Still hurt. Still die. All it would take would be the right bullet, the right sword, the right circumstance, and he'd die just as dead as everyone else.

Nor could his magic grant invincibility to those around him. His best friend could still crash. Still lose his leg and possibly his ability to walk if his other leg didn't heal correctly.

And it could still all be Fieran's fault.

Before his brain spiraled further, he shut the door on those thoughts and emotions. He couldn't deal with them right now.

Time to get back to a clinical discussion of his magic.

Fieran turned his gaze back to Nylian. "And you're sure I have the same resilience you've observed in my dacha? I'm not…less resilient because I'm half human?"

"No, I do not believe so." Nylian shook his head, that frown deepening until his cheeks and brow were both deeply furrowed. "You have the magic of the ancient kings. You have its gift of resilience to the same degree that you have its power."

If that were the case, then perhaps Fieran was marginally less resilient than Dacha in the same way that his magic was marginally weaker.

And yet…

"That doesn't make sense." Fieran gestured at himself as best he could with his good hand. "I've been getting dizzy spells when I use my magic in large quantities. I had one at Fort Defense after wielding a lot of magic, and the healer there determined that it was because I was half-human and wielding the magic of the ancient kings was taking a toll on me."

"I highly doubt that is the case." Nylian shook his head even more vehemently this time. "I am far more familiar with you and your magic, and I can safely say it is not your human side weakening you. At least, not in the way that healer meant. While I do not wish to disparage another of my profession, I suspect they took the easy answer instead of looking deeper."

"Then why…" Fieran waved at himself again. What was going on? Was there actually something seriously wrong with him?

"How long do the dizzy spells usually last?" Nylian steepled his fingers, his gaze sharpening.

"Not long. Sometimes they even pass during the battle.

and I can go back to fighting without issues." Fieran tried to remember the exact timeline of the handful of times he'd felt that weakness and dizziness. "I've been able to wield more power each time before it hits. The last time, it didn't hit until I held back the full force of Dacha's power for several minutes. Yet I was already feeling better by the time the healer examined me. He said the only thing wrong he could sense was that my body showed signs of physical strain."

Nylian made a thoughtful humming noise as he tapped his steepled fingers against his chin. "That is interesting. I do not believe you need to worry that anything deeper is wrong with you or your magic. If that were the case, you would grow dizzy every time you used your magic, and it would likely last far longer."

"Then what is going on?" Fieran couldn't help the bite to his words. It was just so frustrating not having an answer to this. Especially when what he thought was an answer actually wasn't.

"I will have to ponder this more, but I suspect it could be because you are human, but not in the way that other healer made it sound." Nylian spoke slowly, as if he was trying to put his words together very deliberately. "Until now, your use of your magic has been in a very human way. Your largest expenditures of your magic have been in filling magical power cells, a human invention mostly used to power more human inventions."

"Except for training with my dacha." Fieran glanced at where his swords rested now, leaning against the wall beside the table, still in their canvas wrappings.

"Yes. Even then, would I be correct in assuming that it did not feel like training for war?" Nylian raised a single eyebrow.

Fieran hesitated, then shook his head. "No. Not to me, anyway."

He'd been a lackluster student back then. Treating that time with his dacha and his sisters as more a game than serious training.

"You and your sisters are the first generation to have been raised with this particular conception of the magic of the ancient kings." Nylian eyed Fieran. "That is not to disparage the way your dacha raised you. Your dacha was raised on a battlefield, and it caused him other problems with his magic. But it is the case that most of the warriors with the magic of the ancient kings were raised with war and battle in mind."

"Why would that affect my magic like this?" Fieran felt like he was back in the classroom, not quite getting the concept the professor was trying to teach him.

"It could be that you have not built up the magical stamina to wield great quantities of your magic in battle." Nylian's tone remained patient. "Battle demands a very uncontrolled, very powerful unleashing of your magic, yet until now your magical practice has focused on using controlled, small quantities for practical purposes. The more magic you wield, the less dizziness you should experience. But it has nothing to do with your half-human side, and everything to do with building up a stamina of a very powerful magic. Such a thing takes time."

"That would explain why the dizziness goes away so quickly." Fieran spoke slowly, not sure if he dared believe such a simple answer.

"But it could also be the way magic is wielded." Nylian eyed Fieran. "Dwarves use magic in conjunction with tools. It is crafted. Those few humans with magic must also craft it and are by far the most separate from magic. Elves, however, wield magic from the heart. It flows directly from us, and because of that, it is deeply tied with our emotions and perceptions of ourselves. If you were to hold a more human perception as you tried to wield the elven magic of the ancient kings, that would cause difficulties."

Fieran slumped onto his pillow, his mind reeling. Were those dizzy spells because he was, subconsciously, attempting to wield the magic of the ancient kings more like a human than an elf? Or because he *felt* more human than he did an elf most of the time? "So it's all in my head?"

"No. I am not dismissing the dizziness and weakness. Those are real. But whatever is causing the disconnect between your heart and your magic so that wielding your magic puts a strain on your body is also real."

"Then why haven't I experienced this before? Or had other difficulties with my magic?" He'd never feared his magic. He'd learned control easily enough and hadn't struggled with it the way his dacha said he had.

"Your magic has never been tested in this way, used at this kind of full strength, nor put to its true purpose before." Nylian rolled his shoulders in a hint of an elven shrug. "It is quite logical that such difficulties would manifest now when they had not before."

Great. Another thing to add to the roiling mass of emotions and thoughts he needed to sort out. Once he was out of this bed. Out of this hospital. Away from everyone who could judge him for breaking.

His magic crackled through his chest, threatening to burst from his fingertips. He desperately needed a good run. Or, better yet, a good fighting bout. Something to unleash everything bottled up inside him.

Nothing he could do about that now until he was healed and out of this hospital.

FIVE

Fieran gritted his teeth as he leaned on the orderly on one side and his mama on the other. He tottered the last few steps toward the silver roadster, which was parked in front of the hospital.

Mama reached past him and opened the passenger door. "In you go."

Fieran all but collapsed onto the plush leather seat, unable to fully stifle his groan. He shouldn't be this tired and sore just walking from the door of the hospital to the motorcar waiting for him.

But he was up. He was walking. At this point, he was grateful for that much. As the healers kept telling him, he was taking to the healing magic very well, considering he'd only been in the hospital for less than five days.

After tucking his swords into the footwell next to him, Mama closed the door, circled around the roaster's shiny fenders and grill, and slid into her own seat behind the wheel. She smiled at him before she turned on the engine. "Let's get you home."

"You have no idea how much I want my own bed."

Fieran slouched in the seat so that he could lean his head against the seat. "Or how thankful I am to be wearing clothes again."

It had been a struggle, shimmying into trousers for the first time since his crash. But worth it to be out of that hospital gown.

"Now you sound like your dacha." Mama laughed as she tied a scarf over her hair.

"I can't imagine Dacha being happy being stuck in a hospital gown either." Fieran let his eyes fall closed. He'd only been up for a few hours, and already he wanted a nap.

Once her hair was protected from the wind, Mama glanced both ways, put the roadster into gear, and pulled into the lane. After a few moments, she eased the motorcar into the bustle of one of the main roads of Aldon, the traffic moving at a crawl thanks to the clogging mix of horse drawn carriages, steam vehicles, magically-powered motorcars, bicycles, and pedestrians.

The noise of all the traffic made more conversation impossible. It also made napping impossible.

After at least half an hour, the motorcar left the city, and Mama sped up on the macadam stretching into the countryside. Rolling hills and farm fields spread to either side, broken by the occasional tree-lined ditch or creek. Prosperous farmhouses with wooden shingles stood next to large barns while other, smaller homes had mere thatched roofs and a shed for animals. The road wound through the occasional village with its accompanying manor house perched on the outskirts.

Despite the wind in his face and the roar of the engine, Fieran dozed for much of the hour drive. Sleeping was better than dwelling on the churn of thoughts in his head.

When they pulled off the main road in the village closest

to home and took the turn toward Treehaven, Fieran shoved himself more upright. He swallowed at the lump in his throat as Treehaven's brick walls and thick green treetops came into view.

Who knew that he'd get all emotional just seeing home again. It wasn't like he'd never expected to return from the war, except for those few minutes when his aeroplane had spiraled from the sky.

The guards opened the wooden gates for the roadster, and Mama turned the motorcar onto the drive inside. The tires crunched on the gravel, shadows splashing over them from the tree branches overhead.

Mama parked the roadster in front of the house instead of pulling around back to the carriage house.

As she pushed her door open, an older man with silver hair and a sturdy frame strode from around the side of the house. He opened Fieran's door. "Let's get you inside."

"Uncle Eugene?" Fieran blinked up at him, not taking the arm he offered.

Uncle Eugene wasn't actually Fieran's uncle any more than Uncle Iyrinder or Uncle Lance were. He was Aunt Patience's brother, making him Merrik's uncle by blood. Yet Uncle Eugene had served as the head guard here at Treehaven for as long as Fieran could remember, and it had felt only right as a kid to call him "uncle" right along with the other adopted uncles.

Uncle Eugene had never married, too dedicated to taking care of everyone else around him to take on a family of his own, and he seemed quite content with his choice. Thanks to being an elf friend to both Dacha and Uncle Iyrinder, he had aged more slowly so that he was still serving as the head guard even though he was in his nineties.

Fieran took Uncle Eugene's arm and let him leverage him

from the vehicle. It was galling to need so much help from the elderly, but Fieran wasn't sure he could have gotten out of the roadster without help.

Uncle Eugene just made it worse by holding out a wooden cane. "Patience keeps giving these to me. Seems to think I need them. Here, you might as well put one of them to use."

Fieran took the cane and, giving in, used it to steady himself. "Thanks." He hesitated as Uncle Eugene turned toward the house, not sure how to voice this question. "Shouldn't you be…in Estyra?"

"Patience thought it would be best if only she and Kari went instead of crowding Merrik." Uncle Eugene's gaze swung away from Fieran to stare into the forest. "And once she got there, well, Merrik isn't doing well. He will barely talk to anyone. Patience thought it best if I stayed away."

Fieran stumbled, his stomach sinking into his toes. He swallowed at that lump in his throat again.

He should be there for Merrik. Merrik shouldn't have to go through something like this alone.

But Fieran was the last person Merrik would want to see right now.

Uncle Eugene hurried to tug Fieran's arm over his shoulder to better support him, and Fieran didn't want to admit how much he had to lean on both Uncle Eugene and the cane. Mama hurried to catch up, carrying Fieran's swords and further steadying him with her free hand.

The walk up the steps, into the house, and down the hall seemed endless. Fieran didn't even protest when Uncle Eugene steered him straight for the lift instead of taking the stairs to the second floor. When they finally reached his bedroom, he sank onto his bed with a groan. His hips and legs ached after sitting upright so long in the car. Yet he resisted the urge to lie flat with both his mama and Uncle Eugene there.

Uncle Eugene patted his shoulder and left.

Mama pressed a kiss to Fieran's forehead. "Get some rest."

"I'm fine, Mama." Fieran worked up a smile. He was just sore. Just tired. And just trying really hard not to let the emotions churning inside him consume him.

Mama left, closing his door softly behind her.

As soon as she was gone, Fieran swiveled to lie flat on his bed, groaning again at the way his soft mattress supported his aching bones.

He fell asleep within moments.

FIERAN WOKE to the warmth of sun on his face. For long moments he simply lay there, soaking up the comfort of his plush bed.

A shadow moved between him and the sunlight. Was that the branch of the tree outside his window?

No, he didn't think so. There was something off about this shadow. And he could feel eyes on him.

Fieran peeled his eyes open and squinted into the brilliant sunlight. A small figure perched in his windowsill, knees drawn up to his chest, long hair silhouetted by the sun.

With a grin, Fieran lifted a hand and nudged Tryndar's foot. "Hey, Monkey."

"I am not a monkey," Tryndar mumbled into his knees, his tone lackluster and automatic.

"I don't know..." Fieran gathered his strength, sat up,

and swept his brother from the windowsill. A twinge of pain lanced through him, but he ignored it.

Tryndar shrieked, his giggles growing louder as Fieran tickled him.

"You shriek like a monkey. And perch in my window like a monkey. You must be a monkey."

Tryndar rolled out of Fieran's reach, then scrambled to the end of the bed. He smoothed the strands of his silver-blond hair, though it somehow hadn't gotten ruffled in the tickling. His tone held his usual indignation as he crossed his arms. "I am not a monkey. I am an elf."

Fieran probably shouldn't be so envious of his little brother's certainty. If Fieran felt as much an elf as Tryndar did, he likely wouldn't be having any problems with his magic.

"Of course. I see now. You are definitely an elf." Fieran leaned a shoulder against the wall to prop himself upright as another twinge of pain jolted through him. He had overdone it, sweeping Tryndar off the windowsill like that. His little brother wasn't that heavy, but he was probably heavier than what Fieran should be lifting.

Tryndar's indignant pout faded, his eyes going wide and liquid again as he poked Fieran's foot. "Does it hurt?"

Fieran resisted the urge to grimace. He must not have done a good enough job of hiding his pain.

Yet there was no way he was going to tell his little brother the truth. Perhaps lying wasn't the moral option, but it felt like the right one in this case. "Nah. I'm just tired."

Tryndar eyed him with his huge green eyes as if he didn't believe him. "You look like it hurts."

Fieran really must look a frightful sight. He certainly felt bad enough, and even just sitting upright now was making his hips hurt. He plastered a grin on his face. "I'm fine, Tryndar. Really. Mama kissed it better, and you know how well Mama's kisses work."

Tryndar's face screwed up for a moment as he thought about that, then he nodded, as if that made perfect sense to him.

With a sigh to cover his wince, Fieran eased back so that he was lying down once again. He patted the bed next to him where he could better see Tryndar without craning his neck. "Do you want to hear about how Dacha rescued me?"

Tryndar crawled from the foot of the bed to the new spot near Fieran's waist, taking a cross-legged seat once again.

"There I was after my crash behind enemy lines. I thought I was done for." Fieran gestured as he spoke to add to his storytelling. That was all the details he would give Tryndar about those moments lying in the mud, wracked with pain and feeling his life draining from him. "And then Dacha was there. He stepped from the fog with his swords drawn and his magic blazing."

This story would have been better if Fieran could have used his magic to illustrate it. But he was under strict instructions not to use his magic because it would burn away the healing magic that had been pumped into him before he'd left the hospital.

Still, Fieran made his best approximation of the crackling magic sounds.

Tryndar's eyes had widened, and he leaned forward with his hands on his knees. "And then?"

"All the bad guys ran away screaming." Fieran gave an exaggerated, humorous-style screaming, as if he were a story villain running away. "That's how much Dacha loves us. He will take on a whole army just to rescue us."

Those words weren't enough for what Dacha had done. He'd charged into an army, not even knowing if Fieran was still alive. He might have done all of that merely to retrieve Fieran's dead body.

Tryndar gave a solemn nod, his eyes so liquid that he looked about to cry. "I miss him."

Despite the pain, Fieran propped himself onto one elbow and wrapped his other arm around Tryndar in a hug, tugging him to his chest.

Tryndar stiffened for a moment—he wasn't big on hugs, after all. Then he leaned forward and wrapped his arms around Fieran's neck, pressing his face into his shirt. "I miss him lots."

"I know he loves all the pictures you've been drawing for him." Fieran patted Tryndar's back. "He has them tacked to the wall in his room where he can see them all the time. I really like the ones you've sent me."

Though, Fieran lived in a tent so the sketches Tryndar sent were currently stashed in his footlocker.

Tryndar swiped at his face and squirmed in Fieran's hug. Fieran released him, thankful to sink back onto his pillow.

A knock sounded on Fieran's partially open door a moment before Mama's voice called softly from the corridor, "Fieran, are you awake?"

"Yeah, I'm awake." Fieran swiped a hand over his hair, but it likely did little good. He was in desperate need of a shower. Washcloth baths only did so much.

Mama pushed the door farther open. "Have you seen…" Her gaze rested on Tryndar. "There you are. I told you to let your brother rest."

"He wasn't bothering me." Fieran nudged Tryndar's knee again. "At least, not once I woke up to find him perched on my windowsill watching me sleep."

Mama sighed. "Tryndar. What have we talked about

when it comes to entering someone's room while they're asleep?"

"Not to do it." Tryndar slid from the bed, hanging his head.

"And why don't we do it?"

"Because…" Tryndar's face screwed up as if he was struggling to remember.

"Because when someone is asleep, they can't give you permission to enter their room." Mama rested a hand on her hip, giving Tryndar a stern look. "And you should always make sure you have permission to enter a room that isn't yours."

Tryndar vaulted from the bed, dashed across the room, and launched himself at Mama.

She caught him with an *oomph*, stumbling back half a step. "You're getting so big."

"I am sorry, Mama." Tryndar hugged Mama.

"I'm not mad." Mama hugged Tryndar, then tipped her head at Fieran. "And I'm not the one who needs an apology."

Tryndar turned his face toward Fieran. "Sorry, Fieran."

"It's all right. Just knock next time." Fieran grinned to show Tryndar that he wasn't mad. He truly hadn't minded finding Tryndar there, but he could see why Mama needed to use the moment for a lesson.

"I did knock. You did not answer." Tryndar sounded so sad about it that Fieran could have given him another hug, if he wasn't already in Mama's arms.

"Mama?" Ellie's voice came from the hall before she stepped into the doorway. Her red hair was in two braids today, and she clutched the new Star Forest novel to her chest. Her smile widened as she caught sight of him. "Fieran! You're awake!"

He held out an arm to her, and she rushed across the room, giving him a hug. He didn't even mind that her book knocked into his cheekbone at one point.

This war had to be especially hard on Ellie and Tryndar. Most of their family had left essentially overnight. And now their big brother had come home beat up and wounded.

Fieran's childhood had been filled with long, peaceful days. He'd never worried that one of his family members wouldn't come home. Even during the few weeks when Dacha would be gone, attending one of the war games organized by Uncle Julien and Aunt Vriska, Fieran never worried about him.

Mama set Tryndar back on his feet. "Now that Fieran's awake, it's time for supper. What do you say to a picnic in Fieran's room?"

"Do I get to eat in bed?" Fieran gestured at his blankets. No eating in bed had been a rule growing up.

"Tonight, you aren't allowed to eat anywhere besides your bed." Mama grinned back, then rested a hand on Tryndar's shoulder. "And I used our sugar ration to make chocolate chip cookies. You can have one for dessert."

"Cookies!" Tryndar dashed past Mama, disappearing down the corridor.

"I'll get a picnic blanket!" Ellie dashed out the door on Tryndar's heels, her braids flying behind her.

"Sugar ration?" Fieran half-pushed himself onto his elbow again.

"It's not too arduous yet." Mama shrugged, the movement shifting her long red braid from her shoulder to her back. "It ensures that the army has what it needs."

All those donut and ice cream nights, the treats available in Little Aldon, the baked goods in the mess. The army had an abundance, and it hadn't occurred to Fieran that such a thing could only happen if those back home were rationing their own portions.

Mama crossed the room, halting beside the bed. "How are you feeling?"

"Fine. The nap helped." Fieran lowered himself back onto his pillow.

Mama rested a hand on his shoulder, her green eyes going soft rather than sparkling with her usual humor. "If you can't sleep tonight, or any night, there will be plenty of hot chocolate and cookies in the kitchen. No matter our rations. All right?"

There seemed to be something more to those words, but Fieran couldn't quite discern what it might be. All he could do was work up a smile. "Thanks, Mama."

She patted his shoulder. "I'll be back shortly with our picnic."

Fieran smiled and nodded. A picnic in bed didn't sound all that bad. Knowing his mama, she'd have all of them laughing so hard they'd be snorting their food out their noses before the evening was out.

He was falling. Aeroplane spiraling. Hitting the ground.

Fieran jolted awake, gasping for breath. He tore at the blankets restraining him. They were tight. Too tight. Too tangled.

His breathing increased as he yanked at the blankets, a tightness squeezing his chest. He needed to get out. Everything was too constricting. Too stifling.

His legs finally tore free of the blankets, and he stumbled from his bed. He sank onto his knees, gasping as if he'd just ruck-marched for twenty miles at double time.

The half-moon splashed silver light onto his bed and floor. He couldn't tell what time it was or how long he'd been asleep, but it couldn't have been that long.

He eyed his bed. The soft mattress called to him, but the memories still lingered, threatening to grab hold of him the moment he tried to sleep. It seemed his brain had decided he was finally in a safe space to start processing everything that had happened.

Using the bed to leverage himself to his feet, he fumbled

for the cane Uncle Eugene had given him. Once he found it, he leaned on it to steady himself as he shuffled from his bedroom and into the hall.

As the oldest, his room was at the end, farthest from the stairs. He tried to keep his movements quiet to avoid waking up Ellie or Tryndar. The last thing he wanted to do was answer questions from his siblings about why he was awake at this time of night.

At the end of the hallway, he reached the landing at the top of the stairs.

The stairs. For a moment, Fieran just stared. They looked as insurmountable as a mountain at the moment. He was going to be lucky if he didn't take a tumble.

There was a lift just down the hall toward Dacha and Mama's room, but despite all of Dacha's efforts, the lift rattled and whined when used. Fieran would wake up the whole household for sure if he took it.

The stairs it would have to be. He'd just have to fall quietly if he did take a tumble.

With a firm grip on the rail, he took it one step at a time, using the cane both to steady himself and feel for the next stair.

He was breathing hard from exertion rather than panic by the time he reached the bottom. But he'd done it. That was an improvement.

The walk to the kitchen at the back of the house felt like a mile. By the time he approached the door, his legs were shaking, and he gritted his teeth just to stay upright.

A glow shone from beneath the kitchen door. Had Mama left a light on for him?

Fieran pushed the swinging door open, the hinges soundless as if they'd been regularly oiled. As a kid, he'd never found that odd the way he did now.

He halted in the doorway, his hand holding the door from swinging back at him.

Wearing her green dressing gown, Mama sat at the table, bathed in the glow of the lamp set in the middle of the worn work table. She cradled a steaming mug in her hands while a plate with a half-eaten cookie rested on the table before her. Two more plates, one holding several cookies and one empty, had been placed across the table with a mug and chocolate pot sitting nearby. Her eyes were closed, and her mouth moved silently, almost as if she were murmuring to herself.

Or communicating with Dacha through their heart bond. Fieran had seen his parents do it often enough growing up to recognize the look on his mama's face.

Perhaps he shouldn't interrupt. Despite the distance between his parents, this moment seemed too intimate for him to intrude.

"You can come in, Fieran." Mama didn't open her eyes or otherwise move.

For a moment, he remained in the doorway, frozen with the same uncomfortable feeling he'd had when he'd caught his parents kissing a few times as a child.

But Mama had told him to come to the kitchen if he couldn't sleep, and she'd invited him to interrupt.

He shuffled into the kitchen and collapsed into the chair across from his mama and nearest the plate of cookies.

Mama opened her eyes, though she remained where she was, holding her mug of hot chocolate in both hands. "Couldn't sleep?"

"Must have napped too much today." Fieran grabbed a cookie and set it on the empty plate. He couldn't bring himself to meet Mama's gaze. She'd already set out a plate and mug for him, expecting him tonight. He didn't want her to see how right she'd been. "I'm sure all this sugar will help."

"Absolutely." Mama's voice remained cheery, light, even as her gaze rested too heavy and searching on Fieran. When she spoke again, her tone had changed to something more somber. "I'm here if you need to talk. Or if you'd prefer silence."

He didn't want to talk. Or, well, he did, but he wasn't sure how to start. Or which of the things churning through him he wanted to talk about.

Stuffing everything back with the same control he used when dealing with his magic, he took a bite of his cookie, chewed, and with the fortification of sugary goodness, finally had the courage to meet Mama's gaze. "How is Dacha?"

Mama hadn't just been waiting here for Fieran. The weary tilt to her mouth and the weight in her eyes said as much.

The sight brought up dusty, nearly forgotten memories from his early childhood. Those nights when he'd woken to the sound of screams, as if someone was in pain. A nightmare, his mama had told him. Nothing to worry about. His dacha was fine.

And those mornings when Dacha had been quiet and closed off, not smiling and not responding to Fieran the way he usually did.

Facing him, Mama's smile was small, not reaching her eyes, as she regarded him over the rim of her hot chocolate mug. "Your dacha will be fine. We've faced many a dark night before and come out on the other side. We'll do it again now. You don't have to worry."

Her reassurance not to worry just clawed the worries deeper into his chest. When he'd been a child, he'd believed her reassurances. He hadn't worried, and eventually those scary nights and tough mornings had become few and far between.

But now he'd faced war and carried the weight of all the lives he'd taken. He knew enough to worry. Looking back, he now realized his dacha's nightmares likely hadn't gone away entirely. They'd simply become manageable enough to more effectively hide from his children.

And yet what could Fieran do about it? Was it even his place to worry? Dacha and Mama were still his parents, even now that he was grown. Should they still protect him from their own shadows? Or was that something he should be expected to carry?

Mama's smile remained as she reached out and rested a hand on Fieran's arm. "He is fine, Fieran."

If only he could bring himself to believe it. But he'd caught glimpses of the look on Dacha's face as he waited at Fieran's bedside. If Dacha faced darkness tonight, then it was Fieran's fault.

Another failing to add to the ever-growing tally to Fieran's name.

Some of the twinkle returned to Mama's eyes as she leaned back in her chair and picked up her cookie, still holding her mug in her other hand. "He's jealous of the chocolate chip cookies. I couldn't quite figure out exactly what happened, but I gathered the mess is either all out of cookies or only has oatmeal raisin left. And their hot chocolate offerings are rather dismal at this time of night, even when a general is requesting it."

Fieran huffed as much of a laugh as he could manage. "Dacha detests oatmeal raisin cookies."

Well, all of them did. Raisins did not belong in cookies.

"Thus the reason I could sense the lack through the heart

bond." Mama gave a soft laugh and sipped her hot chocolate.

What must it be like to have a heart bond like that? Fieran clamped down on his question before he voiced it. To ask a question like that would mean bringing up Pip, and he wasn't ready to talk that situation over with his mama just yet. He needed to talk with Pip first.

Fieran sighed, reached for the chocolate pot, and poured himself a mugful. His body was aching, especially his hips, at sitting up in a wooden chair. He didn't have long before he'd have to go back to bed. If he was going to talk about some of what was bothering him, he'd have to do it soon.

After taking a sip of his hot chocolate, Fieran set down his mug and flicked a glance at Mama. "Merrik blames me for his crash."

"Is it your fault?" Mama's gaze didn't waver nor did her steady tone. No judgment. No false cheeriness.

"Yes. Maybe." Fieran nudged his cookie around his plate, though he didn't pick it up. His stomach churned with the few bites he'd taken. "I don't know."

"Tell me about it." Mama set down her own mug.

That prompt was all it took. Fieran found himself pouring out the whole story. Or, almost the whole story. He glossed over exactly what he and Pip had been discussing. And left out that almost kiss. Actual kiss? He wasn't even sure what to call it.

Mama nodded at the right moments, but she didn't interrupt.

"I was distracted. I rushed into the battle." Fieran flexed his fingers on his mug. His hot chocolate had long gone cold. "If my propeller was already cracked and if the mechanics could have discovered it before I took off, then I could have prevented my crash. And if I hadn't crashed, Merrik wouldn't have crashed. It's all my fault."

He sagged against the back of his chair, his words spent, his whole body aching.

For a long moment, Mama searched his face. Then she asked in that same, too quiet and steady tone, "If you hadn't distracted your mechanic, would she have inspected your aeroplane?"

Fieran closed his eyes, running the events of that day through his head. His aeroplane had still been out on the airfield. Even if Pip had been working instead of talking to him, she wouldn't have gotten to his aeroplane before the red alert sounded. "No, she wouldn't have. But after the red alert sounded, I could have waited a few minutes for her and Mak to run out and…"

Even as he said it, he realized just how that sounded.

Mama raised her eyebrows. "And how many of that other captain's squadron would have died while you delayed on the ground?"

The five or ten minutes it would have taken for Pip and Mak to inspect his and Merrik's aeroplanes didn't sound like much. But during a battle? That was an eternity. Even with Fieran getting his aeroplane into the sky as quickly as possible, Captain Kentworth and too many of his pilots were killed. How many more might have died if Fieran had delayed even five minutes? "I don't know. But likely several."

Yet if Fieran had taken the time to have his aeroplane inspected, how many of those who were killed after he'd crashed could he have saved? Would that have balanced out those who would have been killed in the delay?

"And what about the army?" Mama's gaze didn't waver. "What did your orders and army regulations require?"

That was just it. According to the army, he'd done everything right. Pip's inspections weren't an army requirement; they were hers. As far as the army was concerned, as soon as that red alert sounded, it was his duty to get his aeroplane into the sky as soon as possible. Sooner than possible, really.

If he'd delayed and his fellow pilots died because of that delay, he would have been in trouble. Possibly even court-martialed. No one would realize that the alternative would have been a crash. Instead, they'd see deaths that he could have prevented by getting into the air more quickly.

The army didn't blame him for the pilots that had been killed because he'd crashed. His crash was an accident. Their deaths were the cost of war. Same for Merrik's injuries.

"According to the army, I did everything I was supposed to do." Fieran tapped his fingers on the rim of his plate. "But if I did everything right, then why do I feel responsible?"

"You survived, and you feel guilty for it when Merrik and others are suffering far worse consequences." Mama leaned forward once again, her green eyes regarding him so steadily that he couldn't have looked away if he'd tried. "But you aren't at fault. At least, not in this. Merrik lost his leg because of war, not because of you. Yes, you were brash. You charged into that battle with less prudence than you probably should have. Take responsibility for the things that are actually in your control and let go of the rest. Holding guilt for things that aren't your fault and aren't in your control will destroy you if you let it."

Nodding, Fieran released a long breath, trying to force her words to stop merely ringing in his head and actually mean something in his heart.

Perhaps that sort of healing wasn't something that could be smoothed over in a few moments. He'd have to apply his mama's words over and over again until they stuck.

He wasn't the reason Merrik lost his leg. The war stole Merrik's leg. The enemy caused his crash.

Yet Fieran was still at fault for dragging Merrik into the Flying Corps. If not for Fieran, Merrik likely would have joined the elven infantry. He would have fought at his dacha's side. He would have been safe, or as safe as he could have been in war.

Instead, Fieran had selfishly made the decision to join the Flying Corps for the two of them. Sure, Merrik hadn't had to follow him, but Fieran hadn't even asked what Merrik wanted. He'd just expected Merrik to follow. Fieran's decisions had cost Merrik his warrior hair and now his leg.

First Merrik, then Pip. Fieran had been trampling over those around him, and he hadn't even realized he'd been doing it.

Oblivious, yes. But also selfish. Arrogant. Too wrapped up in himself to truly pay attention to those around him.

He'd never not liked himself before. It was a rather uncomfortable feeling, and he wasn't sure what to do with it.

"Maybe I'm not at fault for his crash. At the very least, I'm not the only—or even the main—cause of it." Fieran nudged his half-eaten cookie around on his plate. Crumbs crushed, gritty, beneath his finger. "But there's plenty that I *am* at fault for. I've been pretty selfish when it comes to Merrik."

And Pip, but he still wasn't ready to bring her into this conversation.

"All of us are prone to selfishness, and we must make a conscious effort to choose sacrifice and unselfishness instead of our natural inclinations to pride and self-absorption." Mama's smile tilted almost wryly, though it lacked sharp edges. "Those of us with large personalities and ease with people have to be especially aware that we use our charisma to lift up those around us rather than overshadow them, ignore them, or, worse, hold them down."

His mama had always been a shining example of sacrificial love of others. She and Dacha were still beloved by the Escarlish people because of their unselfish caring.

"You have a good heart, Fieran." Mama leaned forward to rest a hand on his arm again. "Maybe it's my rosy perspective as your mother, but you are a good leader and a good man, despite your mistakes. And because you are a good man, you'll strive to do better going forward."

"Thanks, Mama." Fieran released a long breath. He couldn't go back and fix his mistakes.

But he could strive to do better going forward. Make better choices. Actually stop and *think* before he acted, as his dacha—and Merrik—had been telling him for years.

"Will Merrik forgive me, do you think?" Fieran traced his finger over the rim of his plate.

"I'm afraid that's up to him." Mama's tone somehow softened even more as she leaned her elbows on the table. "You can and should apologize for the things that are truly your fault, and you can let him know you're there for him. But you can't make him forgive you, nor should you push. It's his decision when he's ready to forgive you and restore your friendship. If he's ever ready."

If. The bleakness of that word stabbed into his chest. He couldn't imagine a world where he wasn't friends—no, brothers—with Merrik.

"Mama, I—" Fieran swallowed, not sure what to say. "Thanks."

As they lapsed into silence, he glanced around the familiar kitchen, taking in the large white stove with its ceramic polished to a shine. The pots and pans hanging from a rack nearby. The wooden cupboard and countertop for prepping meals and baked goods.

Except…he took in the door to the outside. He pointed. "There's a gun hanging over the door."

That hadn't been there when he'd been growing up. Mama and Dacha never would have kept a weapon so within reach.

Mama's mouth pressed into a tight line, and she didn't answer for a long moment, as if she didn't want to tell him. Finally, she sighed, her gaze still on the rifle over the door rather than on him. "The Mongavarians have been dropping agents into Escarland. They've realized the best way to eliminate warriors of the ancient kings is to get to them *before* they come into their magic. Either kill them or kidnap them to raise. They aren't picky."

Ellie. Tryndar. Fieran's chest squeezed. The Mongavarians wanted to either kill or kidnap his youngest siblings. He swallowed. "Have they…have they gotten close?"

"No. Your dacha's barrier around Treehaven has kept them out, and we capture them before they can do much more than prod at the defenses." His mama gave him a grin that somehow was mischievous as well as grim. "One would think wielding the magic of the ancient kings would be enough, but the intruders always take me more seriously when I'm pointing a gun at them as well."

Fieran tried to say something. Anything. But he couldn't seem to find the words. He somehow hadn't pictured his mama going to confront these Mongavarian agents in person.

Instead, he finally asked, "Does Dacha know?"

He couldn't imagine his dacha would blithely remain at Fort Defense if Mama, Ellie, and Tryndar were being put in danger like this.

"Yes." Mama's jaw worked, her eyes flashing. "But he knows I have it *handled.*"

She said it with an extra, growled emphasis, as if she wasn't just talking to Fieran. Perhaps she was conveying the sentiment to Dacha through the heart bond.

The Mongavarians really should take the hint. Don't mess with Fieran and his siblings. His parents were downright terrifying when they were defending their children.

SEVEN

Fieran woke to bright sunlight and a loud chorus of birds. Pushing to his elbows, then upright, he leaned a shoulder against the wall next to his window and simply took in the cheeriness of the morning.

Normally, he would have been up long before now. Here at Treehaven before the war, he would have already been in the back clearing, practicing his magic with Dacha and itching for more adventure. At Fort Defense, he would have been up and going about his duties. Perhaps also training with Dacha, just with more focus than he'd ever had here at home.

He swept a glance around his room, taking in the blankets he hadn't bothered to fold before he'd left for the army piled on a couch. Some random paperwork lay strewn over the desk in a haphazard fashion. The small collection of books with folded pages and bookmarks at various spots because he never could seem to finish them scattered on several of the surfaces.

This room was a huge part of his childhood, the fingerprints of his innocence all over the items on display.

It didn't feel like it belonged to him anymore. He wasn't that boy who had dreamed of war and adventure any longer.

Now he'd watched squadron mates die. He'd taken too many lives to count. He'd cost his best friend his leg. Possibly both of them, if the elves couldn't save his other one enough for him to walk on it.

He couldn't go back to the person he used to be. And as much as he missed the innocence when it came to death and destruction, he didn't want to go back to being so obliviously selfish either.

With a sigh and a groan, Fieran rolled out of bed and to his feet. He'd pushed it too hard last night. Now his muscles and bones ached, every step shaky with weakness.

Still, he forced himself to gather clean clothes and shuffled to the attached water closet. There, he managed to prop himself up long enough to take his first shower since his crash, the hot water washing away the feel of mud and blood from his skin much better than the washcloths and bowls of water with which he'd been making do.

As much as he wanted to linger, taking a shower in less than three minutes was so ingrained in him that he found himself toweling off and tugging on his clothes almost before he'd realized it.

Before reaching for his shirt, he paused, taking in the sight of the new scars dotting his chest. He cataloged each of them, ending with the largest on his abdomen, where that piece of shrapnel had speared him. When he twisted, he could just make out the pink, still healing splotch where it had come out his back.

Even his body was unfamiliar to him. New scars puckered skin that used to be unmarred. His bones jutted in a way they hadn't before he'd lost weight in the past few days.

Elven healing magic could do much, but it still took a toll on a body. And right now, his body showed that cost.

Once he finished dressing, he located his cane and tottered from his room. In the daylight, the stairs weren't as much an obstacle as they had been in the dark the night before, and he made his way to the kitchen without too much trouble.

There, he found the leftovers of breakfast covered with a towel and set in the oven to keep them warm.

Outside, laughter rang, punctuated by voices. Mama must have taken Ellie and Tryndar outside to let him sleep.

He could have joined them and eaten there. Instead, he sat down at the small table beneath the black telephone. His stomach churned, his hand trembled, but he picked up the earpiece and jiggled the lever to ring the operator.

When the operator spoke, he gave directions to Uncle Iyrinder and Aunt Patience's house in Estyra.

He waited while a series of operators made the connections between Treehaven and the house in Estyra until finally the telephone rang far away. He poked at his breakfast with a fork, but he couldn't bring himself to take a bite.

Would anyone be there? If Merrik was still in the elven hospital in Estyra, Aunt Patience would likely be with him. Merrik's little sister was probably staying with Merrik's elven aunt and uncle.

Yet after only three rings, there was a click, then Aunt Patience's voice came over the crackling line. "Hello, this is Patience."

"Hello, Aunt Patience." Fieran gripped the earpiece tighter as he leaned forward to speak into the receiver.

"Fieran." Aunt Patience breathed his name out on a sigh weighty with relief. "We've all been worried. How are you?

You must be recovering well if you're home and able to get to the telephone."

"Yes. I came home from the hospital yesterday." Fieran hesitated before he could bring himself to ask. "How is Merrik? Is he still in the hospital?"

"He's home, but I'm afraid he won't be able to come to the telephone." Aunt Patience's pause held the weight of words she hesitated to say. "It's only been a week since both of you crashed. He's understandably still struggling, even if he is physically healing well."

Fieran slumped even more against the table, stirring the now cold eggs around on his plate. Why had he hoped for a different answer? Merrik had lost his leg. His other leg was so mangled the elves had barely saved it, and they hadn't been able to promise he would be able to walk on it even once it healed.

Yet he'd still hoped.

"Can you let him know I called?" Fieran's voice scratched roughly in his throat. "And that I'm here if he wants to call back. Once he can get to a telephone."

"I'll let him know." Aunt Patience's voice was soft, barely carrying over the crackle in the line.

"Thanks." Fieran swallowed, trying to clear his throat. "Can you transfer me to Adry? If she's home?"

"I don't know if she's in, but I'll transfer you." Aunt Patience's tone steadied.

After they exchanged farewells, a few more clicks sounded. Another telephone rang.

A click, and then Adry's voice. "Hello?"

"Hello, Adry." Fieran rested his forehead on his hand, something inside him easing at hearing his sister's voice. She'd been the only family member he hadn't seen or spoken with since his crash, and he hadn't realized how much that had mattered to him until just now.

"Fieran!" Adry all but shouted into the telephone. "You're all right. You're calling. *Are* you all right? Hearing about the crash…"

"I know. And I'm sorry." He couldn't imagine how hard it must have been for her, getting the news from either Dacha or Mama. And she was stuck so very far away in Estyra. "But I'm fine."

"Good." Adry said that single word with such feeling that the emotion carried even across the long telephone lines.

"I just talked with Aunt Patience." Fieran couldn't make himself say more than that.

"Yeah." Adry sighed. She, too, didn't say more than that.

"Can you…can you be there for him?" Fieran stabbed at the eggs on his plate. They were unappetizing, rubbery lumps by now.

"Of course I will be. He's my friend too." Adry almost sounded insulted that he would suggest that she wouldn't be there for Merrik without Fieran's prompting.

"I know, I know. I just…it kills me that he's going through all this, and I'm not there for him." Fieran scrubbed a hand over his face. They were like brothers. In any other circumstances, Fieran would have been there every step of the way for Merrik's recovery. And Merrik would have been there for him.

Instead, they were separated by miles and anger and it was just *wrong*.

"He won't be alone in this. I promise." Adry's voice held a soft fierceness that reminded Fieran of his mama the night before.

"Thanks, Adry." Something in Fieran's chest finally

unwound. He was still worried for Merrik, of course. Still dying a little that he couldn't be there when his brother was hurting so much.

But Merrik wouldn't go through this alone. Adry would see to that.

After talking a few minutes more with Adry, Fieran hung up. Gathering his strength, he pushed to his feet and carried his plate to the main table, where that morning's newspaper lay waiting for him.

As he read, he ate the cold eggs and toast since he didn't have the energy to reheat them. It wasn't the worst thing he'd ever eaten. Not by far. Funny how much lower his standards for food had gotten since joining the army.

As he finished, the door opened, and Mama strode inside. When her gaze rested on him, she smiled. "Good morning. Did you sleep well?"

"Yes." It turned out that eating chocolate chip cookies and talking through difficult things had a way of tiring a body out.

"And how are you feeling?" Mama briefly rested her hand on his shoulder before she collected his empty plate.

"I'm fine." He started to swivel on the chair to stand, but a stab of pain lanced through his hips and into his legs.

He must not have hidden his wince well enough because Mama paused, her smile fading. "You overdid it last night."

"Maybe a little." Fieran remained sitting rather than getting up.

Mama set his plate and fork in the sink and turned back to him. "I'm going to take you in to the hospital so the healers can take a look at you." When he opened his mouth to protest, she speared him with one of her *looks*. "I know you're probably fine, and it's just a precaution. But if nothing else, you should get another dose of healing magic."

He snapped his mouth shut. She had a point. More healing magic wouldn't hurt.

"All right." Fieran shifted in the chair, trying to find a more comfortable way to sit. "Can we stop at the AMPC afterwards? There's someone I need to talk to."

Mama's smile returned, a glint in her eyes. "I'll pull the car around once I see if Eugene can keep an eye on Ellie and Tryndar for a while."

Pip had her head and upper body stuck in the engine compartment, the rest of her crammed into the footwell with the control column squishing uncomfortably into her side. At least the rudder bar had been removed since they didn't need it for what they were designing. "What if we made this linkage here more...adjustable? That way it can be fine-tuned when installed on each aeroplane to take into account the variations of models and engines?"

"That...might work." Louise stood beside the aeroplane's fuselage, bending over as she fiddled with the gear above Pip's head. "That would solve one problem, at least?"

"Doesn't solve the other problems." Bennett perched on a stool pulled up to a table on the other side of the fuselage. Various gears and linkages spread out before him as he assembled yet another prototype.

"Don't be such a downer. Each problem we solve is one step closer." Louise shrugged and spun the gears, testing the way they moved.

Pip wasn't sure she shared either Louise's optimism or

Bennett's frustration. The three of them had made progress in the past few days. The model they'd come up with worked…at least some of the time. The army would probably be satisfied with it. After all, working some of the time was far better than none of the time.

But all of them felt they could do better. There had to be a way to make a synchronization gear that worked all the time. Or at least, worked as reliably as could be expected for a piece of machinery.

"Hello, Louise. Bennett. Is Pip around?" Fieran's voice came from somewhere beyond the fuselage.

Pip jumped, then yelped when she bumped her head on the underside of the engine.

Through the opening in the fuselage, Pip could see Louise's grin a moment before she spun, likely to face Fieran. "She's in the aeroplane."

Pip wiggled out of the footwell and sat up in the space where the seat would have been, if this had been a functional flyer. She reached up to check her hair, only to find that her bun had half-fallen out, and some of her hair was sticking out in all directions.

Argh. She needed a mirror. And a few minutes to compose herself before she faced Fieran.

She wasn't going to get either of those. He was standing there next to his sister, leaning on a cane and grinning at Pip in that way that did something squiggly and squeezing to her insides, uncomfortable and yet delicious all at once.

If there was no help for it, she might as well play things casual. She lifted a hand. "Hey."

"Hey." Fieran stumped closer, leaning on the cane in a way that showed he was still healing. After all, he'd fallen from the sky only a week ago. The fact that he was up and walking was a testament to the strength of elven healing magic.

Pip placed her hands on either side of the cockpit and levered herself to her feet. Even with the fuselage sitting flat on the ground, she still struggled to step up and over the high side of the cockpit, her toes barely brushing the floor on the other side. As she lifted her other foot free, she had to give a couple of hops so that she didn't fall over.

As much as she wanted to rush to Fieran's side, Pip faced Louise, trying to keep her tone nonchalant. "Do you mind if I take my lunch break now?"

"Go on. Don't worry about the time." Louise grinned and waved her hand breezily.

How much did Louise know or suspect? Too much, given the way she was smirking.

Pip wasn't going to question her now. Instead, she hurried past Louise to Fieran's side.

Fieran tilted his head, then started walking in the direction he indicated.

Pip fell into step with him. For once, she was the one having to shorten her stride to slow down. She was so used to always walking fast or trotting to keep up with everyone that it was a struggle to slow down.

While they walked, she reached up, took the pins out of her hair, and did her best to gather all the strands back into a neater bun. Not only was she fixing her hair, but it gave her something to do with her hands. Otherwise she might reach for Fieran's hand, and she wasn't sure she wanted to make that kind of statement in front of his sister. Not until she and Fieran had talked.

He led her to the glass-covered courtyard alley Louise had shown her on her first day there, then into the building next to it.

Inside, rows upon rows of shelving filled most of the space while a room had been walled off with wood to their right.

As they neared, the door to the room opened, and an elf woman with long blonde hair bustled out of it. Pip had seen her from a distance a few times during lunches in the alley, and Louise had said she was her Aunt Illyna.

Illyna's gaze swept past them, then swung back to them. A smile creased her face. "Fieran! It is good to see you up and about."

"I'm enjoying being out of bed." Fieran shifted from foot to foot, strain at the edges of his smile.

Pip edged a little closer, ready to prop herself under his arm if needed. Was this his usual fidgeting or a need to sit down?

"You are a similar height to Merrik, right?" Illyna swept a glance over him, as if making mental calculations in her head.

"I think I'm an inch taller, maybe." Fieran rocked back on his heels, his smile dropping entirely.

Pip eased close enough to brush her fingers against his, letting him know that she was there. That she understood why any mention of Merrik was difficult right now.

"Do you have a moment?" Illyna reached into a pocket, pulling out a measuring tape. "I would like to take a few measurements. I will still need to make a few adjustments once I fit the prosthetic for Merrik, but your measurements will help those making the prosthetic get it close."

Fieran hesitated for a moment before he bent in stilted movements and began untying his boot. "Uh, of course I'll help."

Pip shifted, not sure if she should walk a few steps away or continue to stand there awkwardly.

Illyna glanced at her and smiled. "I do not know if we have officially met. I am Illyna Marion. I oversee one of the AMPC's charitable foundations and the manufacturing of prosthetics." Illyna lifted her prosthetic left hand. "I am rather invested in that part of the business, after all."

Pip had seen Illyna from a distance both with and without her prosthetic hand in the past few days. She nodded, not sure what else to say to that.

Oh, wait, she probably should introduce herself. "I'm Pip. I'm here on temporary assignment from the army."

Fieran sat in one of the nearby metal chairs and tugged off his boot, though his gaze remained on the floor. "You are working on his…you are helping him personally." It was as if he couldn't bring himself to say *Merrik's prosthetic* out loud.

"Yes. I will be leaving for Estyra in a few days, once several options are finished for him to test out." Illyna's gaze rested on Fieran, her voice and gaze filled with compassion. She held out her hands—both the one made of flesh and blood and the wooden one glowing green as she moved the fingers with her plant magic. "I know what he is going through right now. He needs the time and patience to pick up the pieces and put himself back together. It is hard, but he will be all right eventually."

Pip swallowed at the lump in her throat, blinking rapidly. She hoped so. Hearing the despair and bitterness in Merrik's voice had hurt. He was her friend, after all. One of her flyboys.

Fieran nodded and stood, wobbling slightly. "How would you like me to stand?"

"Just like that. Stand straight and stay still." Illyna knelt and began taking measurements with the flexible measuring tape, her wooden fingers glowing even more green as she moved them with her magic. She jotted notes on a piece of paper as she went. After a few minutes, she stood. "All done. Linshi."

"Of course. Anything for Merrik." Fieran sat again to put on his boot, concentrating almost too much on the movements.

Pip lingered at his side, her stomach churning more with every moment. All this talk of Merrik was just going to remind him of all the reasons they shouldn't be together. She'd distracted him, and Merrik had lost his leg because of it.

As Illyna hurried off, saying something about passing along the measurements, Fieran gestured toward a lift, which sat to one side of the wooden wall blocking off the back corner of the space. "Anyway. Uh, let's head for the garden."

Fieran shuffled toward the lift. As soon as he stepped inside, he leaned against the cage wall next to the lift controls as if he needed the extra support.

"Should you be walking this much?" Pip halted on the other side, torn between going to him and keeping some space.

"Probably not." Fieran gave a smile and a shrug as he tugged the control lever up. The magically-powered motor engaged, gears spun, and the cable lifted the cage from the ground. "But I was just pumped full of healing magic. I'll be fine."

They remained silent as the lift rose higher and higher until they passed through the ceiling into a glass-enclosed structure on the roof.

As Fieran brought the lift to a halt, then locked it in place, Pip gaped around at the greenhouse filled with a variety of plants, both herbs and blooming flowers, stretching before them. "Louise said there was a garden on this roof, but I didn't expect…this."

"Aunt Illyna has been expanding it for years." Fieran led the way off the lift into the sweltering greenhouse, walking the gravel path between the plants. "It started as a garden for the herbs she uses for making her elven shampoos and conditioners. But then she added the flowers for the scents and eventually transformed the whole roof into a place to relax here in the bustle of Aldon."

"It's amazing." Pip stopped to smell a few of the flowers as she followed Fieran through the greenhouse. She recognized some of them, like roses, but others she couldn't name. She might be half elf, but she'd grown up surrounded by trains and mechanics. While she could recognize and name trees, she wasn't as familiar with other plants.

Fieran reached the outer greenhouse door and pushed it open, holding it for her while he stepped aside.

She strolled into the sunlight, the summer warmth feeling almost cool after the heat inside the greenhouse. Outside, the whole rooftop was one big garden with even more herbs and plants.

Fieran let the door swing closed and tottered off down a path that led around the greenhouse. "A few of the other roofs have been turned into spaces for various yard games, but Dacha and Uncle Iyrinder have been talking about trying to convert some of the other empty roofs into more green spaces."

"That would be nice. Spots of green in all of this." Pip gestured at the skyline of Aldon stretching before them, a patchwork of brick buildings, tiled roofs, and chimneys. "Not that I mind all the brick and stone the way some elves would."

To one side, the city center had more green swaths, from

the expansive back gardens of the nobles' townhouses to the various public parks. Winstead Palace formed a large section of green amid all the brick, including a small forest, and the famous Kingsley Gardens created a patch of vibrant color.

"No. I don't either." Fieran turned into a small alcove formed by a rose-covered arbor shading a backless wooden bench. He lowered himself to sit on it with a stifled sound that might have been a groan, leaning the cane next to him.

Pip sat on the other end of the bench, leaving enough space between them that only their knees briefly bumped when she half-turned to face him.

This was it. She couldn't put off this conversation any longer. Not that she wanted to linger in this slow misery of uncertainty, but she wasn't sure she'd like the fallout either.

She hated this. Hated the person she became in moments like this. She could be so confident with a wrench in her hand, but the moment she had to deal with any kind of personal conflict, she quailed like a wilting flower.

Her chest tightened, and she stared at her hands in her lap, too cowardly to meet his gaze. "Fieran, I'm sorry. I'm sorry I distracted you. You were right. I shouldn't have—"

"Shh. Pip." Fieran gripped her shoulders, gentle and yet firm enough that she couldn't help but peek up at him. His brilliant blue eyes held hers with an intensity she'd rarely seen from him. "It's not your fault."

"But I—" She couldn't speak around the lump rising in her throat. She couldn't break. Not now. Yet the tears building in her chest didn't seem to be listening.

"No. No, Pip. Don't blame yourself. Please." Fieran's thumbs rubbed the tops of her shoulders, a soothing motion that dragged her gaze back to him.

"But I demanded that conversation right then. I should

have waited. I—" Her head was whirling, her chest caving in.

"And you wouldn't have needed to demand that conversation if I'd handled things better from the start. That's *my* fault, not yours." Fieran held her gaze, not a trace of a smile to his mouth. "If anything, I was the one distracting you. As soon as I landed, I was back to standby. You were the one with actual work to do."

"And I should have been doing it." A tear trickled down her face, hot against her skin. "Not demanding a conversation."

Fieran released one of her shoulders and brushed away her tear with the backs of his fingers. "You couldn't have known we were about to be attacked. Our aeroplanes weren't supposed to go back up until the next day. Besides, we were talking for what, five minutes? Maybe ten? How many aeroplanes would you have inspected in that time? Keep in mind, you didn't know an attack was coming. You wouldn't have been rushing."

She closed her eyes, mentally running through her inspection routine. "One. Maybe."

Which aeroplane would she have inspected? In the chaos after the battle, she hadn't heard if any other pilots had crashed because of mechanical failures. Perhaps no one knew, given how many had been shot down once Fieran had crashed. Had a pilot died because of her?

"And would you have had a chance to even fix any problems you found in your inspection?" Fieran's tone remained comfortingly steady, keeping Pip from fully falling apart.

Pip swallowed, her throat rough. "No. I would've just noted problems but not fixed them. But I could have grounded any aeroplane that had a problem too serious to send back up."

She'd never know if she'd sent a pilot into the air with a faulty aeroplane. That guilt tore through her chest, and she might have curled in on herself if Fieran hadn't been holding her with one hand on her shoulder, the other now cradling her face.

"That aeroplane wouldn't have been mine." Fieran's thumb traced over her cheek. "My aeroplane was still on the airfield, and it wasn't like the ground crews had been distracted. Besides, even if you had inspected my aeroplane, you wouldn't have caught a crack in the propeller unless it was visible to the eye. You would've had to call over Mak or one of the elven mechanics for that, and that would've taken even longer. Time we didn't have. You did nothing wrong, Pip. Nothing."

"Then why does it feel like I did?" The words were a rough whisper past the squeezing in her chest and throat.

Fieran gathered her into his arms, sliding her gently on the bench so that she was tucked against his side.

She wrapped her arms around him, pressing her face against his shoulder, clinging to the comfort he was offering.

"We lost friends in the squadron. Our friend lost his leg. It's natural we'll feel guilty." Fieran spoke into her hair as he held her tight. "But it's a lie. My mama told me last night to take responsibility for what was actually in my control and let go of the rest. That goes for you too. And you have far less to regret than I do."

Pip squeezed her eyes shut, two more hot tears leaking from the corners of her eyes to soak into the front of Fieran's shirt.

Perhaps she wasn't at fault. She'd done nothing wrong.

Yet that almost made it worse. It meant that even when she did everything right, she couldn't protect her flyboys. Her friends could still die. Fieran could still crash. And there was nothing she could do to prevent it because war was terribly cruel like that. No matter how hard they fought, how much magic they wielded, how brave they were in the face of the enemy, war would take and take and take, glutted on blood and death, never satisfied.

Yet war wasn't an impersonal monster just gobbling up those caught in its unwitting control. War was controlled by those who had all the power and yet had to pay none of the cost.

What else could they do but keep fighting? If the Alliance lost, the Mongavarian Empire would expand into their borders. And that would bring nothing but pain to the people living in the Alliance kingdoms.

Pip tightened her grip around Fieran. "If I did nothing wrong, then you didn't either."

"Not according to the army, maybe." Fieran's sigh stirred her hair. "But I still selfishly dragged Merrik into the Flying Corps without once stopping to ask him what he wanted, and it cost him his long hair and his leg. I was still rash that day, throwing myself and Merrik into that battle without even stopping to consider if there was a better way to go about it. I was the one to suggest attacking the gun emplacements, which provoked the Mongavarians to attack."

"The generals rubber-stamped that attack. They knew the chances of retaliation." Pip dug her fingers into the back of his shirt. "That's not on you."

"It still feels like it is." Fieran rested his cheek on the top of her head. "And I know there wasn't time for me to wait for Mak or an elven mechanic to inspect my propeller. It wasn't like I would've known it needed checking, and there's a good chance I might have been disciplined or worse for delaying while Capt. Kentworth and his men were dying. But I still wonder... still think that if only..."

"We don't know your propeller was damaged in your attack on the gun emplacements." Pip shifted, turning her head so that she wasn't speaking into his shoulder. "There's a good chance your propeller wasn't cracked before you went up the second time. If that were the case, even having Mak inspect the propeller wouldn't have made a difference. You still would've crashed. It was all just a tragic accident of war."

"Yes, but if Mak had inspected it, then we'd know." Fieran's voice roughened, his arms tightening around her. "I'd know if there was something I could've done. If I could've prevented all of this."

Then they'd both have a lot more peace.

Pip breathed in the scent of Fieran's shirt before she exhaled slowly. She snuggled into the warm strength of his arms around her.

As she did, the painful tension inside her finally eased for the first time since she'd watched Fieran's aeroplane fall from the sky. Maybe…just maybe…things would be all right.

After another long moment, Fieran shifted, making another of those groans of pain in the back of his throat.

Pip straightened out of his arms. "Are you all right?"

"I'm fine." Fieran's gaze dropped away from hers, as he braced himself on the bench. His face went even more pale beneath the smattering of freckles across his nose and cheeks.

"You don't look fine." Pip reached for him, but he scooted back along the bench until he was at the very edge. "Should I call Louise? Get you to the hospital?"

"No, no. I'm fine. Just need to lie down." Fieran spoke in a rushed, staccato tone as he half-fell, half-lowered himself from the bench.

She wasn't sure what to do or how to help, and she

ended up just sitting there, her hands awkwardly hovering in the space between them. This was why she was a mechanic instead of a nurse.

With a sigh, he stretched out on the ground, his legs underneath the plants to one side of them and his head on the pavers by Pip's feet where the arbor and bench cast a patch of shade. He tucked a hand beneath his head as a cushion. Only then did he peer up at her. "I'm fine. Really. Just still healing. Sometimes my bones start aching if I sit for too long, and I just have to lie down."

It looked rather uncomfortable, lying there half on the pavers, half on the dirt. Pip glanced around, but she couldn't find a cushion or pillow or anything soft tucked behind the bench or within reach. Probably wise, given this was an exposed rooftop. But still, she couldn't just leave Fieran like that, trying to use his own arm as a pillow.

"Here." Pip knelt on the pavers next to him. "Lift your head."

Fieran's eyebrows rose, but he raised his head.

She settled into a sitting position on the pavers with her legs stretched in front of her and her back against the bench behind her. Her rear end would go to sleep if she sat like this too long, but it was worth it.

Fieran eyed her, then he lowered his head onto her lap with another soft moan, as if even that much movement hurt.

Pip wasn't quite sure what to do with her hands. She tentatively lowered one hand to rest on Fieran's shoulder while she kept the other planted on the ground next to her.

Fieran reached up and clasped the hand she'd placed on his shoulder. "Are you all right? None of this has been easy on you."

"I'm okay, I guess." Pip leaned her head against the

bench behind her, blinking at the tears threatening to rise once again. "It was just…really hard. First I saw your aeroplane fall from the sky. And then Merrik's aeroplane flew overhead, burning. He crashed, and when we pulled him out…it was bad."

She sucked in a shuddering breath and squeezed her eyes shut. Yet that didn't help. All it did was call up the memories of Merrik's dacha lifting him from the wreckage. Laying him on the ground. Merrik's pale face. His mangled legs. So much blood.

"Pip." Fieran's fingers touched her cheek as his other hand squeezed hers.

She shook the memories away and forced her eyes open.

Fieran's gaze was searching her face. "I'm sorry you've been going through so much, and I've been too drugged and wrapped up in my own recovery to be there for you."

"It's all right." Somehow, Pip's other hand—the one not clasped in Fieran's—found its way to stroking the short strands of Fieran's red hair. "You fell out of the sky. You probably shouldn't even be alive. You needed to focus on healing. I'm not so fragile that I couldn't get by. Besides, I wasn't alone. My brother was there for me, as were the other flyboys."

"I'm glad." Fieran's smile tipped his mouth in a way that made her think about that kiss they'd shared. Or almost shared? It had been so brief it didn't really count.

But now probably wasn't the time for kissing. Not that she didn't want to kiss Fieran. But their relationship was more than just about kissing, and right now she needed to know the foundation was solid before she thought about kissing again.

"So…" Pip ran her fingers through his hair as she cradled his head on her lap. "Where does this leave us? We were

talking about *us*, but then the attack, and you crashed, and…
I just need to know where we go from here."

"Pip." Fieran lifted a hand again, brushing the back of his fingers across her cheek. "When my aeroplane went into its death spiral, *you* were my only regret. Yes, I regretted that my parents and siblings would mourn. I regretted that I wouldn't be there for the Half-Breed Squadron. But I knew I'd loved my family well. I knew I'd done my best for the squadron. But when it came to you, I had so many regrets. I've made so many mistakes."

She stilled. Fieran's touch on her cheek sent tingles through her.

"I *never* should have made you feel like a distraction." Fieran's gaze remained locked on hers, the look in those blue depths arresting. "I was treating you like a mild flirtation that I could just brush aside for a while. But you are more than a mere distraction. You deserve so much more."

Her mouth went dry, and she couldn't have said anything even if all her words hadn't fled her brain like a flock of starlings taking off.

A flirtatious, grinning Fieran sent flutters to her stomach. But a sincere Fieran was the kind of man she could truly fall in love with.

Fieran rolled into a sitting position, his hand dropping from her face though he didn't let go of her hand with his other one. Once he was upright, he met her gaze. "I want to do this *right*, Pip. I want a relationship like the one my parents have. Like the one your parents have. I want to see if we can have that together. Because you are the most amazing, clever, tough, smart woman I've met, and I think I've been falling for you since the moment I saw you head-down in an engine."

All Pip managed was a breathless, squeaky sound. She

really should say something. Anything. She peeled her dry tongue from the roof of her mouth, trying for a light tone. "I know just how much you've been falling for me. You told me. Sang it for me, actually."

The look of utter confusion that wrinkled his forehead and widened his eyes nearly had a giggle bubbling up inside her. "I did what?"

"You sang a ditty about how much you loved me. With your dacha sitting there and witnessing the whole thing." She had to bite her lip to stop her giggles at the horrified look on Fieran's face.

"I've been hoping those hazy memories were dreams." He grimaced. "How badly did I embarrass myself?"

"Terribly, I'm afraid." Pip leaned closer, wrapping her arms around his neck. "Though I think your dacha was the more embarrassed."

Fieran groaned and leaned his forehead lightly against hers. "Next time I'm drugged out of my mind, just gag me or cover my mouth or something."

"I wanted the ground to swallow me at the time but now…" Feeling rather brave, Pip brushed her fingers through the hair at the nape of his neck. "Now I find it hilarious. And rather cute. Even while you were drugged, that's all you could say the moment you saw me. That you love me."

"It's high time that not-drugged me tells you that I love you." Fieran lowered his voice until he was speaking nearly at a whisper. "And that I'd really like to kiss you."

She wasn't quite sure which of them started the kissing. Maybe him. Maybe her. A spark lit in her chest and burned through her, stealing all her senses except her sense of him.

She tugged him closer, molding herself to him. But

instead of deepening the kiss, he gave a pained groan that had her immediately pulling back. "Sorry, sorry. I forgot."

"It's fine. I'm okay." Fieran sat back to lean heavily against the bench. He closed his eyes as he let his head drop onto the bench. "Sorry. I wanted this to be a lot more romantic"

"You're still healing." Pip claimed one of his hands again, threading her fingers with his. "And I thought that was plenty romantic."

"Good." He tilted his head to look at her, and his eyes had a look to them that she'd never seen before. He was so somber. So lacking in any trace of his usual mischief and humor. "May I court you? For real? No hiding. No sneaking. Just you and me building a relationship the right way."

She opened her mouth, tried to speak, closed her mouth, and swallowed. "Yes." The word came out such a squeaky croak that she sucked in a breath and tried again. "Yes!"

Mindful of his injuries this time, she steadied herself with the bench as she kissed Fieran.

But she kept the kiss short. All she'd needed in these past few days was the reassurance that she and Fieran were good, and she had that now. It was time to look after Fieran.

Pushing to her feet, Pip tugged on Fieran's hand. "Come on. You need to head home and go back to bed. You clearly shouldn't be up this long yet."

Fieran huffed a breath that was somewhere between a laugh and a groan. Even with him using the bench to lever himself upright, Pip still had to brace herself to haul him to his feet.

Once he was upright, he leaned heavily on her. "I know I just asked to court you less than a minute ago, but my mama is here and waiting to meet you. And since we aren't hiding anything, we're going to have to tell Louise."

Only courting for a minute, and she was already going to meet his family.

Yet she wasn't afraid. Or at least, not in the way she would've expected. She wanted to meet his mama and hug Louise as Fieran's girlfriend and not just a random mechanic who needed a place to stay.

"I'd love to meet your mama." Pip wrapped an arm around Fieran's waist, the better to keep him upright as they shuffled along the path around the greenhouse. "Besides, I already met your dacha. Meeting your mama can't be any more terrifying than that."

Fieran tried his best not to lean too heavily on Pip or betray just how much pain he was in, even with the healing magic coursing through him.

But pushing himself had been worth it. He and Pip had needed that conversation. He'd needed to undo some of the mistakes he'd made with her. Fix some of the damage he'd done with his selfishness. Finish that kiss, even if he'd interrupted it again.

More than that, Pip had said yes. She was officially his girlfriend.

He would have shouted it from the rooftops…if he hadn't been about to keel over.

The lift ride to the ground floor and the walk from one warehouse to the other had never felt so long. By the time they reached the fuselage where he'd found Pip, he was clenching his teeth and trying not to let his breathing turn into ragged panting.

Mama was standing next to the fuselage, quietly chatting

with Louise and Bennett. As Fieran and Pip approached, all three of them turned in their direction.

Fieran kept his arm around Pip's shoulders, hoping it looked more like a romantic embrace than that she was holding him upright. "Pip, I'd like you to meet my mama. Mama, this is Pip. My girlfriend." He could feel his grin widen as he said it.

Louise squealed and bounced on her toes. Bennett's eyes widened, more bewildered than anything, and he muttered something before he hurried away.

Mama stepped forward with that graceful ease of hers. As Fieran withdrew his arm, Mama gave Pip a quick hug. "It's a pleasure to finally meet you."

"And to meet you. Fieran has told me a lot about all of you." Pip smiled as she returned the hug.

"He finally made everything official!" Louise grinned and hugged Pip as soon as Mama let her go. "You have no idea how hard it has been not to pester you with questions." She shot a look at Fieran. "You should be impressed by my forbearance."

Fieran braced a hand against the fuselage as he sent an exaggerated, annoyed look at Mama. "Dacha told you, didn't he?"

"Yes. Of course he did." Mama's grin widened as she gave Fieran a hug as well.

Right. Because Dacha told Mama everything. The two of them had no secrets

Great. That meant Dacha would have told Mama the whole singing a love ditty thing. He was never going to live that down.

Then something struck him. "Wait. You're the reason Dacha arranged for Pip to be sent to the AMPC, aren't you? I knew meddling wasn't like him."

It made so much more sense that it had all been Mama's idea.

"Yes and no. I might have inspired the idea and urged him to do it, but believe it or not, the actual idea was your dacha's." Mama gave him and Pip a more hesitant glance. "I'm sorry if we overstepped."

"No, not at all." Fieran shared a look with Pip. He certainly wasn't sorry his parents had meddled to make sure Pip was here in Aldon while he recovered.

Pip shrugged and smiled. "I'm glad I'm here."

So was he. He couldn't have imagined waiting until he returned to Fort Defense to finally sort things out with Pip. Nor would he have wanted her to remain in that almost tormented state that she'd been in when they'd first begun talking.

"And Mama told me, of course." Louise's grin was huge as she hugged Fieran. As she did, she spoke quietly enough so that Pip wouldn't hear. "I like her. You'd better not mess this up. I want her for a sister."

Fieran sucked in a breath so quickly that he choked on his own saliva. He covered his mouth and coughed.

Louise stepped back from him, though her grin didn't get any less mischievous. "We spent that night scouring your letters for any mention of Pip, trying to read between the lines and figure out everything we could about her."

Fieran gave another cough, his ears burning, as he shot another look at Pip. Maybe introducing her to his family wasn't the best idea after all.

She was shifting from foot to foot, her face flushing red.

"All good things, of course." Mama gave Pip a smile before she looked away, her smile slipping just a bit. "It was a good way to pass that night. Neither of us would have gone to bed right away anyway."

Fieran couldn't help the lopsided smile, even if his ears still felt a little too hot. It was strangely comforting, thinking about his mama and sister re-reading his letters for any mention of Pip. That was far better than thinking of them sitting there long into the night worrying over him after his crash.

"And of course I had to volunteer to host you as soon as I heard you were coming to Aldon." Louise turned her grin on Pip. "I've been *dying* to ask you everything, but Mama said not to interfere. But now I can. So as soon as they leave, I'll need you to tell me *everything*. Well, not everything. If you kissed my brother, I *don't* want to hear about it. But everything else."

Fieran felt his ears go even more red as he glanced away from Louise. Considering he had just been kissing Pip a few minutes ago, there was actually something to tell her about. Or not tell her about, as the case might be.

Pip's face flushed scarlet, but she managed a smile. "Will ice cream be involved?"

"Of course." Louise gave Pip another hug. "I've been saving up my ice cream ration."

"Then, it's a deal." Some of Pip's agitation seemed to ease as she returned Louise's hug. She and Louise must have been getting along well, if Pip was willing to confide in her.

Fieran smiled at that. There was just something so *right* about seeing the way Pip was fitting into his family.

"Oh, you know what?" Louise turned to Mama. "Pip should come to Treehaven with me this weekend." Louise whirled to Pip with barely a pause. "I go home to Treehaven every other weekend. Bennett goes home the other weekends. I stay the whole weekend before returning to work the next week."

"Yes." Mama smiled at Pip, waving a hand. "You would be very welcome."

"Oh, I…I couldn't impose. I…" Pip glanced from Mama to Louise to Fieran, as if searching for help.

"You don't have to." Fieran worked to keep any trace of disappointment from his voice. He didn't want to rush Pip. "But I would love to show you my home. And introduce you to my youngest siblings."

"Please say you'll come. I'd feel bad leaving you all alone back here at the AMPC." Louise gave Pip her pleading gaze, the one Fieran could never refuse.

"All right. I'll come." Pip smiled at Louise before she shot a look at Fieran. Traces of something like fear still lingered in her eyes, but her smile was warm. "I'd like to see where you grew up."

With the way she was looking at him, he would've liked to kiss her again. But perhaps a hug would have to do, given that they had an audience.

Fieran took a step away from the fuselage, but as soon as he did so, his knees wobbled.

"All right, that's it." Mama hurried to his side and tugged one of his arms over her shoulders. "Time to get you home."

Pip hugged her arms over her stomach as Fieran guided the roadster down the road toward the tall brick wall that surrounded Treehaven Estate. Louise had the back seat while their bags for the weekend had been placed in the trunk when Fieran had picked them up from the train station in the village.

Ahead, tall trees formed a thick, green foliage within the wall, an island of trees amid all the rolling farm fields.

This was it. Pip flexed her fingers without uncrossing her arms. Her chest squeezed tight, and her heart beat harder than it should. She shouldn't be this nervous. She'd already met Fieran's mama, and it wasn't like his youngest siblings would be scary.

At least she was wearing a lovely green dress Louise had lent her, the skirt shortened so that it worked for Pip's height. A cute dress always made a girl feel more confident.

The gates opened as they neared, the guards waving to Fieran. As the roadster passed through, Pip felt the shiver of Prince Farrendel's magic where it was embedded into the ground, just waiting to spring into a mini Wall at the first sign of danger.

Ahead, a tall, brick manor house sat to the right of the drive. More or less across from it behind a screening layer of evergreens stood a stately wooden house with gray clapboard siding, white trim, and dark blue accent trim.

Fieran turned the wheel as he guided the motorcar down the smaller drive toward the wooden house, pulling to the side where a carriage house sat with its double doors wide open. After pulling the roadster into the carriage house, Fieran shut off the engine and shot Pip a grin. "We're here."

Her stomach twisted. She wasn't ready. This was a big step. A huge step.

And yet she was ready. She was falling for Fieran, and his family was a big part of who he was, the same as her family was to her. He'd already come to know her brother, her only sibling. She'd love to introduce him to her parents just as soon as they returned from their diplomatic mission to the dwarven mountains.

Fieran reached for the door handle on his side, still moving far more slowly than he usually did.

Pip was too nervous to sit there waiting for him to totter his way around the vehicle. Besides, Louise in the back seat needed to get out her side as well.

Instead, Pip climbed out of the motorcar and shoved her seat forward to let Louise climb out by the time Fieran was even partway around the roadster.

"You'll at least let me carry your bag, right?" Fieran raised his eyebrows as he switched his direction to head for the back of the motorcar.

"As long as you don't fall over in the attempt." Pip eyed the way he occasionally reached a hand out to the roadster, steadying himself, as he strode toward the trunk. At least she'd left her wrench at the AMPC. Her bag didn't weigh all that much with only a few clothes, toiletries, and odds and ends in it.

"I'm fine. Really." Fieran's grin might have been more convincing if he hadn't paused at the rear of the motorcar, leaning against it. He was likely trying to pass it off as waiting for Louise to get out of the way, but he wasn't all that convincing.

Louise already had the trunk open as she retrieved her own bag. She grinned first at Fieran, then at Pip. "I'll let everyone know you're here." With that, she slung her bag over her shoulder and strode from the carriage house.

Fieran grabbed Pip's bag and shut the trunk. He stood there for a moment, as if he wasn't sure if he should offer her an arm or his hand.

Pip wasn't sure either. She hadn't seen him since they'd officially started courting. How was a courting couple supposed to act?

Who cared how they were supposed to act? She and Fieran had such an easy friendship before they'd started courting. No reason for things to get awkward now.

"Well, I'd better hold your hand. Just to be on the safe side." Pip sidled to him and took his free hand as casually as she could manage.

"Come to think of it, I am feeling a bit wobbly." Fieran strolled steadily out of the carriage house, swinging their clasped hands. "You'd better stick close and hold tight."

"Just to clarify, if you start falling over, I'm letting go and jumping out of the way. I don't want to be squished." Pip grinned up at Fieran and lengthened her quick stride to match his long-legged amble.

"Good plan." Fieran shared a grin with her before he faced the gravel drive and gestured at the gray clapboard stately house with the hand holding her bag. "As you probably guessed, this is Treehaven House, where I spent much of my childhood when we weren't in Estyra. That brick manor across the way is Treehaven Manor, the original manor house for the area and where Uncle Lance, Aunt Illyna, Bennett, Liliana, and Maria live. I don't think you've met Liliana or Maria yet?"

Pip shook her head. "No, I haven't. I'm not sure I can even say I've truly met Lance Marion yet either. He's been pretty wrapped in his inventions every time I've run across him at the AMPC."

"That's Uncle Lance. And Bennett. He takes after his father." Fieran shook his head.

Pip laughed. "Very true. It took a couple of days until Bennett remembered my name. I'm pretty sure he mentally thinks of me as 'iron magic girl' or something like that. Not that I mind. There are worse things to be known for."

Fieran laughed, a sound that encouraged those around him to laugh along. How Pip loved that sound.

Then Fieran's laugh and grin faded as he pointed again. "We can't see it from here, but Treehaven Lodge is tucked into the trees behind Treehaven House. That's where Uncle Iyrinder, Aunt Patience, Merrik, and Kari live."

Treehaven Lodge was empty now, all its occupants scattered.

A lump filled Pip's throat as the images crowded her mind again. Merrik's too pale face. The bloody mangle of his lower legs. The grim way his dacha tightened the tourniquet.

She shook the images away. She'd break if she dwelled on those thoughts.

Clearing her throat, she forced a lightness back to her tone. Neither she nor Fieran were at a point to talk about

Merrik. "Treehaven Manor, House, and Lodge? Isn't that confusing?"

"Somewhat, yes. The whole estate is considered Treehaven, so when Dacha and Uncle Iyrinder had the House and Lodge built, they needed a way to distinguish each home from the others." Fieran rolled his shoulders in a shrug, though it was still more tense than easy. "We still sometimes get mail and telephone calls to the wrong house, but it's easy enough to sort out."

By this point, they neared the house. The larger gravel drive wound to a circle drive by the front door while a smaller path branched off beneath a white lattice arbor to head toward the back of the house.

Pip's steps slowed, hesitating, as she eyed the two paths. Would Fieran take her around to the front? Or to the back? The one signified a more formal introduction to the family. The other a warmer, informal meeting, as if she was already a part of the family.

She shouldn't have doubted. Fieran turned down the path beneath the arbor without a pause in his stride.

The two of them walked through a blooming garden, the flowers bursting and colorful in a way that made Pip almost wish she could name more than a handful of them.

As they turned the corner toward the back of the house, the gravel path transitioned to brick where it led up to a broad patio extending from the back of the house. The landscape dipped into a large hill descending from the house, and both the path and the patio were edged with black, wrought iron railings.

Large windows at the back of the house overlooked the patio and the forested hill beyond while two sets of double doors led into the house.

A pale, almost ghostly face appeared in one of the

windows of the second story, but as soon as Pip glanced that way to get a better look, the face vanished.

Fieran marched right up to one of the sets of doors, though he had to pause for a moment to juggle her bag and turn the knob. He led the way inside and closed the door behind them.

This particular set of double doors led straight into what seemed to be a parlor, all done in rich deep greens and gold accents.

A girl in a light blue dress, which contrasted with her long red hair, sprawled on one of the couches with her feet propped on the armrest and her head on a pillow, a book in her hands. She didn't so much as glance away from the book at the sound of the doors. Perhaps she hadn't even registered the sound.

"That's my youngest sister Ellie." Fieran gestured toward the girl.

Her name must have caught her attention because she arched her back, tilting her head to peer behind her without getting up. Taking one hand off the book, she gave a brief wave. "Hello."

"Hello." Pip gave a wave in return, but Ellie had already returned to her book. Pip smiled, something in her relaxing at the casualness of the gesture. It would have been more awkward if Ellie had made a big production of welcoming her.

More than that, it was exactly what Pip would have expected, given all Fieran had told her about Ellie, especially while they'd been waiting in line to get Star Forest novels signed. It was almost as if Pip already knew Fieran's family, even if she hadn't met all of them in person yet.

Fieran strode across the room, and Pip trotted at his side through the large, framed doorway into a hall. Directly in front of them, a wooden-paneled stairway wound upward while the hall stretched in either direction.

A small boy with silver-blond hair and large green eyes peered between the rails at the top of the stairs. Likely the face Pip had spotted in the window earlier. As before, when Pip glanced at him, the boy disappeared back out of sight.

"That's Tryndar. He's shy." Fieran's smile held a wry tilt. "He's most like Dacha in that way. Most of us ended up more gregarious like Mama."

Pip opened her mouth to reply, but footsteps sounded down the hall before Fieran's mama Princess Elspeth strode into sight.

Princess Elspeth gave Pip a warm smile, her eyes twinkling. "Welcome to Treehaven House, Pip. I'll show you to your room so you can get settled."

She turned and strode back the way she'd come. The corridor was too narrow for walking side-by-side, so Pip rather reluctantly released Fieran's hand so she could follow his mama. Fieran took up the rear, still carrying her bag for her.

The princess led all the way to the end of the hall, where the final room on the left opened into the base of the corner turret of the house. The many windows set into the walls overlooked the forested hill behind the house. A very elven view, here in Escarland.

The room itself was done in pale pinks and greens. A white four-poster bed stood along one of the few windowless walls, spread with a quilt made of floral fabrics. The drapes on the windows were pink overlaid with white lace, and the rest of the furniture was white on top of the green rugs.

It was an adorable guest room. A bit frilly and pink, but in a comforting, homey kind of way. Not the type of room

Pip would have decorated for herself, and yet exactly the kind of guest room she'd love to stay in.

"Make yourself at home." Princess Elspeth gestured around the room. "The kitchen is at the end of the hall back the way we came. Feel free to ask if you need anything. The water closet is through the door there. Towels are on the shelves in the cabinet while there are spare toiletries as well. Help yourself. Thanks to Illyna, we always have extras."

Fieran set Pip's bag on the bed before he retreated into the hallway. "Once you're settled, Pip, I'll show you around the estate grounds. We can take the zip lines."

"Zip lines?" Pip turned right around and headed for the doorway. It wasn't like she had anything she really needed to unpack. She planned to just live out of her bag for the weekend.

"Supper is in an hour," Princess Elspeth called after them as Pip hurried after Fieran.

"Got it," Fieran called back without turning around or slowing his pace.

Pip hurried to catch up and took his hand, smiling when he clasped his fingers with hers.

Despite her worries for the squadron, her frustrations over the interrupter gear, and her nerves at meeting Fieran's family, she was going to enjoy this perfectly lovely weekend where she could just fall in love and forget about the war for a few blissful hours.

FIERAN RELAXED into his seat on the couch in the parlor, his stomach filled with supper, his hand resting in the space between him and Pip. They'd taken seats next to each other, yet they weren't holding hands. Nor had he dared put his arm around her shoulders. Not with his family watching. Even Tryndar had made an appearance—drawn out by food —but he was huddled by Mama and simply stared at Pip with wide eyes.

"And then he ran smack-dab into the door. Not the flat side of the door. No, the door was open so he ran into the end and gouged his forehead on the latch." Mama shook her head, her smile wry as she told the familiar story from Fieran's childhood.

"I still have a faint scar from that one." Fieran tipped his head toward Pip and pointed at his forehead. It was just a barely discernible line that looked more like a wrinkle than anything else.

Pip's eyes scanned his forehead for a moment before she met his gaze, the look switching from mirth to something with more longing.

Mama pushed to her feet. "Come along, Tryndar. It's time for bed."

As if that was the signal, everyone else got to their feet and scattered. Ellie retrieved her book and mumbled something about reading in bed. Louise headed off to her own room with a stack of blueprints clutched in a bag.

Fieran rose to his feet and held out a hand to Pip. He was somewhat sore from all the zip line traveling that afternoon —annoying how something that simple now did him in— but he still had a bit of strength left in him. "Would you like to go for a walk?"

"Yes." Pip hopped to her feet as if she'd been waiting all day for just that.

Together, the two of them meandered out the double doors, across the patio, and down the stairs until they reached a faint path winding between the trees.

Fieran kept his pace slow and ambling so that he didn't

make Pip run to keep up with him. Not that he could have managed a faster pace, stiff and sore as he was.

As they walked, they shared stories of growing up. The mischief. The good memories. The bad ones. All of it.

With most people, Fieran found himself talking too much. But with Pip, he rather enjoyed staying quiet as he listened to her talk.

He pointed out one of the large, rambling maple trees as they passed. "I fell out of that tree. One of the times I broke my arm." The smile dropped from his face as the memories filled him. "Merrik tried to catch me and got dragged out of the tree after me. He broke his arm too."

It seemed Merrik had always been trying to catch him when he fell. And always paid the price for the attempt.

Pip squeezed his hand and briefly leaned her head against his arm. "I'm sorry. Merrik forgave you for that. With time, he will forgive you for this too. Or realize that it isn't really your fault."

Fieran wasn't so sure. Merrik had yet to answer any of Fieran's letters. Nor had he called Fieran back, even though he was healing well enough that Aunt Illyna left a few days ago to see about fitting him for a prosthetic. Even Adry had begun to be cagey and not give him information when he talked to her on the telephone.

Anything Fieran knew about Merrik right now came secondhand through the family grapevine. It wasn't right, but short of traveling to Estyra himself, there wasn't anything Fieran could do.

He didn't want to talk about Merrik. Not even with Pip.

They reached a forest glade not far from the outer wall. Here, a swing hung from one of the sturdy branches, the bench seat wide enough for two people to comfortably sit, though it was small enough to encourage cuddling.

Fieran took a seat on the bench, then tugged Pip down next to him.

She snuggled into his side, her head leaning against his shoulder, her hand still clasped in his. "This is a rather convenient swing."

"Yes." Fieran leaned his head against hers. "All of us kids learned quite early on not to follow when Dacha and Mama wandered in this direction. Not if we didn't want to catch them"—he dropped his voice into a scandalized hush—"kissing."

Pip huffed and gave his arm a light shove. "Thanks a lot. I didn't need that image in my head."

Fieran gave in to the urge to press a light kiss to her hair. "I was hoping the mention of kissing would be inspirational."

"Not when you mention your parents and kissing in the same sentence." Pip gave another grumbling huff as she lightly shoved her shoulder into him.

That might not have been his best strategic move. But now he had no choice but to plow forward. "Did you never catch your parents kissing?"

"That's just it. Dwarves are not as retiring and proper as elves." Pip shook her head against his arm. "Nor do they have the same ideas of what is improper that humans do. It isn't that dwarves lack standards. But kissing in public—and other public displays of affection—are completely normal for dwarves. So, yeah, I've seen my parents kissing way more than my elven half would like."

Fieran laughed softly into her hair. "Traumatizing."

"And reassuring, I guess. We never had to wonder if our parents still liked each other." Pip's voice lowered, softening, as Fieran gently rocked the swing.

She had been right. He definitely didn't want to talk

about either set of their parents kissing. It was sidetracking them from the main thing. Namely, actually kissing.

By the time he and Pip finally meandered their way back to Treehaven House, pausing to kiss a few times along the way, a light shone in the parlor, and only the double doors into the parlor remained unlocked.

Fieran held Pip's hand as he eased the door open and tiptoed inside.

Mama sat on one of the couches, a book in her lap. She glanced up as they entered before her gaze returned to her book. The slightest curve to her mouth betrayed that she knew exactly what he and Pip had been doing.

Fieran cleared his throat, his ears burning. It wasn't like they'd crossed any lines they shouldn't have. And they hadn't *only* been kissing. There had been a lot of talking too.

He resisted the urge to glance at Pip. Her face was likely red as his was. "Goodnight, Mama."

"Goodnight." Mama flipped a page in her book. "Pip, I'll be up for a while yet, if you need anything."

Beside Fieran, Pip bobbed her head and mumbled an unintelligible assent.

Fieran hurried from the room with Pip in his wake. He didn't halt again until he reached the base of the stairs, where he turned to Pip.

For a moment, the two of them met each other's gazes.

And then Fieran smothered a snort of laughter. Pip, too, pressed a hand over her mouth as her shoulders shook with silent laughter.

It took several moments for the two of them to get their mirth under control. Once they did, Fieran gave Pip one last kiss before he climbed the stairs to his room and she retreated down the hall toward hers.

TEN

When Pip strode from the guest room the next morning, she nearly tripped over the small figure sitting cross-legged right outside her door. Only the fact that she made a habit of looking for those few who were shorter than herself saved her from falling.

"Tryndar?" Pip blinked down at Fieran's little brother. The boy hadn't said two words to her all yesterday. "What are you doing here?"

"Sitting." Tryndar gazed up at her with large green eyes. "Because I am not supposed to go into someone's room while they are sleeping. It is not nice."

"I...see." She was glad he hadn't invaded her privacy that much.

Tryndar kept staring up at her. "Are you going to marry my brother?"

How was she supposed to answer that? She and Fieran had just started courting. Sure, that was where Pip believed this was headed. But nothing was certain just yet.

"I don't know yet. Maybe. We're courting." Pip held Tryndar's gaze rather than look away. She wasn't sure how much sincerity the little boy could read in her gaze, but she would be as open as she could.

Tryndar gave a nod. He paused for a moment, his hands gripped on his knees. "Do you want to see my toy soldiers?"

This seemed like a make or break moment for winning over Fieran's little brother.

Pip smiled and nodded. "Of course. I'd love to."

Tryndar popped to his feet, grabbed her hand, and tugged her down the hall. "Come on."

Pip found herself led upstairs and into the first room down the hall. There the bed tucked beneath the window was made rather neatly for a young boy. The chest of toys and the items on the bookshelf were set with a rather meticulous order, down to the rows of soldiers on the lower shelves.

Tryndar darted around his room, pointing out various items and telling her about them. She hadn't known the half-elf boy could string so many words together. He held up one elf figurine. "This one is Dacha. And this one is Uncle Weylind. And this is Uncle Rharreth." He paused, frowning at the line of figurines. "I do not have one of Fieran."

He sounded so despondent that Pip had to smother a laugh. Then she whirled, heading for the door. "Wait there. I'll be back in a moment."

Pip hurried from the door and nearly ran into Ellie, who was walking down the hallway while holding a book before her face. How she was reading and walking at the same time, Pip didn't know.

Dodging around her, Pip dashed down the stairs, down the hall, and into her room. She dug through her bag until she found the section of metal she'd tucked into her bag when she'd left Fort Defense. She'd never unpacked it at the AMPC, and it had made its way here.

She hadn't been sure what to do with the piece of shrapnel, all that was left of Fieran's aeroplane. It had been a sweet—if a bit macabre—gesture on Fieran's part. But Pip didn't really want to keep a piece of metal that had impaled him.

She wouldn't tell Tryndar that part. But he'd find it neat to have a piece of Fieran's aeroplane.

After taking a moment to reshape the metal with her magic, she hurried back the way she'd come.

Louise was meandering from her room as Pip reached the top of the stairs again, and she gave her a raised eyebrow look as Pip ran by.

Pip knocked on Tryndar's open door. "I'm back."

Tryndar was sitting on the edge of his bed, swinging his legs. "You may come in. You are not supposed to go into a room until someone says that."

Pip strode inside with a hand behind her back. "I brought you something."

"A gift?" Tryndar slid off his bed and crept closer.

Pip brought her hand from behind her back and presented the small metal aeroplane she had crafted from the piece of shrapnel. The biplane's wings were thinnest metal while the struts had more weight to them. She'd even created a little metal pilot in the cockpit, complete with goggles and flight cap. "This was made from a piece of Fieran's aeroplane."

Tryndar's eyes were wide as moons as he took the tiny aeroplane. For several moments, he examined the aeroplane from every angle. He spun the propeller and the wheels, making her glad she'd thought to create them so they moved.

Pip smiled, watching him. She'd never had a younger sibling to spoil before.

Something inside her ached, and she wasn't sure if it was a good ache or a bad ache. She was falling for Fieran, yes, but after this weekend she was falling for his family too.

A knock sounded on the open door as Princess Elspeth halted just outside. "Breakfast is ready."

Tryndar bounded across the room, holding up the toy aeroplane. "Look what Miss Pip gave me!"

Princess Elspeth smiled at Tryndar, her gaze taking in the aeroplane. "Did you thank Miss Pip?"

"Linshi." Tryndar didn't even glance over his shoulder, still too enamored with the aeroplane.

Pip took that as a compliment. "You're welcome."

Tryndar made buzzing, zooming noises as he held the aeroplane up and raced past Princess Elspeth and into the hallway.

Princess Elspeth smiled and shook her head. "I'm sorry about Tryndar kidnapping you this morning."

"I don't mind. I'm just glad he's warming up to me." Pip followed the princess from the room.

The two of them entered the hall just as Tryndar clambered onto the stair railing. Still holding the toy aeroplane, Tryndar slid down the banister. Beside Pip, Princess Elspeth just shook her head, as if she was rather inured to wild elf children by now.

Too bad Pip couldn't create a fully metal aeroplane for Fieran. She could make something like that more impervious to bullets, not to mention capable of conducting his magic even better than the shielding wires.

Yet everyone knew aeroplanes needed to be as light as possible. It was difficult enough to get a heavier-than-air aeroplane to fly as it was without making it even heavier.

Someday, maybe mechanics and science would develop enough to make such a thing possible. Until then, Pip needed to concentrate on the things she could develop. Like the incredibly stubborn synchronization gear.

If only she could just work her magic on that as easily as she had the scrap of metal. But magic didn't seem to be the answer this time around.

Or was it...Pip froze in the corridor, her mind whirling. What if...if they...

She hurried past Princess Elspeth with a murmured "Pardon me," before she raced down the stairs. Bursting into the kitchen, she skidded to a halt by the table, where Louise was already helping herself to pancakes from the stack on the plate. "We've been coming at the gear all wrong."

Louise froze, her gaze swinging to Pip. "What do you mean?"

"We've been trying to make it purely mechanical. But what if it needs to be powered?"

"A magical solenoid! Of course!" Louise shoved away from the table. "If we routed the magic through..."

She kept speaking out loud as she headed for the door, as if she planned to grab her bag and leave for Aldon right that minute.

Princess Elspeth stepped into the kitchen, took one look at Louise, raised her eyebrows, and pointed toward the table. "I'm not sure what I missed, but both of you need to eat breakfast before you go anywhere. If you don't eat for your sake, then at least let our guest have a chance to eat."

Louise blinked, then turned back to Pip as if she'd forgotten Pip was there. "Oh, right. Sorry, Pip."

As she settled into her seat once again, the back door opened, and Fierar stepped inside.

Pip caught her breath, her mouth going a little dry at the sight of him. He wore his swords strapped across his back, his red hair tousled and a hint of perspiration at the hairline. With his green, elven-style clothes and those swords, he looked far more elven than he usually did in his Escarlish uniform.

It was really too bad that she wasn't brave enough to kiss him in front of his family.

PIP THREW herself into Fieran's arms when he stepped into the main invention warehouse. "We did it."

He caught her, his arms wrapping around her waist and holding her against him, even as her feet dangled above the floor. "The synchronization gear?"

"Yes! It works. It finally works." Pip hugged him around the neck. "Not just works, but it's reliable. Much better than the Mongavarian version."

He never would have crashed if his propeller hadn't broken. She couldn't prevent all the reasons for a crash. She couldn't control all the factors in a war. But this was one thing she had fixed.

Fieran grinned at her, his face only inches from hers. "I knew you could do it."

"Louise and Bennett did most of it. I just gave a few suggestions here and there." Pip shifted her elbows to better support her weight against Fieran's chest since her feet were still rather far from the floor. She was definitely not going to think of the feel of his muscles and the way his face was so very close and kissable.

"They still couldn't have done it without you." He was all but beaming at her, his grin wide, his blue eyes sparkling.

"Then do I get a congratulations kiss?" After all, what was the point of officially courting if congratulations kisses weren't a part of the deal?

Fieran's grin widened before he finally kissed her. She wiggled her toes in her boots and kissed him back, her grip tightening around his neck.

Now this was the perfect way to celebrate. Even better—barely—than the bowls of celebration ice cream she and Louise had gotten during their lunch break. It had been really good ice cream.

When she pulled back to end the kiss, Fieran lowered her feet back to the floor. His grin faded into a rather serious expression, given the kissing of a moment before.

Pip rested her hand on his arm. "What is it?"

Fieran pulled a piece of paper out of his pocket. "I've been cleared for duty and given my new orders. I'll be flying out in a few days, escorting a squadron of the new bomber aeroplanes to Fort Defense."

"Oh." Pip's hands dropped to her sides. All the heady rush of their courtship dropping as quickly as an aeroplane from the sky.

She'd known Fieran would be returning to Fort Defense soon. He was too integral to the war to remain here a moment longer once he was fully healed. And by the way he hadn't flinched when she'd jumped into his arms and he'd held her without trouble, he was healed and definitely strong enough to fly an aeroplane.

Yet she didn't have orders to return to Fort Defense. Perhaps they would still be coming, now that she had helped solve the synchronization gear problem.

Unless her work with the synchronization gear had proved to the higher-ups that her skills could be put to more use here than at Fort Defense as an aeroplane mechanic. She could find herself separated from Fieran for the rest of the war.

Not just Fieran. But Mak. Her flyboys. The whole squadron. She *needed* to return to Fort Defense.

"Hey. It'll be all right." Fieran grasped her shoulders, rubbing his thumbs over them in a way that sent tingles down her back.

He'd done that before. Did he know how comforting she found the gesture?

He studied her expression as he held her gaze. "You can stay here. I know we wouldn't see each other as often, but you'd be safe. And you'd be able to work at the AMPC."

She could stay. It would mean more ice cream nights— and afternoons—with Louise. Probably more weekends spent with Fieran's family. Days here at the AMPC surrounded by magic and mechanics in a way she'd only dreamed about when growing up. There would be far fewer bombings. Less danger. No more watching her flyboys fall from the sky.

Perhaps that was a life for someday. But right now, she couldn't imagine letting Fieran fly into danger without her. She couldn't abandon her flyboys.

Pip shook her head. "No. I'd like to return to Fort Defense. I can't abandon the squadron."

Fieran exhaled a long sigh and pulled her to him, wrapping her in an embrace. "I don't want you in danger again, but I'll be glad to have you watching my back."

She wrapped her arms around his waist and rested her head against his chest. "But will they send me back? What if they think I'm too valuable here?"

"If my family was so keen to meddle to get you here, then they had better meddle to send you back to Fort Defense." Fieran's huff stirred her hair.

Very true. After all, she likely wouldn't have even been here if not for their very appreciated meddling.

She might not return to Fort Defense right away, but hopefully she'd rejoin Fieran sooner rather than later.

FIERAN SWALLOWED, his stomach far too knotted, as he faced the airfield outside of Aldon.

Last year, this had merely been a farmer's field. But in the past few months, it had been requisitioned by the army, due to its location and overall flat terrain, and turned into a makeshift aerodrome. Large tents and half-finished structures filled one side of the field while aeroplanes lined up at the end.

Most of the aercplanes were huge biplanes, their wings stretching for nearly a hundred feet compared with the nearly thirty-foot wingspan of the type of aeroplane Fieran flew—apparently they were calling those fighter aeroplanes now to distinguish from these new bomber aeroplanes.

The bombers had three seats, including one for an onboard mechanic, three engines with two of the engines out on the lower wings, and three machine guns, two forward and one pointing backward. Cleats for six bombs were attached inside a hollow in the belly of the bomber aeroplane, to be dropped by a lever controlled by the person in the second seat. That person had a rudimentary bomb sight to attempt to land the bombs on the target.

Piloting those aeroplanes must be something else. They looked like they would fly like unwieldy turtles.

Several of the bomber aeroplanes were already rumbling down the airfield before lifting into the air. More were spinning up, waiting for their turn to take off.

Fieran's new aeroplane waited behind the bomber aeroplanes. It had a cowling painted in black and white stripes while the rest of it was a nearly flat gray-blue like the rest of the Alliance aeroplanes, the red, green, and gray circles painted on the wings. Without the nose art, it seemed rather plain.

On the undersides of the wings, new cleats held spots for four bombs, much smaller than the ones the bomber aeroplanes could carry. The bombs on his new aeroplane would likely be rigged as incendiaries to take out airships, but they could also be anti-personnel bombs to be dropped on ground troops.

Besides the bomb cleats, this aeroplane also had two machine guns built into the nose rather than the single machine gun on his previous aeroplane, making this aeroplane faster, more maneuverable, and more lethal.

Fieran swallowed again as he faced his new Defender. He loved flying. He did.

And yet when he looked at that aeroplane, something inside him shook with the memories of the whirling, spinning, falling, crashing…

No, he couldn't think of it. He'd survived. He would not fear flying.

"I do not want you to go." Tryndar's teary voice brought Fieran back to himself.

He turned around, back to where Pip, Mama, Louise, Ellie, and Tryndar waited next to the roadster that they'd somehow all packed into. It was a sign of how haphazard this airfield was that his family had been allowed onto it so easily.

Tryndar leaned against Mama's legs, his green eyes big and liquid.

Fieran crouched to put himself eye level with his brother. "I know. But I have to go. I'll write and call as much as possible, and I will love any pictures you send me."

Tryndar nodded before he flung himself forward, wrapping his arms around Fieran's neck.

Fieran hugged him tightly, a lump knotting in his throat to match the one twisting his stomach. As much as he wanted to return to his squadron, this goodbye with his family was almost harder than the one when he'd left for the army.

Probably because he actually knew the dangers now. He'd spent several hours over the past few days writing *If I Die* letters for each of his family members—and one for Pip —and he'd entrusted those letters to Mama to distribute if the worst should happen.

She'd taken them with that far too solemn look on her face before she'd stowed them in Dacha's desk, right by a pile of letters in Dacha's hand. The top one had Mama's name across it, and if Fieran were to guess, those were Dacha's *If I Die* letters.

Somehow, Fieran had never realized that Dacha, too, would have a stack of letters like that. A will. Preparations for what would happen if he were killed in this war.

It had simply never occurred to Fieran that his dacha was anything but invincible any more than it had registered that he wasn't.

After setting Tryndar down, Fieran hugged Mama, Louise, and Ellie, trying not to let himself think that this could be the last time he hugged them. The last time he saw them. If he crashed again…

He wouldn't. He would fight to get back to them with all the strength of his magic.

Once he reached Pip, he held out his hand. "Walk me to my aeroplane?"

Pip took his hand, giving him a small smile.

He paused long enough to retrieve the stack of his

flight gear from the back seat of the roadster. He hesitated a moment before he also grabbed his swords. The rest of his gear had already been passed to a member of the ground crew to load into the second seat of one of the bombers, since only some of the bombers had a second seat gunner.

Then Fieran and Pip strode between the various bombers spinning up. They didn't speak until they reached Fieran's new aeroplane.

Pip let go of his hand as she walked around the aeroplane, occasionally patting the side or peering closer at a section of it. "A brand new Soarwing Defender with the latest Dymman engine."

"I'm going to miss the old one." Fieran eyed the aeroplane. The canvas covering the fuselage and wings was so taut and painted so glossy that it almost appeared to be sheeted in metal. Not a single scratch or bullet hole.

But this wasn't the aeroplane he'd flown for so many miles, until the control stick had been worn to his fingers and the seat in the cockpit molded to him.

Yet he'd never fly that aeroplane again. He'd blown that one to bits.

"Me too." Pip's eyes never left the new aeroplane, as if she was already itching to open the engine compartment and start wrenching on it. "But this is a beautiful machine."

Fieran swallowed, set the stack of his flight clothes on the wing, and dug into his pocket for the box he'd stowed there. "Pip, I...I got this for you."

He held out the brown paper wrapped box, sporting a white ribbon tied in a bow.

Pip took the box, her eyebrows scrunching as if she was puzzled about what he'd get her.

He rocked back and forth from heels to toe and clasped

his hands behind his back to hide the fact that he was struggling to keep his magic from twining around his fingers.

Pip slid the bow from the box before she took off the lid. She gasped as she lifted the necklace out of the box. "Fieran, this…it's…"

It was a deceptively simple necklace. Just a chain with a single pendant dangling from it. Except that the pendant was in the shape of a wrench, and he'd had the jeweler set three gems along the wrench's handle. A ruby, an emerald, and a diamond. The Alliance colors.

"Are these *real?*" Pip gawked, first at the necklace, then at him.

"Uh, yes?" Fieran shrugged and winced. "Is that okay?"

He hadn't been sure what was the correct price range for the first jewelry gift for a girlfriend. He suspected whatever he considered a normal amount was still on the higher end.

Pip stared at the necklace for another moment before she smiled. "It's perfect. Linshi."

She stood on her tiptoes, and he drew her in for a quick kiss. He would have loved to give her a longer kiss, but there were too many people around.

Once he stopped kissing her, he kept an arm around her waist as she unclasped the necklace and quickly put it on. It fell onto her blouse, the gems winking in the sunlight.

The bomber aeroplanes in line before Fieran rolled forward as the aeroplanes before them moved into position to take off next.

"I'm next." Fieran didn't want to let her go.

"Then I suppose you should get dressed in your flight gear." Pip didn't step away either.

"I should." Fieran wrapped her in his arms for one last embrace as he pressed a kiss into her hair.

Then he forced himself to let her go and step back. He

turned away and busied himself with pulling on his warm flight boots that covered all the way up to his thighs, his flight coat that went to his knees, a flight cap, goggles, and finally his scarf around his neck.

Of course, none of these were *his*. They were all as new as his aeroplane. This jacket wasn't the one he'd broken in until it was flexible and comfortable. The boots were still stiff when he moved. The cap wasn't worn to fit his head just right.

Lastly, he picked up his swords in their sheaths. He probably should have stowed them in his trunk, but he found he couldn't bring himself to entrust them to one of the other pilots, especially as green as these bomber pilots were.

He met Pip's gaze as he climbed onto the wing. "I'll see you at Fort Defense in a few days."

"I'll be counting them down." She backed away from his aeroplane.

As he'd hoped, his family had come through. Orders had come that she was to take the train to Fort Defense with the first batch of new synchronization gears in a few days.

The upper wing crowded closer to the cockpit on this new aeroplane, and Fieran had to bend and maneuver his way into the cockpit more than he had on his old one. When he settled in, the dimensions weren't familiar, the scant leather padding beneath his butt not yet broken in. Even the control column didn't feel the same, as it had an additional trigger lever for firing the two machine guns mounted side-by-side on the aeroplane's nose. No more having to let go to reach the triggers on the guns themselves.

Leather straps were bolted on the inside of the aeroplane, likely to hold an additional rifle or a spyglass for scouting missions. Fieran stowed his swords alongside him and strapped them in place before he reached for the belt to strap himself in.

When he flipped the switches to turn on the engine, it roared to life with a power that vibrated through the whole frame around him. The engine spun up more quickly than his previous aeroplane's, and the propeller soon beat the air with a humming whir.

When it was his turn to take off, the ground crew removed the wheel chocks and dashed away as his aeroplane rolled forward.

Fieran steered the rolling aeroplane to the end of the airfield. When he straightened the aeroplane out, he poured on the power. The aeroplane bumped and bounced over the cropped grass. He could feel the ridges where the farmer must have plowed the field at one point, and the aeroplane's wheels automatically followed those ruts down the length of the airfield.

The aeroplane grew light around him, the air firming beneath the wings. His breath caught, and he braced himself to take to the skies once again.

Then it lifted off, and the knots in his stomach eased along with it. He whooped as the aeroplane soared upward, gliding on its shiny wings.

Once he had enough altitude, Fieran looped his aeroplane upside down before he threw it into a corkscrew. When he came out of that, he swooped lower over where Pip and his family still stood by the roadster, waving at him as they gazed upward. He flew upside down to wave back. He could see Tryndar, jumping on the back seat, the toy aeroplane Pip made for him in hand, as he waved with both arms.

"Capt. Laesornysh, stop showing off and take up your

escort station." The voice on the radio rang with a disgruntled authority.

He must have been someone on the ground. Likely the aerodrome's commanding officer since none of the pilots flying the bombers outranked Fieran.

"Yes, sir." Fieran pulled his aeroplane back to right side up before he pointed the nose toward the swarm of bombers assembled in the sky as they headed for Fort Defense.

ELEVEN

His aeroplane's wheels touched down on the familiar airfield on the bluff, the grass so dead and brown that clouds of dust billowed behind him and coated the pristine paint of his new aeroplane. When he turned his aeroplane, he had to steer it into the dust cloud to head toward the hangar.

The bombers were already parked in a long line beside the hangar, their wings too wide to fit inside the double doors. Along the right side of the airfield and perpendicular to the current hangar, the frame of a new building was going up. Probably a hangar for the new bombers.

Fieran let his aeroplane roll to a stop before the door to Bay 4. The ground crew dashed forward to claim his aeroplane even before he unbuckled himself and his swords.

He started to lever himself out of the aeroplane, but a spasm seized his leg muscles. He gritted his teeth and fell back into the aeroplane seat.

Bother. He'd known that long flight was going to be hard, but it turned out he wasn't nearly as back to full strength as he'd hoped.

"Captain?" Lije appeared at his side, balancing on the footstep. "Are you all right?"

"Fine." Fieran sucked in a breath as he kneaded first one calf muscle, then the other. "Muscles locked up. That's all."

With another steadying breath, Fieran braced his hands on the sides of the cockpit and levered himself upright. Once Lije stepped down from the aeroplane, giving Fieran room, Fieran swung his leg over the side. His toes found the step, and he grabbed his swords before he lowered himself from the aeroplane to the ground. If he kept a hand on the wing to keep himself steady, hopefully no one would notice.

The heat from the summer sun beat down on him, almost instantly roasting him within his layers of flight clothing. He peeled his goggles and cap off as a mob of flyboys rushed from the hangar.

They halted before him, pausing to give him a proper salute. The elves followed at a slower, more orderly pace before they, too, saluted.

Fieran leaned against the aeroplane behind him so that he could lift his hand from the wing to return the salute. He took in the familiar faces, something in his gut easing at the sight of each one. Lije with his gap-toothed grin. Pretty Face with a smirk twitching his thin mustache. Tiny with hints of his ice magic playing around his fingers. Stickyfingers standing on tiptoes to see past the others. Aylia, Murray, and more.

Except...

"Where's Lt. Rothilion?" Fieran glanced over the assembled squadron, even as he peeled off his far-too-warm flight jacket. Lt. Rothilion and a handful of elven pilots were missing. "And the others?"

"They're on patrol." Lije grinned, as if there was something humorous about that.

After shucking his flight boots and setting his gear on the wing, Fieran slung the straps of his swords over his shoulders and buckled them in place with a few practiced moves. The weight settled against his shoulders, familiar yet not comfortable.

He eyed his grinning flyboys. "What aren't you telling me?"

"Nothing too important." Pretty Face smirked, as if he and the others shared an inside joke. He pointed upward. "Actually, looks like Lt. Rothilion is coming in for a landing. You can see for yourself."

An aeroplane scared overhead, the engine humming, the propeller setting up that deeper thrum, as it lined up on the airfield, which was now cleared of bombers and other aeroplanes.

Fieran turned to get a better look, squinting into the setting sun. That was a two-seater, not Lt. Rothilion's normal aeroplane.

The aeroplane touched down lightly, then rolled with its momentum. As it slowed, it turned and coasted back to the hangar until it finally came to a halt only a few yards away.

The aeroplane's pilot climbed out, revealing Lt. Rothilion's honey-blond hair as he removed his cap and goggles. His long hair was tied back and tucked underneath his flight jacket to keep it from tangling.

Rather than stroll toward Fieran, Lt. Rothilion waited beside the aeroplane as the passenger in the second seat climbed smoothly down, the grace of the movements proving that his passenger was an elf.

There was something familiar about those movements. Yet it wasn't until the passenger pulled off his flight cap and goggles and revealed silver-blond hair, similarly tied back and stuffed beneath the flight jacket, that Fieran started. "What's my dacha doing flying with Lt. Rothilion?"

"Pretending to be you." Pretty Face shrugged, as if that was a perfectly normal set of words. "He volunteered, and we conducted our first flight only a few days after you'd been sent back to Aldon."

"First flight?" Fieran braced himself more firmly against his aeroplane behind him, his legs going even more wobbly.

"Yeah, we've done five or six of these." Lije gestured to where Dacha and Lt. Rothilion were striding toward the rest of them. Both elves were busy freeing their hair from the ties. "Your dacha realized that the Mongavarians wouldn't know how badly you'd been wounded, and they have no way to tell your magic apart from his. So he's been going up, putting on a show of his magic, to make the Mongavarians think that you've been here the whole time."

"It worked." Pretty Face grinned again. "We've had a nice, quiet two weeks."

Fieran released a breath, an ache disappearing from his chest. He'd been worried that his squadron would be in danger without him and his magic there to protect them.

Yet his dacha had stepped in to protect the squadron for him.

As Dacha reached them, the pilots all turned and saluted. Yet there was something about the way they did so, as if they weren't quite as terrified of Dacha as they had been before.

Fieran hurried to straighten and salute as well, still reeling at the sight of his dacha in flight clothes.

"At ease." Dacha returned their salutes, his gaze locking on Fieran.

Last time Fieran had arrived at Fort Defense, he hadn't hugged Dacha, too mindful of all the eyes watching. This time, he didn't hesitate. He embraced Dacha, throwing in a back slap for good measure.

After the first stiff moment, Dacha returned the embrace before he stepped back, gripping Fieran's shoulders. His gaze flicked over Fieran, as if taking in everything from his stance to the swords on his back. "You seem to have healed well, sason."

"Nylian worked wonders, as usual." Fieran grinned with all the memories of past trips to Nylian when growing up. He released Dacha's shoulders and gestured at the two-seater. "You've been flying with my squadron."

He was dying to ask all about it, especially how it had come about that he was flying with Lt. Rothilion of all people. Rothilion came from a stuffy elven noble family who hated Dacha. While Rothilion had come around to respecting Fieran, that didn't necessarily extend to Dacha.

Or did it? Fieran suspected neither Lt. Rothilion nor Dacha would own up to anything in front of the rest of the squadron.

Dacha gave that graceful elven shrug and—wonder of wonders—his mouth twitched with a hint of his smile. "I can see why you love it, sason."

Was Dacha...bonding? Over flying? Fieran was actually going to keel over if his dacha kept surprising him like this.

With one more nod, Dacha stepped back, his gaze swinging to someone out of Fieran's sight.

Uncle Iyrinder strode between the ranks of flyboys and elven pilots, setting off another round of salutes.

As he approached, Fieran met his gaze. "How is Merrik? Have you heard from him?"

He hated how much his question betrayed. Perhaps Fieran should respect Merrik's wish for silence, but he had to know how Merrik was doing. He was still Fieran's best friend.

Uncle Iyrinder dipped his head. He had weary lines creasing his face and a slump to his posture. "He seems to be doing better these past few days. He has started the process of strengthening his leg to learn to walk again."

"And the healers think he will? Walk again?" Fieran clenched his fists at his sides. He should have been there at Merrik's side. He should have known exactly what Merrik was going through and how to help. There shouldn't have been this silence between them. Not during a time like this.

At least Adry was there in Estyra. Merrik wouldn't be alone. Sure, he had his mama, sister, and elven aunt, uncle, and cousins there. But he'd have a friend as well, even if that friend wasn't Fieran.

"Yes, they do." Uncle Iyrinder's smile was forced, not reaching his eyes. "But it will take work and time."

Not unexpected. But that gnawing need to be there ached inside Fieran again.

"General Laesornysh!" A huffing clerk dashed between the crowd of pilots.

Dacha gave just the slightest sigh before he and Uncle Iyrinder strode after the clerk, headed back for headquarters and whatever crisis of paperwork awaited them.

With the higher-ups gone, everyone seemed to release a collective breath as shoulders sagged, postures relaxed, and grins returned.

Fieran pushed away from the aeroplane and clasped Lt. Rothilion's shoulders. "Thank you for looking after the squadron."

Lt. Rothilion dipped his head. "It is good to have you back, Captain."

"Good to be back." Fieran strode between his pilots,

accepting the various back slaps as he passed. He jabbed a thumb at the line of new bomber aeroplanes. "My footlocker was loaded in the second seat of one of the bombers."

"We'll fetch it and see that it's brought to your tent." Several of the flyboys rushed off. Since it would only take one or two to tote the footlocker, Fieran wasn't sure how all the others planned to assist.

Fieran passed the stack of his flight gear to another eager flyboy, who rushed away to put it in his tent as well.

As Fieran headed for the hangar, the rest of his squadron trailed after him as if they were ducklings who had lost their mother and they weren't sure what to do about it. "What else did I miss?"

"You'll need to get your name added to the waiting list for a gas mask." Lije gestured at the strange contraption hanging from his belt. It was made of green canvas with glass goggles set in it and a canister over where a person's mouth and nose would be. "It protects against chlorine gas. That's the chemical the Mongavarians unleashed the day you crashed."

"The army requisitioned as many gas masks as they could from factories, but there's still a shortage." Pretty Face grimaced as he motioned at his own, rather empty belt.

"It hasn't been too much of a problem." Stickyfingers, too, lacked a gas mask on his belt. "Thanks to King Weylind and some of the other elves. And there haven't been too many gas attacks yet. Your dacha has seen to that."

Fieran made a mental note to check in with the weapons supply sergeant after he reported to Colonel Dentley. "Anything else I should know?"

"Little Aldon is in the process of disbanding." Aylia caught up with them and gestured in that general direction. "The army will only provide gas masks for military personnel. Right now, the danger is somewhat negligible, given that King Weylind is here and able to shield the base from chemical attacks. But the army no longer wishes to be responsible for civilian safety."

"It's made things rather dead boring." Pretty Face heaved a sigh as he grimaced. "There's very little to do on days when we don't have a patrol."

"Are most of them setting up shop outside of base?" Fieran tilted his head toward the west, farther into Escarland.

"Yes. It's calling itself Defense City." Stickyfingers shot a look toward Tiny of all people.

"It is not so easy to simply walk there, even when leave is given." Lt. Rothilion did not sound too disappointed by that. After all, he had not been so enamored with the entertainments offered in Little Aldon.

This would change the feel of the base. It was truly becoming a military operation with the defense complex locked down.

He'd only been gone a little over two weeks. And yet it seemed like far longer had passed, given all the changes.

Lije grinned and also shot a look at Tiny, who had dropped to the back of the group. "Not that the long walk has stopped Tiny."

"Yeah, he and the donut girl—" Pretty Face started to say something, but Tiny swung a punch at him. Pretty Face dodged with a yelp, his hands going to his face. "Not the nose!"

Tiny rolled his eyes. "Don't say stuff that deserves a punch."

"I wasn't going to, this time! Besides, I can't help it if I'm leery of getting hit in the face." Pretty Face gestured at his own face before he sent a smirk Fieran's way. "After all, I have it on good authority that I have a rather nice nose."

Fieran groaned and ran a hand over his face. "Don't tell me. I made some comment while drugged."

Seriously, someone should have stuffed a gag in his mouth. He struggled to filter his words when he was fully aware of what he was doing. Apparently he had absolutely no filter when drugged out of his mind.

Pretty Face smirked and tapped the side of his nose. "You've apparently always liked my nose."

Fieran groaned again and ran a hand through his hair. "Let's get back to Tiny and this girl in Little Aldon…"

That sounded like a much better topic than whatever Fieran might have blurted or, worse, sung while he'd been out of his head.

"Well, after your crash and you were sent home, we went into Little Aldon…" Lije trailed off, a sadness in his eyes.

"Looking to drown our sorrows in soda and donuts." Pretty Face took up the tale readily enough, though he stayed out of Tiny's swinging range. "That's when we ended up in a donut shop run by a troll man and his daughter. And Tiny…"

Tiny shot Pretty Face another look that had Pretty Face dodging to put Stickyfingers between himself and Tiny's fists.

"When word came that Little Aldon had to disband, we volunteered to help them move their shop." Stickyfingers grinned before he patted his stomach. "They thanked us for our help with donuts."

Pretty Face smirked in a way that made his thin mustache waggle. "And she thanked Tiny with a kiss. Probably inspired by all the muscles he was showing off."

Tiny muttered under his breath, his gray skin darkening with his embarrassed flush.

"Well, good for you, Tiny." Fieran dropped back long enough to give Tiny a slap on the back.

This would've been a good moment to bring up that Fieran and Pip were courting, but Fieran bit back the words. Pip had wanted to be there when they told the flyboys together, and he wasn't going to spoil that for her.

All of them stepped into the hangar, and Mak met Fieran with a back slap that had Fieran staggering forward a step. "Good to have you back."

"Good to be back." Fieran returned the gesture, trying to pretend he wasn't still trying to regain his balance. He really wanted to sit down and rest, despite the fact that he'd been sitting for hours while flying.

But he couldn't rest just yet. He nodded to his pilots as he turned toward the door that led toward the other bays in the hangar. "I'd better report in to Colonel Dentley."

The flyboys finally stopped following him as he strode through the hangar bays until he finally reached Bay 12, which Colonel Dentley had turned into a command room and office for the three squadrons.

Colonel Dentley stood near the back of the room with his adjutant Lt. Busher at his side with his clipboard. The table with the charts and maps had been moved out of the way to create more space in the center of the room.

Capt. Fleetwood, who was now the senior captain, stood on the other side of Colonel Dentley with Lt. Hadley from the late Capt. Kentworth's squadron beside him. He must be the new commanding officer for that squadron.

A few of the bomber pilots were filing from the room, and Fieran halted and waited for them to exit before he stepped inside.

After marching across the room, he stood at attention before the colonel. "Capt. Laesornysh reporting for duty."

"At ease, Laesornysh." Colonel Dentley nodded to him. "It will be good to have you in the skies again, although General Laesornysh has stepped in rather admirably."

"So I saw." Fieran tried to keep his tone professional, but his shock over that still leaked through.

At another nod from the colonel, Capt. Fleetwood and Lt. Hadley stepped forward, greeted Fieran, and filed from the room, leaving Fieran alone with Colonel Dentley and Lt. Busher.

Colonel Dentley swept a glance over Fieran. "While you have been cleared for duty, I'm putting you on light duty for at least the next week, perhaps longer. I will not risk you or your squadron by putting you on long patrols before you're ready."

"Yes, sir." Fieran nodded. As much as he wanted to argue, he could feel his own lingering tiredness. It was the right call, even if he wanted to pretend he was back to full strength.

"In a week, we will also be receiving new recruits." Colonel Dentley clasped his hands behind his back. "Most of them will be going to fill in the losses sustained by the other squadrons. But I will be assigning four of the new recruits to you."

Fieran waited. Based on Colonel Dentley's tone, there was something else going on.

"After a great deal of debate, army policy was changed to allow Escarlish women to join Alliance Flying Corps units. As your squadron is currently the only integrated Alliance Flying Corps squadron at the moment, I have no choice but to assign them to you." Colonel Dentley's voice held the barest trace of something beneath his professional tone. If

Fieran were to guess, he was one of those who disapproved of allowing women to serve.

"I'm happy to have them." Fieran had no trouble with adding a few Escarlish women to his squadron. He already had female elf pilots and a female mechanic. He might as well add four human female pilots to his motley squadron.

After all, many of the early aviatrices had pushed the boundaries just as much as the male aviators like Capt. Arfeld. He saw no reason to bar them from serving. Many of them had far more flight hours than the male pilots currently being rushed through training.

Besides, Escarlish women were allowed to serve in the navy, either on ships or airships, as long as they were an integrated Alliance ship where elf or troll women already served. It only made sense to open the Flying Corps the same way.

Fieran had to suppress his grin. Aylia and Pip were going to be thrilled.

CHAPTER
TWELVE

Fieran buckled his swords onto his back over his fatigue shirt, the morning chill wafting around the flap to his tent door. When he stepped outside, the gray dawn held the scents of damp earth, yet a promise of the warmth to come built in the humidity clinging to Fieran's skin.

He glanced at the tent next to his, but Merrik didn't step out to join him as he had every morning practice they'd gone to at Fort Defense.

Giving himself a shake, Fieran strode alone through the hangar and into the hills on the far side. When he crested the rise, he found Dacha standing alone. Uncle Iyrinder was likely somewhere nearby, but Fieran didn't spot him.

As Fieran approached, Dacha's gaze flicked over him, as if assessing his movements.

Fieran halted and spread his arms. "I'm fine, Dacha. The healers patched me up just fine."

"Yes." Dacha drew his swords. "But we will not engage in a battle today. Instead, we will stick to the basic sword forms."

"Is that really necessary? I'm *fine*." Fieran drew his own swords, adjusting his hands. They were sure to be sticky with sweat soon thanks to the humidity.

"You were healed by elven healing magic, which prevented your muscles from weakening from a long recovery." Dacha held out his swords in the first sword stance, a guard with one sword raised, and the other in a block. "But such healing still takes a toll on your body. You are healed, yes. But your body will not be back to full strength for weeks yet."

Fieran copied the movements, as he'd done so many times before. This was, after all, how Dacha had trained him since the very first day Dacha had pressed a pair of wooden swords into Fieran's small hands and guided him through the motions.

Yet as Fieran held the first stance, he could feel the ache in his muscles that came far sooner than it should. Perhaps Dacha had a point.

Of course he did. Dacha was, after all, speaking from experience.

After holding the first stance for a full minute, Dacha gracefully swept into the next form.

Fieran matched him, stepping forward into the movement. His shin bone twinged, reminding him again that he wasn't as recovered as he might feel. He had, after all, crashed only two and a half weeks ago.

Dacha would gladly perform the whole routine in complete silence. But Fieran wasn't going to manage it. Not when he still had so much to tell Dacha. The brief phone calls while he'd been recovering hadn't been enough.

Fieran tried not to let his arms quiver as he held the stance. "Thank you for protecting my squadron while I was gone."

Dacha gave a nod, though he didn't glance at Fieran, too focused on his sword. "They are clearly important to you, and you are important to them. I saw that after you crashed."

Meeting new people wasn't Dacha's preference, and yet Dacha had actually made an effort to get to know Fieran's squadron in the past two weeks. He'd flown with them. Made a point of figuring out why Fieran loved flying so much.

Fieran worked to stuff back his smile. If Dacha would go to such lengths with the squadron, how much more would he take the time to get to know Pip? "I'm courting Pip. Officially now."

That made Dacha's sword stance wobble, just a moment before he caught himself. He cleared his throat as he glided into the third form. "Good. I...good. You will have to invite her to join a morning practice, once she returns to Fort Defense."

Fieran had asked her once before, more a joke than a true invite since he'd known Pip would refuse.

But it was a big deal for Dacha to extend the offer. Morning practices were nearly sacred. Only for family or those so close they were like family.

"I'll do that." Fieran grinned as he matched Dacha's stance, his arms and legs already aching. But it was a good ache. "Thanks for seeing to it that she was sent to Aldon with me. And that she is coming back to Fort Defense."

Dacha gave another throat clearing noise. "Your uncle Lance did most of the work for her return. Rather reluctantly. He, Bennett, and Louise were quite impressed with her."

"She is impressive." Fieran clamped his mouth shut

before he waxed eloquent on all of Pip's many amazing attributes and skills.

The two of them lapsed into silence as they moved through several more forms. The familiar routine was strangely soothing, even as his muscles burned with the exertion.

Perhaps it was the silence or the peace of the morning. But Fieran found himself blurting, "While I was in the hospital, I had a talk with Nylian. About those dizzy spells."

"And?" Dacha glanced at Fieran, giving him that raised eyebrow look that never failed to make Fieran confess whatever he might have done wrong when he'd been young.

Fieran moved into the next form as Dacha did, sweeping one sword down and the other out. "He doesn't think they're caused by the fact that I'm half-human. He said I might simply need to increase my magical stamina or that they might be caused because I'm trying to wield my elven magic like a human."

For a long moment, Dacha remained silent as he swept into the next stance. Then he exhaled a sigh in time with his movements. "Sason. I—"

"My doubts aren't your fault. Yours or Mama's." Fieran cut his dacha off before he could apologize. Perhaps some of Fieran's struggles with his magic were because of the way his parents raised him. Maybe his dacha had been so focused on making sure Fieran didn't experience the same trauma with his magic that Dacha had growing up that he instead made other mistakes.

But Fieran wouldn't trade his childhood for anything even with its imperfections, and he wouldn't have his dacha apologize for what Fieran wouldn't want changed.

Instead, he shrugged, making his stance wobble for a moment. "I don't know why I don't feel enough like an elf.

Or why I can't seem to embrace that side of myself the way I can my human side."

Dacha sighed again as he moved into the next form. "When you were born, your macha and I feared that you would struggle, being half-human, half-elf. We hoped that the fact that you would be surrounded by others like you growing up would help, but it seems you all were locked in the same struggle."

Not that Merrik seemed to struggle with it the way Fieran did. Or perhaps his struggles were simply the opposite of Fieran's.

"It did help, I think." Fieran matched Dacha's movements. The sun peeked over the horizon, already burning away the coolness of the night. Sweat slicked down his back, and he tried not to let his muscles shake. "I never had such problems growing up. Or I was too happy to realize I had them."

Dacha let another pause fall. Then he glided into the next stance. "Close your eyes, sason."

Fieran did as he was told and squeezed his eyes shut.

"Feel the slight breeze in your hair. Breathe in the scent of the earth. Plant your feet on the grass and feel it beneath your boots."

Fieran tried. He really did. But the sun was hot, and he was sweating. "It's not working."

"No talking, sason. Just listen." Dacha's voice remained even. After a moment, the grass crinkled, and Fieran guessed Dacha had moved into the next stance.

Fieran eased his arms and feet into the next form, holding it as he breathed slowly, steadily. The whispering breeze was scented with dry grass and dust, gunpowder and grease.

This wasn't working. He wasn't going to magically feel

more connected to the earth or whatever elven lesson Dacha was trying to teach him.

There was a whisper of fabric and crackle of grass as Dacha moved again. "When I was growing up, I felt out of place. I was illegitimate. Most elven magic involves healing and growing, and yet mine killed and destroyed. I hated my magic. The more I hated it, the more I lost control. And the more I lost control, the more I hated my magic."

Fieran had heard all of that before, yet now he actually understood in a way his younger self hadn't.

"There were many times I did not feel like a true elf. I was not like those around me." Dacha's voice remained as steady as his movements.

Now that hit harder than Fieran would like to admit.

Except that Fieran hadn't always felt like this. Or hadn't realized those feelings were buried deep inside him. Yes, he felt lacking. But he felt it because he couldn't measure up to his dacha, not because he felt alienated from everyone and everything.

"I needed your macha's help and more years of perspective before I finally came to terms with my magic." Dacha gave a sigh, and there was a tightness in his voice that betrayed just how much emotion was behind those words. "It took seeing your macha wield my magic and eventually you and your sisters before I began to love my own magic. I could not hate it when wielded by her or by you, and thus I could not hate it when it was wielded by me."

Fieran risked cracking his eyes open and peeking at Dacha.

Dacha had his eyes closed as well as he moved into a new stance with fluid movements, his hair floating across his shoulders. His jaw was hard in a way that gave away just how hard the words were for him.

Fieran squeezed his eyes closed again and hurried to match Dacha's current stance.

"The truth is that all elven magic has the ability to kill and destroy, not just yours and mine. Plant magic can kill trees as easily as grow them, and elves with that magic have used it in battle for generations. Healing magic can kill, and such killing is considered so terrible that healers take oaths to prevent it."

Fieran hadn't considered elven magic in quite that way before.

"If all elven magic kills, then all elven magic also protects. Plant magic's purpose is to protect the forest. Healing magic protects the body." Dacha's voice strengthened again, that edge of emotion disappearing. "And our magic's purpose is to protect the kingdom's people."

Fieran had experienced that aspect of his magic many times over now. He'd come to terms with that long before now.

"If my magic has essentially the same purpose as all elven magic, then I am just as true an elf as an elf with plant magic or healing magic." Dacha's voice changed, as if he'd turned toward Fieran. "And you, sason, are just as much a true elf as I am."

Fieran opened his eyes and dropped from his stance as he faced Dacha. "Half of me is a true elf."

Dacha lowered his swords and held Fieran's gaze. "You cannot always divide yourself, as if dissecting yourself into the pieces that are human and the parts that are elven. That is not how a body or soul works. You are an elf. And you are a human."

"I'm not a whole elf or a whole human either." Fieran shook his head before he sheathed his swords. "I'm a messy mix of both, and apparently that is messing with my magic."

Dacha's gaze searched Fieran's for a moment before he, too, sheathed his swords. He waved a hand in the direction of the hangar. "Why is your squadron named the Half-Breed Squadron?"

Fieran blinked at the non sequitur, but he shrugged. "Because we have so many half-breeds as a part of the squadron, including me as their leader."

"Yes, but from where I stand, the name means more than that." Dacha gestured again. "Your squadron is itself a half-breed. Half-elf, half-human. And yet it is a whole squadron. One unit, undivided, made all the stronger because of its mixed parts."

Ah, now Fieran saw what his dacha did there.

He huffed a sigh and gazed in that direction. There wasn't much he could say to argue against that metaphor.

But that still begged the question. How did he embrace his elven side the way he'd managed to embrace both halves of his squadron? And would that fix the problem he had with his magic?

THIRTEEN

Pip hefted her bag higher on her shoulder as she stood on the train platform within the AMPC's secure boundaries. Troll and human workers loaded crate after crate filled with new synchronization gears—as many as AMPC and several other manufacturing companies could put together in the past few days.

Instead of patenting the item, Louise had made the plans available to other manufacturers so that more could be made on a short timeline. While they hadn't managed to make enough for even a full squadron, more gears were being made every day. Luckily, most of the parts were standard parts from other sources, so only a few pieces needed to be made specially for the gear.

"That looks like the last of it." Louise examined a clipboard she'd been handed before she signed the paper on it. She handed it back to the clerk, who scurried off to tend to the next item on his list.

"Thank you for seeing to it that I was sent back to Fort Defense with this shipment." Pip shifted closer to the train.

The sooner she boarded, the sooner she could be on her way back to Fieran.

"I like you. I'm invested in you and Fieran." Louise grinned, sharing a look with Pip.

Pip grinned back, though she wasn't sure what to say besides, "I'm glad."

And she was. Louise already felt like a sister, and Pip was rapidly coming to love Fieran's whole family. How could she not, when Tryndar had hugged her around the legs that morning and cried at having to say goodbye to her too?

Though Fieran's dacha was still intimidating. She wasn't sure if she'd be able to get so much as a word out the next time she saw him.

"Besides, everything I included in my report was true." Louise turned back to the train as the workers slid the door closed. "It will be helpful for you to be there with your squadron to install the new gears and monitor their effectiveness. We tested the gear as much as we could, but it hasn't been tested as rigorously as I'd like. A mechanic with your training and skills needs to be on hand in the field. Not just for this, but for anything else we send your way."

Pip nodded, edging another step closer to the train. She'd helped with the new radios when those had arrived at Dar Goranth, and now she could help with this.

That record would, hopefully, mean that she would stay at Fort Defense with Fieran for the rest of the war. Lance Marion, Louise, and Bennett had things well in hand here. Another inventor might help, but not enough. Not the way she could help at the front lines with real-world testing.

The train gave a whistle. A warning that it was leaving soon.

"I need to board." Pip turned to Louise. Should she hug? Elven hug? Just wave?

Louise didn't seem to have any hesitation as she hugged Pip with the enthusiasm of a sister. "Stay safe. And keep Fieran safe, even though I know that's a tall order."

"I'll do my best." She knew all too well that she couldn't promise anything more than that.

After returning Louise's embrace, Pip stepped back, gripped her bag, and boarded the passenger car. She found a seat at the back. Right now, she was the only military passenger headed for the front, but she'd heard they'd be stopping to pick up a unit of infantry also bound for Fort Defense.

Within a few minutes, the train pulled from the station, the gates set in the wall opening to let them through.

Pip watched as the buildings and sprawl of Aldon flashed past the window. As this was a military train, it didn't stop at any of the stations, though it remained at a slower speed until it left the last of the city behind.

She settled down for a nap. After all, today would be a long day of travel.

When the train slowed and pulled into the station at Fort Charibert, Pip roused and scrubbed at her eyes. The train car was about to become very crowded and very noisy. Her nap was definitely at an end.

After several minutes, she could hear the barking of sergeants outside of the train. Then a column of men in olive-green uniforms marched into the train car. They filled the train car from the front to the back until one of the men broke ranks to take the seat next to Pip.

Pip scrunched closer to the wall to give him more space. She had expected to have to share a seat, but she wasn't in the mood for chitchat.

The young man had brown hair, brown eyes, and a complexion that had burned slightly pink instead of browning in all the time he must have spent out of doors during basic training. He smiled at her before he stuck out a hand to her. "Myles Kinsley."

"Pippak Detmuk-Inawenys." She shook his hand firmly, not sure why he was bothering with introductions. They would just be seat mates until Fort Defense, then they'd go their separate ways.

At her name, his grin broadened. "I thought so. Fieran's girlfriend, right?"

"How…" Pip blinked, staring at the stranger next to her. How in Tarenhiel could this random man know that?

He glanced around before he lowered his voice. "I'm Fieran's cousin. Well, cousin a couple of times removed. My grandfather is Fieran's first cousin."

Wait…if he was fully human and his grandfather was Fieran's cousin…there was only one branch of Fieran's family that fit that description.

"Then you're a prince." She gawked at him as the train shuddered into motion. "Aren't you in line for the Escarlish throne?"

"Yes and yes." Myles flashed that grin. Even though he was a cousin so far removed, the grin still reminded her of Fieran's. "But I'm sixth in line for the throne. Far enough down that I'm allowed to join the army and contribute to the war effort."

Sixth in line. He said it so casually. And here Pip had been intimidated by the fact that Fieran was somewhat in line for the Escarlish throne and seventh in line for the Tarenhieli throne.

Myles heaved a sigh. "Though I'm probably going to be stationed in headquarters as a clerk or adjutant or something. They aren't going to send me to the front lines."

"Be glad. The front lines are giant, dug-in mud pits." Pip

suppressed a shudder. Not that she'd seen them up close. But she'd gotten glimpses of them from the top of the bluffs, and she'd seen the mud-spattered clothing of those returning after the battle to rescue Fieran.

"Still." Myles slumped against the seat behind him, his grin disappearing as he stared at the rows and rows filled with men before them. "My unit will be stationed there. I should be with them. Not given special treatment because my great-grandfather wears a crown."

Now *that* Pip understood. She'd had the opportunity to stay in Aldon, but here she was, returning to the danger of Fort Defense to be with her unit. Because she couldn't imagine her boys going into danger without her having their backs.

"I'm sorry. But I'm sure Fieran will appreciate having one of his cousins around." Pip settled more comfortably on the seat. "Which brings us back to my original question. How did you know Fieran and I are courting?"

That had only become official a week ago. How had this random cousin learned it while at basic training?

"The family grapevine." Myles grinned and stretched his legs out as far as he could under the bench in front of them without kicking the feet of the man sitting there. "Louise talked to my sister who talked to me on my last call home before being sent to the front. My sister and I figured out that I was being sent on the same train as you."

"Fieran wasn't kidding when he said the family grapevine is scary." Pip hugged her bag tighter to her stomach. She'd been worried about all the titles and fame in Fieran's family. Turned out the family gossip chain was by far the more intimidating.

"It's a force to be reckoned with, for sure." Myles tilted his head to rest it against the back of the seat. He closed his eyes, as if settling in for some shut-eye of his own. "The only reason Uncle Farrendel hasn't heard already is that everyone is under strict instructions not to blow the surprise before Fieran has a chance to tell him in person."

Pip blew out a long breath and sagged against the back of the seat. "Everyone knows? Even King Averett?"

"Pretty much." Myles cracked an eye open and gave her that lopsided grin again without stirring from his slouch. "But don't worry. All I've heard are good things about you."

Great. Pip squeezed her eyes shut and pretended to sleep. She'd known courting Fieran would be complicated. And yet this still threw her.

FIERAN TRIED NOT to bounce on his toes as he waited for the train to chug its way into a stop.

The train station at Fort Defense was strangely crowded with some of the higher-ups, including Uncle Julien. Someone important must be arriving.

With a hiss of its air brakes, the train settled to a halt. At one end of the platform, crews descended on the cargo cars, opening the doors and loading crates onto various carts.

The door to the passenger car opened, and a sergeant stepped out, barking orders. He was followed by ranks of marching infantrymen dressed in crisp, olive-green uniforms.

Fieran blinked. Was that...no, it couldn't be cousin Myles. But when the man was pulled aside by Uncle Julien's adjutant, Fieran got a good look at his face. Yep, that was Myles. He must have volunteered for the army, and of course he would be stationed somewhere in headquarters.

Fieran would have to track him down to swap basic training stories when he had a chance.

Then Pip stepped from the train, and Fieran forgot all about his cousin, his uncle, and the audience crowding the platform. It didn't matter that he'd only been separated from her for a few days. He dashed forward, wrapped her in his arms, and kissed her right there in front of everyone.

When he set Pip back on her feet, she sent him an expression that was somewhere between a grin and a grimace. "As if your family grapevine didn't have enough to gossip about."

"Sorry. Should I have waited to kiss you?" Fieran took another half step back. He and Pip hadn't had much time to discuss what kind of boundaries they wanted, especially when it came to public displays of affection. She'd said dwarves were more exuberant than elves, and he was naturally exuberant, but he wasn't sure what she'd prefer.

"Yes. No." Pip huffed a breath and adjusted her bag on her shoulder. "It's just...my parents don't even know yet, and apparently most of your family has already found out. And it's not like it's a secret. That's the whole point of finally courting. It's just...a lot to learn a cousin of yours I hadn't even met yet already knew." Pip's voice dropped even further. "Apparently even King Averett knows."

Fieran winced. He could see how that would be intimidating. "Sorry. We'll have to tell Mak as soon as possible. Before he finds out from someone else."

"Yes." Pip jabbed a finger at where the workers were unloading the crates from the train. "I need to see to it that the new synchronization gears are properly delivered to our hangar, then we can go tell Mak and the flyboys."

Fieran held Pip's hand as the two of them strolled from the tram to the hangar. His heart hammered harder in his chest, but that was mostly just from holding her hand.

As soon as they stepped inside the hangar, the flyboys hurried toward them. But they halted in their tracks as, almost as one, their gazes dropped to Fieran's and Pip's clasped hands.

"Finally!" Lije grinned.

Stickyfingers swatted Tiny's arm. "Told you."

"It was rather obvious." Pretty Face smoothed his mustache.

Deeper in the pack, a few of the flyboys exchanged money. As if they had been taking bets. Even some of the elven pilots exchanged looks, as if they had been expecting this.

"You all...knew?" Pip stepped closer to Fieran, her eyes wide.

Lije crossed his arms and huffed. "Duh. The two of you were obvious as sunflowers in a wheat field."

"Why do you think none of the rest of us so much as flirted with Pip?" Pretty Face pointed a finger at his own chest. "Not even me."

Aylia strode between the others and smirked at Fieran. "And why do you think I never flirted with you?"

"Yeah, the two of you have been walking around with big *Taken* signs." Stickyfingers jabbed a finger first at Fieran, then at Pip. "No one dared get between you."

Fieran shifted and shared a look with Pip. They really hadn't been all that subtle.

Mak strode between the flyboys, halted in front of Fieran, and crossed his arms. "So. You're courting my sister."

Pip huffed, losing that hunched look. "Mak. Don't you dare go all big brother on him."

"It's my job. I'm obligated." Mak's gaze didn't waver from Fieran's. "Don't hurt her."

Fieran held his gaze, his own stance firm. "I won't."

"Then we won't have any problems." Mak held out his hand, and Fieran gave it a firm shake.

Pip just huffed again and rolled her eyes, as if she was rather fed up with their male posturing.

Lije grinned and bumped Pip's arm with his. "Well, it's good to have you back, Pip. Things haven't been the same without you here. You and Fieran."

Fieran forced his smile to remain in place. Things wouldn't be the same again. Not with Merrik fighting to walk again in Estyra. He might never return to active duty, much less flying in their squadron.

Pip drew her hand out of Fieran's and planted her hands on her hips. "All right, I'm glad to be back, but I need to get to work. There's a shipment of new synchronization gears that will be coming up the tram any moment. I'd like to get them installed as soon as I can so there will be no more crashes from broken propellers."

Several of the flyboys cheered.

Fieran grinned and gestured in the direction of the tram platform. "Since everyone is so excited, who wants to volunteer to help haul the crates to the hangar?"

The groans were more exaggerated and halfhearted than real as the squadron trooped toward the platform.

FOURTEEN

Fieran kept a firm grip on the control column of his new Defender as it climbed higher into the sky. This new aeroplane was far more touchy. The more powerful rotary engine created more torque and kept wanting to tip his aeroplane over if he wasn't careful.

This high up, he could see the smudge of shapes on the horizon, the new Little Aldon re-forming upriver.

Four other aeroplanes circled in the sky. Two of them were at the far end of Fort Defense near the Wall while the other two were headed in the direction of the airfield, preparing to land as soon as Fieran and his wingman were in the air.

He pushed the rudder bar with his feet as he worked the ailerons, turning the aeroplane to circle over Fort Defense. The familiar buildings flashed below, and he further relaxed into the new aeroplane's seat.

"That new Defender is *fast*." Pretty Face, his aeroplane taking up Merrik's wingman position behind Fieran, spoke into the radio. As he was in the older T-05 Soarwing, his aeroplane was lagging behind, especially as they were still climbing to altitude. "When do I get one?"

"I heard they'll be delivered shortly." From what Fieran heard, the female pilots who hadn't been added to his squadron had been turned into an auxiliary unit to deliver aeroplanes throughout the Alliance. Perhaps not the job they'd wanted, but it was a role that was sorely needed. Without it, Fieran and his squadron would be back to having to put together their own aeroplanes as they'd done at Dar Goranth. "But be warned. These new aeroplanes are finicky."

"You just need to know how to woo them." Pretty Face somehow managed a sultry tone over the crackling radio.

Fieran rolled his eyes, even as he smiled. He'd missed his squadron. "Since you love the new Defenders so much, you can see to it that my new aeroplane gets nose art once we're done with our patrol."

"Gladly." Pretty Face sounded cheerful, as if he didn't mind the extra work Fieran was giving him. "I've already set aside the paint."

"And you can help paint over the nose art on the T-05 Soarwings." Fieran tightened his grip on the control stick as a wind gust tossed his aeroplane about.

"If I have to. Though it seems such a shame." The cheer left Pretty Face's voice.

It did, at that. Pretty Face and the others had worked hard on the nose art back in Dar Goranth. It hurt having to erase the work and the memories.

Yet they couldn't send back the T-05s with the custom nose art. Their old aeroplanes were going to be put to use for training new pilots, as they were more stable and thus easier to fly than the Defenders.

At least the elven half of the squadron wouldn't need

new nose art since they were currently keeping their Yshendar aeroplanes.

As he and Pretty Face neared the Wall, Fieran turned his aeroplane, paralleling the Chibo River. On the Escarlish side of the river, the bridges that had been built during Fieran's rescue remained jutting into the river, though they ended abruptly at the Wall. The Alliance armies must have dismantled the bridges on the Mongavarian side when they returned back to Escarland. It made sense not to leave such easy crossings over the river for the enemy, even if the Wall made such a thing impossible.

The dots of Alliance airships trundled along the Wall to the south. In the wake of the previous battles over Fort Defense, the navy had redistributed the airships to longer patrols over the borders, ceding the main air defense of the fort to the Flying Corps squadrons.

At the Hydalla River, Fieran turned his aeroplane to the west, following the familiar routine. If he ignored the strangeness of the aeroplane around him, Pretty Face's voice in his ears instead of Merrik's, and the ache in his muscles as the patrol continued, he could almost pretend he'd never crashed.

Pip had her head in the engine compartment of Fieran's new aeroplane as she installed the synchronization gear. His aeroplane would be the easiest to do. She'd wait on the others until headquarters swapped out the old T-05 Soarwings with the new T-07 Defenders. Supposedly they'd be arriving in a week at the most.

There came the expected scuffing of footsteps behind her,

and she grinned down into the engine. "You had better not be staring at my rear end."

Fieran gave a cough, his footsteps shuffling more than striding for a moment. "You know I've always found you rather attractive in coveralls and wrenching on an engine."

With the way her face heated, she was glad she was head-down in the engine where no one could see. Sure, the two of them had been thinking stuff like that for months now, but how was she ever going to concentrate now that Fieran had decided to start saying stuff like that out loud?

"Distracting me already." Pip wiggled her hand into the narrow spot between the top of the aeroplane and the new gear. "You're not supposed to do that while I'm working."

"Right. Sorry." The ladder wobbled slightly. Fieran must have rested a hand on it. "So…would you like help? If you don't find my presence too distracting?"

"Don't flatter yourself." She wouldn't pander that much to his ego. Even if her face was flaming and she was fiddling with the wires to pretend she wasn't struggling to think about what she should do next when her mind was filling with thoughts of kissing. Nope. Focus. She wasn't some young girl who couldn't function when falling in love. "This is strictly professional."

"Of course. Keeping flirty comments to myself." Fieran's laugh betrayed that he was grinning. "You won't even know I'm here. Just another set of hands to fetch your tools for you."

"I'll believe it when I see it." Pip hoped her tone came across as snarky instead of the breathy, mushy puddle she really was. "Since you offered, I need a nine-sixteenths wrench, more wire, and two more three-eighths bolts with nuts and washers."

"As you wish." Fieran's bootsteps trotted off.

Just like old times. Her working on an engine. Him fetching parts and tools.

Except that Merrik wouldn't wander by, interrupting before things got too close to romantic. He wouldn't be there to joke with her and Fieran.

For a moment, Pip had to brace herself against the sides of the engine compartment while she caught her breath. Would she ever adjust to the gaping hole in the squadron that Merrik left behind?

Heavier bootsteps sounded on the cement floor a moment before Mak's voice came from beside the aeroplane. "Where do you want me?"

Maybe she should set him to work on a different aeroplane so she and Fieran could enjoy more alone time.

But Mak's presence would keep her and Fieran from getting too distracted.

"Could you start on the insulators for rigging the shielding wire?" Pip extracted one hand so she could flap vaguely at the side of the aeroplane without looking. "And figure out how to rig it without disrupting the aerodynamics or the lines of this aeroplane. It's too beautiful to mess up."

Mak laughed as he set to work. When Fieran arrived, he fell right into the friendly banter they'd always had. Before too long, Pretty Face joined them with paints and brushes and grand plans for the nose art.

It wasn't the same without Merrik. But Pip wouldn't choose to be anywhere else.

FIERAN TOOK in the gleaming Defenders as the ground crew wheeled them into the hangar. Pip and the other mechanics directed each aeroplane into its spot.

"I'm in love." Pretty Face leaned against the wing of his new aeroplane, as if embracing it.

"Me too." Stickyfingers had climbed into the cockpit of his new aeroplane, and he was now caressing the twin machine guns with a slightly maniacal gleam in his eyes.

The other flyboys were similarly acquainting themselves with their new aeroplanes. At least none of them seemed as sad as they had an hour ago when they'd said farewell to their old flyers. The shiny, brand-new aeroplanes had quickly won them over.

Outside, the whine of aeroplanes taking off filled the air as the auxiliary pilots took off in the old aeroplanes to take them back to Fort Linder for use as training flyers. No one even looked up to watch their old aeroplanes disappear, each one sporting elf ears and "with love from the Half-Breed Squadron" painted on the side. Fieran hadn't seen Pretty Face's handiwork until it had been too late to change it.

"You're going to paint new art on my aeroplane, right, Pretty Face?" Tiny patted his aeroplane.

"Yeah, got to make sure the Mongavarians know the Half-Breed Squadron is still in town," one of the other flyboys called out from across the bay.

Other flyboys shouted out their suggestions for artwork. Some wanted the same thing they had before. Others wanted something completely new.

With the march of boots on cement, Lt. Busher strode into the hangar bay, followed by four female pilots dressed in the army-green uniform and their hair in tight buns at the back of their heads.

Those would be his new recruits. Fieran crossed the hangar before Lt. Busher drew more attention. The last thing the new recruits needed was to be mobbed by the whole squadron on their first day.

From somewhere behind him, one of his flyboys started to wolf-whistle before the sound was smothered. When Fieran shot a glance over his shoulder, he spotted Pretty Face of all people pressing a hand over a flyboy's mouth and giving him a lecture on how to treat women.

"Capt. Laesornysh." Lt. Busher and the four pilots came to attention. When Fieran gave them leave to stand at ease, the adjutant gestured behind him and rattled off the pilots' names.

Fieran grinned and took in the four women. One appeared to be in her thirties while the other three were younger. From the paperwork he'd been sent, all four of them had been aviatrices or barnstormers before joining the Flying Corps. The other squadrons were missing out, taking the rather untrained male recruits. "Welcome to the Half-Breed Squadron. I'm your captain, and you'll be serving in Flight B. Lt. Daemaer?"

Lingering by the door as she had been, Aylia jumped to join them, already grinning. "Yes, sir?"

"Please show our four newest pilots to their quarters and give them the tour of the hangar and Fort Defense." Fieran nodded from Aylia to the four pilots.

"With pleasure." Aylia grinned back, as if she'd been waiting for just that. She leaned closer to the pilots. "I'm so happy we'll have more females in the squadron. We've been a little outnumbered. Come on, I'll show you to our barracks."

The four new pilots trailed after Aylia as she led them toward the nearest door to the outside.

"Are those the new recruits?" Lije spoke from just behind Fieran.

Fieran jumped and spun, only to find Lije, Stickyfingers, and Pretty Face lined up behind him.

"It sure is going to be nice to have a few more women in the squadron." Pretty Face's eyes tracked something behind Fieran, as if he was still watching Aylia and the new pilots.

Fieran wagged a finger at him. "Don't even think about flirting with any of them. They're your colleagues as much as any other pilot."

When Pretty Face didn't stop looking, Stickyfingers punched his arm. "You'd think you would've learned after Fieran's cousin punched you. Just remember. You like your nose as it is."

"Right." Pretty Face ran his fingers over his nose as if checking that it was still straight.

Fieran could only shake his head. The four new pilots would change the dynamics of the squadron, that was for certain. But he wasn't sure that would be a bad thing.

FIERAN TRAILED at the back of the group of flyboys as Tiny led the way with eager steps through the new dirt streets spreading out from the river. The buildings of Defense City were even more ramshackle than Little Aldon had been since most lumber and steel had been requisitioned for expansions on Fort Defense. The civilians here had to make do with the castoffs.

This was the first pass he'd had since returning to Fort Defense over a week ago. Not that he'd done much to deserve time off just yet. He and the Half-Breed Squadron had been patrolling the skies over Fort Defense, leaving the duty of escorting the new bomber aeroplanes on runs into Mongavaria to the other two squadrons. The longer patrols guarding the border had been almost entirely turned over to the airships and to additional Flying Corps squadrons now operating out of newly formed aerodromes.

This leave was especially disappointing because Pip had to stay behind while she, Mak, and the other mechanics worked to install the synchronization gears in the new Defenders. Fieran had offered to stay behind with her, but she'd shooed him off.

Without Pip at his side and without Merrik, he drifted, hands in his pockets, letting Tiny and the others direct their path and fill the silence with chatter.

That was how he found himself at the back a few steps behind the others with Lt. Rothilion more or less at his side as the elf lieutenant trailed along in their group's wake.

Fieran glanced at Lt. Rothilion. They'd been slowly easing him into their group, but perhaps it was time Fieran worked to build more of a friendship with the lieutenant. Not just because he was missing Merrik but because Rothilion really could use a few friends.

"Thanks once again for flying with my dacha while I was gone." Fieran hesitated, not sure if he dared ask even now how that had come about.

"It was necessary to protect the squadron and Fort Defense." Lt. Rothilion's shoulders went somewhat stiff, his gaze locked ahead. "He is an elf general. It was only right he fly with an elf of the Tarenhieli Flying Corps."

And Lt. Rothilion was the highest ranked among the elven pilots. But it was still odd, given the history between their families.

Fieran remained silent, waiting, hoping. Perhaps Rothilion would say more. Maybe he wouldn't. But Fieran let the unspoken invitation remain between them.

After a long moment, Rothilion sighed, although the stiff

set didn't leave his posture. "He is unlike what my family has made him out to be. He took on an army for his son. My damasha…" Rothilion trailed off for a moment, a hint of roughness and bitterness in his tone. "My damasha has threatened to disown me for willingly serving under a half-elf."

Fieran halted and turned to face Lt. Rothilion, causing him to stop as well. "I am sorry."

He'd known Rothilion's family were sticklers and not happy that he was associating with Fieran and his family, but for his own father to threaten to disown him over his choice to remain in Fieran's squadron was mind-boggling.

While Fieran had experienced pressure to live up to his family, it was nothing like the pressure Rothilion was under. If Fieran's family placed the burden of expectations on him, it was the expectation to do the right thing and live with honor. Even when he made choices like joining the Flying Corps instead of fighting at Dacha's side in the infantry, his parents had still supported him.

But the pressure Rothilion was under was simply *wrong*.

Rothilion's expression shuttered again, his posture so stiff he might as well be a tree about to crack under a windstorm. "I do not want your apologies. Or your pity."

"It's not pity but an acknowledgment of what being under my command has cost you." Fieran didn't look away, even if Rothilion wasn't meeting his gaze. "If you would like to transfer, I'll submit the paperwork along with a glowing recommendation, even if the Half-Breed Squadron would be sorry to lose you."

"No." Lt. Rothilion all but spat the word, and he finally looked at Fieran. "No, I will not bend to appease them this time. They are in the wrong. I am not. Yes, it may cost me my family, but to do otherwise would cost my honor. I will not do that. Not again."

Fieran had been wrong. Rothilion wasn't the stiff tree about to crack. He was an oak standing strong against the storm, refusing to break.

He swallowed back his instinctive urge to tell the elf lieutenant he was sorry for him again. Instead he held out his hand. "You are a good elf, Saranthyr. I'm honored to have you in the squadron, and I'd be even more honored if you would accept my friendship."

For a moment, Rothilion hesitated. Then he slowly reached out and took Fieran's hand, giving it a single shake. "It would be my honor, Laesornysh."

Fieran grinned, not taking it personally when Rothilion yanked his hand back and scrubbed his palm on his trousers. "Just be glad I didn't decide to seal that friendship with a spit handshake."

"So unsanitary." Lt. Rothilion shuddered as the two of them set off walking once again, the others now well ahead of them and turning the corner into another dirt alley. "Is a handshake containing saliva a normal human practice?"

"No. But Merrik and I read it in a book when we were kids, and we—well, I—thought it was a fun idea. Better than sealing our brotherhood with blood, at least, which even I had the sense to know our parents would not approve of."

Rothilion was giving him a look that was somewhere between exasperated and bewildered. "You are a strange elf, Laesornysh."

"I'm well aware." Fieran grinned and lengthened his stride. If he wasn't such a strange elf, he might not get dizzy when he used large quantities of his magic. But that was something he didn't want to think about while on leave. "We'd better catch up with the others."

He and Rothilion rounded the corner into the alley as the rest of the group stopped at what appeared to be the back door of one of the ramshackle sheds making up this part of Defense City.

Tiny reached to knock on the door, but before he could, the door swung open, revealing a young female troll of around their age. She was at least half a foot taller than Tiny with a plump, well-built frame that was made all the more beautiful when she smiled at Tiny, her eyes lighting. "Donkyn! You got leave! And you brought your friends. Come in, come in. I thought I'd teach you—all of you—how to make donuts."

Lt. Rothilion sighed and muttered only loudly enough for Fieran to hear, "This is bound to be messy."

"Yep." Fieran grinned, although he let that grin fade as he halted to face Rothilion again. "If you ever need a place to stay in Estyra or Aldon, you'll always be welcome with my family."

"Linshi." Rothilion's vulnerability vanished, and he almost seemed to be packing himself back inside his impassive mask. He gestured at the shack ahead of them, where Aylia was waiting, holding the door for them. "Shall we?"

Fieran nodded, but he made sure to fall into step behind Rothilion to make sure the elf lieutenant followed the others into the tiny space that served as the bakery of the donut shop.

By the time they trooped out again, all of them were covered in a fine layer of flour. Lt. Rothilion had dough in his hair, and he was muttering as he picked at it. Aylia, Pretty Face, Stickyfingers, and Lije chatted about their grand plans for using the stovetop Fieran and Pip had cobbled together to fry donuts for the whole squadron, once they could get their hands on the ingredients. Tiny lingered in the doorway, clutching a glass jar of sourdough starter to his chest as if it was the most precious gift he'd ever received.

Fieran held a paper bag with the two donuts he'd saved for Pip and Mak. They'd turned out somewhat lopsided, but at least these ones were fully cooked and not burned. That was more than could be said of the first few attempts.

Now he just needed to get his hands on the bottle of root beer he'd promised her. By the time he returned, night would have fallen. Perhaps a starlit walk with donuts and root beer would be just the thing.

FIFTEEN

As the sunrise splashed the horizon behind her pink, the sun not yet peeking over the horizon, Pip tromped next to Fieran up the hill behind the hangars and swallowed at the bubbling, churning feeling filling her gut. The sun-burnt summer grass crunched beneath her boots while the thin coating of dew wasn't even enough to get her boots damp.

She had to extract her hand from Fieran's to swipe her palms on the front of her trousers. "You're sure your dacha doesn't mind?"

Fieran held his hand out, waiting for her to clasp it again. "He's the one who invited you."

"And you don't mind me taking away your time with your dacha?" Pip couldn't look at Fieran, and she definitely couldn't think of his dacha as anything but his dacha. Not as Prince Farrendel Laesornysh.

She was going to join a morning practice with *Prince Farrendel Laesornysh*. Her heart hammered in her ears again.

"No, I don't mind at all." Fieran halted and studied her. "You don't have to come if you don't want to."

"I know, I know." Pip tried to take deep breaths to steady herself.

"Pip." Fieran cradled her face with his free hand, tipping her chin up so she was looking into his blue eyes. "I'd like you and Dacha to get to know each other. But if you aren't ready for that yet, it's all right. I know it is a little unfair that you've met both of my parents, and I have yet to meet yours."

Because her parents were still somewhere in the dwarven mountains, trying to negotiate a closer treaty with the dwarven kingdoms.

"I'd like to get to know your family better too. It's just…" Pip released a long breath, hating how it shuddered out of her.

"He's not just a normal dacha." Fieran also sighed, as if he understood all too well. His thumb traced over her cheek.

"No, but…" Pip drew in a deep breath and forced her shoulders straight. "I can do this. I've talked to him before. Surely I can do it now when your life isn't hanging by a thread."

"As I don't intend to make nearly dying a habit, that would be best." Fieran's smile sent a sparkle to his eyes. "If you're ready?"

"Yes." She faced the top of the hill again and marched up it. She could do this. She was just going to demonstrate her magic to her childhood hero. Worse, her childhood hero was Fieran's dacha, and she really, really needed him to like her. No big deal.

And if he didn't like her or if she broke Fieran's heart, then she could just kiss any future working at the AMPC goodbye.

Nope. Don't think about kissing. Not around Fieran's

dacha. Were her ears red? Her ears were definitely red. Her whole face was probably red.

Then she and Fieran reached the top of the hill, and she found herself facing a hollow on the far side. At the bottom, Prince Farrendel stood with his silver-blond hair drifting around the hilts of his sheathed swords. Despite his resemblance to Louise—or her resemblance to him—there wasn't a trace of the ever-present smile that Louise and Fieran wore. Prince Farrendel's jaw seemed rather hard, his eyes flinty.

Pip squeaked and half-ducked behind Fieran before she caught herself. No hiding. She could do this. Be confident. The rest of Fieran's family seemed to like her. At least, the ones she'd met. She hadn't met his sister Adry yet.

"He's going to be impressed," Fieran whispered into her ear, his breath stirring her hair.

She forced her legs to move, though her steps remained stiff, as Fieran strolled down the hill. At the bottom, Fieran gestured between them. "I know you've met before, but, Pip, this is my dacha, and, Dacha, this is Pip."

Fieran's dacha tipped his head to her, but he didn't speak. He flicked a glance to Fieran, and something in it was almost...pleading. But surely that couldn't be right. Why would Prince Farrendel be scared?

Fieran grinned and released Pip's hand. "Why don't we start with Pip showing what she can do? Pip, would you please create a shield around us?"

Right. A shield. Something simple. She called up her magic and cast a shield. It shimmered in the early morning sunlight, a solid bubble around them.

She'd kept it close, close enough that Fieran had no trouble reaching out and placing a hand on her shield. A heartbeat later, his magic flared over his hand, then raced over her magic in that eager way it had.

Prince Farrendel still had that hard and impassive expression on his face as he took in the play of magic overhead. After another moment, he reached out one of his hands, his magic already twining around his fingers. "May I?"

Pip swallowed, nodded, and poured more of her magic into the shield.

A moment later, Prince Farrendel touched the shield. His magic crackled over hers with that electric taste of power that she recognized from the handful of times her magic had interacted with Prince Farrendel's during battle.

Yet it was even more intimidating, the depth of power more terrifying, in person.

Her shield held as Prince Farrendel's magic danced over it rather than consuming it, just as Fieran's did.

For the first time that morning, something flickered in Prince Farrendel's gaze. "I have never seen another magic interact with the magic of the ancient kings like this."

"Amazing, right?" Fieran's gaze was locked on Pip rather than on the magic around him.

Pip's face warmed, and she had to look away before thoughts of kissing made her lose control of her magic.

"It is." Prince Farrendel stepped closer to the shield, as if to study the magic in more depth. "How much magic can you contain?"

"A lot, but I haven't tested my full limits when it comes to the magic of the ancient kings." Pip couldn't believe she'd managed to get out a full sentence, even if her voice was still squeakier than she'd like to admit.

"Would you be willing to hold a shield over our practice?" Prince Farrendel turned to Fieran, that hard edge back in his expression. "We have not practiced your magic lately, sason."

Fieran heaved a sigh and shot a glance at Pip. "Practice, practice, practice."

His light tone made it easier for her to grin back. "If your dacha thinks you need the practice, who am I to argue? I'll just find a seat over there and watch."

She settled herself down on the grass just outside of the bubble of her magic so that she just needed to focus on holding the shield, rather than worry about protecting herself on top of it.

"Speak up if you start to get tired or can't hold the shield anymore." Fieran sent her another lopsided smile before he faced his dacha, his smile vanishing.

Prince Farrendel faced Fieran, dropping into a stance with his hands held before him. "Just magic, sason. No swords. Perhaps we can test some of your limits to see if stamina is the issue."

The issue? Was he talking about that dizziness Fieran had experienced when using his magic?

As Fieran and his dacha unleashed their magic, Pip poured even more magic into her shield. The competing, powerful magics exploded against each other as Fieran and his dacha dodged and ducked, flinging about enough magic to level an army.

And she was holding back all that power. It probably shouldn't feel as old hat as it was.

She settled more comfortably on the grass, her gaze focused on Fieran. She was his girlfriend now. Appreciating his muscles as he sparred with his dacha was rather expected now, wasn't it?

Fieran held Pip's hand as the two of them strode back toward the hangar. His muscles were sore from all the dodging and movement, even if sparring with magic wasn't as physically strenuous as doing the same with swords.

Better yet, he hadn't gotten dizzy, despite the amount of magic he'd expended. Although, he wasn't sure if that proved anything. Unleashing his magic in practice with his dacha wasn't like doing it in battle.

Pip peeked up at him, swinging their clasped hands. "So…you and your dacha are trying to figure out the source of that dizziness you've had when using your magic."

"Yes." Fieran sighed and slowed their pace. "While I was in the hospital, I talked with the head elf healer about those dizzy spells. He doesn't think they are being caused by the fact that I'm half-human. Well, not entirely. He thinks it's either because I'm still building my magical stamina or that I'm trying to use my elven magic like a human. Or maybe a mix of both issues."

Pip just kept walking at his side, her gaze encouraging. The rising sun splashed highlights through her dark hair.

"And, I don't know, maybe I wanted to believe that my human side was the cause. That was the easy explanation. The one I already believed, deep in my gut." Fieran couldn't bring himself to look at her and instead swung his gaze toward the hangar ahead. "But that's the problem, isn't it? Because I believed that, I made it so. I don't know how my beliefs about myself are messing up my magic, but it seems they are."

Pip still remained quiet, but she squeezed his hand.

"If you'd asked me before I joined the army, I would have said I was perfectly fine with my dual heritage. I was comfortable with my magic and who I am." Fieran shook his head, trying not to squirm at the way sweat trickled down his spine beneath his fatigue shirt. "It turns out I wasn't. Not as much as I thought I was, anyway. But I don't know how to fix it." He paused and finally met Pip's gaze again. "What about you? You also have a dual heritage. Yet you don't seem to have problems with your magic."

"It's different for me." Pip matched his pace as he slowed still further. "I have iron magic like a dwarf, but I wield it like an elf. Perhaps I'm not so torn as you are because my magic is both in the way that I am both."

He hadn't thought of her magic that way, but it made sense. "I would have said I was both as well. My parents did a good job of making sure I was raised knowing and experiencing both cultures. I spent just as much time in Estyra as I did Treehaven."

"Yet you feel more human. Despite your elven magic, you've managed to embrace your human side more than your elven side." Pip halted and peered up at him. "That's not a bad thing. You are who you are. If you prefer short hair and human clothes, that's all right."

"But it isn't all right. Not if it's interfering with my magic." Fieran huffed a breath that came out far louder and more frustrated than he'd intended.

"You were raised in the heart of both Escarland and Tarenhiel. You experienced both kingdoms at their cultural center." Pip dropped her gaze to stare at the hangar. "But I was raised on the western rail terminal. I merely visited the dwarven mountains and my elven grandparents deeper inside Tarenhiel. While I experienced and knew both cultures, I was never a part of them the way you were. Things are different at the edge of Tarenhiel. We had our own little world where we had our own culture. A little dwarven. A little elven. Even a little human influence thanks to having the human tribes just across the river. I never felt I had to choose between parts of myself. Not the way you did. I was just…me."

He'd thought he'd been that comfortable within his own skin. Yet here he was, wrestling within himself. "That sounds like a great childhood."

"It was." Pip smiled, though it faded after a moment, the expression soft as she peered up at him. "Your childhood sounds pretty great as well."

"I wouldn't change anything about it." He wouldn't. His parents had given him and his siblings the very best of childhoods. It certainly wasn't their fault if he struggled with figuring out how to meld his human and elven sides within himself.

Maybe that was part of his guilt. They had given him a great childhood, a great life. There was no reason he should be struggling.

Stickyfingers grew up in the slums of Aldon. Pretty Face was the son of a wastrel nobleman who led him to follow those wayward footsteps. Lije spent part of his childhood in a home with a dirt floor. Lt. Rothilion came from one of the snobbiest elven noble families.

Compared to that, what did Fieran have to struggle with? Just his dacha's trauma, his parents' fame, and the indescribable weight that came from carrying their legacy. Yes, it was a lot of pressure. But he'd never lacked. Not for food and certainly not for love.

"But I don't want you to think I never struggle with having a dual heritage." Pip shrugged as they kept moving again. "I have the opposite problem from you. I've never truly felt a part of either my dwarven side or my elven side. It's lonely sometimes, not fitting in anywhere."

"I'm sorry." Fieran tugged her closer as they neared the

hangar, yet he resisted the urge to pull her into a hug. Too many people were around for that.

"It is what it is." Pip shrugged, as if letting the weight roll off her shoulders. After a moment, she swung their hands again, a hint of a smile returning to her face. "I've realized something about you."

"What?" Fieran was more than ready to return to a lighter topic.

"You probably would have been the type to become rebellious, except that you respect and love your parents far too much." Pip shook her head, that smile still there. "So instead, you just do these little rebellions, like joining the Flying Corps, and seek your parents' approval afterwards."

Fieran wasn't sure if he should laugh, roll his eyes, or grimace at how on the mark she was. He settled for chuckling and bumping her arm with his. "You make me sound rather ridiculous."

Pip's grin turned even more teasing as she picked up her walking pace again. "Just calling it like I see it."

"Ouch." Fieran pressed his free hand over his heart as he steered them through the large door in the side of the hangar. "We've barely started courting, and you're already pointing out my flaws."

"It's part of my job description as..." Pip's grin faded as she swallowed. She blinked up at him, her posture hesitant. "As your girlfriend."

Girlfriend. Just hearing her claim the title sent his head reeling and his heart beating harder. And if his smile went sappy, well, courting her was worth whatever ribbing he might get.

SIXTEEN

"Keep a wary eye out, everyone." Fieran spoke into the radio as he guided his Defender in a circle while he waited for the bomber aeroplanes to lumber into the air. The rest of the Half-Breed squadron had formed up behind him with Pretty Face once again taking Merrik's spot as Fieran's wingman. "Especially our green pilots."

"Watch who you're calling green, Captain." The oldest of the flygirls spoke in a light drawl that earned a few chuckles over the radio. "I was flying when most of these flyboys were still learning their letters."

Below, two more bomber aeroplanes lifted into the sky to join the formation circling over the fields to the west of Fort Defense.

"You don't know what it's like flying in close formation until you've flown a barnstorming act." Lt. Nellie Blair, another of the flygirls, piped up. She was a short, petite young woman who appeared too small to see through the windscreen, much less fly the aeroplane. But she and the others were plenty competent at their jobs, even in the finicky new Defenders. Fieran had paired her with Stickyfingers as his wingman. Well, wingwoman.

"We're thankful to have experienced new recruits join our ranks." Fieran led the circle around as more of the bombers made their lumbering way into the sky.

Two days before, one of Capt. Fleetwood's new recruits had crashed during takeoff, and another had lost control of his Defender and spiraled into Escarland's front lines, killing himself and wounding several nearby infantrymen. Several more had come perilously close to taking out some of their fellow pilots while in the air on patrol.

At least Fieran could count on his new pilots to keep their aeroplanes in the sky.

"But…" He kept talking before Lt. Blair or the others had a chance to interrupt. "You're still green when it comes to battle. Yes, I know you've pulled off incredible stunts in aeroplanes. But those stunts never involved another aeroplane shooting at you and actively trying to kill you. You don't know how you'll react until you face your first battle."

That sobered up the whole squadron, and they lapsed into an uncharacteristic silence on the radio. Probably not Fieran's best motivational speech before going into battle.

The last bomber aeroplane crawled into the sky, and a new voice crackled over the radio. "Capt. Laesornysh, Bomber Squadron A assembled and ready for our run."

"Acknowledged. Half-Breed Squadron, take your positions." Fieran swung his aeroplane over, then glided his aeroplane lower, followed by the flyboys—and flygirls—of Flight B. Lt. Rothilion and Flight A took up a higher position.

As the bomber formation set out over Fort Defense, headed east toward Mongavaria, Fieran's squadron formed a sandwich above and below them. Lt. Rothilion's Flight would protect the bombers from above while Fieran's would protect from gun emplacements below.

"Get ready. Magic incoming." Fieran let his magic twine around his fingers, then down the control column. As he unleashed more magic, it jumped eagerly to the shielding wires Pip had run over his new aeroplane.

Once his magic was steady over his own aeroplane, he pushed it outward until it wrapped around the nearest aeroplanes.

Pretty Face gave a whoop. "I missed going into battle like this."

"Didn't my dacha use his magic while flying with the squadron?" Fieran glanced over the side as the Wall flashed by below.

"Yes, but we stayed on the Escarlish side of the Wall. It was more demonstration than battle." Lije joined the conversation. He also had one of the flygirls for his wingwoman. Fieran hadn't wanted to pair any of the flygirls together until he'd assessed how they handled themselves in battle.

"And your dacha is scary when he wields his magic." Pretty Face sounded like he was giving an exaggerated shudder. "So silent. No jokes over the radio."

"It was quite serene," Lt. Rothilion, of all people, added, his tone so flat and unamused that it was clearly a joke, coming from him.

"Quite scary, you mean," Stickyfingers chipped in, before adding as if worried he'd offended Fieran, "Not that your dacha doesn't seem nice. He seems nice enough. For a general and all that."

Just how many attempts at bonding with the squadron had Dacha attempted?

Fieran shook the thoughts away as the Mongavarian front lines rushed below. They were set farther from the Wall and the Chibo River than they had been before, the previous trenches left abandoned and water-filled.

A few of the gun emplacements boomed out, but the fire was limited as the Mongavarians were still rebuilding their entrenchments after Dacha had destroyed them. Fieran had heard the Alliance had conducted a few other lightning raids into Mongavaria, further hampering efforts to refortify.

"Pretty Face, let's take out the guns while we're at it." Fieran eased up on the control column, and his aeroplane rolled into a dive almost of its own accord.

Taking out the guns would make future bombing runs easier, especially for the other two squadrons who weren't protected by Fieran's magic.

Fieran's connection to his magic wrapped around the other aeroplanes stretched, but he stayed close enough that he didn't lose control of it.

As another gun barked shells at the bombers, Fieran unleashed his magic still more, following the line of bullets back to the gun. Another burst of his magic, and the gun exploded.

The other guns fell silent, as if the gunners realized they would be better off simply letting Fieran's squadron go by rather than give him an easy way to destroy more munitions.

If destroying the guns had been Fieran's mission, he would have swooped lower and finished the job. But right now, protecting the bomber squadron was his primary goal. He couldn't put them at risk for side destruction.

Fieran peeled away and pointed his aeroplane's nose upward again, Pretty Face following in his wake. The two of them rejoined Flight B, taking up the spot at the fore of the formation.

The Mongavarian countryside crawled by below. Now that they were past the front lines, the land sprawled in a patchwork of farm fields and tree-lined rivers. It looked so much like the Escarlish side of the border that Fieran almost could have fooled himself that he was flying over his own backyard instead of enemy territory.

Above him, the formation of bombers flew in a cluster, their wings loaded with the bombs they planned to drop on the target within Mongavaria. The entire squadron of bombers could only hold as many bombs as a single airship, but the bombers could make a dash into Mongavaria and return in a few hours while the same run would take an airship a full day.

Today, their mission was to bomb an army base and airfield two hundred miles into the Mongavarian countryside. Part of a defensive line Mongavaria had set up several hundred miles within their own borders.

This was the most ambitious bombing run the Alliance had conducted yet. They'd done some small bombing runs on various army bases and airfields, using airships, since the war had begun. Not to mention numerous scouting missions in recent weeks. In the days since the first bomber aeroplanes arrived, Capt. Fleetwood and Lt. Hadley had escorted the bombers to destroy the airfields nearest the border out of which all the attacks on Fort Defense were flown.

But for this run deep into Mongavaria, headquarters had waited until Fieran was ready to provide protection.

Hopefully he was ready. He stretched his legs as best he could in the cockpit without accidentally sending his aeroplane into a turn by twitching the rudder. His body felt fine, but he'd have to see how he felt after the planned four hours of flying.

Fieran settled in, and the next hour and a half proved to be rather boring as the countryside rushed by below. Some of the flyboys made nonsense chitchat, and Fieran joined in occasionally. But it wasn't the same without Merrik chipping in.

"Capt. Laesorrysh." Lt. Rothilion's sharp tone cut through the chatter. "Enemy incoming ahead. Coming in high. Moving to intercept."

Fieran scanned the sky. From his position below the bombers, he couldn't see the enemy coming down at Flight A.

A look at the landscape below showed more empty fields and small villages. He couldn't see far enough to know if there was a gun emplacement somewhere ahead, but he doubted there would be anything until they got closer to their target. Mongavarian aeroplanes didn't have the range of the Alliance aeroplanes, and the Alliance hadn't executed a raid quite like this before.

"More enemy coming from the rear! They're trying to use the sun as cover." Aylia's voice rose in pitch.

Some of the Mongavarian aeroplanes must have circled around. The Alliance raid had been spotted and reported.

Fieran veered his aeroplane to the right to get out from under the bombers. "Flight B, break off formation and move to assist Flight A. We'll come up on the enemy from below."

It was a move only these new, faster Defenders could pull off. The old Soarwings hadn't had the power to ascend as steeply and were more prone to stalling. The Mongavarians, too, couldn't maintain enough airspeed to effectively attack from below.

The aeroplanes of his Flight scattered either to the right or the left to go around the formation of bombers, and Fieran had to drop his magic from around some of them.

Pretty Face stuck close to Fieran's tail as the two of them pointed their noses upward. As Fieran cleared the shadows of the bombers, he spotted the two formations of

Mongavarian aeroplanes swooping down from both the east and the west. Flight A had broken into two as they raced to face the attacks.

Which attack should Fieran head off? No matter which he chose, he'd leave the other half of his squadron facing the enemy without his magic.

The attack to the rear. His squadron would need their retreat clear, more than they needed their line of attack open.

"I'm taking on the enemy to our rear." Fieran aimed his aeroplane in that direction. He quickly rattled off names, dividing his Flight. He sent most of them to reinforce Lt. Rothilion and those fending off the frontal attack, keeping only a third of his Flight to reinforce himself.

As he neared the attack to the rear, he shoved his magic outward once again, re-engaging his shield around the aeroplanes of his squadron. Each time his magic touched Pip's familiar magic, he wrapped his magic around the wires, protecting that aeroplane.

Yet Pip's magic wasn't the only magic he sensed. As bolts of his power brushed the enemy aeroplanes, it skidded off with the taste of that foreign magic he'd encountered before.

"Their aeroplanes are shielded." Fieran tilted his aeroplane still more steeply upward, right at the edge of how steep he could go without stalling out.

An enemy bore down on one of the elven pilots. The pilot's wingelf was already swooping around to come at the enemy from the side, but Fieran squeezed the new trigger lever on his control column.

His twin machine guns barked, their rhythm different than what he was used to from before. Either because they were a different gun or because of the interrupter gear, he couldn't tell. At the very least, there was no familiar clang of bullets hitting the metal reinforcing the back of the propeller.

He coated his bullets with his magic, but as soon as they neared the enemy aircraft, they almost seemed to deflect away, missing instead of striking.

Fieran bit back a curse as his line of bullets shot off into the sky, thankfully missing the wingelf's aeroplane, which swooped down, firing. Her bullets struck without deflecting, so that foreign magic wasn't yet a solid shield like what Pip could create even if it was stronger than it had been before.

Was it his magic that caused the problem? Fieran fired again, this time without adding his magic. His bullets slammed into the enemy, catching the aeroplane in a cross-fire. The engine burst into flames, the pilot slumping, before the aeroplane rolled into a death spiral.

Fieran tipped his own aeroplane into a roll, the move almost scarily easy since the aeroplane had wanted to turn in that direction anyway. He swooped around to target a cluster of enemy aeroplanes that were converging on a pair of elven pilots. As they were far enough away from his own men, Fieran blasted his magic outward.

His magic just skated over the aeroplanes and ricocheted in all directions. Where it struck one of Fieran's squadron, the magic was just absorbed into the protective shield. When it struck an enemy, the magic skidded off again, bouncing around the sky until finally dissipating.

"That foreign magic is stronger than before." Fieran growled the words between his gritted teeth as he gripped the trigger and bore down on the enemy. "I won't be able to just wipe out the Mongavarians."

"At least it doesn't seem to affect your protective magic," Lije added as his aeroplane roared at an angle below, followed by his new wingwoman. "You might not be able to incinerate them, but they can't shoot us."

"A true dogfight it is." Pretty Face almost sounded

cheerful about that. He swung his aeroplane higher than Fieran's, the bullets from his machine gun shooting over Fieran's head.

The enemy turned toward them, machine guns blasting. Yet the bullets were nothing but bright flares against his protective magic surrounding his aeroplane. Under the combined fire from Fieran and Pretty Face, the other enemy flyer burst into flame.

Perhaps…Fieran wheeled his aeroplane to chase another Mongavarian aircraft…perhaps Fieran didn't need to actively target the Mongavarian aeroplanes. His own squadron was immune to his magic, thanks to the shielding wires.

Instead of following the line of bullets from his barking machine guns, Fieran let his magic explode outward, filling the sky with a haze of crackling magic. He didn't try to pinpoint anything, simply letting his magic hang in the sky.

His magic curved around his squadron but radiated in starbursts from the enemy aeroplanes as whatever magic they had on them deflected it.

But he could sense it. The way the constant deflecting wore down that foreign magic. It was strong, but not strong enough to continuously bat away his magic.

"Uh, Fieran." Lije's voice came over the radio. "Were you trying to make it harder for us to shoot back?"

Oops. Fieran fired his machine gun and winced as his magic in the sky ate the bullets before they got far. "Not my intention. It's burning through that other magic."

Which was more important? Making sure his flyboys and flygirls could shoot back or that he destroyed that other magic? If he could get past that magic, he could end this attack in a moment. But in the meantime, his squadron and the enemy were just wheeling in the sky, ineffectually shooting at each other.

"Get closer to the other aeroplanes." Stickyfingers whizzed so close to an enemy aeroplane that the other aeroplane bobbled as it tried to dodge. "The magic doesn't get in the way as much."

Tiny and his wingman Murray flashed by. They dove at an enemy aeroplane, and Murray tossed one of his magical water globes down at the enemy. Tiny shot out his magic, and the water globes turned into shards of ice that sliced through the enemy, shredding the canvas of the wings and fuselage.

An enemy aeroplane dove at Fieran, and Fieran swung his aeroplane, trying to bring the nose up to target the incoming enemy.

Before he could, Pretty Face came in from the side, machine guns barking. This close, Fieran could part his magic to prevent it from incinerating the bullets.

Movement out of the corner of his eye drew his attention. Several Mongavarian aeroplanes had peeled away from the dogfight and swooped down on the lightly defended bomber aeroplanes. One of the pilots seemed to be fumbling with something, turning in his seat as he hefted something out of a back compartment.

"They have bombs!" Fieran let his aeroplane go into a roll before he pushed it to dive as steeply as the wings would allow. The force of it pressed on him, and he clenched his muscles to resist it. He bore down on the aeroplanes attacking the bombers, Pretty Face in his wake.

The Half-Breed Squadron had bombs tucked under their wings as well, but theirs were all rigged for ground detonation to drop in support of the bombs in the assault on their target.

The pilot of the lead enemy aeroplane dropped something large and cylindrical from the aeroplane. It plunged from the sky downward at one of the bombers.

Fieran lashed out with his magic, grabbed the bomb from the air, and slung it back at the enemy aeroplane.

The bomb exploded even before making contact, spewing fire in all directions with more force than he would have expected. The aeroplane swerved, its left wings on fire.

"They're incendiary." Fieran lashed out to catch a second bomb from one of the other aeroplanes attacking the bombers. "And I think they're on some kind of timer."

They'd likely been armed with incendiaries to combat Alliance airships, but such bombs would work just as well on the bombers. All they'd have to do was get the bomb somewhat close, and they'd set the bombers on fire.

The second bomb burst within his magic, and his power absorbed the splashing fire. He could taste the sense of human magic, likely fire magic to ensure that the fire from the bomb wouldn't be easy to put out. At least this magic was something he recognized and could easily overcome.

Fieran wrapped his magic in a denser storm around the enemy aeroplanes attacking the airships, keeping it just far enough away that he wasn't actually touching the foreign magic. The foreign magic deflected his for a full minute, bouncing the bolts away, until, finally, that other magic began to weaken.

Gritting his teeth, Fieran poured more power into the magical storm. He couldn't relent. Not until he'd destroyed these aeroplanes.

Finally, his magic touched the flammable lacquer on the canvas, and it latched on, consuming it as greedily as the magical fire of the incendiary bombs would have the bombers if given the chance.

"Lt. Blair!" Stickyfingers shouted into the radio. "Stop!"

Fieran scanned the skies, squinting into the brilliance of his magic. When he couldn't see Stickyfingers or Lt. Blair, he tilted his aeroplane to peer upward at a better angle.

Lt. Blair's aeroplane was diving out of the cloud of Fieran's magic, following an enemy aeroplane with the single-minded tenacity of a falcon on a hunt. Yet two more Mongavarian aeroplanes were breaking away and diving after her, seeing an opportunity to pick off a lone aeroplane.

She was headed away from the rest of the dogfight, in the opposite direction of the bombers. Being lured away, if Fieran were to guess. A mistake by a pilot too green to realize the danger she was putting herself in.

Almost directly above, Stickyfingers had been left alone, and three Mongavarian aeroplanes converged on him. Even with Fieran's magic protecting him, there was a chance that many concentrated bullets could get through.

"Pretty Face, I've got Lt. Blair. Go help Stickyfingers." Fieran raced his aeroplane in the wake of the enemy chasing Lt. Blair. His magic tugged as he was pulled farther from the fight, and he could feel it slipping off some of the aeroplanes farthest from him.

"On it." Pretty Face's voice crackled over the radio, but Fieran didn't turn his head to see Pretty Face veering his aeroplane to assist Stickyfingers.

The two Mongavarian aeroplanes converged on Lt. Blair, blasting at her with their machine guns. Fieran's magic absorbed most of it, but he was stretched thin, trying to hold magic on his scattered squadron and burn away that other power.

"Lt. Blair!" Fieran gripped the control stick, still too far away to help, as the aeroplane Lt. Blair had been chasing flared its wings and flipped around to join in the attack on her.

She didn't bother to answer, likely so focused that she wasn't even hearing what was being said on the radio. She juked her aeroplane, dodging the streams of bullets before her machine guns blasted. At the last moment, she flipped her aeroplane over and turned on the enemy behind her.

She could fly, Fieran would give her that. But that didn't excuse her recklessness, even if it was a mistake many of them had made in the early days.

And…he couldn't believe he was the one thinking that. How this war had changed him.

The two chasing aeroplanes scattered away from her before heading out again.

Lt. Blair turned again to chase all three enemy aeroplanes, as if not caring that they were luring her still farther away from the rest of the squadron. Even worse, they were slowly dropping lower in the sky. Perhaps they realized that if they lured her far enough away, she'd lose the protecting magic. They'd catch her in a deadly crossfire.

And if she got far enough away, Fieran would have to let them. He couldn't leave the squadron or the bombers unprotected. They would be his priority, not one reckless pilot.

"Lt. Blair, halt your pursuit and turn around now." Fieran tried his best impression of his dacha's hard, unyielding tone, hoping his voice would cut through whatever battle haze was currently gripping her. "That is a direct order."

For another long moment, she continued chasing the Mongavarians. Then she wheeled her aeroplane around, headed back toward Fieran. When the radio crackled, her voice held a trace of disorientation, as if she hadn't realized just how far she'd gotten from the squadron. "Yes, sir."

An honest mistake made in the heat of battle, but Fieran

would have to take her aside once this was all over and impress on her just how much of a mistake it had been.

The Mongavarians wheeled around as well, but they did so at a more leisurely pace. They weren't giving chase, not with Fieran right there.

"Bomb! Bomb!" Stickyfingers shouted. More shouts came over the radio.

Heart in his throat, Fieran yanked his aeroplane over to point his nose the other way, just as a fireball exploded within the cluster of aeroplanes wheeling in the sky.

He was too far away. His magical protections had gone weak around them, slipping entirely off the farthest aeroplanes. He couldn't reach out and grab the bombs. He couldn't suppress the fire and shrapnel that tore into the nearest aeroplanes.

Another incendiary bomb burst, showering flames in all directions.

Fieran pushed his aeroplane as fast as he could, ignoring the way the power gauge leapt far too close to the red line. He didn't bother to check if Lt. Blair had fallen into place as his wingwoman. At this point, he didn't particularly care if she followed his order or went off on her own again. Because of her, he was out of position.

"My aeroplane is hit." Pretty Face's voice sliced through the tumult on the radio, even as an aeroplane peeled away from the others, one of its wings on fire.

"Hold on another moment. I can suppress the flames once I'm closer." Fieran's gaze locked on the aeroplane dropping from the sky in a controlled, wide spin.

He'd already lost Merrik because he wasn't there to protect his back. He couldn't lose Pretty Face too.

"Wouldn't do any good." Pretty Face's voice had gone extra tense, as if he spoke through gritted teeth. "It knocked out something in my engine too. I have to set down."

The words were a rock landing in Fieran's gut. They were hundreds of miles into Mongavaria. There would be no setting down in Alliance territory. No way to even send in a rescue party.

For a moment, the radio waves fell silent.

Another aeroplane shadowed Pretty Face's dying aeroplane—Stickyfingers, most likely, protecting Pretty Face. A moment later, Sticky's voice came over the radio. "Just set down safely. You can sneak back to the Alliance."

"They will expect you to head west for Escarland." Lt. Rothilion's voice remained steady, even now. "It will be about the same distance to head north for Tarenhiel."

"Whichever direction, keep your head down and stay wary." As Fieran neared, he got a better grip on his protective magic again, strengthening it. Once that was done, he wrapped his magic over the last of the enemy aeroplanes still in the sky. He wasn't going to let a little bit of mysterious magic prevent him from taking down the enemy.

"Will do." Pretty Face's voice was taut, his aeroplane circling even lower in the sky. Black smoke rose from his wings, the fire spreading.

Would he be able to put down before the fire engulfed him? Or the wings gave out?

Fieran tightened his magic on the enemy as it ate through the last of the other magic. He didn't even look as his magic incinerated wood and canvas, blood and bone. He kept his gaze focused on Pretty Face's aeroplane as he glided down, down, down until he was lined up on a large field.

There was a chance whatever was wrong with the engine wasn't serious. Fieran might even be able to fix it, if he set down and took a look at it. He could fix it and both he and Pretty Face could take off once again.

But doing so would leave the squadron and the bombers vulnerable as they were nearing their heavily fortified and protected target.

"Capt. Laesornysh." Lt. Rothilion's voice was almost gentle. "The bombers are getting ahead of us."

Fieran squeezed his eyes shut for a moment, his chest tightening. He wanted to stay. He should stay to protect his friend.

But duty demanded that he leave.

"Sticky, Lije, Tiny, Murray, stay with Pretty Face until he's on the ground. Everyone else, form up around the bombers." Fieran turned his aeroplane away, pointing his nose toward the squadron of bombers.

Lt. Rothilion and those who had fought off the frontal attack were already there, spreading out into a protective formation once again.

For several tense minutes, Fieran waited. His knuckles white as he gripped the stick. His breath catching. If the engine fully cut out before Pretty Face could make a good landing…if he hit the ground hard enough to set off the four bombs under his wings…

"He's on the ground!" Stickyfingers all but shouted over the radio.

"I'm setting the engine to overload, then I'm bailing out." Pretty Face's voice was back to something almost cheerful. "Happy flying, Half-Breed Squadron."

Fieran caught up with the last of the bombers, and he dove once again to provide protection from below.

Moments later, a large burst of static filled the radio.

"Stickyfingers, did he get out? Did he get far enough

away?" Fieran took up his position at the head of the Flight below the bombers, his heart hammering even as it ached.

"He got out, but I can't see him." Stickyfingers almost sounded like he was crying. "I can't see him."

"I think he found cover in those trees." Lije's voice, too, rang roughly over the radio. "The aeroplane is destroyed."

Those were the new orders, which had come down from headquarters. If they set down behind enemy lines, they needed to overload the engine to blow up the aeroplane to keep the new synchronization gear and the magical power cell from falling into Mongavarian hands.

"Good. Rejoin the squadron." Fieran worked to keep his voice steady. He needed to be strong. Be the squadron's leader. Finish the mission.

SEVENTEEN

When Fieran climbed down from his aeroplane, he just stood there for a long moment, staring at the bright artwork painted on the nose. The swirling flames that almost looked like red hair. The bolts of blue magic threaded between them. The images of some of his victories. All painted by Pretty Face.

"What's going on?" Pip hurried up to him, her eyes wide as she took in the returning aeroplanes. "What happened?"

Of course she could tell something had happened. The squadron wasn't buoyant, as they normally would be after a successful mission.

Fieran didn't care that most of his men and women were still there, trudging back to the hangar. A few of them had bloody bandages wrapped around arms or legs where they had been caught in the shrapnel blasts, but none of the injuries were serious. The only pilot they'd lost had been Pretty Face.

Fieran wrapped his arms around Pip, holding her close. Who cared if everyone saw them having a moment? Today was a day for holding loved ones close because one never knew when the war would snatch someone away.

"Fieran?" Pip leaned into him, her arms coming around him.

"Pretty Face's aeroplane was damaged, and he was forced to set down in Mongavaria," he murmured into her hair, holding her close. "We think he escaped his aeroplane before it blew up but…"

But he was now on foot, alone, somewhere deep within Mongavaria. It would be a miracle if he evaded the enemy long enough to get back to either Escarland or Tarenhiel.

When they'd flown over the spot on their return from successfully bombing the Mongavarian airfield—with Fieran further destroying buildings, grounded aeroplanes, and airships with his magic—the Mongavarian army had already been at the crash site, combing through the wreckage.

Fieran led a small strafing run, dropping the handful of bombs he and the others of the squadron hadn't needed to use during the attack on the target and sending the Mongavarians scattering. He also sent his magic over the pieces of Pretty Face's aeroplane, further incinerating it. He couldn't do anything about any parts that the Mongavarians had already carted away, but there looked to be little that survived the initial explosion.

There had been no sign of Pretty Face. No way to know if he'd gotten out of there before the Mongavarian army arrived.

Pip's arms tightened around him as she buried her face against Fieran's chest. "No. No, not Pretty Face. Not him too."

Fieran rubbed her back, his own throat squeezing. He'd lost those under his command before. Pretty Face likely wasn't even dead.

But with Merrik gone, losing Pretty Face hit that much harder.

Fieran let himself soak up the comfort of having Pip in his arms for another minute before he forced himself to pull back.

She glanced up at him, tear tracks glistening on her cheeks.

He swiped one of the tears from her skin. "I know it's a lot to ask, but could you look after the squadron for me? I need to report in to Colonel Dentley."

And reprimand a certain new pilot.

"Of course." Pip straightened her shoulders, her jaw firming in that way that showed she was pulling herself together.

Fieran pressed a kiss to her forehead before he forced himself to release her shoulders, turn, and march away, heading toward the nearest hangar door.

But as he neared, his gaze landed on the figure standing just outside the door. His dacha, dressed in his elven armor with his swords strapped to his back.

Fieran's feet dragged still further. He should have expected to find his dacha waiting for him, especially after a long mission like that. A little bit of hovering by his dacha was rather expected after his crash.

He halted in front of his dacha and just stood there, silent, for a long moment.

Dacha, too, didn't break the silence, merely regarding Fieran with the too knowing gaze of a warrior who had seen too many battles and lost too many of his fellow warriors on his watch.

Finally Fieran released a breath. "We lost a pilot. A friend. Pretty Face. He isn't dead, but…"

Dacha tipped his head, something of recognition in his

eyes as he looked away from Fieran for a moment. "I am sorry, sason."

Fieran swallowed and nodded, but he couldn't find the words for any more than that. But this was his dacha. Communicating without words was his thing.

Was there something Fieran could have done differently that day? Perhaps he should have sent Pretty Face after Lt. Blair and gone to help Stickyfingers. But then Lt. Blair and Pretty Face might have been ambushed. Likely one or both of them would have crashed. Or he could have simply let Lt. Blair fly to her death and focused on protecting the rest of the squadron.

No matter what choice he'd made, he would have lost someone that day.

Dacha reached out and rested his hand on Fieran's shoulder briefly before he turned and strode away through the hangar.

After gathering himself, Fieran stepped into the hangar as well. Lt. Rothilion stood only a few feet inside, as if waiting for him. When Fieran headed for where Lt. Blair stood, alone, in the empty space of the hangar, Lt. Rothilion followed, not speaking.

Fieran halted before Lt. Blair, and her shoulders remained somewhat hunched even as she came to attention. "Lt. Blair, you left your wingman in the middle of a battle and because of that action, one of our own is now fighting to survive somewhere in Mongavaria."

"I know. I'm sorry. I was so focused, and the enemy was right there, and I thought if I could just chase them down for another minute, but then…" She shuddered, and tears welled in her dark eyes, spilling down her cheeks.

Great. Now she was crying. How was he supposed to give her a proper reprimand when she was crying?

She sniffled and seemed to be trying to pull herself together. "I understand what you meant about being green. I didn't think I would react like that. But then…I'm sorry."

"Don't let it happen again." Fieran waited one more moment before he let his tone and posture soften. He waved to where Stickyfingers, Tiny, Murray, Lije, and many of the others had gathered. "Go on. Join the rest of the squadron."

"They won't want to talk to me. They'll blame me for… for what happened." Now that he'd essentially dismissed her to stand at ease, she wrapped her arms over her stomach. Her straight, dark brown hair had partially fallen from its bun to straggle around her face.

"They might. For a few minutes. But we've all done something reckless our first few battles." Fieran didn't think she would've been able to hear the soft snort Lt. Rothilion gave behind him at that.

Lt. Blair hesitated another moment before she bobbed her head to him and made her shuffling way over to the others. They parted for her, but the moment she began speaking with more tears pouring down her face, Stickyfingers and Lije stepped closer, likely saying something comforting.

Lt. Rothilion strode to Fieran's side. "You have come a long way, Capt. Laesornysh."

"It used to be you giving me a dressing down for being reckless." Fieran sighed and shook his head. Perhaps if he'd learned his lesson sooner, Merrik wouldn't have crashed and lost his leg.

"Yes." Lt. Rothilion tilted his head. "Your arrogance was in your own abilities and your belief that you and only you had the capacity to gain the victory. You were reckless when you believed that recklessness would save lives. Neither your arrogance nor your recklessness was for your own advancement but rather for the good of others. That made it understandable, even if it needed to be tempered with wisdom."

The words settled deep inside him. He hadn't liked the parallels he saw between himself and Lt. Blair, but at least he could depend on Lt. Rothilion to tell him the truth.

Fieran worked up a smile, even though it still felt out of place after the events of the day. "That almost sounded like a compliment, Rothilion."

"Do not let it go to your head." Lt. Rothilion gave another tip of his head, even as his mouth curved with a hint of a smile. "You are finally becoming tolerable."

"Tolerable. Really. I knew we were friends." Fieran clapped Lt. Rothilion on the back.

Rothilion stiffened, though he didn't shy away from the gesture. It was more as if he didn't know how to respond to the very human gesture. "Do not push it, Laesornysh."

"Wouldn't dream of it." Fieran gave Rothilion one more slap on the back before he stepped away.

The joking words weren't like Rothilion, but perhaps he'd known Fieran had needed the bit of levity after Pretty Face's crash.

His smile faded a moment later as he made his way through the hangar to report to Colonel Dentley. After that, he'd have to face the rest of the squadron as they processed Pretty Face's loss.

PIP MEANDERED between the various clusters of flyboys, flygirls, and elves sitting on chairs or on the floor of Hangar Bay 4. She paused at each group to ask if they needed anything.

It was the least she could do, even as an ache settled deep within her own chest.

Pretty Face had been part of the core of the Half-Breed Squadron. Generally liked by everyone and a leader among them, especially in the past two weeks when Fieran had been absent. A gaping hole had been left, now that he was gone.

Gone, but not dead. She repeated that to herself yet again. Gone like Merrik was gone. But not gone like the others who were dead and gone.

She glanced around, taking in the faces who were still there, seeing all the echoes of those who were not. Fieran's training squadron had started with thirty-eight back in Fort Linder. Through all the losses, they were down to twenty-one of that original group, counting Merrik and Pretty Face in those losses. A few of those who'd been lost in the attack on Bridgetown were also alive gone and not dead gone.

Seventeen, wounded, lost, or dead. And that was only the losses of Flight B.

It wasn't even the worst losses experienced by a squadron. The late Capt. Kentworth's squadron had been all but gutted, only a handful of the original members still remaining.

They were only months into the war. How many more would they lose before the war was over?

She shook that thought away, pasted on a smile, and moved to the next group. As she paused before them, she waved to the table at the other side of the hangar. Paperboard boxes filled the table while halves of oil drums sat below the table, filled with ice created by Tiny. "There are donuts and sodas, if you want some."

She, Mak, and Tiny had made a trip to Defense City, and Tiny's girlfriend had been happy to provide the donuts.

Some more scrounging had located enough sodas for the squadron.

She finally made her way to where Fieran sat with Mak, Stickyfingers, Lije, Tiny, and Aylia. Lt. Rothilion sat a few feet away, not quite a part of the group but not fully alone either.

Without Merrik and Pretty Face, the group seemed small. Empty.

All of them already had sodas and donuts, although the donuts were only nibbled and the sodas were mostly full.

Pip sank to the floor next to Fieran, close enough that she could lean her head against his shoulder. "How are you holding up?"

"About as well as you are." Fieran wrapped his arm around her shoulders, easy and loose rather than tugging tight. "Thanks for rounding up donuts and sodas for everyone. I appreciate it."

"Mak and Tiny did most of the work." Pip tipped her head in her brother's direction.

Mak gave a roll of his shoulders that didn't even slosh the root beer he held. "It was your idea. I just provided the grunt labor."

"Still. I appreciate how you look after the squadron." Fieran laced the fingers of his other hand with hers.

"It was the least I could do." She could repair their aeroplanes. Scrounge up a feast of donuts and sodas. Be here for Fieran.

But she couldn't repair the gaping hole Pretty Face left behind in the squadron.

They lapsed into silence for a moment, as if lost in thought. Stickyfingers, especially, stared sightlessly at the floor. He probably felt partially responsible.

Lije rolled his unopened soda from hand-to-hand. He

probably shouldn't open it anytime soon. "Should we...for Pretty Face?" He held up his bottle of soda.

Pip swallowed. Right. The tradition of leaving a full glass for a fallen comrade.

"No." Stickyfingers sat up straighter, life flaring back to his eyes. "He's not dead. He will get back to the squadron."

"Yes, he will." Tiny slapped Stickyfingers on the back. "Pretty Face is smart."

Not a word Pip would have applied to the flirtatious nobleman when they first met. But he'd proved he was more than a just a pretty face, especially recently.

Aylia gave something of a snort. "This is Pretty Face we are talking about. He will charm a farmer's daughter and probably convince her to lend him a horse or wagon so he can ride out of Mongavaria in style."

"And thanks to our efforts, he will probably even be respectful about it." Lije knocked Sticky's shoulder with a fist. "Which will improve his chances of actually charming her instead of insulting her to the point of her turning him in."

"You're right." Stickyfingers gave an approximation of a grin, though Pip could see even from across their little circle that the expression didn't fully reach his eyes. "He will be back before we know it."

"That he will." Fieran raised his soda—the raspberry one that was his favorite. "To Pretty Face."

"To Pretty Face," the others echoed as they also held up their sodas.

Lije reached to twist the metal cap of his soda bottle.

Pip straightened, reaching for him even though she was too far away. "No, don't—"

Lije twisted the cap. Soda shot upward, bubbles spraying everything and everyone nearby.

EIGHTEEN

Fieran strode between the aeroplanes in the hangar, his new gas mask bumping against his leg.

Around the hangar, the flyboys and flygirls lounged about as they waited on standby. Beside the far wall, Stickyfingers and Lije consulted the donut recipe and double-checked their ingredients, debating whether they had enough to attempt donut-making. Tiny gripped four glass jars in his arms, stopping every flyboy and flygirl to attempt to convince them to take some of the sourdough starter off his hands.

Shaking his head, Fieran headed toward where Pip was currently fiddling with something on her workbench near his aeroplane. Her dark brown hair frizzed from her haphazard bun, a smear of grease on her chin.

The wail of the red alert siren blared through the hangar, echoing off the steel and cement in a way that made him wince, even though he didn't have the sensitive hearing of a full elf.

He spun on his heel and instead ran toward the opposite wall, where one of the mechanics was sliding into the seat behind the spare radio Pip had set up back when they'd first arrived at Fort Defense.

Fieran skidded to a halt next to the chair. "What's going on?"

"A small formation of Mongavarian aeroplanes is coming over the mountain pass south of Fort Defense." The mechanic grimaced as more static and voices came through the speaker.

"More aeroplanes! Coming over the Wall into Tarenhiel to the north." The unknown voice gave the location. Perhaps he was the radio operator on one of the airships patrolling that section of the border.

Fieran did the calculations, mentally finding the spot on a map. He spun, turning toward the flyboys. "Suit up, everyone!"

As soon as Fieran and his squadron had shrugged into their flight gear, orders came from Colonel Dentley for their squadron to stagger takeoffs with Capt. Fleetwood's squadron. Capt. Fleetwood would go after the enemy to the south while the Half-Breed Squadron would take on the Mongavarians to the north. Lt. Hadley's squadron would remain on station above Fort Defense.

Within half an hour, Fieran gripped the control column as his aeroplane winged over the Hydalla River along the Tarenhieli-Mongavarian border. Lt. Blair had the spot as his wingwoman since he didn't trust her enough yet to assign her to anyone else. Flight B trailed after him while Lt. Rothilion led Flight A in a formation flying several miles inland.

Fieran scanned the skies ahead in all directions. "Anyone spot the enemy?"

"Not yet." Lije held station above and behind Fieran.

More trees flashed by below, not giving any landmarks

for Fieran—or anyone else—to navigate by. Good thing they were sticking by the river, otherwise even Fieran would likely find himself pretty much lost over Tarenhiel.

"Enemy spotted." Lt. Rothilion's voice came over the radio, crisp and cool. "They are flying north-northwest."

"Moving to intercept." Fieran turned his aeroplane in that direction. He should come up behind the enemy and slightly from the side, cutting off the enemy's avenue of retreat.

A distant glint of sun on something human-made—certainly nothing elven—provided him a more exact heading. Within another minute, the shapes of aeroplanes appeared out of the brightness of the morning.

Fieran pushed his aeroplane harder as he bore down on a small cluster of Mongavarian aeroplanes.

Strange that there were so few of the enemy. Before, Mongavaria had sent over large raids, trying to wipe out Escarland's air defenses. Not that those large sorties had ever succeeded in anything but sacrificing Mongavaria's most experienced pilots to Fieran's magic.

Was this merely a scouting run? A small bombing run?

Lt. Rothilion swooped down on the lead enemy aeroplane, machine guns blasting.

The Mongavarian shot back, one of the other Mongavarians trying to loop around to come at Lt. Rothilion from the side. Aylia, as Lt. Rothilion's wingwoman, cut off the enemy.

Fieran took a moment to scan the skies again, searching the rising sun for the telltale dark dots of more incoming aeroplanes. He couldn't see any, but he'd keep a wary eye out.

As he neared the fight, Fieran released his magic, letting it coat his aeroplane before he blasted it outward. His magic danced over the protective wires, protecting the other members of his squadron.

The lead Mongavarian aeroplanes flared into swift turns, protected by the aeroplanes coming up behind them. Before Fieran could even reach them, the whole group of them had performed a coordinated turnabout as they beat a retreat.

Fieran joined Lt. Rothilion and the others in chasing the Mongavarians back to the border. As the Mongavarians kept fleeing, Fieran gave the order to hold at the border rather than pursue. The small raid might be bait to lure them across the border into a trap.

"Capt. Laesornysh to Fort Defense, the northern raid has been turned back." Fieran held the button on the control column. "Do we need to assist on the southern raid?"

"No, that one has been turned back as well." Colonel Dentley's voice filled the radio waves. "Patrol the border to make sure the Mongavarians don't come back."

"Yes, sir." Fieran acknowledged. He and his squadron had just pulled long hours the day before on another bombing run, but they'd be up for a day of patrols if needed.

PIP MEANDERED through the aeroplanes parked in the hangar.

The large hangar doors were open to let in the somewhat cooler evening air, although the lack of a breeze left the night nearly as sweltering as the late summer day had been. Strands of her hair stuck to the back of her neck, and she tugged her shirt away from her body, flapping it to try to cool herself.

The bustle of the day had gone quiet, and only a few mechanics still lingered as they cleaned their tools. She held up a hand to Mak but didn't stop to talk.

She rounded the last aeroplane and finally spotted Fieran. He was propped against the inner wall separating Bay 4 and 5, his flight cap, goggles, and scarf set beside him. Despite the heat, he still wore his flight jacket and boots, as if he hadn't had the energy to take them off. His eyes were closed, his chest rising and falling as he slept, slumped right there against the wall.

Poor Fieran. Poor all of the flyboys and flygirls.

For the past three weeks, Mongavaria had been sending small sorties over the Wall, usually just far enough from Fort Defense that it would take the Alliance squadrons longer to respond. Even with additional, new squadrons now stationed along the Tarenhieli border and farther south along Escarland's border, Fort Defense was still covering a lot of territory. And, of course, Fieran and his squadron were sent up more than any of the others, thanks to Fieran's magic.

Yet every time Fieran, his squadron, or pilots from one of the other squadrons chased down the Mongavarians, the enemy only engaged for a few potshots before they turned tail and ran.

Worse, these small sorties just kept coming. No sooner would Fieran and his men land after chasing down the enemy in one section of skies than another raid would be reported. All three squadrons here at Fort Defense were being kept busy, nearly constantly in the sky from dawn to dusk. Occasionally, Mongavaria would overlap so many raids that they'd manage to get in a small bombing run over Fort Defense, usually dropping gas canister bombs.

The change in strategy made far too much sense. Mongavaria had finally learned that sending large waves against Fieran was just a waste of lives.

But this new strategy was wearing everyone thin. They couldn't catch a break. Couldn't relax.

Even worse, the Alliance command was still pushing for more bombing runs of their own, and the squadrons had to fly protective formations around the bombers for the long bombing runs on top of having to turn back the Mongavarian raids.

Pip had barely seen Fieran and the flyboys in the past few weeks. There'd been no donut making. No relaxed dinners. By evening, all of them were too exhausted to do more than fall straight into bed.

About the only good news in the past three weeks had been word that the Alliance naval fleet had won a smashing victory over the Mongavarian Navy. Retributions for the losses at Dar Goranth, or so the newspapers were saying. At least Fieran's cousins must be fine this time, for neither of the Generals Ardon had been called away.

Pip halted before where Fieran was sleeping, hesitating as she looked down at him. As much as she wanted to let him sleep, he would wake with a crook in his neck and an ache in his back if he slept the whole night sleeping propped against a wall.

She rested a hand on his shoulder and shook him. "Fieran."

Fieran's breathing hitched, and he blinked up at her. "Hey."

"Hey." She smiled and held out a hand. "Come on. You should get some sleep. In a proper bed and not just slumped against the wall. You should have already headed there."

"I was waiting to talk to you." Fieran smiled in return, though the expression just highlighted the dark circles beneath his eyes. "Are you up for a nighttime walk?"

"As long as that walk is in the direction of your tent, then yes." As much as Pip wanted a romantic walk with Fieran, he needed his sleep more than she needed time with him

She'd known what she was signing up for when she said yes to courting Fieran while this war was ongoing.

"All right." Fieran released her hand as he shrugged out of his thick flight jacket. He wiggled out of his flight boots, revealing the uniform he wore beneath. After shoving his feet into his military boots, the laces tucked inside rather than tied, he grabbed the pile of flight gear before he held out his hand again.

Pip laced her fingers with his, falling into step with him as they strolled between the sleeping warbirds, lit only by the low lights around the work stations.

Fieran tilted his head. "How are the aeroplanes looking?"

"Just fine. Despite all the hours you've been putting in the air, the lack of dogfights has left me very little to do." Pip tried to keep her boredom out of her voice. She wasn't going to complain. She'd take bored over losing another one of her flyboys. "But you're in the sky so much I can't even fiddle with anything to make improvements."

She didn't dare risk having an aeroplane in a state where it wouldn't be ready to go up at a moment's notice.

"Hopefully this won't last much longer." Fieran tugged her closer. "I can't imagine the Mongavarians can keep up this pace any more than we can. It has to be as exhausting on them as it is on us."

She could only hope. After all the experienced pilots Fieran had taken out early in the summer, Mongavaria had to be hurting for pilots, even if that foreign magic protecting their aeroplanes meant fewer of them were getting killed lately.

As they stepped into the night, Pip drew in a deep breath of the somewhat cooler air.

Fieran halted, also inhaling deeply. "I'm sorry we haven't

had much time together lately. I haven't even had the energy to fetch your tools and pretend to help."

"It's okay." Pip let go of his hand so that she could wrap her arms around his waist instead, leaning into him. "You've barely been out of your aeroplane in the past three weeks. You haven't even managed morning practice with your dacha."

"We're courting. I need to make time for you." Fieran embraced her in return and leaned his head against hers.

"We're at war. Everything else needs to take the rear seat, even a courtship. I get it." Pip would have snuggled closer, but she was growing all the more aware of how Fieran hadn't had a shower yet, and he'd been sweating in that flight jacket for the past few hours. She tried to take shallow breaths as she eased just a bit away from him so that her face wasn't pressed against his sweaty shirt.

"I just wish it didn't have to be like that." Fieran held her for another long moment before he pulled back. "Sorry. I smell, don't I?"

"Terribly." Pip took another step back to drag in a breath of the fresh, nighttime air. "It's a sign of my love that I actually hugged you when you are this gross."

"Then I'd probably be pushing my luck if I kissed you." Fieran gave her what he probably thought was a smoldering look, though it looked more puppy dog pleading than smolder.

Pip eyed him, debating. On the one hand, he was rather gross. On the other hand, she didn't know when they'd have another moment alone for stealing kisses. This was war. She had to take her opportunities where she could get them.

Fieran's smolder turned into a lopsided smile. "If you have to debate that long, then the answer is no." He lifted his shirt, sniffed at it, and grimaced. "Perhaps after I take a shower? I don't fancy marinating in my sweat all night."

As hot as it was likely to be tonight, they all would be doing just that, regardless of their prior cleanliness. She resisted the urge to shudder.

"I don't want to waste what time we have." Pip drew in a deep breath, holding it, as she eased closer. "Perhaps if we—"

"Capt. Laesornysh!" Lt. Busher hurried from the hangar, a clipboard in hand. He halted and gave Fieran a salute. "If you could spare a moment, sir."

And…they'd lost their moment.

"Yes?" Fieran turned, returning the lieutenant's salute.

Pip faced the adjutant as well. Somehow, his uniform was crisp and neat, despite the day's heat, nor had the scorching day managed to melt his starch.

Lt. Busher held the clipboard out to Fieran. "Colonel Dentley asks that you peruse this form. He will only give his approval and signature if you also do so."

Fieran took the form, his eyes flicking back and forth as he scanned the paper. He stilled, his eyebrows rising before he glanced up at Lt. Busher. "Is this…he's…" Fieran's gaze dropped back to the paper, staring at it.

What was on that paper? Pip clamped her jaws shut to stop her questions. Technically, it wasn't any of her business what was on that paper, and she didn't dare ask in front of Lt. Busher.

Lt. Busher somehow managed to stiffen, his back even more starched straight. "Colonel Dentley realizes these are unusual circumstances, which is why he is seeking your approval for this return to combat. But as you do not seem bothered by unusual cases—"

"I'm not arguing. I'll sign. Where's a pen?" Fieran fumbled to take the pen the lieutenant held out to him, his hand shaking as he scrawled his name. He handed the clipboard back. "How soon can we expect everything to go through?"

"Soon. Headquarters is motivated to get as many experienced pilots as possible to the front to turn back this latest wave of attacks." Lt. Busher saluted and, once Fieran gave him a salute in dismissal, he spun on a heel and marched back the way he'd come.

"What—" Pip turned toward Fieran.

"He's coming back." Fieran rested his hands on her shoulders before he pulled her in for a hug, as if he couldn't quite contain himself.

"Who?" Pip found herself once again squashed against Fieran's sweaty shirt, and this time she hadn't had the time to take a decent breath beforehand.

"Merrik." Fieran's arms tightened around her. "He requested to return to duty. The healers cleared him, and the commander of the reserve squadron in Estyra certified that he can still fly. So he's coming back."

Pip hugged Fieran tighter, a lump filling her throat so thickly that she wasn't sure she could speak, even if she could find the words.

Merrik was coming back.

She would have snuggled into Fieran's hug, but…he was still very gross. After a moment, Pip pressed her palms to Fieran's chest and pushed back, easing out of Fieran's embrace as he released her. She kept her hands on his chest as she studied his expression. "He still hasn't answered any of your letters, has he?"

"No." The joy leached out of Fieran's voice on his sigh. He shook his head, his gaze dropping from hers. "Nor sent me a message through his dacha, even though I know Uncle Iyrinder has talked with him."

"I'm sorry." That lump was back in her throat. Merrik hadn't sent a message to any of them in the squadron. "But it must be a good sign if he's coming back, right? He could have easily taken an honorable discharge or a transfer to the reserve squadrons in Estyra or Aldon. He didn't have to come back to the Half-Breed Squadron if he didn't want to."

In fact, returning to the Half-Breed Squadron was by far the hardest option. Merrik would've had to fight to return, as demonstrated by the fact that Colonel Dentley and Fieran had to give their stamp of approval on the paperwork.

Surely he wouldn't do that if he wasn't healing from the bitterness that had made him push them all away after his crash.

"Maybe." Fieran took another step away from her, shaking his head again. "I just hope…"

"Yeah. Me too." Pip reached out to take his hand, the ache in his eyes and voice mirroring the one in her heart.

Merrik had been so hurt and bitter. Would things be the same when he returned?

After another moment, Fieran released another long breath. He straightened his shoulders, a smile returning. "We'd better tell the others the good news. At least, anyone who is awake."

The ruckus of celebrating flyboys would wake everyone up, no doubt. But Pip forced a grin of her own and hurried at his side toward the row of tents.

NINETEEN

Fieran stood on the grass a few yards away from the tram platform, trying to still his jitters. The late afternoon sun beat onto his face and the back of his neck, reminding him that he probably should have put on his service cap but he'd been in too much of a hurry.

He'd wanted to meet the train, but Uncle Iyrinder had—probably wisely—insisted that he meet the train alone to give Merrik space rather than everyone swarming him upon arrival.

Fieran had acquiesced. It was, after all, the same reason he was waiting here alone. He'd asked everyone, including Pip, to wait for Merrik in the hangar rather than overwhelm him the moment he stepped off the tram.

He would step off the tram, right? Surely he wouldn't have been allowed to return to Fort Defense if he hadn't regained his ability to walk.

But Fieran didn't know. He didn't know what had been going on with Merrik outside of the short updates Uncle Iyrinder provided during the few mornings when Fieran snatched a morning practice.

At least Mongavaria had let up on attacks today, so Fieran wasn't in the air for the first time in weeks.

The tram clattered its way up the hill before easing to a halt beside the platform. The doors whooshed open, and various men and women poured from the tram, most of them headed in the direction of the headquarters building.

Finally, Uncle Iyrinder strode from the final tram car, his long chestnut hair flowing over the shoulders of his evergreen elven uniform. He carried a large, wooden contraption under one arm and a large bag in the other.

Then a familiar figure with matching long chestnut hair stepped from the tram, dressed in the olive-green uniform of the Escarlish Flying Corps. Even from this distance, Merrik's face seemed somewhat haggard, his gait hitching in a way it hadn't before. A large canvas bag was slung over one shoulder while his sword rested at his hip. He carried a cane in his free hand, though he wasn't using it at the moment.

Merrik halted and swept a glance over the tents and the hangar before his gaze snagged on Fieran. But he almost immediately looked away, turning back to Uncle Iyrinder.

Uncle Iyrinder set down the items he was carrying and clasped Merrik's shoulders in an elven hug, saying something to him.

Merrik gave a slight nod, his shoulders stiff, as if he was caught somewhere between defensive bristling and weary slumping.

Then Uncle Iyrinder glanced at Fieran, gave him a nod as if to signal him, and strode off the platform, heading in the direction of headquarters.

For a moment, Fieran still hesitated, unable to force his feet to move. He wasn't even sure what to say to Merrik.

Which was ridiculous. This was Merrik. His best friend since they were both babies.

With a deep breath, Fieran strode forward, hopped onto the platform, and halted in front of him.

Merrik leaned the cane against his side before he crossed his arms, regarding Fieran with a hard, impassive look that gave nothing of his thoughts away.

Fieran opened his mouth but for a moment all the words he needed to say lodged in his throat. He needed to apologize. To make things right.

Instead, he found himself all but babbling, "I hope your train ride was good. Everyone is excited to have you back. Do you need anything? Can I carry something?"

Merrik remained silent for another moment, arms still crossed, eyes and jaw still hard. When he spoke, his expression didn't change. "I kissed your sister."

The words were so incongruous that Fieran didn't even know how to respond. It wasn't like Merrik to use family to needle someone, but who knew where his head was at?

Fieran gave a forced, rough chuckle. "Ha, ha. Very funny."

Merrik just kept staring at him, his jaw and eyes hardening further. "I would not joke about something like that."

Oh. *Oh.* He was serious.

Fieran spun away from Merrik, running a hand through his hair. Merrik and…Adry? Kissing? When he'd asked Adry to look after Merrik, this was *not* at all what he'd meant.

He glanced at Merrik. "You…and Adry."

That bristling stance was back in Merrik's posture. "Yes."

Fieran swiped his hand over his face, dropping his gaze. The next words out of his mouth would either heal or break his friendship with Merrik. Sure, Merrik wouldn't use family for a joke, but he wasn't above using his relationship with Adry as a test.

Adry and…Merrik? Fieran tried to get it to compute. Merrik was like a brother to them. Sure, he wasn't actually related by blood. But still. It was just…weird.

And yet not. Merrik was family already. Fieran couldn't think of anyone more honorable, more worthy, to court his sister. He certainly couldn't question if Merrik would treat Adry right.

Fieran forced an easy grin as he turned back to Merrik. "Good. That's…good."

Merrik's stance finally eased. It was only a fraction, but at least it was a start.

"Pip and I are courting." Fieran tried to keep his tone light, as if they were just having a normal conversation as they would have before.

"Finally." Merrik relaxed another fraction. He gestured down at the wooden contraption and bag Uncle Iyrinder had been carrying. "Could you grab those?"

"Sure." Fieran hurried to heft both items, all too aware of the lingering tension.

Merrik strode across the platform, his gait unfamiliar even if he was walking mostly steadily. He hesitated at the edge of the platform, lowering his right foot—the pant leg on that side glowing slightly green as Merrik used his magic —down first as if he wasn't sure his feet would hold.

Fieran waited, close enough that Merrik could reach out a hand to steady himself if needed, although Fieran didn't offer or presume to grab Merrik's arm. This seemed like something Merrik needed to do himself, even if Fieran had to tighten his grip on the items in his hands to resist helping.

As they set off across the grass, Fieran matched Merrik's slower pace. Neither of them spoke as they made their way down the road toward their tents.

By the time they neared Merrik's tent, Merrik was

breathing slightly hard, his face tightening again, this time with pain. At the platform beneath the tent, Merrik hesitated once again. He tried to step up, but he wobbled, reaching out a hand.

Fieran hurried to position himself next to the step, and Merrik planted a hand on Fieran's shoulder. Fieran held still as Merrik levered himself up.

Once Merrik stepped into the tent, Fieran followed, maneuvering the bulky items in his grasp inside without knocking Merrik over.

Merrik sat on the cot, massaging his right leg, his shoulders hunched.

Fieran set down his burdens in the corner before he sank onto the single chair next to the table across from the cot. He barely kept himself from asking if Merrik was all right. "Is there anything I can do? Anything I can fetch?"

"No." Merrik's tone was short, his shoulders going tense again.

Fieran braced himself. No putting this off any longer. "I'm sorry. For the crash."

"It was not your fault." Merrik's words were clipped, his head still bowed as he massaged his leg.

"Perhaps the crash wasn't my fault. But I'm sorry for all the times I was reckless, and you were the one who got hurt because of it." Fieran swallowed at the lump in his throat. "I dragged you into the army—"

"That was *my* choice." Merrik's words held a heat as he shot a glare at Fieran. "Do not take away my part in that."

"Yes, but I didn't even consider that you would make another choice besides join up with me." Fieran rubbed his sweaty palms on his thighs. He needed to get this apology right. Not just because he wanted things to go back to the way they were, but because he wanted this friendship to be better than it was. Merrik deserved that. "I always just assumed you'd follow wherever I led. I should have listened to you. Or perhaps followed you for a change. I'm sorry."

For too many years, Fieran had treated Merrik as his sidekick. Someone who existed only to follow him around.

But that wasn't right. That wasn't how a good friendship worked.

For a long moment, Merrik remained as he was, stiff and hunched, his gaze on his feet instead of on Fieran.

Then he sighed and straightened, lifting his head to look at Fieran. "I am sorry too. I said some things I should not have after my crash. I did not even realize how much I had been holding against you until…until the crash brought it all to the surface."

"There was a problem. It took crashing for me to see it." Fieran pressed his palm to the table beside him, feeling as if he needed the steadiness of solid wood.

"I know. I read your letters. They…helped." Merrik looked away again, heaving a long sigh. "I am sorry I never answered them. At first, I was too angry. Then I was trying to sort through everything. Not just the bitterness toward you, but all of it." He made a gesture down at his feet. "And when I started to piece myself back together, it had been so long, I just did not know what to say."

"How is…all of that?" Fieran, too, gestured at Merrik's legs. He wasn't sure how to go about asking. Would Merrik even feel comfortable sharing those details? He just didn't know where they stood, metaphorically. "You're walking. So it must be going well."

"Well enough." Merrik rolled up his right pant leg, revealing the wooden leg currently wearing his sock and boot. Merrik pulled up his pant leg all the way above his knee and unbuckled a leather strap tightened around the stump of his leg. When he pulled off the cuff of the prosthetic, he had to disentangle a network of roots that threaded through holes in the sock he wore over his stump. He probably used those roots to send his magic into the wooden prosthetic, making it move. "I am still getting used to wearing the prosthetic, and my stump is adjusting. I have enough magic that I can move the wooden limb to walk more smoothly, as long as my stamina holds out. I am told I will be able to move it even more naturally and for longer the more I do it."

Fieran swallowed, not sure what to say.

Merrik tugged up his other pant leg, showing a wooden brace that stuck out above the top of his boot. "And this leg is still weak."

"I'm surprised the healers allowed you to return to duty." Fieran spoke softly, not a trace of his normal joking in his tone. Six weeks was a short amount of time to return to duty after the injuries Merrik had suffered.

"They were not in favor of it." Merrik rubbed first at his stump, then at the calf of his other leg. "But I argued that I could practice walking here just as well as there. It will just take time."

Perhaps, but such practice seemed like it would be better done in the safety and peace of Estyra, where he could get ample rest. Here at Fort Defense, the demands on him wouldn't give him a lot of time to rest after pushing himself. Especially right now with the way Mongavaria had been constantly attacking.

But Fieran was too happy to have Merrik back to argue. "We'll do whatever we can to help. Just let us know what you need. The squadron is here for you."

"That is good because..." Merrik sighed, not meeting Fieran's gaze, and pointed at the wooden contraption. "I am going to need a few accommodations. When my leg or my magic gives out and I cannot walk any longer, I still need a wheelchair to get around."

Now that Merrik had pointed it out, Fieran could see that the item was a wheelchair, its wooden frame folded so that it lay flat with its two large wheels pressed nearly together. The smaller front wheels were tucked within.

"Not a problem." Fieran gave a shrug. No one would care if Merrik had to occasionally use a wheelchair.

Merrik shot him another look, that edge returning to his eyes as his mouth pressed flat. "The hangar floor is cement, but there is a three-inch step to get into it. As there is for the showers and latrines. I cannot stand on my weak leg for a full shower just yet, so I will need a stool to sit on. My tent is a whole foot off the ground, as is the tram platform."

Oh. Right. All those little steps that Fieran walked up every day without even thinking about them. They were now obstacles to Merrik.

"Then it's a good thing I'm used to modifying our billets without asking the army's permission." If he asked the army for permission, the war would end before the proper authorization came through. He was still waiting on the official permission to make the tents livable—something he and his squadron had done themselves months ago. "I'm sure Mak and a few of the elven pilots can make ramps. Perhaps Pip can add a steel ramp or two where needed."

They wouldn't be able to do that everywhere. The mess hall, for one. But anywhere here by the hangar would be no problem.

"Linshi." Merrik dropped his gaze again, his shoulders slumping as if the fight was going out of him. "I know I am asking a lot. You will have to make exceptions for me. I can fly. I do not even need to use my magic on my prosthetic for that. But I am still re-learning how to run, and I will not be able to scramble into the sky as quickly as before."

Fieran stood, the space so small that he simply had to turn to sit on the cot next to Merrik. "We're just glad to have you back. The squadron hasn't been the same without you."

"It is good to be back." For the first time, a hint of a smile creased Merrik's face, though it faded quickly. "I heard about Pretty Face."

"It's been hard without him, but he's still alive, as far as we know." Fieran tried to keep his tone hopeful, ignoring the gnawing in his stomach.

It had been weeks since Pretty Face had landed in Mongavaria. Even taking into account that he would be walking only at night and hiding during the day, he should have been close to the border by now. Every day that went by without word that an Escarlish pilot had walked across the border increased the likelihood that Pretty Face was already captured or dead.

For a long moment, Fieran and Merrik lapsed into silence. Then Fieran worked up a grin, and it didn't even feel that forced. "So. You and Adry."

"Yeah." Merrik breathed out the word, that hint of a smile returning and staying this time.

"It's serious?" Fieran wasn't sure how to go about asking what he really wanted to know. Merrik had only been in Estyra for six weeks. That was an awfully short time to go from friends-who-were-like-family to courting. To *kissing*.

He trusted Merrik, yes. But Adry was still his sister. He had to be sure.

Merrik's smile tipped wryly as he glanced at Fieran, as if he could read exactly what was going through Fieran's head. He probably could, given how long they'd been friends.

"Yes, it is serious. We would not have started anything, given how close our families are, if we were not."

Fieran waited. That still did not fully explain how they'd gotten to that point.

Merrik huffed a sigh as he shook his head. "We have both liked each other for a long time, but neither of us was willing to make the first move, not knowing how the other felt and not wanting to ruin anything. But after all this..." Merrik gestured at his legs. "We could not hide our feelings from each other any longer. After that, well..." The tips of Merrik's ears went pink.

"I don't want to hear about it." Fieran gave an exaggerated shudder. It was just too weird hearing about his best friend kissing his sister. It was strange enough realizing how much he hadn't noticed when it came to Adry, Merrik, and the feelings they'd apparently been hiding right under his nose. "You realize the position you've put me in, don't you?"

Merrik's gaze narrowed with that bristling heat again. "Do not make this about you."

Fieran blew out a breath, even as he stuffed down the defensive heat that rose in his own chest. The habits of how he treated Merrik would be hard to break, and he'd have to be intentional about it.

"I know, I know. Just...I'm asking for patience, all right?" Fieran waved at Merrik. "I'm all for...this between you and Adry. But if Adry had been courting anyone else, I would've been giving him a hard time. But I can't because you're...you. And if you'd been courting anyone but Adry, I'd be offering to be your wingman to help you and her sneak off together, but she's my little sister. It's just a bit awkward."

Merrik gave a soft snort, the heat vanishing back into a smile. It wasn't quite the easy laugh he'd had before, but it was enough. "Adry said the look on your face was going to be priceless. I will have to describe it to her."

"Yes, yes. Get a good laugh out of it." Fieran gave an exaggerated roll of his eyes. But after a moment, he stilled and searched Merrik's expression. "I'm surprised you came back here, when it meant leaving Adry."

Fieran couldn't imagine having to make that choice. He'd nearly had to, if Pip had decided to remain in Aldon rather than return to Fort Defense. Fieran would have made the same choice Merrik had, leaving his girlfriend behind in relative safety to protect his friends. But it would have been hard.

Merrik shrugged. "You know how much Adry wants to be sent to the front. With the way the war is going, she will get her wish sooner rather than later, and I would rather already be here when she does."

"Right." Fieran didn't want to think about his little sister being thrown into this world of blood and death. Of her taking a life and feeling the weight on her soul that he now carried. That Dacha carried. But she had an intensity inside her that wouldn't be satisfied until she followed in Dacha's footsteps.

"Besides, I could not abandon the squadron." Merrik shifted, as if he had been about to elbow Fieran but hesitated to do so.

"It hasn't been the same without you." Fieran didn't hesitate. He gave Merrik a light nudge with his elbow.

Merrik's smile made a brief appearance, there and gone in a blink. He hung his head again, his hands braced on either side of him as he stared down at his foot and stump. "And I had to come back for myself. I needed to fly again. I had to reclaim that piece of myself."

There was an ache to Merrik's voice, one Fieran somewhat understood from those difficult first days after the crash even though his recovery had been nothing like Merrik's.

Fieran glanced down at Merrik's stump and the prosthetic sitting on the bed on Merrik's other side. "Are you all right?"

Merrik's fingers tightened on the edge of the cot, his shoulders stiffening. "I am…getting there. Some days, I do not feel like myself. As if the person I was before died in that crash, and now I do not even know who am I anymore."

"I'm sorry." Fieran briefly rested a hand on Merrik's shoulder before letting it fall back to his side. "I would've been there if I could have."

"I know. But Adry was there." Merrik's smile returned, soft and wistful. "Some days were so hard and yet so good at the same time. Those days…those days I felt more myself than ever."

"That's good." Fieran could understand that. Those first days after the crash, wracked with pain, had been so hard. And yet going back to Aldon, spending time with his family and finally resolving things with Pip had been so good. He wouldn't trade that time for anything.

"And you?" For the first time, Merrik turned to him and seemed to truly study him. "Are you all right? You nearly died too. I did not let myself think about how I nearly lost my brother as well as my leg. It was easier to be angry."

"It took a week of healing at the hospital and even longer to regain my strength, but I'm fine now." Fieran shrugged and grinned, not wanting Merrik to see how hard it had been. "And I had Pip. She helped. A lot."

"Good." This time Merrik smiled, more of a reaction than he'd shown at the tram platform when Fieran first mentioned that he was courting Pip.

Fieran searched Merrik's face again, holding his gaze. "So? We're good?"

"Yes." Merrik seemed to brace himself, a grimace replacing the smile for a moment, before he held up his right hand and spat on it. He held it out to Fieran. "Brothers."

"Brothers." Fieran spat onto his own hand and shook Merrik's hand firmly, their warm spit squishing.

Someday, perhaps, they'd be brothers for real, if Merrik married Adry. A definite perk to his best friend courting his sister. He'd get over a lot of the awkwardness to make that happen.

After a moment, Merrik yanked his hand free and swiped it on the front of his trousers, that grimace twisting his expression. "That is still highly unsanitary and immature."

"Agreed. I think that should be the last time we do that." It was high time they came up with something else besides spitting on their palms. Besides, Merrik didn't like it. That should be enough reason to find a new brother handshake. Fieran scrubbed his own hand clean before he braced his hands on his knees. "Now, are you ready to head to the hangar to greet the rest of the squadron?"

Merrik nodded and reached for his prosthetic. "Thanks for talking them into giving me space for a few minutes. I am assuming that was you?"

"Yes." And it wasn't that hard, once Fieran convinced them to throw a welcome back party in the hangar to keep everyone busy. Fieran pushed to his feet and pointed to the folded-up wheelchair. "Will you want this?"

Merrik glanced up from buckling on the prosthetic. "Yes, but I can carry it."

"I got it." Fieran picked up the wheelchair once again.

Merrik rolled down his pant leg. "I am not an invalid. I can carry my own wheelchair."

"I know." Fieran kept a firm grip on it. "But I wasn't able to be there for you for the past six weeks. Please let me do this much."

"Fine." Merrik sighed, shook his head, and headed for the flap of his tent. "Just do not make a habit of it."

Fieran hurried after him. They might be good, but he still wasn't sure what to do with this new, more prickly Merrik. "I'll try not to. Besides, this isn't just me helping. It's practical. You'll need your hands free once we get to the hangar for all the hugs, backslapping, handshaking, and, well, you'll see."

Fieran wasn't quite sure how to explain the current sourdough situation, except that he was pretty sure the squadron had gone half-crazy in the past few weeks because of all the raids. Too much stress and too little sleep made people do interesting things.

Easing the step down from the platform to the ground, Merrik grimaced more at Fieran's words than he had at the spit handshake. "I do not suppose we could sneak in and just skip all the attention?"

"Nope. Sorry." Fieran fell into step with him, the dead grass crunching beneath his boots. "The only way I could distract everyone long enough to give you these few minutes was to let them go all out in putting together a welcome back party. Like I said, everyone is very glad to have you back. Prepare to be mobbed."

Merrik heaved another sigh, though a hint of his smile returned. "I guess I can put up with it for a few minutes."

At the road, they had to pause to let a column of army trucks go by. Fieran covered his mouth and nose with his sleeve, even as he took in the stretch of grass and the gravel road that lay between the tents and the hangar. How difficult would those be for Merrik to navigate with his wheelchair? The grass was dead, the earth hardpacked, but Fieran wasn't sure how easily the wheelchair rolled over anything that wasn't concrete.

It was a new way of looking at the world. One Fieran would have to learn, for the sake of his friend.

As the last truck rumbled past, Fieran hefted the wheelchair higher. "You know, it wouldn't be that hard to add a small magically powered engine to this."

"Do not even think about it." Instead of bristling as he'd done earlier, Merrik gave Fieran's arm a slight shove. "The only ones I would trust to do that would be Louise and Pip. Perhaps Bennett and Uncle Lance. But I would break my neck for sure if you were the one to do it."

Fieran exaggerated a wince. He *had* gotten an image of a wheelchair speeding through the hangar. Perhaps Merrik had a point. "You wouldn't trust Adry? She has the same experience and degree that Louise, Pip, and I have."

Merrik snorted, true mirth in the sound, as he set off across the road. "Not a chance. I love her, but I would trust her to fiddle with it even less than I would trust you."

Fieran had to work hard not to react at the casual way Merrik used the l-word in regards to Adry. Yes, she was Fieran's sister. But it was fine. It wasn't awkward. Much.

"True. I wouldn't trust either of us with something like that." Fieran gestured at the hangar ahead of them. "Ready?"

"Not really." Merrik shared a lopsided smile with him, braced his shoulders, and stepped through the hangar door.

Grinning, Fieran followed.

"Merrik!"

The shouts came from around the hangar, which had

been mostly cleared of aeroplanes to accommodate the party. Flyboys, flygirls, and elven pilots swarmed from every direction, and many of them held jars of the dubious-looking and somewhat noxious smelling sourdough starter.

Lije reached Merrik first and thrust a jar at him. "Please say you'll adopt George the Twenty-fifth."

"No, take Trevor. He's far superior." Stickyfingers lunged past Lije and shoved a jar at Merrik.

"Don't listen to him. Beatrice the Beautiful is the best." Tiny presented Merrik with one of his jars, this one decorated with a scrap of silk from a torn scarf.

Merrik gaped from the flyboys to the jars and finally shot Fieran a glance as if begging for help.

Fieran just waved his hand helplessly. The sourdough situation was well out of his hands at the moment. The stuff just kept growing and growing and dividing, and a few of the flyboys had become downright obsessed with tending their jars of it. Tiny's girlfriend was supplying some of the flour, but Fieran could only guess where the rest was coming from. He wasn't quite sure how to get things back to a normal level of crazy.

But Merrik was back. That was all that mattered right now.

A BOTTLE of soda in each hand, Pip wound her way through the various groups of flyboys and flygirls as they lounged about Bay 4, which had been mostly cleared for Merrik's party. A large banner made of scrap paper proclaimed "Welcome Back, Merrik" while a table held a bounty of donuts and the sodas they'd scrounged.

To one side of the hangar bay, Lije, Stickyfingers, Tiny,

and Aylia stood by the makeshift stove. Aylia and Tiny dropped coils of dough into cooking oil bubbling in the oil drum pots Pip had created while Lije and Stickyfingers pulled out the finished, fried donuts. At this rate, they'd have enough to share with the other two squadrons. Even with their efforts, they'd barely put a dent in the sourdough starter, which formed rows upon rows of glass jars that had taken up one of the workbenches.

Lt. Rothilion and many of the elves had claimed a spot by the large open door, chatting quietly while the night breezes tossed their long hair.

In the center, one of the largest groups of both humans and elves was playing a round of "Guess that quote" with one flyboy reading a quote from a Star Forest novel, and the others guessing who said it. Nellie Blair must just about have that book memorized since she was shouting out the answers almost before the flyboy finished reading. The others were talking about banning her from playing.

Pip reached the side of the room where Merrik sat in his wheelchair in the shadow of one of the aeroplanes. He had ice provided by Tiny wrapped around his stump, his prosthetic tucked in the bag hanging from the back of the wheelchair. Shadows still lingered in his eyes, even when he smiled, while his face was drawn and thin.

"Hey." Pip held out one of the sodas to Merrik. "It's good to have you back."

"Good to be back." Merrik took the soda with a smile that didn't quite reach his eyes.

He'd managed the initial round of welcome backslapping, handshaking, and story-swapping well enough. He'd even been persuaded to show off his new wooden leg, gaining oohs and aahs over his ability to wiggle the wooden toes with his magic.

But then he'd drifted to the sidelines, hiding even more from the bustle than he had before.

Pip sank onto a seat on the cement floor next to him. "How are you?"

"Well enough." Merrik shrugged, not glancing at her as he uncapped his soda.

"Probably getting very tired of everyone asking you that." Pip opened her own soda before taking a small sip.

"Just a little." Merrik's smile returned, a wry curve to his mouth.

"Well, just let me know if there's anything I can do to help." Pip took another sip of her soda.

"Linshi." Merrik sipped his soda, and silence fell between them for a moment. Then he gave her another smile, one that very nearly reached his eyes. "I heard you and Fieran are courting. It is about time."

"Isn't it?" Pip grinned, her grin widening as she heard Fieran's and Mak's footsteps clomping on the concrete toward them. "Took him long enough."

"Took who long enough?" Fieran flopped down onto the concrete next to her, his legs sprawled out and his arms braced behind him.

"You to finally ask to court me." Pip poked his stomach, earning her an *oof*. "Where did you and my brother get off to?"

Mak lowered himself to the concrete floor on the other side of Merrik. "Installing a few ramps."

"There's now a ramp on that hangar bay door." Fieran pointed at the door of Bay 4 that led toward the tents. "The other side is already level with the dirt for getting the aeroplanes in and out. There's also a ramp to your tent and to the showers and latrines."

"Linshi." Merrik's smile vanished as quickly as it had come, those shadows deeper in his eyes.

"Now about that engine…" Fieran reached past Pip to tap one of the wheels of Merrik's chair.

"No." Merrik sent Fieran a glare, even if his mouth now twitched with a smile. There seemed to be some kind of joke there, but Pip was missing something.

"Fine, fine." Fieran just grinned before he rested his hand over one of Pip's. He glanced at her, tilting his head toward Merrik. "Did he tell you that he had the gall to start courting my sister the moment my back was turned?"

"No, he didn't." Pip glanced between Fieran and Merrik, not sure if she should laugh or brace herself for an argument. Since she and Fieran had been in Aldon with Fieran's youngest two sisters, that left only Adriana, the one sibling Pip hadn't met yet.

"Yep. Kissed her and everything. The cheek." Fieran gave Merrik a glare just as fake as the one Merrik had given him a few moments ago.

On the other side of Merrik, Mak gave a snort before he burst into chuckles. "Now you know exactly what it feels like."

Fieran gave a wince.

Pip shook her head, rolling her eyes. Brothers.

TWENTY

In the cool of the morning, Fieran stepped out of his tent, his swords strapped to his back. He glanced at Merrik's tent, but no one stirred.

For a moment, it was too much like every morning for the last four weeks. No Merrik. A lonely walk from the tent to the hill beyond the hangar.

It should hopefully be the last walk like this. Merrik told Fieran the night before that he would be leaving for morning practice early. Fieran would have assumed Merrik was avoiding him, except for the pink flush to the tips of Merrik's ears. Ridiculous of Fieran to assume this had anything to do with him.

Shaking off the weight, Fieran set off over the dead grass, cutting through the hangar to reach the hills beyond. He waved at a few of the mechanics, although he didn't see Pip yet.

On the other side of the hangar, he hiked up the rise and over the crest of the hill, giving him a view into the hollow where he and Dacha usually practiced.

Down in the valley below, Dacha and Merrik faced each

other, just talking. Uncle Iyrinder lingered in the forest beyond, well out of earshot.

Fieran hesitated at the crest of the hill. He shouldn't interrupt. Not if this discussion was what he thought it was.

But then Dacha reached out and gripped Merrik's shoulders in the elven hug. He said something Fieran couldn't hear from that distance, but the words had Merrik ducking his head before giving a nod. After another moment, Merrik returned the elven hug gesture.

Dacha stepped back, his gaze swinging up to where Fieran stood at the top of the hill. He didn't make a gesture as obvious as a wave, but the tilt of his head, the twitch of his hand, beckoned Fieran forward.

Fieran strolled down the hill, trying to keep his gait casual, his expression neutral, when all he really wanted to do was grin at Merrik. And maybe tease him about how the whole "talking to his girlfriend's father" went.

Then again, Fieran probably should hold off on the teasing, and not just because Merrik's girlfriend happened to be Fieran's sister. But also because Fieran had yet to go through that proper step with Pip's dacha. He had yet to even meet Pip's parents.

Fieran reached the bottom of the hill just as Uncle Iyrinder approached from the copse of trees.

Merrik ducked his head again, not reaching for his sword as he avoided looking at anyone. "I am not sure I am up for much of a practice today."

Fieran slung an arm over Merrik's shoulders. Merrik flinched, but he didn't shove him away or pull back, so Fieran didn't withdraw his arm. "My dacha hasn't even progressed me to full fights yet. Something about me still regaining my strength and reconnecting with my elfness or something like that."

Dacha gave him a dour look that didn't fully hide the faint curve upward to his mouth. "It has been necessary, sason."

"So you won't be the only one not yet up to fighting." Fieran slapped Merrik's back, though he kept the gesture light, before he stepped back. "We can all go through our sword stances together."

Merrik nodded, though he still didn't meet Fieran's gaze as he drew his sword.

The rest of them all drew their swords, forming a line with space enough between them. With Merrik mirroring Uncle Iyrinder's single sword stances and Fieran copying his dacha's forms with the double swords, they moved through the various stances.

Merrik began to breathe heavily by only the third stance, and he stumbled on the sixth.

"That will be enough for today, sason." Uncle Iyrinder lowered his sword, sheathed it, and rested a hand on Merrik's shoulder.

Merrik lowered his sword, but his jaw knotted as if he wasn't happy with having to admit weakness.

Fieran would have moved to the next sword stance, but a blaring siren cut through the morning, the sound somewhat faint all the way out here in the hills. He dropped out of the form and hurried to sheathe his swords. "I knew the break in raids was too good to last. They're getting an early start today."

Dacha sighed and lowered his swords. "Yes."

Fieran spun toward the hangar, but he paused, glancing at Merrik.

Merrik waved at him. "Go on. I will follow as quickly as I can."

With a nod, Fieran took off at a sprint, not looking back

even as an ache filled him at having to leave Merrik behind to go at his own pace.

The ground crew were already pushing aeroplanes out of the various hangar bays, and several aeroplanes from Lt. Hadley's squadron roared down the airfield.

Fieran dodged around an aeroplane and skidded into Bay 5, where the elven pilots of Flight A calmly glided toward their aeroplanes. "What are our orders?"

"Fleetwood is to head north and west, Hadley south." Lt. Rothilion dragged on his flight clothes over his uniform. "The colonel wants us to remain over Fort Defense. So far attacks have only been reported to the west and south, but we know Mongavaria's current strategy."

That they did. Very likely, an attack on Fort Defense would be coming, once Mongavaria ensured the Alliance squadrons were distracted elsewhere.

"Got it." Fieran pointed first at Rothilion, then at Aylia. "Lt. Rothilion, you're with me. Aylia, wait for Merrik. We'll switch once everyone is in the air."

Perhaps slightly unconventional, but he wanted one of the best pilots to take off with Merrik. He didn't want to risk any accidents. Not with Merrik.

"Understood." Rothilion tugged on his flight jacket, smoothing it over his uniform.

From beside her aeroplane, Aylia grinned. "Will do."

That taken care of, Fieran raced from Bay 5 into Bay 4, finding a more chaotic rush than in Bay 5, although not in a fearful way. Just in the more noisy, tromping way of humans.

Nearby, one of the flyboys jostled the workbench piled high with jars of sourdough starter. As the flyboy frantically tried to steady the tower, several of the jars toppled, then fell to the cement floor with the splintering of shattering glass.

Shards of glass scattered amid the gooey spatter of the starter.

The nearby flyboys froze, staring first at the mess, then at Fieran.

Fieran heaved a sigh and jabbed a hand at the disaster of glass and fermenting dough. Time to finally take this in hand. "Leave it for now. But when we get back, all of this is going to have to go. Give it to the cooks at the mess hall, throw it away, lob it at the enemy, I don't care. But it needs to go. From now on, if anyone wants a donut, you'll just have to wait until you get a pass to go into Defense City."

It wasn't like Tiny, the one who had started this whole debacle, would care. He'd already been visiting his girl in Defense City every chance he got, regardless of how many donuts the squadron fried up.

The squadron had had their fun with their foray into donut-making endeavors, and it had served its purpose to keep them somewhat sane during those weeks of near constant raids. But it was time to wrangle things back into good order.

The flyboys muttered their assent before they raced away to see to getting into their fly gear and into the sky.

Fieran came across Lije as he hurried through the hangar bay. "Pass the word. Flight A will be taking off first. I'd like all of you to take off afterwards and make a swing south before coming back north."

"Got it." Lije raced off, halting by each aeroplane to pass the word through the rest of the Flight.

Fieran ran for his own aeroplane in its station closest to Pip's workbench by the wall.

She was up on a ladder, the engine compartment open, as she gave the engine a quick look over, even though she'd already given it a thorough inspection the day before after he'd landed.

"How's everything looking?" Fieran reached for the bundle of his flight clothing he'd left on the floor next to the aeroplane.

"All set." Despite her words, Pip continued inspecting the engine, her hands and eyes moving rapidly as she worked to finish before the ground crew arrived to wheel out his aeroplane. There was something almost obsessive in the way she scanned the parts of the engine.

"Hey." Fieran paused in hiking up his flight boots and reached for Pip. As she was standing on a ladder and he was hunched with the fur-lined leather boots halfway up his thighs, he settled for briefly resting his hand on the side of her calf. "The engine is in perfect working order."

"I know, I know. I just…" Pip didn't withdraw.

Fieran hopped a bit as he pulled the boots the rest of the way up, hooking the straps to his belt. Then he gripped her waist and lifted her off the ladder.

Pip yelped and squealed as her feet left the ladder.

Fieran set her on her feet on the cement floor in front of him. "You've done all you can. I'm not going to crash."

Pip wrapped her arms around his waist and buried her face against his shirt. "It's a lot harder to watch you fly into danger after…you know. I thought I was getting better at pushing the memories aside, but seeing Merrik again…"

Her words choked off, but he didn't need her to finish. It was good to have Merrik back, but Merrik was still dealing with the consequences of that day in a way Fieran wasn't.

Fieran ran a hand up and down her back while he buried his other hand in her hair, the thick waves curling around his fingers. "I'm going to be all right. Even if I crash again—

even if I'm not all right this time—it's my duty. I need to go up."

Pip nodded against his hand, blinking as she did so.

Fieran pressed a kiss to her forehead. "I need to go."

Pip gripped the front of his shirt, stood on her tiptoes, and kissed him before he straightened. When she stepped back, releasing him, her shoulders had straightened, her face smoothing. "Just bring my aeroplane back in one piece. And I mean the whole aeroplane. Not just one tiny piece of it."

Fieran just grinned at her as he bent, picking up his flight jacket. That was a promise he couldn't make.

She climbed the ladder again to close the engine compartment. As she clambered down once again and pushed the ladder out of the way, the ground crew arrived to wheel the aeroplane to the airfield.

Fieran wrapped his scarf around his neck, tugged on his cap and goggles, and gave Pip one last quick kiss before he hurried to follow his aeroplane outside.

By the time he climbed into his aeroplane and let the engine spin up, most of Lt. Hadley's and Capt. Fleetwood's squadrons had already taken off, headed for their longer flights to turn back the distraction attacks. When Fieran glanced over his shoulder, Lt. Rothilion's aeroplane had taken up the spot behind him, ready to take off once the airfield cleared.

Finally, the crew took out the wheel chocks, and Fieran's aeroplane rolled forward. He steered his aeroplane to the end of the airfield, even as the final two of Fleetwood's squadron lifted into the sky on the other end.

Fieran's aeroplane bumped and rolled over the dead grass as it gained momentum. The aeroplane grew light a moment before the wheels lifted off the ground. He poured on the power as he tipped the nose toward the sky.

Lt. Rothilion's aeroplane lifted off in his wake, following him as they climbed higher into the sky.

"Enemy incoming!" The mechanic serving as the radio operator shouted over the static and sounds of the other two squadrons communicating with each other. "Mongavarian aeroplanes have been spotted by the watch tower, headed for Fort Defense."

After leveling out his aeroplane with Lt. Rothilion at his back, Fieran raced over Fort Defense, his dacha's blue magic flaring to life below. Ahead, the black dots of enemy aeroplanes appeared on the horizon, glinting in the rising sun.

More of Flight A took off, trailing after them. But for the moment, Fieran and Lt. Rothilion were on their own.

It was too much like before. And yet Fieran couldn't do anything but make the same decision as he had that day.

"Rothilion, I'll come at them straight on." Fieran kept his hands poised on the control column as he studied the small formation of enemy aeroplanes nearing the Wall.

"I will circle around to come at your target from the side." Rothilion's clipped tones cut through the crackling static.

Fieran bore down on the Mongavarians as they crossed over the Wall. The Mongavarians were scrambling to release the bomb canisters secured under their wings or drop bombs over the sides from the cockpit, as if they couldn't get rid of their load fast enough.

The canisters tumbled downward, headed for the Alliance front lines. Dacha's magic reached for them, but the canisters burst as soon as they came into contact with it. Clouds of odd-colored smoke billowed, sinking toward the ground despite the magic Dacha poured into his shield.

A gas attack.

Green magic joined Dacha's blue bolts down below.

Uncle Weylind, using his plant magic to sweep the air, cleansing it the way a tree freshened the air of a forest.

After calling up his magic, sending it out over his aeroplane, then Rothilion's, Fieran lined up on the lead Mongavarian aircraft. He squeezed the trigger of his machine guns, even as the Mongavarian facing him did the same. The flares of the bullets hitting his magic filled his vision, blurring the sight before him.

Then Lt. Rothilion swept in from the side, his bullets slamming into the enemy's engine. Smoke burst from the engine, and the Mongavarian turned his flyer back toward the border, as if he hoped to get back over before he went down.

Fieran wished the man all the luck. He knew the feeling all too well.

The Mongavarian's wingman roared in, his bullets targeting Rothilion. Fieran turned his aeroplane, triggering his machine guns again.

This time, the enemy dodged his stream of fire. The other Mongavarian aeroplanes roared past him, engaging with the incoming aeroplanes of Flight A.

As the others came into range, Fieran stretched out his magic, adding them into his protective network. Every time his magic brushed a Mongavarian aircraft, that foreign magic made his magic skate off.

Fieran looped his aeroplane to turn around, sweeping behind the nearest enemy.

"Coming in hot!" Aylia whooped into the radio, her voice a cheerful counterpoint to the otherwise silent elven pilots.

Fieran had forgotten how dull it was flying with Flight A without the constant banter of Flight B.

He took a shot at the enemy, but the aeroplane dodged out of his path. Fieran didn't waste time chasing the

Mongavarian. Instead, he maneuvered through the whirling aeroplanes, Lt. Rcthilion behind him, until he reached Aylia, Merrik in his new Soarwing Defender flying behind her.

"Ready to swap wingmen?" Fieran overshot Aylia and Merrik, casting his magic around them, before he looped his aeroplane again.

"Yep! Here is Merrik back." Aylia sounded as if she was grinning. "Good flying with you, Merrik."

"You too." Merrik's voice was a welcome sound over the radio.

Lt. Rothilion turned his aeroplane around, falling into place in front of Aylia. The two of them shot off to the left, chasing down a Mcngavarian aeroplane.

Fieran took up the spot as Merrik's wingman. If Merrik got into trouble, Fieran wanted to be able to spot it right away. "Lead the way, Merrik."

Merrik dove at one of the attacking enemy aeroplanes. "You are not going to simply wipe them out?"

Right. Merrik wouldn't know how much stronger that strange protecting magic had become. Fieran grimaced as he mirrored Merrik's maneuver, sticking slightly above to shoot over Merrik's head. "That foreign magic has gotten stronger. It's quicker to shoot them down than it is to take them out with my magic."

"That is disappointing." The machine guns on Merrik's aeroplane barked.

"At least my magic still protects us from their bullets." Fieran squeezed his trigger, also targeting the enemy.

"A good thing." Merrik rolled his aeroplane as another Mongavarian aeroplane dove at him, as if intent on ramming him.

Fieran strafed that enemy with his machine guns before

he matched Merrik's roll, coming out onto his tail once again.

"Flight B, reporting for duty." Lije's voice came over the radio as the formation of Flight B soared in from over the Wall. They had formed up before setting out.

The Mongavarians were now surrounded, their line of retreat cut off by Flight B.

"Good to have you in the sky, Flight B." Fieran grinned as he whipped his aeroplane upward in Merrik's wake. "Cut off any Mongavarians who try to escape. Flight A, let's take these aeroplanes down. We need to bring down at least one of them over Fort Defense so that the foreign magic can be tested. If I do it with my magic, there won't be any magic left to test."

The various pilots of both Flights acknowledged, the radio filling with voices in elvish and Escarlish.

The Mongavarians, as if realizing their peril, were trying to escape. Three bolted northward; two others raced toward the south. Still more grouped together, heading straight west for the border that likely felt tantalizingly close.

Lt. Rothilion and half of his Flight raced after the Mongavarians heading north. More of his Flight peeled off toward the south, aided by part of Flight B.

Merrik swept toward the main formation of the remaining Mongavarian aeroplanes.

Fieran gripped the control column as he followed, pressing the talk button. "I'm going to try something."

"A good something or an *I should be worried* something?" Merrik's tone held dry humor, even over the radio.

"Good. I think." Fieran eased his aeroplane into position slightly lower than Merrik's.

"*I should be worried* it is." Merrik pulled up slightly so that he and Fieran were level. "Where do you want me?"

Would Merrik be safer in front of him or behind him?

"Stay above me but put a little more space between us. I'm not sure how steady I'll be able to hold my aeroplane while I'm doing this." Fieran reached into his chest, letting his magic build.

Unleashing more of his magic, he shoved it outward, surrounding three of the enemy aeroplanes ahead of him. He didn't try to touch them and instead merely surrounded them in a cloud as he had before.

Now for the tricky part.

Fieran squeezed tighter with his magic. The foreign magic fought his, trying to repel it away. But since he wasn't actively trying to incinerate the other aeroplanes, the opposing magic acted more like a magnetic repulsion.

Perfect. As he'd hoped.

Yanking on his magic, he dragged the aeroplanes backward, fighting against the force of the enemy's engines. His magic burned in his grip, the forces pulling at him blurring his vision.

No. He was not going to give in to the dizziness. He could do this. He was a warrior of the magic of the ancient kings, and his magic was strong enough for this.

With a yell, he yanked, forcing the aeroplanes lower.

A few swear words filled the radio.

"Are you...dragging those aeroplanes right out of the sky?" Merrik's voice held more of a trace of a laugh than the awe in the others' words.

"Yes. Now don't distract me." Fieran resisted the urge to squeeze his eyes shut. He had to remember to fly his own aeroplane, even as he fought the other aeroplanes for every yard. Just a little bit lower. Lower.

Dacha's magic lashed upward, wrapping around Fieran's.

Fieran released a breath, relaxing slightly as Dacha's vast, reassuringly strong magic took over, dragging those aeroplanes the rest of the way to the ground. "There. Got three aeroplanes to Escarlish lines."

"You were right. It is quicker to shoot them down than use your magic." Merrik's aeroplane appeared back in Fieran's vision, winging overhead as he cut off a Mongavarian aiming for Fieran.

Fieran gathered himself, realizing he'd let the protective magic on the others go thin as he poured so much into taking down those three aeroplanes. He blasted his magic back through the protective network, his magic eagerly following the wires reinforced with Pip's magic.

Blinking away the last of the blurring from using so much power, Fieran took in the dogfight again.

Only a handful of Mongavarian aeroplanes remained in the sky. Columns of black smoke rose from crashes just on the Mongavarian side of the Wall while a few enemy aircraft had set down on the muddy, marshy field just over the border.

But some wreckage had come down over Escarland. The aeroplanes that would have crashed into Fort Defense had been caught and either dragged to the ground or incinerated by Dacha. An enemy aeroplane floated in the Hydalla River while another bit of wreckage stuck out of the shallow Chibo on the Escarlish side of the Wall.

Surely in some of that wreckage—not to mention the aeroplanes Fieran had taken to the ground—there would be enough pieces to test for that foreign magic. He was getting really sick of not knowing what it was.

After the last of the Mongavarians were taken down, Fieran and Merrik remained in the sky while the rest of the squadron landed. Capt. Fleetwood's squadron was the one on duty, with Lt. Hadley on standby. Both of their squadrons had chased off the distraction attacks easily enough. As their aeroplanes returned, they took up station over Fort Defense once again.

When it was Fieran and Merrik's turn to land, Fieran led the way with Merrik shadowing him. Fieran craned his neck to keep an eye on Merrik, nearly bumbling his own landing because he was so busy watching Merrik's.

Merrik set down more heavily than he usually did, his aeroplane bouncing over the ground as it slowed.

Fieran's aeroplane rolled to a halt by the end of the airfield, and he unbuckled his belt and climbed down. When he glanced at Merrik's aeroplane, Merrik was still sitting inside the cockpit, not getting out.

Why wasn't he climbing out? Had he been shot and Fieran hadn't noticed?

Fieran dashed for Merrik's aeroplane, his heart hammering. He flung himself upward, his toe finding the step on the side by long habit. "Merrik? What's wrong? Are you hurt?"

"I can't...I can't get out. Legs won't work." Merrik's hands were braced on the sides of the cockpit, a faint sheen of sweat on his forehead, his breathing ragged.

Fieran gripped Merrik's shoulder and squeezed hard enough to make Merrik look up at him with eyes that were too wide, too panicked. Fieran gave him a slight shake. "Breathe. Deep breaths, Merrik."

It was the same thing Dacha had told Fieran when he'd been panicking, and Dacha seemed to know what he was talking about when it came to that.

Merrik leaned his head back against the leather padding at the rear of the cockpit. He squeezed his eyes shut, his breathing not slowing for several more long moments.

Fieran kept his hold on Merrik's shoulder, hoping the

contact helped the same way Dacha's grip on his shoulder had kept him from falling apart.

Merrik's breathing eased, but he didn't open his eyes. "I cannot get out."

"It's all right. We'll—"

"No, you do not understand. You do not know what it is like, lying there in bed unable to so much as get to the lavatory by yourself." Merrik's eyes remained shut, his hands clenched so tightly on the sides of the cockpit that his knuckles were white.

Fieran clamped his mouth shut. He'd been in wooden bracing from his ankles to his hips for nearly a week. He'd been there, unable to move, unable to care for his own most basic needs.

But it had been less than a week for him, and he'd been told right from the start that he would walk again. He'd simply had to wait it out, then he was back on his feet, just as good as before.

His experience hadn't been quite like Merrik's, even if he'd gotten a taste of it.

"I still fear getting back to that place. The wheelchair rolling out of reach. The prosthetic placed somewhere I cannot get it. My leg giving out if I try to hop. I have two working knees, and I know I can crawl if I must, but…" Merrik's voice cut off, as if he couldn't finish that sentence. He swallowed, still not opening his eyes. "I nearly did not get on the train to come back here. The fear of being in a place where I could not control my surroundings—where I might end up stuck, unable to get myself out—was nearly too much."

Fieran gave his shoulder another squeeze, his own chest tight. It was a fear he couldn't banish for Merrik with a few empty words. He could make sure there were ramps. He could make sure the things Merrik needed to get himself around were within reach. But he couldn't battle this fear for Merrik.

Merrik had come back too soon. He wasn't fully healed, physically, mentally, or emotionally. He should have taken far more time to heal in the peace of Estyra rather than forcing himself to return so quickly.

Yet perhaps it was foolish, but Fieran wasn't going to force Merrik back to Estyra, much as he probably should.

Members of the ground crew halted a few yards away, as if unsure what to do since Merrik was still in his aeroplane.

Fieran waved them forward before he gave Merrik a slight shake again. "I can't promise that we can control things so that you aren't ever in that position. But I'll do my best. Today, the ground crew can wheel the aeroplane into the hangar, and I'll help you out. You are not stuck."

Merrik released a long breath, nodded, and finally opened his eyes. "Linshi."

The men of the ground crew shot Fieran a look, but they put their backs into wheeling Merrik's aeroplane toward the hangar, a more difficult task thanks to Merrik's and Fieran's extra weight.

But Fieran didn't climb down, even if it would have made the crew's job easier. They were experienced enough that the extra burdens didn't pose too much of a problem for them.

Once the aeroplane was parked in its spot in the hangar, Fieran released his grip on Merrik's shoulder and instead held out his hand. "We've got this, all right?"

Merrik nodded, gripped Fieran's arm, and together the two of them levered Merrik upright. Fieran steadied Merrik as he climbed down.

By the time they both stood on the cement floor, Pip was

there with Merrik's wheelchair. Merrik sank onto it with a sigh before scrambling to unbuckle his flight boots. Once he had those off, he rolled up his pant leg, revealing where his stump had swollen at the cuff of his prosthetic.

Merrik sighed, but his voice sounded far more normal, a note of something almost like humor in it. "My other new fear. That my leg will get stuck on."

Fieran's huff wasn't quite a laugh, but he patted Merrik's shoulder as Tiny hurried over, an ice chunk already forming in his hands.

Merrik had a long road ahead of him. But the Half-Breed Squadron would be there for him.

TWENTY-ONE

Fieran stood in his dress uniform, complete with the various medals properly placed, just behind the row of Alliance commanding officers. The sun beat down on his head and shoulders, extra sweltering in his layers of stiff wool. His feet were sweating so much in his perfectly polished shoes that his socks were getting damp and sticky against his skin.

Not that his shoes were all that perfectly polished anymore since he'd been standing in the dusty dirt surrounding the train station at Fort Defense. Unlike around the hangar where the mostly dead grass made a valiant effort to cling to the earth, the train station, warehouses, and docks were surrounded by nothing but bare earth and gravel from so much traffic.

In the first row of officers, Dacha, Uncle Weylind, Uncle Julien, and Aunt Vriska had the place of prominence. Not that Fieran minded being tucked in the second row where he could stand with Merrik and Uncle Iyrinder on one side, his cousin Myles on the other. While Myles was only a lieutenant, he wore a red sash across his chest, marking him as an adjutant stationed at headquarters under the Escarlish generals.

Fieran probably shouldn't even be a part of this elaborate welcome ceremony. Everyone there knew a lowly captain would only be invited because of his family ties. Colonel Dentley wasn't even here.

Worse, Pip and Mak had been placed farther down the line, so Fieran couldn't even stand next to her nor whisper back and forth while they waited.

So maybe it was a good thing he and Pip had been separated for something this official.

Pip looked even more uncomfortable to be included in this welcome ceremony than he did. Her face was pale, and she kept swiping her hands down the front of her good trousers. She wore a leather vest over her white shirt, the geometric pattern in the leather a hint at her dwarven heritage.

She and Mak had been invited because they were the only dwarves—well, half-dwarves—here at Fort Defense and their parents had been the ones to negotiate the new treaty with the dwarven kingdom of Dalorbor.

The result of that treaty? A regiment of dwarven warriors, sent to reinforce the Alliance.

A few of the other dwarven kingdoms had been willing to increase their trade in iron and other raw materials, as well as continue to send work crews to the Alliance. But only Dalorbor, her muka's kingdom, had been willing to sign a treaty and join the war on the side of the Alliance.

With a whistle, the train finally chugged its way into the station, the air brakes hissing as it settled to a halt by the platform. A military band struck up a song as Uncle Weylind, Uncle Julien, Aunt Vriska, and several other assorted Escarlish, elf, and troll generals stepped forward.

The door of the first train car opened, and Uncle Rharreth strode onto the platform, his antler crown resting against his white hair and a sword buckled at his side. He wore pauldrons and chain mail, the image of a troll warrior.

Rhohen, his long black hair loose down his back, strode behind Uncle Rharreth. Something about the set of his shoulders beneath his pauldrons and chain mail was less slouchy than the last time Fieran had seen him. He wore a pair of swords across his back, their blades shorter and thicker than the ones Fieran wielded. Yet these swords were not the ones he'd carried when Fieran had fought that bout against him at Dar Goranth.

Merrik's elbow dug into Fieran's side, as Merrik spoke in a whisper, still facing forward and not otherwise breaking his military stance. "Be the more mature cousin."

"Of course. I am the picture of maturity," Fieran murmured back, not breaking his at attention stance either. Still, if their drill sergeant at Fort Linder had caught them moving their mouths even that much, they would have been in trouble. Good thing the only senior officers close enough to hear them were Dacha and Uncle Iyrinder, and neither of them would rat them out.

Out of the corner of his eye, Fieran caught the sideways look Myles was sending him. He'd probably caught at least Fieran's half of that conversation.

After King Rharreth and Rhohen stepped out of the way, a male dwarf marched from the train, his black beard long down the front of his chain mail. His leather bracers and pauldrons had geometric designs that Pip would probably recognize, even if Fieran didn't.

He risked glancing her way, but he wasn't close enough to read her expression.

After that dwarf, another dwarf stepped from the train,

followed by an elf with long brown hair braided at the sides in the style common among the elves in western Tarenhiel.

This time when Fieran glanced at Pip, she was grinning, leaning forward as if it was taking all her self-discipline not to run onto the platform. Next to her, Mak, too, was grinning.

Fieran studied the elf again. That must be Pip's dacha. And that dwarf next to him must be her muka. The dwarf's figure was rather curvy, her black beard braided with even more elaborate braids than the male dwarf, her skin a shade darker than Pip's.

Her parents. Fieran swallowed hard, his chest squeezing tight. They were here. Right here.

Yes, he wanted to meet them. They were Pip's parents. And he wanted to court her properly.

But still, they were her *parents*. Meeting them was a big deal. A big step.

Merrik gave him another elbow to the side.

Right. Focus. He needed to remain at attention for a while longer.

A few more dwarves exited the train car. A round of handshaking between the various dignitaries commenced, followed by a round of speeches about a new era of cooperation and victory and stuff Fieran couldn't care about while standing there, baking in the sun.

Finally, the speeches finished. The black-haired dwarf who had exited first clapped his hands together twice.

The doors on the rest of the train cars opened. The pounding of a drum—deep and resonant—sounded, and dwarves marched from the train carriages. They formed up in the space next to the platform, ranks upon ranks of the stout, bearded warriors with glints in their eyes and huge weapons in their hands.

As soon as the last dwarf stepped from the train, the drum beat changed. The dwarves marched forward with a pounding step, their faces as hard as their glinting weapons.

Aunt Vriska and several other of the senior army officers fell into step on one side of the marching column of dwarves. Pip and Mak's parents, too, strode at the head of the dwarves.

"That's my cue." Myles shot a grin at Fieran before he hurried to join the senior officers, trailing after them along with the other various adjutants and aides.

Fieran glanced without moving his head at Pip once again. She and Mak were hugging their parents, even as their parents were tugging them to join the line of marching dwarves.

Pip met Fieran's gaze over her muka's shoulder. Fieran broke his stance enough to give her a small "go on" wave with his hand. As much as he wanted to meet her parents, he didn't mind putting it off a while longer. Besides, she and her parents should have a few minutes to catch up before he was introduced.

Once the last of the dwarves had marched by, headed for their new billets in what used to be Little Aldon, Dacha took a step forward, although he glanced over his shoulder. "Come, sason."

Fieran trailed after Dacha, Uncle Iyrinder and Merrik with him, as they crossed the dirt road and climbed onto the platform to join Uncle Weylind, Uncle Julien, Uncle Rharreth, Rhohen, and the black-haired dwarf.

While Dacha was introduced to the dwarf commander, Fieran faced his cousin. He could sense Merrik hovering just behind him, as if prepared to yank him out of there if things got out of hand. "Rhohen."

"Fieran." Rhohen's shoulders went stiff, though his gaze

flicked away toward the retreating dwarves as if he had somewhere he'd rather be. But it was only a moment before he met Fieran's gaze again with flashing dark eyes and a tick to his jaw.

Yet as Fieran held his cousin's gaze, he couldn't call up the bristling annoyance he usually felt around him. He had nothing to prove. Not to Rhohen. Not to anyone.

Besides, there was more than enough blood and death and war to go around. If Rhohen wanted a piece of it, he could have it.

Fieran stuck out a hand. "Welcome to Fort Defense."

For a moment, Rhohen eyed Fieran's hand, as if he expected Fieran was tricking him somehow. Then he grasped Fieran's hand, squeezing tightly, and gave it one firm shake. "Linsh."

The abbreviated, troll version of the elvish *thank-you* was brief and sulky. But even that much was an improvement in their cousinly relationship.

"Rhohen." Uncle Rharreth called for him with a sharpness in his tone, as if he expected Rhohen and Fieran would come to blows if left unattended for too long.

Rhohen stalked to his father's side without another glance at Fieran.

Merrik took his place at Fieran's side. "That was… surprisingly mature of you."

"My feud with Rhohen just seems kind of trivial now." Fieran shrugged before he sent Merrik a smile. "Besides, it isn't like I'll even have to see him much, if at all. He will be at headquarters or up in the mountains with the troll warriors; I'll be at the hangar. Fort Defense is big enough for the two of us."

"I will believe that when I see it." Merrik matched Fieran's lopsided smile.

Fieran resisted the urge to grimace. He wouldn't have believed himself so easily either, not with his and Rhohen's record of fighting whenever they were in the same room together. "Yes, it's a stretch. But I'll behave."

After all, he had a set of parents to impress, and getting into a childish brawl with his cousin wasn't likely to do that.

"I can't believe you're here." Pip gave Muka another hug, sinking into the familiar feeling of her muka's scratchy beard, which wafted the faint smell of grease and iron.

Ahead, the column of dwarven warriors marched down the road, metal chain mail clinking, weapons glinting, that deep drum booming out a steady rhythm.

The occasional human—even shorter than most of the dwarves—marched among them. Humans who were on the short side, sometimes deemed an oddity and mistreated by their fellow humans, were always welcomed into the dwarven clans as one of them, and it was rare for a clan to not have a bit of human in them somewhere.

Something swelled inside her chest, and Pip found herself standing straighter. She'd told Fieran that she didn't feel particularly connected to either her dwarven or elven heritage.

And yet as she stood there, watching the dwarves march past to the beat of the drum, she felt that rhythm deep in her bones. Perhaps she was more dwarf than she had let herself believe. With that drum beat pounding in her chest, she was ready to pick up an axe and join them.

Or maybe her favorite head-bashing wrench. That would serve as a good bludgeoning weapon in a pinch.

Muka released Pip to wrap Mak into a hug. Short as she was, Mak bent down to hug her properly.

Dacha rested his hands on Pip's shoulders in the elven hug. "It is good to see you again, sena. We missed you greatly while we were gone."

"I missed you. So much." An elven hug wasn't enough. Pip stepped in and hugged her dacha around his waist. She'd been cut off from her parents for so long.

So much had happened since she'd last talked to them. Everything at Dar Goranth. Everything with Fieran and Merrik and their crashes. She had a boyfriend.

Even before Dar Goranth, her letters had been lacking in details, mindful as she had to be about what she said. She didn't even know how much of what she'd written had gotten past the army censors.

Dacha patted her back before he stepped out of her hug. "Come. Let us find our accommodations, and we will talk. Are the two of you free?"

"Yes. We're off duty for the rest of the afternoon and evening." Mak shot Pip a speaking look.

She gave him a look back, shaking her head. He had better not spill the nail jar about Fieran before she did.

Fieran's cousin Myles jogged up to them, his olive-green uniform crisp beneath the bright red sash across his chest. "Ambassadors Detmuk-Inawenys?"

"Yes?" Dacha turned toward Myles, his tone and expression that impassive, elven one he used when being particularly official.

"The two of you have been allotted Building 42." Myles consulted a paper on a clipboard before he motioned with a pen. "Just head down the main street, take the third right, and you'll find the building clearly labeled and on the left."

"Thanks, Myles. We'll find it." Pip set out along the

familiar road toward Little Aldon, her chest still strangely bubbling and tight with tension. As if she just had to hurry her family along.

A dust cloud hung over the area after all the tromping boots. Pip had to breathe lightly, even as she gazed around at the buildings on either side of the street.

It was strange being back here in Little Aldon now that it had been fully cleared out of all the civilians. For several weeks, these buildings had been empty and hollow where once this had been a bustling part of Fort Defense.

So many memories. There was the café where she'd eaten with the flyboys. There was the photography studio where the whole group had gotten those costumed photographs.

Now, large numbers in army green had been painted on the front of each building. Dwarves bustled about as they settled into the various shops-turned-barracks. Some of the larger restaurants were now the scattered mess halls for the dwarven warriors.

She and her family turned down one of the side streets, this one filled with smaller shops. Clusters of dwarves—including many from Detmuk—bustled between the buildings as they settled in. She caught snatches of conversation, mostly the boasting of warriors about what they'd do once they had a chance for battle and some mentions of a shipment of dwarven vehicles arriving in a day or two.

Building 42 was a small shop with large front windows. When they entered, they found a couple of tables and a small kitchen area on the main floor while the upper floor was the lavatory and bedroom.

Almost as soon as they entered, humans arrived, carrying Dacha's and Muka's trunks. Mak and Muka both nodded their thanks, grabbed a trunk, and carried them upstairs.

"This will be quite adequate." Dacha turned in a circle on

the main floor. Muka and Mak were tromping about on the upper floor, their footsteps ringing heavily on the ceiling overhead.

"How long will you be staying?" Pip wrapped her arms over her stomach. She didn't want to admit how much she was already dreading having to say goodbye to them again.

"Only a day or two. We will see the dwarven regiment settled, then we must return to the western rail terminal." Dacha settled his hands on her shoulders again. "We will need to make the most of the time we have."

Pip nodded, swallowing. Her stomach twisted. She needed to tell him. But she probably should wait until Muka returned. She should tell them together.

Muka tromped down the stairs, followed by Mak. "These are fancy digs."

"Nicer than the army barracks, that's for sure." Mak grinned before he met Pip's gaze over Muka's head.

Pip narrowed her eyes back at him. She didn't need her brother rushing her. She'd get to her news when she got to it.

Dacha slid into a seat at one of the largest tables, this one with four chairs already around it. "We have some time before supper. The two of you should tell us what has happened since we last saw you."

Pip forced herself to pull out a chair and sit across from Dacha. Muka and Mak sat to either side of her.

Mak met her gaze, then tilted his head toward Dacha.

Pip sucked in a breath, opened her mouth, closed it. She swiped her hands on the front of her trousers again. "I have news."

Dacha's gaze searched her face, his eyes warm and brown. "That sounds serious."

"I…" She chickened out. "I'm the head mechanic for my squadron."

"That's my girl." Muka punched her arm, grinning broadly.

"Well done, sena." Dacha tilted his head in a nod that was almost a salute.

Mak narrowed his gaze at her, crossing his arms. "That isn't all."

"Mak!" Pip scrubbed her hands against her trousers yet again. She was going to either leave large sweat stains on the fabric or wear a hole right through it.

Why was she so scared? She loved Fieran. And he was a good guy. It wasn't like her parents were going to disapprove of him.

"So...I'm..." Pip's voice squeaked. Ugh. Why was this so difficult? She'd faced bombings. Sneak attacks. Crashing aeroplanes. Her courage shouldn't fail her now, not when all she was doing was telling her parents about her new boyfriend. "I'm courting."

Her parents blinked at her, their expressions not changing from mildly confused.

She'd probably blurted that out so fast the words had been unintelligible.

With a deep, steadying breath, Pip fixed her gaze on the table instead of looking at either of her parents. "He's one of the flyboys from Fort Linder. Fieran. I think I mentioned him in my letters?"

When she peeked at Dacha, he tipped his head, though his expression had gone neutral. Muka's beard was twitching with the beginnings of her grin.

"But I didn't tell you his last name." Pip blew out a breath. She couldn't. That was a bit of a military secret. "He's Fieran Laesornysh."

Dacha bolted upright. "Son of Prince Farrendel Laesornysh?"

"Yes." Pip's voice squeaked.

Muka's guffaw made Pip jump. Muka gave Pip a light punch to the arm. "Now isn't that quite the unlikely vein of gold in the rubble. You're courting the son of your childhood hero. Have you met his dak just yet?"

"Yes." She wasn't going to mention she was still working on trying to actually *talk* to Prince Farrendel.

"Is this Fieran a good man? Is he respectful?" Unlike Muka, who was still grinning, Dacha was frowning, grooves lining his forehead and bracketing his mouth.

"Of course." Pip squirmed, shooting a look at Mak. He'd helped start all this. The least he could do was help her out.

"He is. I haven't had to beat him up or give him more than a *treat my sister right* speech." Mak's arms were crossed, but he was grinning. Getting far too much enjoyment out of her squirming, no doubt.

"I can invite him to supper tonight." Pip popped to her feet, nearly tripping over the chair in her haste to back away from the table. "Why don't I go right now? Mak can fill you in."

She didn't wait for her parents' agreement. She all but bolted out the door.

TWENTY-TWO

Fieran leaned closer to the tiny mirror by one of the sinks in the shower building. He carefully eased the razor across his cheek, scraping away the hint of red peach fuzz.

Another reminder of how he wasn't fully an elf. Neither was he fully human enough to actually grow a decent beard. Instead, he had to shave every few weeks; the random bristles and patchy fuzz just looked ratty if he didn't.

He drew the razor over his jaw. There, that should do it. After rinsing off the razor, he wiped the lather from his face with a damp towel.

After grabbing his uniform shirt from a hook, he shrugged into it, buttoned it, and tucked it in properly. As this wasn't a ceremony, he was wearing his good, normal uniform and not his dress uniform.

Just as well. The dress uniform looked nice, but it was so stiff and tightly tailored he could barely sit down in it. Supper would be uncomfortable enough as it was.

The outer door creaked open, then slammed shut on its spring-loaded hinges. As it was early for the evening shower rush, that was likely Merrik, come to give Fieran a hard time for taking so long.

But instead of Merrik's voice, Dacha spoke from behind him. "You missed a spot."

Fieran glanced over his shoulder, finding his dacha standing only a few feet behind him. Dacha pointed to a spot on his own face just beneath his ear.

Turning his head one way, then the other, Fieran found the spot of lather he'd missed mopping up with the towel and dabbed it away.

Leaning closer to the mirror, Fieran ran his hand over his face, making sure he'd gotten all the patches of bristles. "I think that should do it. I cannot grow an impressive dwarven beard, but at least I can shave closely enough to pass as an elf."

It had been Uncle Edmund who had taught him how to shave since Dacha hadn't known how.

"You are an elf, sason. You do not need to merely pass as one." Dacha's tone was soft, not quite scolding, not quite disappointed.

Fieran didn't dare glance over his shoulder, not wanting to see the look in Dacha's eyes. "I know."

It was just harder to remember that when he was having to shave like a human.

Probably best to change the subject. Fieran smoothed down his damp hair. "What do you think? Slicked down…"

Dacha made a small noise, the closest thing to an undignified snort that he'd make.

"You're right. It isn't me." Fieran ran his fingers through his hair so that it lay more loose with strands trailing across his forehead. "Artfully tousled it is."

He'd delayed as long as he could. At this point, he was just pointlessly primping. He turned, facing his dacha.

Dacha's gaze swept over him before he took a step forward. He tugged at Fieran's collar, smoothing out a wrinkle. "You will do fine tonight, sason. Her parents will not disapprove of you."

No, they wouldn't. But would they *approve* of him? That was the real question. He had a feeling that Pip's parents, like Fieran's, would care far more about how he'd treat their daughter than anything else, including his name and family connections.

Fieran shrugged, trying to call up a grin. "Easy for you to say. You didn't meet Grandmother until after you and Mama were already married."

"That just made the experience more nerve-wracking. Your mama's family were already predisposed to dislike me because I stole your macha away so abruptly." Dacha's mouth curved into that slight smile, his eyes going distant, in that way that said he was sensing his heart bond with Mama. After a moment, Dacha gripped Fieran's shoulders. "But they came around quickly. Be yourself, sason, and you will win over her family just as quickly."

That sounded more like something Mama would say than Dacha. Perhaps it was something Dacha had gotten through the heart bond.

Fieran tried to nod. "Linshi, Dacha."

Dacha squeezed his shoulders and stepped back. "Now, you do not want to be late."

That would certainly make a great impression on Pip's parents.

Fieran spun on his heel and started for the door. Only to remember that he probably should pick up his shaving items and other toiletries to return to his tent.

"Go on. I will see to this." Dacha turned to the sink, his nose wrinkling slightly.

If Dacha wanted to pick up after him, Fieran wasn't going to argue. Dacha must really like Pip if he was going this much out of his way to see that tonight went well.

Fieran hurried out of the showers, only to find Merrik and Uncle Iyrinder waiting there. Merrik leaned more weight on his left leg than his right, lines of weariness around his eyes. But he was standing steadily.

Merrik held out a bouquet of some kind of flowers, tied with a scrap of fabric. "You are welcome."

Fieran took the flowers. Merrik must have grown them as there weren't any flowers to be had at Fort Defense. "I'm going to owe you for this, aren't I?"

Merrik's grin gleamed in his eyes with too much satisfaction. "Yes."

Great. That wouldn't be at all awkward, considering the girl Merrik would expect help wooing was Fieran's *sister*.

Fieran sighed. "Fine. Linshi. Now…"

"Go." Merrik waved a hand. Uncle Iyrinder gave him a nod.

As Fieran turned to go, a small group of the pilots of Lt. Hadley's squadron hurried around him and bustled into the shower building. Even as the door slammed shut behind them, the startled exclamations of "General" rang out as the unsuspecting pilots found themselves face-to-face with an elf general in the communal showers for the low-grade officers.

Grinning, Fieran set off down the road, heading for the tram platform. As he strode past the hangar, various of the flyboys and flygirls leaned out of the hangar doors, calling out teasing advice or merely smirking at him. Tiny, Lije, and Stickyfingers were all grinning as they waved him onward.

He arrived as a tram was pulling in, so he was able to walk right on and take a seat.

After a quick tram ride, Fieran was soon strolling down the road past the mess, the commissary, and the communications building, until he reached the outskirts of Little Aldon. Though perhaps it should be called Little Dalorbor, now that the dwarves had taken over.

The dwarves bustling between the buildings halted to look at him as he strode past, making him all too aware of his height and the very elegantly elven points of his ears. To those dwarves watching him, he likely seemed more elf than human.

The elves and dwarves currently didn't have the animosity that the elves and trolls had had only a generation ago, but that was mostly because they stayed out of each other's spaces. This new treaty—actually fighting at each other's side—was unprecedented.

As he turned the corner onto the smaller side street, he found Pip pacing back and forth across the road, as if to make sure he couldn't slip past her. She wore that same green dress she'd worn in Escarland, and it swirled around her calves each time she spun to march the other way. Her hair lay around her shoulders and down her back in glossy waves while the necklace he'd given her winked when it caught the sunlight.

She reached the far side of the road, spun again, and faced him. As her gaze landed on him, her dark eyes lit, a smile breaking across her face.

He held out the flowers. "For you."

She hurried across the road, took the flowers, and sniffed them. "Linshi. These are beautiful. Where did you get them?"

"Where else?" Fieran grinned, the expression going a touch lopsided. "Merrik."

Pip laughed, shaking her head. "I should've guessed.

He's an excellent wingman."

"He's also making sure I owe him so that I'll be forced to return the favor as his wingman...while he's courting my sister." Fieran gave an exaggerated huff.

"Good for him." Pip's eyes sparkled with mischief. But the expression faded after a moment as she glanced over her shoulder down the side road. "Well, I guess we should go. My parents are waiting."

Fieran's stomach churned, but he pasted on a smile. He held out a hand, his nerves easing when she took it. He would face her parents with her at his side. Besides, they raised Pip and Mak. They had to be people he'd like, once they got past the parental interrogation.

"Yes, but first..." Fieran tugged her closer before he leaned down and pressed a kiss to her lips. He wouldn't be able to do that once they were under the watchful eyes of her parents. When he drew back, he whispered in her ear, "You look beautiful."

Her face flushed as she ducked her head. "It's the same dress I wore in Aldon."

"And you're just as beautiful as you were then. Or as you are in your overalls." Fieran pressed another kiss to her temple before he forced himself to put some distance between them, although he didn't let go of her hand.

Pip cleared her throat and looked away from him. "Stop saying stuff like that or I'm going to be beet red."

Fieran grinned and fell into step with her as they strolled down the road, swinging their clasped hands as they went. "Just to be clear, I'm to stop saying romantic stuff for now. That's not a ban forever."

"No." Pip's voice went a touch squeaky, her face flushing again. She stepped closer to him so she could nudge him with an elbow. "Not helping."

Was it bad that he wasn't at all repentant?

He forced himself to look away to give her a moment and instead took in the street around them.

Dwarves lounged on chairs, stoops, and wooden sidewalks of what used to be cafés and small shops for Little Aldon. Many of the dwarves were sharpening or polishing weapons, laughing and speaking together in their guttural language as they did so.

A large group of them, sprawled across a section of sidewalk, lifted their hands and called out in their language. The only thing Fieran recognized was *Pippak*.

Pip halted, turning toward the group with a grin. She spoke in dwarvish, gesturing at Fieran. He recognized his name in the jumble, but that was it.

Still, the guttural, deeper sounds of dwarvish coming from Pip was strangely startling. He'd known she was half dwarf, but until now he'd only heard her speak elvish or Escarlish. She was so comfortable in human spaces that he'd perhaps begun to see her as half-human like him.

But she was half-dwarf in the way he was half-human, and he shouldn't let himself forget that. She moved more easily through three cultures than he did his two.

He should start learning dwarvish. If he was going to be with Pip, then he would need to be as comfortable with dwarven culture as she was with Escarlish.

Pip glanced up at Fieran, the twinkle in her dark eyes matching her grin. "Fieran, these are a bunch of my Detmuk cousins, distant cousins, and a few aunts and uncles."

Aunts? Fieran eyed the group of dwarves again, this time actually picking out the female dwarves among the males. Everyone having a beard was going to take some getting used to.

"Hello." Fieran waved back at the cluster of Detmuk

dwarves, not sure what else to say. Perhaps he should have spoken in elvish instead of Escarlish? Did these dwarves know either? "Elontiri."

One of the dwarves guffawed and punched another's arm. The two of them shook with their raucous laughter, drawing the others in.

Pip rolled her eyes, huffed, and spoke in dwarvish again. With a flap of her hand, she tugged Fieran onward. "Apparently my uncles find it hilarious that I have the same taste in men as my mother."

"Tall and elven?" Fieran wasn't sure he actually wanted to know.

"Beardless and skinny." Pip gave that huff again.

He wouldn't have shaved, but he'd remembered what Pip had said to Pretty Face about how dwarves found a patchy, wimpy beard even more unimpressive than a lack of a beard.

"Perhaps I should have worn my swords." It was what Dacha would have done. But it hadn't occurred to Fieran that he might need to sport weaponry, besides his military sidearm in its holster at his hip, when meeting Pip's parents. "I would have looked more imposing."

"Only if you managed to keep up a hard look like the one your dacha wears." Pip elbowed him again. "Your grin rather wrecks the look."

Fieran couldn't help but grin back. After a moment's pause while they strode down the street, he tilted his head back toward the group of her Detmuk relatives. "I thought I had a lot of nosy relatives. Aunts and uncles, huh?"

"Well, they aren't all my aunts and uncles, as in, my mother's siblings." Pip gave a shrug. "Detmuk is a clan as well as a mountain. I'm related to all of them, so they're called aunts, uncles, and cousins, even though we're related more distantly than immediate family."

Fieran swung their clasped hands again. "Good thing I'm used to having a big, nosy family around."

"That will certainly make your introduction to the Detmuk clan easier." Pip shook her head, a frown briefly replacing her smile. "But let's get through introducing you to my parents before we worry about meeting the rest of the clan."

Good plan. Fieran tried to keep up his jaunty stroll, even as he and Pip approached Building 42.

This particular shop had a small, porch-like wooden awning over large front windows overlooking the sidewalk. Mak stood on the sidewalk with the brown-haired elf and female dwarf from the train station standing next to him.

Fieran drew in a deep breath, unable to hold his grin in place. This was it. Time to meet Pip's parents. He forced his step to remain steady as he strode onto the sidewalk.

Beside him, Pip had gone back to vibrating with energy. Her voice squeaked slightly as she gestured between everyone. "Muka, Dacha, this is Fieran. Fieran, these are my parents."

"Elontiri." Fieran gave the traditional elven hand gesture of greeting, which involved artfully touching one's hand to one's mouth, then forehead.

"Elontiri." Pip's dacha returned the gesture. "I am Myrdin Detmuk-Inawenys."

"Glorirgoulyn Detmuk-Inawenys." Pip's muka tapped her right fist over her heart.

That must be some kind of dwarven gesture, but Fieran didn't know enough about dwarven culture to attempt to return it. He might do it wrong and instead make an offer-sive gesture.

Instead, he gave a nod of his head. Holding out his hand for a shake seemed too human for the moment. "Fieran Laesornysh."

He could see the flicker in their eyes at his last name. Pip said she'd told them, but it would hit differently coming directly from him.

Mak just stood there, arms crossed, as he grinned. He was enjoying this far too much.

"Come in. The food is currently an edible temperature." Pip's dacha spun on his heel, opened the door, and gestured for everyone to precede him inside.

Mak pushed away from the wall and strode in first, followed by Pip's muka. Fieran fell in behind Pip, and as they stepped inside, Pip's dacha followed after him, shutting the door with a finality that shivered against Fieran's shoulders.

When they sat at one of the round café tables, Fieran found himself between Mak and Pip and facing Pip's parents.

The table had already been set with covered dishes crowding the center. The table hadn't been designed as a family dining table, and with five of them around it, Fieran had to keep his elbows tucked to his sides to avoid bumping Pip and Mak.

For a few minutes, an awkwardly tense silence fell around the table, broken only by the clink of dishes as everyone helped themselves to the chicken, potatoes, and corn that must have come from the officers' mess since it was recognizable as food.

Pip's dacha glanced up from his plate to spear Fieran with a look. "Tell us about yourself."

Where to start? Most of the basics about Fieran's family were public knowledge.

With a glance at Pip, Fieran started talking. It was, after all, something he was good at.

BY THE TIME they finished supper, Fieran had everyone laughing at his stories, and Pip's muka was slapping her knee as she guffawed. Surely that was a good sign for Fieran's chance of a future with Pip.

Pip's dacha stood and tilted his head toward the door.

A clear order. Fieran pushed out his chair, stood, and followed as Mak took over the conversation.

Pip glanced over her shoulder, but Fieran gave her a smile. Everything was fine. Hopefully. This was merely the conversation he'd been expecting the whole night.

They stepped outside, and Fieran closed the door softly after him. Evening cloaked Fort Defense, the sun setting beyond the Escarlish hills in the distance. To the east, the blue glow of the Wall filled the horizon.

Dwarves still lounged on the various sidewalks and stoops, their laughter and boisterous voices filling the street. Yet the groups were still far enough away that Pip's dacha and Fieran had a semblance of privacy.

Pip's dacha led the way around the corner to the alley between the buildings so that they weren't standing in front of the windows where Pip, Mak, and Pip's mother would see.

Once they were around the corner, Pip's dacha turned to Fieran and crossed his arms. He was even slimmer than Fieran's dacha, lacking the lean muscles of a warrior, nor did his face have the hard edges. Yet his brown eyes were still flinty with fatherly determination. "What are your intentions toward my daughter?"

The standard question, but Fieran could hear the implied layers to it. After all, Fieran wasn't just any young elf lad. He was a prince in two kingdoms. He could toy with a girl's affections and leave with few consequences.

As if his own parents would ever let him get away with acting like that.

What were Fieran's intentions? He drew in a deep breath, then let it out slowly as the question settled deep within him. He called up all the memories of his time with Pip, from that first meeting at Fort Linder to holding her hand on the way home to Aldon.

Straightening his shoulders, he met her dacha's gaze and held it. "I'd like to marry her someday. She's the most amazing, talented woman I've met. She's going to go far, and I want to be there when she does. I can't imagine my life without her."

From the way her magic interacted with his to how well she got along with his family, he fell more in love with her the more he got to know her.

Her dacha searched Fieran's face, as if looking for the truth of those words. He must have seen an answer he liked for a smile replaced the flat expression. "Good. Then we will not have a problem."

Even more surprisingly, he held out his hand for a human-style handshake.

Fieran grasped his hand and shook it firmly. "No, we won't."

He resisted the urge to pump his first. Pip's parents approved.

The war was still ongoing. The future was still very much uncertain. But at least he and Pip were on solid ground. As long as they were together, he could face whatever would come.

TWENTY-THREE

"This is Merrik, Lije, Stickyfingers, Tiny, and Aylia." Pip gestured to each one as she spoke, the predawn chill wrapping around her as they stood in the street. "Everyone, these are my parents."

Dacha and Muka made their welcoming gestures, though Dacha's brow had furrowed at the rather interesting monikers for Stickyfingers and Tiny.

A pang filled her heart. If only Pretty Face were here. But there still had been no word about him. He must have been captured by the Mongavarians.

If he was still alive.

She shook off the melancholy thoughts to focus on the flyboys and flygirl here. They'd gotten up early so that they could meet her parents before their standby shift started and before her parents' train departed.

She glanced down the street again, but most of it was blocked with the large army truck waiting to take her parents to the train station. Where was Fieran? He said he'd be here for the farewells.

She turned back to where Muka had somehow gotten

into a discussion of dwarven brews with the flyboys. Sticky's eyes had gone wide while Lije's mouth had dropped open as Muka described the mushroom and rock salt brew that was the traditional drink in Dalorbor.

Pip resisted the urge to roll her eyes. Would the flyboys turn to brewing once the sourdough craze faded? The army would probably have a thing or two to say about that.

An open-topped army truck rumbled down the street. Pip only gave it a passing glance as she moved out of the way. But when it parked behind the larger army truck, she looked again.

Fieran hopped out of the front passenger seat, grinning at her before he turned back to the vehicle. He said something to a person sitting on the other side, blocked from her view by the larger vehicle parked in front of it.

Then Prince Farrendel Laesornysh stepped around the front of the army truck, dressed in full elven armor and carrying his swords on his back.

Her chest seized. Fieran had brought his dacha—*Prince Farrendel Laesornysh*—to meet her parents. She opened her mouth. She should warn them. Tell everyone who was about to show up.

But nothing but a breathy squeak wheezed out of her.

Then Fieran was there, his hands resting lightly on her shoulders as he leaned closer. "I brought a surprise. I hope you don't mind."

"Nope." She muttered the word too fast, her knees still locked.

Prince Farrendel halted next to Fieran and gave her a nod, not a twitch to his face to betray his thoughts. "Pippak."

Fieran's dacha had yet to call her by her nickname. Fieran assured her that his dacha liked her, but he was so hard to read that she couldn't tell. He'd seemed to find her magic impressive that one time she joined morning practice, but he hadn't invited her and Fieran to dine with him in his quarters as her parents had Fieran.

Then again, Mongavaria had been attacking so constantly up until a few days ago that there hadn't been time for dinners with parents.

What did it mean that Prince Farrendel was here? Meeting her parents? That was the gesture of someone who approved of the relationship, wasn't it? But how was she to know?

Prince Farrendel faced her parents, giving a nod.

Pip was still so frozen that she couldn't force herself to move. With a low chuckle, Fieran used his grip on her shoulders to turn her around just in time to catch the look on her parents' faces as they registered the fact that Prince Farrendel was standing there.

Her dacha's eyes widened before he bowed with the graceful flourish of the elves. "Amir, it is an honor."

Muka pounded her fist over her heart before she bobbed her head in the dwarven gesture of respect for one of high standing.

Fieran kept his hands on Pip's shoulders, rubbing his thumbs gently over the tops in that soothing gesture. She worked to unlock her knees and unglue her tongue from the top of her mouth, but her parents were going to be on their own for a bit.

To one side, the flyboys had eased back a step after they saluted, though they weren't quite as in awe as Pip's parents. Prince Farrendel was becoming a familiar enough face that it was more the respect for a general rather than abject terror.

Prince Farrendel glanced at Fieran, then back at Pip's parents. "You run the western rail terminal."

"Yes." Pip's dacha bobbed his head again, his voice stilted.

"The original trading hub there provided some of the first plans for a Tarenhieli rail system, did it not?" Prince Farrendel stepped forward, something in his voice smoothing the more he spoke.

Dacha's mouth worked as he shared a look with Muka. Muka thumped her fist on her chest again. "Yes, we did. I'm surprised you'd remember such a thing."

Prince Farrendel gave a slight, elven shrug. "I found trains fascinating. My dacha gave me the plans to read over."

Pip saw it then. The resemblance to Tryndar in the look in Prince Farrendel's eyes. Or, rather, Tryndar's resemblance to him when he'd held that little metal aeroplane she'd made for him.

The sight finally eased the hero worship paralysis. She sucked in her first decent breath in the past few minutes. Perhaps she could actually join the conversation.

Fieran had been right to bring his dacha here. Their families had a lot in common, if they had the chance to sit down and talk.

She opened her mouth, but before she could say anything, a distant boom broke the silence of the morning, a vibration traveling through the ground beneath their feet. A distant rumbling continued even after that initial boom, the vibration still shaking the ground.

That wasn't an artillery gun or a bomb. She was familiar with the sounds of those.

"What was that?" Stickyfingers was scanning the skies, as were all the flyboys.

"I don't know." Fieran, too, was searching the skies.

Merrik moved, as if by pure instinct, to take the place at Fieran's back.

When Pip glanced upward, the gray skies were streaked with the first rays of dawn.

Prince Farrendel's gaze had gone distant, and he turned toward the Wall rising high on the eastern horizon. "There is something…I sense…"

He didn't finish whatever he was saying. Instead, he spun on a heel and dashed toward the army truck.

Fieran glanced around at them. "Pip, Mak, see to your parents. Everyone else, get to the hangar just in case. I'm going to see what's going on."

With that, he dashed after his dacha. The flyboys were only a few steps behind him, racing toward the lower tram platform.

"Perhaps we should stay." Muka clenched her fists, sharing a glance with Dacha.

"No, the western rail terminal needs you." Mak picked up one of their bags.

"I'm sure it's nothing to worry about." Pip grinned, the expression tense, and grabbed another bag to load onto the larger army truck. "Let's get you on your way."

Yet even as she said the words, her chest tightened. What new awful turn to this war would the Mongavarians unleash?

Fieran flung himself into the front passenger seat of the small, open-topped truck, even as his dacha was putting it into gear.

Beside the truck, an army driver had his hand on the side panel. "Sir, I can drive. I—"

Dacha popped the clutch and sent the truck rolling forward, even as he worked the wheel so they did not hit the larger truck parked in front of them. The truck rumbled down the street, gaining momentum even as it flashed past where Pip stood with her parents.

Fieran braced himself against the dash and the door. "Where are we going?"

"The Wall." Dacha's tone was tight, his gaze focused on the front windscreen. He barely slowed the vehicle as they swerved onto the main road.

Fieran gripped the door, trying to brace himself as the truck careened around the turn. "What's going on?"

"I do not know. But I sense…I do not know. But it is not good." Dacha mashed the accelerator and worked the gear shift into a higher gear as the main road flattened out, heading toward the front lines.

People and other vehicles dodged or swerved out of their way.

Fieran gathered magic in his chest, though he didn't release it yet. He couldn't sense anything amiss. He couldn't even hear if that rumble continued over the roar of the truck's engine. But if Dacha was driving like this, then something terrible must be happening.

Within minutes, they were driving over the dusty, hard-packed roads between the infantry fortifications, the men in their entrenchments staring as they flashed past.

Ahead, the Chibo River rippled, reflecting the rising sun and the crackling magic of the Wall bisecting its waters.

At this time of summer, the Chibo River was already running low. Yet it seemed even lower than it had been the last time Fieran had flown over it a few days ago.

Dacha didn't slow until they were rumbling onto one of the half bridges extending out into the Chibo. He slammed on the brakes, sencing the truck into a screeching, skidding halt only a few yards from the Wall. No sooner had he shut off the engine than he was hopping from the truck and dashing toward the Wall.

Fieran scrambled out of the truck after him, his boots landing hard on the stone surface of the bridge. He jogged to the edge of the bridge and peered over the low side.

The river water seemed to have retreated from the banks, leaving yards of mud, flopping fish, and stranded turtles on either side. Only the center of the river still had water, and even that seemed to be draining away.

"What's going on?" Fieran glanced first to the north, then to the south. The northern end of the river where it dumped into the Hydalla, was turning into a stagnant eddy. The southern end was draining away even as he watched, leaving behind a huge muddy trench a mile wide and only five feet deep at the center.

Dacha pressed his palm to the Wall, his magic crackling around his fingers and merging with the magic he'd embedded into the Wall seventy years ago. "I sense that strange magic. But I do not know what its purpose is."

"Should I…" Fieran let some of his magic curl around his fingers as he waved toward the Wall.

"Not yet." Dacha's eyes went even more distant, as if he was sensing the immense length of the Wall.

Something moved beyond the Wall. Fieran squinted into the blue crackle, trying to make out the shapes.

There seemed to several large vehicles unlike anything he had ever seen rumbling toward them. They appeared to be giant metal boxes set on large rolling treads on either side, of the type he had occasionally seen used by farmers on their tractors.

These vehicles tipped over the lip of what had been the

bank of the Chibo River. They splashed into the gloppy mud left behind, but the treads plowed through the mud, keeping the vehicles from burying themselves and getting stuck.

As they drew closer, Fieran could make out something sticking out of the metal box set on the treads, almost like a pair of wires. Was that some kind of machine perched on top?

Several men walked beside the vehicles, carrying metal shields.

"Should we stop them?" Fieran clenched his fists, falling into a fighting stance almost by instinct, even though he had no weapons besides his magic and his sidearm.

With a glint in his eyes, Dacha unleashed more of his magic, making the hair on the back of Fieran's neck and along his arms stand on end.

Dacha lashed out with his magic, reaching through the Wall toward the line of odd vehicles advancing on them.

Yet as soon as Dacha's magic brushed the vehicles, it stuck there, focusing on the protruding wires rather than consuming the vehicles.

Dacha muttered something under his breath.

"Dacha?" Fieran took a step forward, his magic curling around his fingers.

"It has caught my magic somehow." Dacha almost seemed to be trying to tug his magic free.

The vehicles rolled inexorably forward. The machines on their backs brightened, glowing slightly blue, as a faint whirring sound filled the air over the crackle of Dacha's power.

Dacha cried out, going down onto one knee as he pressed both hands to the Wall. The whole Wall wavered, bending slightly toward the enemy vehicles planting themselves in a line just on the other side.

"Dacha!" Fieran stumbled forward, his magic around his fingers as he reached, though he wasn't sure if he should reach for Dacha or for the Wall. There was a faint tugging sensation, as if something was reaching for his magic. "What should I do? How can I help? Should I attack them too?"

"No!" Dacha's shout was loud, tight. He shook his head, even as he squeezed his eyes shut. His silver-blond hair whipped around him as he unleashed even more power, filling the air with that lightning taste. "Those machines are pulling in my magic. You cannot risk your magic getting caught too."

Fieran squelched his magic, standing there with his hands uselessly at his sides. How could anything overpower his dacha's magic? Dacha had the most powerful magic—the most amount of magic—of any living person. Nothing could defeat him.

Yet magic poured from Dacha, more than Fieran had ever seen him unleash at one time. Fieran had to squint at the brightness, his breaths burning in his throat from his dacha's magic filling the air.

Dacha cried out again, a shout that was both pain and a battle cry, his hands still braced in the Wall.

The Wall itself was flickering, its glow going more white than blue as Dacha poured more power into it.

"Dacha!" Fieran fell to his knees beside his dacha. He should do something. Dacha had told him not to use his magic, but what if they could defeat the foreign magic powering these machines between the two of them?

"Do...not..." Dacha growled the words between clenched teeth. Stray bolts of power flickered over his armor and along the strands of his hair. Magic roared around them in an inferno of power. His eyes were squeezed tight, his shoulders bunched as if straining under an immense weight.

Fieran had to do something. He couldn't just kneel there, helpless, while Dacha fought…and seemed to be losing. "I can help. Together, we can—"

"Fieran." Dacha's harsh tone cut through the storm of magic. "The Wall is coming down."

"What?" Fieran tried to process those impossible words. What was Dacha saying? Surely he couldn't mean what it sounded like. That Wall had stood along the border for Fieran's entire life. It was the greatest magical achievement of the age. It couldn't simply…come down.

Dacha's eyes snapped open. He half-turned his head, his blue, magic-laced eyes meeting Fieran's. "The Wall is coming down."

Those five words made no more sense the second time than they had the first.

Dacha squeezed his eyes shut again, shouted, and blasted so much power into the Wall that Fieran flinched at the feel of it scraping against his skin and into his throat when he breathed.

The Wall exploded.

TWENTY-FOUR

Pip watched as the train eased away from the station, gaining speed as it curved onto the track that would take it under the Hydalla River and into Tarenhiel.

She hugged her arms over her stomach. A part of her already missed her dacha and muka. They'd had so little time to catch up after not seeing each other for months.

And yet she gusted out a breath of relief that her parents were safely on their way, headed away from the dangers of living in an active war zone. Especially with whatever was happening on the front lines. Even as her parents had said their final farewells and climbed onto the train, Pip could taste the storm of magic building only a few miles away, her skin prickling with it.

No sooner had her parents' train pulled away than another one screeched to a halt at one of the other stations, the one for unloading heavy equipment. Instead of large guns or crates, this train was made up of flatbeds, each one holding a large, armored vehicle with an artillery gun pointed out the front.

A contingent of dwarves and Escarlish military personnel

met the train. This must be the shipment of dwarven vehicles she'd heard her Detmuk cousins discussing.

As she turned to Mak, that distant magical storm exploded, a wave of magical blowback sweeping over Fort Defense with such force that Pip staggered. She stumbled into Mak, who steadied her with a hand on her shoulder even though he was swaying on his feet too.

For a moment, she couldn't breathe from the lashing pressure. Then Mak pounded her back, and she gasped in a breath. "What was that?"

Mak shook his head, gave a cough, and set out in the direction of the tram platform. "I don't know. But it can't be good."

The two of them climbed onto the tram, and it shuddered its way up the side of the bluff toward the hangar. Pip slid into a seat, her gaze fixed ahead. If something bad was going down, she needed to get back to her flyboys.

"Pip…" With a strangely taut note to his voice, Mak was bent over as he peered out the windows on the left side of the tram as it rose above the rooftops of the buildings by the river.

Pip crossed the nearly empty tram car to join Mak peeking out the windows on that side. For a moment, she didn't see what had caused that worried tone in her brother's voice.

Then she realized that was exactly what was wrong. It wasn't what she could see but what she couldn't see.

The Wall—the crackling blue wall of power that had dominated the horizon for as long as she'd been at Fort Defense—was gone.

No, not entirely gone. She could see a blue glow on the horizon where the Wall still rose out of the Hydalla River along the Tarenhieli-Mongavarian border.

But the whole Escarlish-Mongavarian border for as far as she could see from the mouth of the Chibo River to the Whitehurst Mountains rising in the distance was empty and unprotected.

As the tram rose higher, the muddy expanse of what had once been a river came into view, an indistinct smudge of brown where once there had been glittering water.

"What's going on?" She breathed the question, not really expecting an answer.

Mak just shook his head as the tram pulled into the station at the top of the bluff.

As soon as the tram doors opened, the two of them dashed off the tram and raced for the hangar.

FIERAN GROANED as he blinked awake. His shoulder hurt, a spot on the back of his head ached, and there was a strange ringing in his ears.

Cold stone pressed against his back and his shoulder. When he blinked again, he struggled to bring his eyes into focus.

He lay on his side on the half bridge, his back pressed against the low wall rising on one side. The bridge ended in mid-air, hanging a few feet over the empty mud of what had once been the Chibo River.

The Wall was gone. As was Dacha.

"Dacha?" Fieran shoved onto his elbow, then into a sitting position. His head swam for a moment, and when he touched the aching spot on his head, his fingers came away smeared with blood. He must have hit his head when the exploding magic had flung him backwards.

Now that he was sitting up, he could see the smoking

wreckage of those vehicles, the machines blown apart. The Mongavarians who had accompanied the vehicles lay prone on the ground, dead or knocked out.

But where was Dacha?

Fieran used the low wall at the edge of the bridge to push himself to his feet. He let just a hint of his magic flow through his veins, steadying him, as he half-ran, half-stumbled across the bridge and peered over the far side.

Dacha lay on the riverbed, unmoving, his silver-blond hair splayed across the mud.

No. *No.*

"Dacha!" Fieran flung himself over the side of the bridge, landing in the mud with a squelch. He sank all the way to his ankles in the muck of what had once been the silty, plant-filled bottom of the shallow river. Slipping and sliding, he scrambled to Dacha's side, falling into his knees in the mud.

"Dacha, wake up. Don't be dead." He pulled his dacha from the mud, even as his dacha's head lolled, his body limp. "Dacha!"

With shaking hands, Fieran pressed his fingers to the side of Dacha's neck.

He couldn't feel a pulse. Not past the pounding of his own pulse beneath his skin. His own heart thundered in his ears, hammering in his chest as if he had a galloping horse lodged behind his ribs.

No. Dacha couldn't be dead. He simply couldn't.

Something whipped past Fieran's face before thwacking into the stone of one of the pillars holding up the half bridge.

His magic reacted, blasting outward around him and Dacha before he'd even registered what it was.

A bullet.

More bullets flared against his shield of magic as they were incinerated. The rumble of gasoline engines and barking of machine guns filled the air past the fading ringing in his ears.

He dragged his gaze away from Dacha and up to the far bank of what had once been the river.

There, a line of men in Mongavarian uniforms jogged forward, carrying their rifles, a dark mass stretching along the river for as far as he could see in either direction. In between their ranks, more vehicles with those tractor treads rolled forward, except these ones had large artillery guns mounted on top of the metal box instead of magical machines.

Enemy aeroplanes roared overhead before diving downward to strafe the Alliance front lines behind Fieran.

This was an invasion. Mongavaria had taken down the Wall, and now they could roll into Escarland with impunity. The Alliance front lines were dug in, but they weren't prepared for a major invasion of this scale.

Right now, Fieran was the only one standing in the way.

He glanced down at Dacha, who lay limp and unmoving, his eyes closed. Surely that was a good sign, right? If he were dead, his eyes would be wide and soulless in that way Fieran had seen far too many times since this war began.

There was no time to pick Dacha up and try to move him to the Alliance front lines. With every moment, those vehicles crawled closer, tipping over the edge of the riverbank and plowing through the mud. Even now, the nearest vehicle lowered its huge gun to take aim at Fieran.

The enemy might have more of those machines that had captured Dacha's magic. Fieran, too, might end up unconscious or dead on the riverbed.

None of that mattered. He would have to make his stand here.

He hadn't worn his swords that morning. He didn't even

have his army issue rifle since he'd left that back at the hangar. But…

Fieran reached out, his heart hammering again. His fingers closed around the hilt of one of Dacha's swords, the leather worn to the shape of his dacha's hands.

He well remembered the first time Dacha had placed the hilt of one of these swords in Fieran's small hands, Dacha's far larger hand closing over his fingers to hold the sword steady.

"A sword is a weapon, not a toy, sason." Dacha had speared Fieran with those silver-blue eyes. "When you draw your sword, you do so with the intent to draw blood. It is not an action to take without thought or honor."

Fieran drew Dacha's sword now, nothing but bloody intent filling his heart. He had to roll Dacha to draw the other blade before he eased Dacha back to the ground, making sure his mouth and nose were clear of the mud.

Then Fieran rose to his feet and faced the enemy, a sword in each hand. As he let his magic twine from his hands and down onto the blades, he sensed the weight of all those past warriors and kings who had wielded these swords before him settling on his shoulders and deep within his heart.

He was Laesornysh. Warrior of the magic of the ancient kings, like his dacha before him. He would stand firm, no matter how much blood and death it took.

The vehicle-mounted gun boomed, lobbing its shell in Fieran's direction.

Fieran lashed out with his magic, grabbing the shell and flinging it back toward the Mongavarian line. Unleashing more of his magic, he shoved it into a storm of crackling bolts filling the space between him and the enemy.

As his magic brushed the smoking remains of those magic-absorbing machines, he could still sense a faint trace of that foreign magic within them. It didn't tug on his magic as it must have Dacha's, as if dormant now that the machines were broken.

More of that foreign magic blanketed the gun vehicles rolling toward him. At least this magic was the strange but familiar magic the Mongavarians had used on their aeroplanes, the one that deflected his magic but didn't otherwise impede it.

A sharp-edged smirk cut across Fieran's face. He knew exactly how to handle these vehicles.

Reaching deeper into his chest, he blasted his magic outward, stretching it to fill the river from one end to the other. His magic raced over the ground, following the faint traces where the Wall used to be.

As the vehicles rolled forward, he strengthened his magic, gritting his teeth at holding so much power.

The vehicles plowed into his magic and halted, their treads spinning trenches into the mud as the magic coating them deflected against Fieran's makeshift wall.

He took a step forward and *shoved*. All along the line, the steel vehicles skidded backward on the slick riverbed, pushed by their own protective magic deflecting off Fieran's magic.

Fieran took another step forward, gathered his magic, and shoved with all the magical strength in him.

Vehicles lurched and tumbled onto their sides or crashed backward. Men—the lucky ones—scrambled out of the way to avoid being crushed by the falling steel behemoths.

A wave of dizziness washed through Fieran, and he had to plant his feet, squeezing his eyes shut for a moment.

No. He wouldn't give in to this weariness. He was not at the end of his power. He wasn't at the edge of his stamina.

He was an elf. This magic was *his*. It wasn't his dacha's.

But his. A part of him, as integral as blood and bone. He was not lessened because he was half-human but he was all the stronger because he was a warrior with both human and elven blood running through his veins.

His whirling head steadied, though some of the dizziness still lingered at the edges. He snapped his gaze open and lifted the swords into a fighting guard stance. Whether this was caused by lack of stamina or lack of faith in his own elven heritage, he wouldn't let it impede him now, not with his dacha's life depending on him.

With his magic so occupied holding back the line of armored, tractor-tread vehicles, he hadn't stopped the soldiers. The first rank of them rushed forward, bayonets flashing on the ends of their rifles.

Fieran steeled himself as he faced the oncoming enemy. His dacha's swords in his hands glinted in the rising sun, the blades coated blue with his magic.

Then he launched himself forward and tore into the enemy. The familiar sword patterns that he'd practiced nearly every morning from the moment his dacha had first placed a wooden sword in his hand no longer merely met air or his dacha's blade. Instead, the swords met flesh and bone.

He'd thought he'd understood death. He'd caused it enough times. Felt it through his magic when he'd killed hundreds while taking down airships.

But this was death so visceral, so all-encompassing, that he couldn't escape it. He could taste it in the spattering blood, feel it in his blades meeting flesh, see it in the eyes of his enemy, live it in a way he never had before.

There was no going back. No staying his hand. His dacha lay prone and helpless behind him. The enemy assembled before him. He carried the duty of blade and battle, and he could not flinch from it.

He wasn't sure how much time passed as he wielded the swords as the warrior his dacha had trained him to be, cutting through the enemy with blade and magic. The rank upon rank of incoming enemy didn't give him time to think or feel. There was just the mud and the death and his dacha's swords in his hands.

With the deep whir of the propellers and the buzz of the magically powered rotary engines, a formation of aeroplanes flashed overhead, diving at the enemy lines. The aeroplanes' machines guns chattered, strafing the Mongavarian soldiers. Several of the aeroplanes farthest away from Fieran dropped bombs, which exploded in gouts of flame and earth among the enemy ranks.

As the aeroplanes swooped upward once again, the rising sun glinted on the artwork painted on them, each one incorporating an elf ear somewhere in the design.

His squadron. Fieran had gained enough space in the fight to lift a sword in salute, only to realize that the sword's blade dripped a rivulet of blood.

A wave of icy magic blasted from behind him, twining with and yet crackling against his magic in that way only the magic of the ancient kings ever did.

With the tromping squelch of boots in mud, ranks upon ranks of troll warriors in gray uniforms adorned with leather or metal armor strode forward, wielding swords and axes alongside rifles and sidearms.

"We've got this now." Rhohen appeared at Fieran's side, his hands laced with crackling icy-white bolts of his magic, a version of the magic of the ancient kings. He gave Fieran that pouty smirk that usually made him want to punch his cousin. Today he might have hugged him.

Uncle Rharreth stepped to Fieran's other side, his sword

in his right hand, his left hand wreathed with sparkling white ice magic. "See to your dacha."

Even as Fieran nodded, taking one step back, then two, Aunt Vriska, dressed in her gray uniform and wielding a sword, shouted orders to the troll warriors as she led the front ranks arrayed to Fieran's right.

To his left, elven warriors in deep evergreen uniforms edged in leather glided forward, interspersed with units of Escarlish soldiers in olive uniforms and carrying rifles. With Rhohen's magic providing a shield, the Alliance army pressed forward, advancing across the riverbed.

Fieran released his magic, turned, and dashed the few yards back to where Dacha lay.

Uncle Weylind knelt next to him and was prying Dacha's limp form from the mud. As Fieran crashed to his knees next to him, Uncle Weylind glanced up, his mouth in a grim line bracketed by deep grooves. "He is alive, nirshon."

Alive. Fieran released a breath that came out with a shudder. "Then why hasn't he woken yet?"

Fieran had only been out for a few seconds. He wasn't sure how much time had passed—likely not that long, despite how it had felt to him—but it seemed like too long if Dacha had been merely knocked out by the explosion.

"I do not know. But magical backlash can be tricky." Uncle Weylind hefted Dacha's limp form, pulling him up and over to drape across Uncle Weylind's shoulders. Mud smeared Uncle Weylind's uniform and into his hair, but he did not seem to notice as he stood, carrying Dacha. "Come. We must get your dacha to the healers."

Still holding Dacha's bloody swords, Fieran trotted after Uncle Weylind, his boots squishing in mud that was now even more churned and soupy from many boots. They passed more ranks of elves, trolls, and humans rushing onto the battlefield to reinforce the first wave of warriors.

Uncle Weylind climbed up the shallow bank, and Fieran jumped up after him to stand on the somewhat firmer ground of what had once been the riverbank. Here the bank was now clogged with various trucks, some abandoned and some with drivers working to turn them around to transport more troops to the growing battle in the riverbed.

His uncle tilted his head toward a nearby small, open-topped army truck identical to the one Fieran and his dacha had taken to the Wall. The truck they'd driven was now lying on its side in the mud, blown off its wheels and over the side of the half bridge in the magical explosion. "You will need to drive, nirshon."

Right. Unlike Dacha, Uncle Weylind hadn't learned. Tarenhiel hadn't embraced motorized vehicles the way Escarland had, and when Uncle Weylind visited Escarland, he always had someone on hand to drive him around, if needed. After all, he was a king. Even Uncle Averett didn't drive himself.

Fieran numbly settled into the driver's seat, resting Dacha's swords in the footwell of the passenger side. Uncle Weylind eased Dacha down so that he sprawled across the back seat before climbing into the back, propping himself under Dacha's head and shoulders to keep him steady.

Mechanically, Fieran turned on the engine, worked the gear shift and clutch, and sent the vehicle rolling and bumping along the road. Behind him, artillery guns boomed, men shouted, and machine guns chattered as the violence of war unleashed its carnage.

TWENTY-FIVE

Fieran braked, halting the truck in a cloud of dust only feet from Dacha's door. Shattering explosions rang behind him, the sirens for red alert and gas attack blaring from all the nearby buildings. As he flung himself from the truck, a boom shook the ground, and he braced himself against the truck's side.

Below the bluff, Mongavarian aeroplanes dropped bombs and canisters of gas onto the Alliance soldiers. Only the hangar was safe beneath the shimmer of Pip's shield. Clouds of gun smoke and gas billowed over the riverbed where Fieran had been only moments ago. Alliance aeroplanes chased after the enemy, firing in bursts.

More Alliance aeroplanes roared overhead, rushing to reinforce the beleaguered pilots battling in the sky.

Uncle Julien dashed out of the lingering dust cloud, glancing from Fieran to Uncle Weylind, who was hefting Dacha's limp body from the back seat of the truck. "What happened?"

"There were these machines with that foreign magic." Fieran braced both hands on the side of the truck as another series of explosions shook the ground. Gouts of dirt and flame burst among the trees where the elven infantry was stationed. Fieran swallowed and forced himself to focus. "They seemed to catch Dacha's magic, and the Wall exploded. Dacha has been unconscious ever since."

"I will send a team to retrieve one of those machines. We need to figure out exactly what they are and how they work." While his tone remained calm and steady, Uncle Julien's gaze locked on Dacha, sprawled across Uncle Weylind's shoulders.

As Uncle Julien's words registered, Fieran resisted the urge to swear under his breath before he heaved a sigh. "From what it looked like, the machines were mostly destroyed in the magical explosion. You'll need a mechanic with magic to know if the one the team is retrieving has enough magic and mechanics left to study."

"Do you have someone in mind?" Uncle Julien's gaze tore from Dacha and Uncle Weylind to settle squarely on Fieran.

Fieran bit back the words he wanted to spit out again. He didn't know of any mechanics with magic in the airship crews, and even if there were, Uncle Julien—as a general in the army—wouldn't be able to quickly requisition them for a retrieval mission since they would officially be under the navy.

No, the best person for the job was Pip. But if Fieran mentioned her, he would send his girlfriend off into that inferno of bombs and gas and bullets engulfing the riverbed.

Fieran swallowed and nodded. "Yes."

"Send the mechanic to headquarters." Uncle Julien glanced at Dacha one last time before he whirled and dashed back toward the headquarters building.

Fieran turned to go as well, though he hesitated, glancing

over his shoulder to where Uncle Weylind was navigating through the door into Dacha's quarters with Dacha on his shoulders. "Should I…"

Uncle Weylind gestured to him. "Go, nirshon. You need to get into the sky."

Fieran shot one last glance at his dacha's unconscious form, something inside him tearing at having to leave Dacha like this.

But his duty was in the sky, and he couldn't shirk it. Not even for Dacha.

He turned and sprinted for the hangar higher on the ridge and shielded by Pip's magic. As he skidded through the hangar door, he found himself in a nearly empty space. Only a handful of aeroplanes remained here in Bay 4 with their mechanics rushing to fix whatever was wrong and keeping the aeroplanes from the air.

From the other, more distant hangar bays, he could hear the shouting, pounding of feet, and squeaky rolling of aeroplane wheels as the other squadrons hurried to finish disgorging their aeroplanes into the air.

"Fieran! What happened?" Pip dashed toward him, nearly falling into him when she didn't stop quickly enough. Mak ran up after her, halting several feet away.

"There were these machines, they captured Dacha's magic, and when everything exploded, it knocked him out. He's still unconscious." Fieran gripped her shoulders, pausing as he worked up the courage to speak the next words, words that would send her into battle. "Uncle Julien is sending a team to retrieve a machine for study. But they need a mechanic with both magic and training to go along."

For a long moment, Pip just stared at him, as if the words didn't compute.

Behind her, Mak crossed his arms, a scowl deepening the shadows formed by his beard. "Not Pip. I'll go."

Beneath Fieran's hands, Pip's shoulders straightened, and her chin came up. She held Fieran's gaze rather than glance over her shoulder at Mak. "No, it has to be me. My magic will be better suited to recognizing what I'm looking at, and I'll be able to shield myself and the team."

She was also the one with the magical engineering degree, although she didn't say that. Fieran wouldn't say that out loud either. He respected Mak greatly, as a friend and a mechanic, but he didn't have the experience on the experimental side of things that Pip did. He wouldn't recognize what he was looking at. Pip would.

Mak's glower drew down even deeper as he glared at Fieran, as if blaming him. "No."

Fieran ignored the stabbing glare. He didn't like the situation either. It went against every protective urge in his heart to send Pip into the maelstrom descending on the lower reaches of Fort Defense.

But she was the best person—only person, really—for the job. He couldn't stand in her way or in the way of the war effort because he was protective. That was exactly what they'd pledged to each other that they wouldn't do when they began courting.

Pip's deep brown eyes locked with his. "I'll deal with Mak. You need to go."

"Uncle Julien is waiting for you at headquarters. Stay safe." Fieran swept her up in his arms and kissed her. He couldn't linger. Couldn't do more than pour out his heart into a brief moment before he released her and stepped back. As he was turning to dash for his aeroplane, he barely heard her mumbled "You too," behind him.

His aeroplane wasn't in its usual spot in the hangar, so he

grabbed a few items of his flight gear and dashed out the far door, quickly locating his Defender by the bright flames of the art painted on the sides of the nose. The ground crew must have pushed it outside to prepare it for takeoff, and it sat off to one side at the end of the airfield beyond the queue of aeroplanes lining up for their own turns down the airfield.

Fieran hopped into the aeroplane, switching on the power even before he buckled on the lap belt. He yanked on his flying cap and plugged in the end of the radio wire. Voices flooded into his ears, a garble of shouting and orders nearly as chaotic as the melee taking place in the sky.

"Half-Breed Squadron." Fieran yanked down his goggles. He hadn't taken the time to dress in the rest of his flight gear, and it would be a cold flight. But there wasn't time, nor did he want to drag on those items over his uniform, which was spattered with mud, blood, and other things that he was trying really hard to ignore. "I'm taking to the skies. I just need my aeroplane to finish spinning up."

Cheers broke through over the other voices.

Lt. Rothilion's voice was faint from distance, barely discernible through all the other chatter and static. "It will be good to have you in the sky, Laesornysh."

To the other squadrons, it might have sounded disrespectful, the way Lt. Rothilion dropped Fieran's rank. But even over that distance, Fieran could hear the elven emphasis in those words. Lt. Rothilion wasn't merely calling Fieran by his last name; he was stating Fieran's elven title. Laesornysh. Death on the Wind.

Then Merrik's voice cut through the din. "I will swing back to fetch you."

"Thanks." Fieran monitored the gauges as the rotary engine gained speed, glancing between his dashboard and the line of aeroplanes taking off two at a time.

Several members of the ground crew directed the aeroplanes from the end of the airfield, keeping the scramble from turning into a confusion.

Fieran was directed into a place in line, then his aeroplane's wheels were chocked. The aeroplane shuddered around him, seeming as eager as he was to take to the skies to defend the rest of the squadron. He watched another pair of aeroplanes take off before he toggled the radio. "There's one more pair of aeroplanes, then I'm next."

"Almost there." Merrik's voice rang slightly louder, easily masking the shouts and voices from the aeroplanes fighting farther away.

Fieran flexed his fingers on the control column as the ground crew members waved the next pair of aeroplanes to begin their run, even as the previous pair was just rising into the sky on the other end. He pressed the talk button again as he counted down for Merrik.

Then two members of the ground crew snatched the wheel chocks free, and he was waved to begin his run. "Beginning my takeoff."

"Coming down for you."

Even as Fieran flashed past the ground crew members directing traffic, he caught a glimpse of them shading their eyes, then pointing toward the sky.

His aeroplane gained speed, the air strengthening beneath the wings until the flyer grew light around him. A warbird on the cusp of flight.

With a roar, a black shadow swooped down over him, leveling out disconcertingly close overhead. Merrik glanced over the side of his aeroplane and gave a small wave before he pointed his aeroplane upward once again.

Fieran laughed even as he pulled back on the stick. His aeroplane rose into the sky, falling into place as Merrik led the way back into the air. "I think you gave the ground crew a collective heart attack."

"I could not leave you to take off alone." Merrik's voice held a trace of humor before he sobered. "What happened? We saw the Wall come down."

As the two of them gained altitude and turned back toward the fight, Fieran gave a brief summary, ending with, "Pip is going with the team to retrieve a machine or two for study."

"Got it," Merrik acknowledged, but then there was no more time for talking as they shot into the edge of the whirling chaos of the dogfight spreading over Fort Defense.

Mongavarian aeroplanes dove as they dropped bombs onto the fort below, some of the canisters even falling among the headquarters buildings on the bluff. A part of the Escarlish officer quarters was burning, a column of gray smoke rising into the sky to join the haze of gun smoke. Clouds of gas drifted over the front lines, spanning from the bluff, across the muddy river bottom, and even onto the Mongavarian side of the border.

Alliance aeroplanes chased and battled the Mongavarian ones, attempting to take them down before they could drop their bombs. Yet without Dacha's magic arching over the fort, the burning wreckage falling from the sky just added to the destruction below.

To the south, Alliance airships lumbered into a defensive position at the border, though they had yet to join the fray.

There was no cohesion or plan to the Alliance aeroplanes' movements. Each pair of pilots were on their own, trying to defend themselves from the attack.

"I'm going to sweep the Mongavarians toward the border." Fieran reached into his chest and tapped the deep well of his magic. Despite all the magic he had expended during the fight on the ground, more still sizzled inside him, just waiting to be unleashed.

"Is that safe?" Merrik still led the way, his machine guns blasting as the nearest Mongavarian aeroplane swung toward them. "If they have one of those machines up here, and your magic gets caught…"

He'd get knocked unconscious, and this time he really would die in the crash.

But they couldn't continue this fight over Fort Defense. Between the bombs and the falling debris, the fort below was getting hammered. Better to take the fight to the enemy skies.

"Those machines were large. I doubt they can mount one on a fighter aeroplane." Fieran let his magic build in his chest, but he held it back for a moment longer as he aimed his machine guns to the side of Merrik's aeroplane to also target the enemy flyer. "But I'm open to suggestions if you have a better idea."

He wasn't going to just disregard Merrik's concerns over the risk. Not again. The last time Fieran had been reckless, Merrik had lost a leg.

There was silence from Merrik for a long moment. The enemy aeroplane's engine caught fire, and it stalled in the air so abruptly that Merrik and Fieran had to scatter—Merrik whipping his aeroplane one way, Fieran the other, to avoid a head-on collision.

When they swerved back to each other, Merrik fell in behind Fieran. "All right. Do it. But if you feel anything off, pull your magic back immediately."

Fieran didn't think such a thing would be so easily done. Dacha hadn't been able to pull his magic back, and anything that could overwhelm Dacha's magic could take out Fieran's easily.

But he wouldn't clutter up the airwaves to say so.

Nor would he point out the glaring problem. If the Mongavarians had one of those machines mounted to an aeroplane, all of them would be in trouble, not just Fieran. They were, after all, flying aeroplanes powered by magic. That machine had seemed to need physical contact to latch on to the magic, but if it only needed proximity, then it could take down any one of their aeroplanes, whether Fieran was using his magic or not.

But Fieran wasn't about to say that out loud on the radio for members of all the squadrons to hear. They needed to focus on fighting, not on the possibility that their engine's power source might be neutralized at any moment.

"Magic incoming." With a deep breath, Fieran blasted his magic outward. He didn't try to wrap it around anything but instead concentrated on forming his own, active version of the Wall in the sky as far as he could stretch it across the open air.

"Capt. Fleetwood, Lt. Hadley." Fieran worked to keep his tone and aeroplane steady as he held the great quantity of magic crackling above, below, and to either side of him. One of the Mongavarian aeroplanes got too close before it sheered off, propelled away by its own deflecting magic. "I will cover as much of the sky as I can to sweep the Mongavarians back, but I might need some help herding them toward the border."

Technically, Capt. Fleetwood was the senior captain, and Fieran was toeing the line of giving an order to an officer who outranked him by wording that as a request rather than the demand it really was.

But someone had to take charge here in the skies, and while Capt. Fleetwood was a good pilot and good squadron leader, he wasn't always the most creative when it came to overall battle tactics in the sky.

"Acknowledged." Capt. Fleetwood's voice had a harried edge to it. "Fighting Second, you heard Capt. Laesornysh. Let's chase the enemy back to the border."

Lt. Hadley repeated the order to his own men.

Fieran couldn't see any of the Half-Breed Squadron nearby. As they had been the first ones up, they appeared to be all at the border, strafing and bombing the enemy lines while trying to prevent more of the enemy aeroplanes from getting past them.

With Fieran's wall of magic pushing the enemy from the center, the rest of the Alliance aeroplanes in the sky rallied, only engaging the Mongavarian aeroplanes that tried to swerve around Fieran's shield in some way.

He swept over the bluff, then over the front lines. Below, great gouges tore into the earth where bombs had struck. Buildings smoked while elves with strong plant magic worked to cleanse the air from the gas attacks.

The muddy expanse of what had once been a river was churned and soupy, with the tiny figures of the dead and dying sprawled in the mire. Despite the carnage, Alliance troops charged across to join the fight on the far side.

The Mongavarians had been pushed back across the river and into the marshy expanse where Fieran had crashed. The sharp line of Rhohen's icy, crackling magic sliced across the land, showing exactly where the battle raged.

Here, the Half-Breed Squadron whirled and fought enemy aeroplanes, though some of them peeled away to strafe the enemy ground troops.

Fieran peered over the side of his aeroplane, tilting it to get a better look. But he couldn't spot the smoking hulks of those machines. "I think the Mongavarians took the machines when they retreated."

"Big pieces of machinery set in a metal box and placed on tractor treads?" Lije's voice rang over the radio from wherever he fought in the dogfight. "Yeah, they hooked up draft horses and trucks to them to haul them away. Lt. Rothilion has been keeping an eye on them."

"They have dragged them along with their retreat, but it appears to be slow going." Lt. Rothilion's crisp voice was slightly distorted and hard to hear with the distance. He must be one of the Alliance fighters farthest out, over the enemy lines.

"It is a good thing we cannot hear them." Aylia's chipper voice held a laugh, even garbled as it was. "They appear to be swearing up a storm. The hulks keep sinking into the mud, giving them a time of hauling them out."

They must be quite determined to keep that technology out of Alliance hands. Something that could take down the Wall would be a closely guarded secret. If they'd had more time, they likely would have set demolition charges to blow up the hulks. But between the pressure from the oncoming Alliance army and their fear of letting even a piece of those machines fall into Alliance hands, the effort of hauling the destroyed vehicles with them would have been deemed worth it.

"It has slowed their retreat," Lt. Rothilion added. "They are putting up a much better stand than they did facing General Laesornysh when he rescued you after your crash."

On another day, Fieran might have made a snide remark about how Rhohen wasn't as intimidating a warrior as Dacha.

But not today. Not while he still wore the gore of combat

and remembered all too well the feel of swords slicing through his enemy.

The Mongavarians hadn't run before him as they had his dacha either. Perhaps he hadn't unleashed the full fury of his magic the way Dacha had, and he'd been hampered by the fact that he didn't want to leave Dacha unguarded. Maybe the Mongavarians were merely less surprised to find themselves facing a warrior of the magic of the ancient kings now that they'd done it once already.

"Where would you like us, Capt. Laesornysh?" Capt. Fleetwood's tone held deference. His words might have been a question, but he was essentially handing over the role of commander in the air to Fieran, and doing it for every member of all three squadrons to hear.

Fieran gave a quick scan of the battlefields, both ground and air. "Capt. Fleetwood, please continue reinforcing the Half-Breed Squadron in defending the sky. Lt. Hadley, send one of your Flights to assist the ground attack while the other continues the dogfight in the air. Lt. Rothilion, take Flight A and keep an eye on those machines. General Julien Ardon is sending a team to retrieve them. When that team arrives, provide air cover and whatever other assistance you can give them."

How Fieran would have rather given himself the job of looking after Pip. But he'd have to trust her safety to Lt. Rothilion and whatever team of soldiers Uncle Julien sent with her. Fieran's duty lay elsewhere.

"Flight B, we're going to hold the border. Don't let any more enemy aeroplanes back over to attack Fort Defense." Fieran could sense the lingering trace of magic in the ground where the Wall had once stood. He positioned his wall in the sky over that, using the marker to hold his shield steady, even as he stretched more magic around himself and Merrik.

"Fieran…" Merrik's voice was tight. "We have a problem."

Fieran glanced around, trying to find whatever Merrik was referring to.

A huge behemoth of an airship rounded the point of the nearest mountain to Fieran's right, escorted by several smaller airships and another swarm of aeroplanes. The blue and white markings on the airships and aeroplanes showed that these were not Alliance reinforcements coming from the south.

"You said those machines were too large to mount on a fighter aeroplane." Merrik's tight tone didn't waver, even as he brought his aeroplane level with Fieran's.

"Yeah." Fieran studied the incoming airship. There seemed to be a large square box mounted beneath the gondola, a hedgehog of wires trailing down. "But it would definitely fit on an airship."

TWENTY-SIX

Pip paused long enough to grab her largest, head-bashing wrench off her workbench and shouted to one of her mechanics that he was in charge before she raced out of the hangar, her heart hammering in her ears.

She couldn't believe she was doing this. Running toward battle. She wasn't a warrior. She was a mechanic.

But right now, a mechanic was what they needed. The Mongavarians had unleashed a machine so terrible that it had taken *Prince Farrendel Laesornysh* out of the fight. She had to do what she could to get her hands on the machine so it could be taken apart and studied.

"There's no way I'm letting you do this." Mak ran at her side, still glaring that big brother scowl of his.

A rather immature part of her wanted to stick out her tongue and tell him he wasn't the boss of her, as she'd done as a kid. In fact, she was technically the boss of him at the moment.

Instead, she flashed a quick shield of her magic, enough to bump his shoulder. "You can't stop me."

All right, so that probably wasn't all that more mature

than sticking out her tongue. But Fieran hadn't doubted her capability. Her own brother shouldn't either.

A boom exploded somewhere nearby, shaking the ground so violently Pip stumbled. A gout of flame erupted from somewhere behind the line of tents and trees standing between her and the headquarters section of Fort Defense.

Hopefully that hadn't been the main headquarters itself, where Fieran's uncle was waiting.

"Fine. Then I'm coming with you." Mak jogged at her side as they slowed to navigate between the tent platforms and line of trees.

"I'm the one with the ability to fend off bombs and gunfire." She didn't add "not you" or otherwise denigrate his magic. But plant magic wielded with dwarven crafting wasn't going to help on a battlefield. Her magic would. She probably would have been sent out on the battlefield long before now if she hadn't been such a skilled mechanic.

"Two mechanics will be better than one." Mak's tone lowered, softened from that belligerently overprotective edge. "You might need an extra pair of hands and a strong back."

"All right." She wouldn't fight him on this. As much as she didn't like knowing that both of them could be killed, the squeezing eased in her chest at having her brother beside her. She'd just have to protect both of them with her magic.

They crested the small rise overlooking headquarters. Gray smoke rose from one of the distant buildings—the Escarlish officer quarters, if she guessed right—but the other buildings appeared relatively undamaged. Beyond the bluff, clouds of gas filled the air, though it hung in the lower lying areas rather than spreading to the flatlands on the bluff.

With a blazing crackle of power, Fieran's magic spread across the sky, the power of it prickling against Pip's skin and through her magical senses. She risked only the briefest peek upward at his aeroplane, a gray-green dot wreathed in blue bolts, before she charged down the ridge, Mak at her side.

Down below, the area around headquarters teemed. Trucks roared up to the headquarters building, only to skid away a moment later. Men on horseback dodged through the fray, delivering messages to headquarters before speeding away again with new orders. A team of trolls with ice magic worked to suppress the fire in the Escarlish officer quarters.

Pip and Mak dove into the crowd by the doors of the headquarters building, shoving their way past the various runners, corporals, aides, adjutants, and other assorted personnel until they stood at the entrance to the central command room.

An MP barred their way with a hand, but Pip could still see past him into the space. A huge table held several maps and charts with a layout of Fort Defense and the surrounding area currently taking prominence. The distant sounds of ringing telephones came from somewhere farther along the sprawling buildings, and a woman in a green uniform shirt and skirt hurried inside and handed a piece of paper to one of the men standing around the table.

The man glanced at it, then moved something on the chart depicting the whole Escarlish-Mongavarian border, even as he said something about troop movements and attacks. The Wall must be down along the whole border, meaning this invasion wasn't isolated to Fort Defense. Escarland was fending off attacks in multiple places.

No sooner had the woman left than two women and an older man hurried in, all of them carrying slips of paper. One said something about the dwarven delivery having arrived.

General Julien Ardon—Fieran's uncle—was only one of

the huddle of green-, blue-, and gray-uniformed men packed around the table. He was running a hand over his beard—likely absently—as he took in the sprawl of the ongoing battles.

"Excuse me." A young man shoved past them to get into the room. Only once he was past did Pip recognize him as Fieran's cousin Myles, begrimed and smelling of smoke. Even his red sash had burn marks scorched into it. He marched up to General Ardon. "The fire has been contained."

The message brought the general's head up, and he nodded to Myles before his gaze swept past him to land on Pip and Mak, still hovering just outside of the doorway.

After speaking in a low tone to the general next to him, General Ardon strode in their direction. "Which one of you is the mechanic Fieran was sending?"

She would have wondered how the general guessed, but both of them wore green, grease-stained coveralls, and she was clutching a giant wrench.

"We both are," Mak replied before Pip could explain the situation.

General Ardon nodded, as if he wasn't going to question being promised one mechanic but being sent two. "I've sent instructions to the dwarven commander. A squad should be assembling as we speak."

Dwarves. Something both uncoiled and yet touched off inside her at the same time. If she had to go into battle, she should march with her dwarven countrymen and women.

General Ardon didn't wait for her or Mak to respond. He gestured to Myles. "Lt. Kinsley, please escort the mechanics there. Then see what you can do to hurry along the unloading of the shipment of dwarven vehicles."

"Yes, sir." Myles spun. Once he was in the corridor, out of

sight of all the generals, he grinned at Pip, then at Mak. "Daring of Fieran to send his girlfriend. All right, come along. I have a truck."

Pip let Mak and Myles go first so that the two of them could plow an opening through the milling tangle of bodies mobbing the building.

As soon as they were free, Myles jogged to one of the small open-topped vehicles parked nearby, still idling.

He hopped into the driver's seat, and Pip claimed the back seat so that Mak could have the passenger seat with more leg room.

Pip gripped the side and braced herself as Myles worked the gear shift and sent the vehicle lurching down the road, his speed curtailed by all the other vehicles, horses, and running men clogging the zigzagging road from the bluff down to Little Aldon.

The smoke from more burning fires filled the air with an acrid taste that lodged in the back of Pip's throat. At least the chemical gas attacks didn't seem to have been directed here, though she had her gas mask clipped to her belt.

Dwarves and more Escarlish soldiers and personnel milled about as they fought the fires or dug into the rubble.

Pip swallowed, looking away from the sight. It was all too familiar from the bombing of Bridgetown or cleaning up Dar Goranth after the battle there.

On the flat flood plain between the bluff and the Hydalla River on the far side of Little Aldon, several large army trucks assembled, the back benches already packed with dwarven warriors, clad in armor and bristling with weapons. More dwarves waited in line to clamber onto the final truck.

Myles halted their truck a few yards away and swiveled in his seat. "Best of luck on your mission. I look forward to having a proper family chat, once this war is over and Fieran brings you around to the formal Escarlish events."

Formal Escarlish events. As in balls and stuff at the royal palace with King Averett and the whole Escarlish court.

Pip's chest squeezed as she tried to make her seizing muscles move. This was ridiculous. Here she was about to go into battle, but it was the thought of a royal ball that had her far more panicked.

She just wouldn't think of it now. She had more important things to worry about.

"Yeah. Uh, thanks." She climbed from the truck, her boots hitting the ground with the crunch of gravel.

With one last wave to the two of them, Myles sent the truck rolling back up the road they'd come down, heading for the railyard.

"Pippak!" One of the dwarves—a brown-haired dwarf with warrior braids in his beard—pounded toward her. "Maktorekk!"

"Uncle Thortrad?" Pip would have hugged him, but he was all armor and weapons at the moment.

Not only were they going with dwarves, but with Detmuk dwarves.

"I wasn't sure what to think when I heard they were sending us a civilian to go on this raid." Uncle Thortrad pounded her on the back hard enough to send her staggering forward. He was strong and well-muscled, even though she was taller by several inches. "Glad to see the two of you. Come on aboard, and we can get rolling."

Draenelynn, Pip's cousin and Thortrad's daughter, leaned out of the cab of the lead truck. "There's room here by me."

Pip climbed into the truck and wedged herself into the

backseat next to her well-armored cousin. The space grew even more squished as Mak climbed in after her.

Uncle Thortrad clambered into the front passenger seat and glanced over his shoulder at them. "Looks like everyone's here. It would've been nice if the tanks had been unloaded so we could take one along, but we'll make do."

"Tanks?" Pip wiggled to try to find a spot where Mak's elbow didn't dig into her ribs.

"Large metal vehicles. Kind of like rolling land battleships." Uncle Thortrad gestured, as if he was struggling to figure out how to describe them.

"Oh, I see. We saw the train arrive after seeing our parents off." Pip shared a look with Mak. Those tanks must have been secretly in development by the dwarves. Neither of them had seen them on their last visit to Detmuk Mountain.

The Escarlish driver clambered in and turned on the truck's engine.

"Masks on, everyone." Uncle Thortrad pulled a gas mask from his belt, struggling to get the mask over his hair and large beard.

Smooshed between her cousin and brother as she was, Pip struggled to reach her gas mask, much less get it on. Draenelynn and Mak also squirmed in their seats, trying to reach their masks, and the three of them were a tangle of elbows for a few minutes until they all got their masks free.

The Escarlish driver pulled his mask on easily, as if he were far more practiced at it. With his short hair and lack of beard, he had an easier time of it than the dwarven warrior.

Pip grimaced as she pulled the canvas over her head. The eye sockets were bulky, falling lower on her face than they should so that she had to keep adjusting the mask to see. When she breathed in, she tasted the scent of charcoal in the back of her throat as the air was filtered through a layer of charcoal and moss enhanced with elven magic.

Both Mak and Draenelynn struggled to get their beards stuffed inside the mask.

Within a few minutes, an order was shouted from driver to driver, and the trucks rumbled forward, away from the safety of Little Aldon, headed toward the roiling smoke, haze of gas, and booming artillery guns.

Pip gripped her head-bashing wrench between her knees and tried not to throw up as the truck lurched and jolted. She was really doing this. Going into battle.

PIP MARCHED at the center of the formation of dwarves as she held a magic shield around them, her heart hammering in time with the tromping of boots on the soft Mongavarian soil.

She was in Mongavaria, the muddy expanse of what had once been a river behind her, the line of fighting before them.

An artillery shell whistled over the battle lines before it smashed into her shield, exploding in a starburst of flames and shrapnel.

She gritted her teeth and held her shield firm.

Beside her, the draft horses they'd requisitioned from an artillery unit once they'd reached the front snorted and tossed their heads. Mak made soothing noises as he reached up to stroke their necks, keeping a tight grip on their lead ropes.

Uncle Thortrad halted the formation and turned back to her, his face no longer hidden by the gas mask. Once they'd been past the section of the front lines hit with the gas attacks, all of them had taken off their gas masks to better see for fighting. "What's our heading?"

Why was he looking at her, as if she was the one calling the shots? Pip swallowed, glancing from Uncle Thortrad to Mak. Neither of them gave her any indication of what she should do.

She scanned the long, seething mass of men ahead of them. Prince Rhohen's icy, crackling magic filled the sky and spread all down the line, reinforced with ice, stone, and plant magic from King Rharreth and the other troll and elf warriors.

Aeroplanes whizzed and twirled overhead. Most of the ones nearest the raging battle were those of Flight A. She recognized the aeroplanes—and the artwork—even from that distance.

Several of them seemed to be circling something on the ground below, as if marking a spot.

"That way." Pip pointed to where one of the Flight A aeroplanes circled nearly directly ahead of them.

Uncle Thortrad shouted orders, and the dwarves shifted, forming a wedge with their shields locked and their axes raised. Uncle Thortrad called out a rhythm, and the squad of dwarves marched forward at double time, setting up a deep chant, punctuated by the pounding of their boots.

Pip matched their pace, her skin prickling as magic built around them.

As they neared the battle, dwarven magic spread before them, similar to her shield in that it was a shield like iron. But this magic was powered by the crafting, chanting rhythm of the dwarves around her, humming with the active power being funneled into it.

She mingled her shield with theirs, as she had with the dwarves in the battle for Dar Goranth.

Trolls filled the battlefield ahead of them, and as they neared, one of the trolls at the rear glanced over his shoulder. When he turned back to the fight, he was shouting orders, though the fighting men and women ahead of him didn't seem to hear.

Not that it mattered. The dwarves reached forward with their magic, then shoved the fighting trolls with the magical shield, carving an aisle to march through.

The rhythm of the chanting and pounding boots changed as the dwarves launched from double time into a charge. Even then, they stayed in rhythm, holding their magic.

Pip found herself yelling as she charged forward, gripping her wrench. She wasn't even sure why she was yelling. Just that it seemed like the right thing to do.

She tried not to look too closely at the bodies strewn on the ground, even as she had to look to avoid stepping on them. Her stomach churned, but as long as she kept yelling, she wasn't tempted to vomit.

Ahead, an Alliance aeroplane swooped down, machine guns chattering, as the pilot strafed the mass of enemy soldiers. It roared back higher into the sky nearly as quickly as it had come.

The lead dwarves smashed into the front line of enemy soldiers, tossing aside soldiers even as machine gun fire pinged off the magical shield around them.

Pip's stomach heaved at the sights. The sounds. The smells.

The dwarven rush slowed as they fought their way through the lines. Pip pressed close to the warmth of one of the draft horses, resting a hand on the horse's shoulder.

As she stepped around one of the bodies lying on the ground, the man, dressed in a blue Mongavarian uniform, began getting up, his hand closing on his gun with its bayonet.

Pip shrieked and whacked the man with her wrench. He collapsed back to the ground.

Had she just…was he…

"Mak…" She froze, staring at the man, at the wrench in her hands. She'd always joked about a head-bashing wrench. But she'd never experienced what it actually felt like to bash a head with a wrench.

She was shaking, her stomach rising into her throat. She couldn't do this. She had to get out of here. Had to escape. It was too much. Too loud. Too much blood.

Then Mak was there, wrapping an arm around her and tugging her to his chest, even as he kept a grip on the horses' leads. "I got you. Just keep your shield up."

Her shield. Pip squeezed her eyes shut and poured more magic into her shield.

Mak led her forward, and she tottered next to him, stumbling over the uneven ground. But she didn't open her eyes more than a peek or two to check on her shield.

Then she sensed it. A strange magic brushing against her shield. It was just a trace of it, not enough to pose a threat.

The hulk of a metal machine lay a few yards away, similar to the dwarven tanks she'd seen but more rudimentary. Huge drag marks carved into the ground while the team of six horses hooked to it were sweat-slicked and breathing hard, too tired to even stir at the fighting going around them.

The dwarves set up a wedge-shaped shield of warriors and magic around the machine, keeping the Mongavarians at bay. They marched in place, knocking the flats of their axes or swords against their shields to maintain the rhythm and the magic held strong before them.

Machine gun bullets pinged off the iron shield. Mongavarian soldiers tried to bayonet it or shoot it, only for their blades or bullets to bounce off.

Pip stepped out of Mak's grip and dashed the last few feet to the hulking thing on the tractor treads. How were they going to get this thing out of here? If those six horses were already exhausted, there was no way the two they'd brought would be able to haul it the other way.

She clambered up the side of the huge vehicle, balancing on the tread as she peered at the machine mounted within.

The actual machine itself was about the size of a large aeroplane engine. Wires connected it to the engine powering the wheels. But she didn't need the whole engine. Just the magical part of this machine.

The wiring and inner workings were still smoking, and this close the acrid scent of burnt-out metal filled her nose. The center machinery was melted and warped in on itself.

"What do you think?" Mak halted behind her.

"I think I can disconnect the machine so we can haul it out of here without taking all of this." She patted the armored side. "But I'm concerned that the inner workings are so fried."

"Let's just grab this one, then see if we can snag a second one." Mak climbed up beside her. "But we need to hurry."

Right. With the shield of dwarven magic, her magic, and the dwarves themselves between her and danger, it was too easy to forget that they were rather exposed, a spearhead into the Mongavarian lines. If the Alliance army retreated, they'd find themselves cut off.

Aeroplanes circled overhead, the elves of Flight A preventing Mongavarian aeroplanes from dropping bombs onto her head.

Still mentally holding her shield, Pip swept her magic

over the machine, melting through any mounting brackets or wires holding the machine inside the metal shielding box. It wasn't pretty, and she could only hope she wasn't leaving something important behind, buried deeper within the engine or frame of the tank.

Once it was free, Mak called over a few of the rear guard of dwarves, and together he and the others levered the heavy machine up and out.

Pip sliced off a section of the metal armor with her magic. Within a few minutes, she and Mak had the machine secured to the piece of metal, which she formed into a sled. Now that it had been removed from the rest of the vehicle, only one horse was needed to pull it.

As soon as the horse was hitched to the sled, Mak shouted to Uncle Thortrad in dwarvish, "We got it."

"Fall back." Uncle Thortrad also called in dwarvish, not looking over his shoulder.

Together, the dwarves took one step back, then another, their shield still steady around them as they kept up their steady rhythm even in retreat.

Within moments, the dwarven squad was back behind the Alliance line. Uncle Thortrad sent two of the dwarves off with the horse and machine before he turned to Pip. "Where to next?"

Pip scanned the sky and the lines again. She found the next circling Alliance aeroplane pointing the way toward another one of those machines. "There. Let's go after that one."

She adjusted her grip on her wrench, swallowed, and faced the horror of battle again.

TWENTY-SEVEN

Fieran sensed the tugging on his magic as the airship steamed closer, clouds of smoke pouring from the funnels set at the rear of the airship as its engines burned fuel. Wires laced over the whole airship; perhaps all of them ran back to that machine.

None of the Alliance airships were anywhere close enough to engage the enemy airship in battle. In past battles, Fieran had demanded the airships stay away. Now he would've cheered to see one moving to head off the enemy.

This time taking down the airship was up to them, and they couldn't use magic to do it.

"Capt. Fleetwood, Lt. Hadley, keep holding off the enemy aeroplanes. I'm going to have to stop using my magic." Fieran eyed the approaching airship. How long did he dare hold the magic and risk getting it caught?

"Understood." Capt. Fleetwood began shouting orders to array his men in a better formation for fending off the enemy without the benefit of Fieran's magic at their backs.

"Flight B." Fieran turned his aeroplane toward the incoming airship. With a sigh, he released his magic, letting it fizzle out even as he drew the magic within him deep into his chest. "We're going to take out the airship."

"Do you want Flight A to assist?" Lt. Rothilion called from where he and his pilots were keeping an eye on the destroyed machines.

"No. Stay with the machines and protect Pip." Fieran wasn't going to leave her without air cover. He'd all but sent her into the carnage of war. The least he could do was ensure she wasn't bombed and strafed while she was at it. "Do you have the incursion team in sight yet?"

"I do." Aylia's voice piped up over the radio. "Looks like she's with a squad of dwarves."

Fieran breathed a laugh into the frigid air this high up. He flexed his fingers, his gloveless hands feeling the cold now that he wasn't using his magic. "Good."

"So what is the plan?" Merrik's voice was steady with just a hint of an undertone to it. A quiet questioning of whether whatever Fieran was planning was wise.

If anyone had earned the right to question Fieran's plans, it was Merrik.

But this time, Fieran wasn't going to be reckless. He wasn't going to rely on himself or his magic. After all, he couldn't even use his magic.

This time, he'd trust in the Half-Breed Squadron.

"We're going to take down the airship. Together." Fieran let a steely determination ring through his voice. "I can't use my magic. Tiny, Merrik, you can't either. All of you, watch those wires. Our engines, radios, and the solenoid trigger system for our machine guns are powered by magic. If you brush one of those wires, you'll probably lose all power."

At least the rudders, elevators, and ailerons were manually controlled. If one of them lost power, hopefully they would be able to glide back to the airfield at Fort Defense.

"Does anyone have incendiary bombs?" Fieran shifted his legs as the chill seeped into him. He'd need to take the airship down quickly before he froze up here without his flight gear.

Negative responses filled the radio. As the Half-Breed Squadron had been the first to get airborne, they'd used up any bombs they'd had by tossing them at the Mongavarian ground troops to hold them off.

"I have one!" A voice—only vaguely familiar—joined the discussion. A few more voices added that they, too, had incendiary bombs.

Capt. Fleetwood rattled off a few names. "Go reinforce the Half-Breed Squadron."

Ah. Those pilots must be a part of the Fighting Second. "Glad to have the help."

"What about my magic?" Murray, the one human magician in the squadron, spoke up as he and Tiny turned their aeroplanes to join Fieran and Merrik.

"Only use whatever you have pre-prepared. Don't try to form any new magic." Fieran flexed his fingers on the control stick. Human magic was even more crafted than dwarven magic. Once it was set into place, it was fully separate from the magician. Murray should be able to safely use anything he had stored without risking the machine latching onto the magic within him. "What do you have stored?"

"Mostly water magic for Tiny, but I have a handful of globes with fire magic that I've been saving." Murray dropped back as Tiny surged forward, taking the lead position.

"Good. Use them." Fieran further clamped down on his magic, making sure there was nothing that machine could take. "Lije, Stickyfingers, Merrik, and I are going to strafe that machine and keep them focused on us. The rest of you, hold off the enemy aeroplanes and create a path for Tiny and Murray."

"I'll need a few good tears in the airship's skin." Murray, with Tiny following him, peeled away to join most of Flight B as it formed up higher in the sky. "My fire magic will do more damage if I can get it inside the airship instead of just burning the skin."

The incendiary bombs tossed out by the pilots from Capt Fleetwood's squadron would also do better if they exploded within the airship instead of just against the outer skin.

The first wave of enemy aeroplanes roared down at them Without Fieran's magic, this would be a knock-down, drag-out dogfight pitting the pilots of the Half-Breed Squadron against those of the enemy squadron. No magic. No advantage. Just a blaze of guns and hail of bullets.

As most of Flight B soared upward and clashed with the enemy, Fieran dove his aeroplane to swerve below the airship's gondola. He pressed the trigger lever on the control column when he was still farther out than he normally would. His machine guns spat bullets, the line of them growing closer to the box hanging just below the gondola.

Even when his bullets reached it, they simply pinged off the metal, ricocheting outward. Without magic, he wasn't sure how he could destroy the machine shielded within. Perhaps taking down the airship and letting it crash on top of it would do it, but there was also a chance the machine would remain undamaged.

Since the airship would likely crash on the Mongavarian side of the border, it would mean leaving one of those machines still active. Sure, the Mongavarians might have loads of machines stored up. But he would like to take out as many of them as possible.

Fieran veered away before he got too close to the trailing

wires, releasing the trigger before he wasted too much ammunition.

Behind him, he heard the chatter of Merrik's machine gun as he strafed the machine's shielded box, followed by Lije and Stickyfingers.

A pair of Mongavarian aeroplanes roared around the airship, speeding toward Fieran, their machine guns already blazing.

Fieran juked his aeroplane to the right, letting the aeroplane flip onto its side as it wanted to do thanks to the power of the rotary engine. The bullets whipped past him, just a few clipping his wheels as he peeled away.

He rolled his aeroplane all the way, coming up slightly beneath the other aeroplane. Gripping the trigger, he stitched a line across the enemy's fuselage.

Bullets from Merrik's machine guns tore through the second aeroplane, and then both enemy flyers were tumbling from the sky.

The Half-Breed Squadron might not have Fieran's magic, but these new Defenders were faster and more maneuverable than the Mongavarian aeroplanes. That didn't make this a turkey shoot, but it gave them the edge they needed.

Before the machine guns on the side of the airship could train on him, Fieran turned his roll into a loop so that he could strafe the metal box around the machine again. Perhaps if he aimed a little higher, he could cut one of the power wires running from the box to the rest of the airship.

Merrik flipped around to fall into place as his wingman while Lije and Stickyfingers continued on, heading off another pair of Mongavarian aeroplanes.

Fieran wrapped his fingers around the trigger again, holding it down as he bore down on the trailing wires and airship again. Bullets whipped between the wires, occasionally hitting one and making it swing wildly, before pinging off the metal surrounding the machine.

This wasn't working. He wasn't doing more than scoring the paint. Hopefully the flyboys and flygirls taking on the rest of the enemy aeroplanes were having better luck.

As he turned away, he glanced over his shoulder as Merrik made his run. His bullets, too, did nothing but wiggle wires and scuff paint.

Behind Merrik, the airship's machine gun was trained on Merrik, the gunner peering through the sight. He pressed the trigger, a line of bullets stitching the air, headed for Merrik's unprotected back.

There was no time to warn Merrik. No time to turn his aeroplane to bring his own machine guns to bear. Both Lije and Stickyfingers were well away from the airship, fighting off enemy aeroplanes and too busy to help.

There was nothing for it. Fieran reached deep into his chest and unleashed his magic, not holding back. Gripping the control column with one hand, he reached over his shoulder and blasted out a bolt of magic.

The wires caught his magic, dragging it toward the machine rather than letting it continue its mission onward.

No. Fieran gritted his teeth and poured even more power through the connection, even as bullets punched holes into the nose of Merrik's aeroplane, each one landing closer and closer to where Merrik sat in the cockpit, trying to turn his aeroplane away.

With a yell, Fieran ripped just enough of his magic out of the machine's grasp to slam it into the airship's machine gun. The machine gun exploded, the shrapnel melting against Fieran's magic. "Merrik. Are you all right? Did any of those bullets clip you?"

Merrik peeled his aeroplane away, glancing over his

shoulder. "No. I am fine." His tone sounded almost like he might have muttered a few less-than-proper words before pressing the talk button. "Is your magic caught?"

Fieran tried to draw his magic back but he just…couldn't. That machine was dragging his magic inexorably into it, and the more it drew in, the stronger the pull. He tried to cut off his magic. Release it. Anything. But nothing stopped the pull. All he could do was grit his teeth and yank back, the sensation blooming into a pounding at his temples and a squeezing in his chest. "Yep. Definitely caught."

"You should not have done that." Merrik's scolding voice held a sharp edge. "If you get knocked unconscious…"

"I know." Fieran struggled to breathe past the tearing of his magic inside of him. He felt like his brain was being rope burned as his magic was yanked through his mental fingers. "I couldn't let them kill you. But don't worry. I'm not going to try to overwhelm this thing on my own."

At least, not unless that was the only option to save his squadron. But he suspected that was what Dacha had done with the others, and it had rendered him unconscious.

Hopefully unconscious. Hopefully still alive. Not dead.

Granted, Dacha had taken out a whole line of those machines, likely stretching across a large chunk of the border. Could Fieran overwhelm a single machine with his magic without getting knocked unconscious?

But Dacha had more magic and all the magic stored in the Wall backing him up. Fieran had just himself.

"What's happening?" The question came from several voices. Lije and Stickyfingers peeled away from where they had just taken down the enemy aeroplanes, rushing to help.

"Minor setback. But the plan remains the same. I trust we'll take this airship down before things get too dicey." Fieran's eyes blurred, and he struggled to hold his aeroplane steady. Was it his imagination, or was the magic tugging his aeroplane closer to the airship even as he was trying to fly farther away? "Murray, how's it coming on the fire magic?"

"We've put a few rips in the side, but nothing big enough to risk a throw just yet." Murray's voice was strained. "Fighting has been fierce up here."

"It is one machine." Merrik paused, as if he wasn't sure he wanted to say this next bit. "Perhaps you cannot overwhelm it on your own, but maybe we all can. It likely cannot stand the mixing of multiple magics from several sources all at once."

"No. I will not risk more of us falling unconscious. Better it be just me." Just getting those words out was becoming harder. His magic was slipping from him faster and faster. He didn't have long to debate this before he would be knocked unconscious regardless.

Perhaps he should just give this machine what it wanted. Surely it wouldn't be able to hold up under the full force of the magic of the ancient kings.

"You said you trust the squadron." Merrik's aeroplane drew alongside Fieran's. "So trust us to help."

He wanted to argue. The last thing he wanted to do was give the order that would risk the others.

But he'd learned his lesson in trying to fight this war on his own. His squadron had always been strongest when they fought together.

"All right." Fieran gripped the control column and, with a supreme effort, turned his aeroplane toward the airship once again. "Tiny, tear into the airship with your magic. Try to rip a large hole before your magic gets caught. Merrik, add your magic as well. Lije, Stickyfingers, keep the Mongavarians off our backs."

"I will need to get closer and actually touch one of those

wires." Merrik swerved to take the place ahead of Fieran, bearing down on the airship. "It might take the magic in my aeroplane's power cell while I am at it."

Fieran wanted to argue, but he was gritting his teeth so tightly that he wasn't sure he could form words.

Merrik bore down on the wires trailing below the airship. His machine guns chattered, even as his aeroplane glowed green with his magic.

"Magic incoming," Tiny called through the radio moments before a wave of icy white magic shot through the airship and added to the glow coming from the machine and lighting up the metal surrounding it.

"Yes! Finally!" Murray whooped into the radio. "There's a huge hole in the airship's skin. Fire magic incoming."

"Bombs incoming after that." Fleetwood's pilot seemed to have fallen in with the squadron easily enough, even mimicking their cheerful cadence. "I wouldn't recommend being underneath the airship when all of this explodes."

Fieran muttered cat names under his breath. That was exactly where he and Merrik were going to be when the bombs went off. But they didn't have much of a choice. With both Fieran's and Tiny's magic caught, they couldn't risk that the machine would avoid destruction in the airship's crash.

Merrik dove into the forest of wires, the ends trailing over his aeroplane's wings and fuselage. The green of his magic pulled away from his aeroplane, running along a wire before disappearing into the machine to join the brightness of Fieran's magic. Less than a second later, Merrik's machine gun fell silent.

"Merrik. Merrik!" Fieran shouted into the radio, but there was no response. Merrik's aeroplane must be dead in the air, its propeller spinning only from its own momentum.

There was nothing for it. Fieran dove into the tangle of wire, reaching into his chest and unleashing his magic. He didn't even try to use his machine gun.

The wires gobbled up the magic in his magical power cell, and the chatter of voices on the radio cut off, leaving him in a silence his cockpit hadn't experienced since they'd installed the radios back at Dar Goranth.

And yet he could feel it. There was less strength behind the tug on his magic. The machine glowed brighter, brighter, sparks flying, a high-pitched whine filling the air even over the noise of battle and the clanking of the airship engines.

He gave one last shove with his magic. With a brilliant burst like sunlight, the machine below the aeroplane exploded, sending a shower of shrapnel in all directions. Fragments of metal tore through the tail of Fieran's aeroplane, and he scrambled to blast his magic, now returned to his control, outward to incinerate the shrapnel before it could tear into him or Merrik.

The sheer relief of his magic releasing was heady. He drew in a deep breath, his mind clearing from the painful tearing of a moment before.

With a great *whump*, an explosion detonated somewhere deep inside the airship. Debris lashed outward in a deadly storm of shredded metal. Flames wreathed the ship, tongues of fire licking out of each of the busted windows and holes in the sides. With a groan of metal, the airship began plummeting toward the earth…and toward where Merrik's and Fieran's aeroplanes were gliding, powerless, through the sky.

TWENTY-EIGHT

Pip tried not to throw up as the squad of dwarves charged through the carnage. Here the fighting was more fierce, farther as it was from where King Rharreth and Prince Rhohen provided a shield for the Alliance soldiers with their magic. The Alliance and Mongavarian soldiers struggled in a chaotic melee, without any discernible line between them. Bayonets, knives, and even a few swords flashed in the sunlight, the blades coated with dripping red.

And the bodies. So many bodies. They had to step over them—or step on them when there was nowhere else to go.

She wasn't built for this. She'd gladly keep the aeroplanes flying. She'd take the dangers of bombing. But she couldn't fight like this on the front lines, despite her powerful iron magic.

But right now, she couldn't retreat. She had to get that second machine, then she, Mak, and the dwarves could get out of here.

"We'll have to fight our way to this one." Uncle Thortrad thumped his axe against his shield.

The dwarves, already in their wedge formation, presented their shields and weapons. As they charged forward, they kept up their magical shield, but they didn't use it to shove the fighting soldiers aside as they had before. Instead the dwarven warriors plowed into the fight, their weapons glinting.

Mak wrapped his arm around Pip, and she pressed her face against him. Perhaps it was cowardly to block out the sights like that. The sounds and the smells were bad enough, and she just couldn't keep going forward otherwise.

Trusting her brother to guide her, she simply held her magical shield in place and clung to Mak. He all but carried her in one arm, still gripping the remaining horse's lead with the other.

"The dwarves! Rally to the dwarves!" That voice shouted in Escarlish.

Pip didn't even peek to see what was going on.

"We're here." Mak's voice spoke near her ear as she was set more firmly back on her feet.

Pip peeled her eyes open and found herself only a foot away from the looming side of the wreck of the armored vehicle. If a team of horses had been hooked to it, they were gone now.

Without looking around at the raging battle, she clambered up the side and peered over it.

This machine appeared in better shape than the other one, with fewer melted parts and a stronger sense of lingering magic. If the Mongavarians had gotten this one back, they might have been able to repair it, assuming they could get past the lingering magic of the ancient kings imbued into every piece and part of the machine. At least this second incursion would be worth the trouble.

She ran her magic around and beneath the machine,

severing all the brackets, bolts, and wires holding it in place, as she had the last one.

But this time when she glanced around, the dwarven warriors were locked in battle with Escarlish soldiers interspersed in their ranks. No one would be able to help Mak leverage the machine out of the armored vehicle.

No matter. She'd just use magic instead of brute strength.

Slicing the side of the armor with her magic, she bent it outward so that it formed a flat surface. Placing a small shield between the machine and the far side of the vehicle, she expanded her magic, shoving the machine with the screech of metal on metal.

Mak reached forward and tugged as well. Between the two of them, they hefted the machine onto the flat metal. He strapped it down securely. With a deep breath, she set up another shield dome beneath the flat plate, sliced it free, and lowered it to the ground, where Mak hitched it to the remaining horse.

He gripped the horse's lead but hesitated.

Pip finally forced herself to glance around, her stomach churning. The fighting extended all the way around them with their retreat cut off. The dwarves held an impenetrable line around them, but they were being pressed back into a smaller and smaller circle.

The Escarlish soldiers fought at the edges of their defensive stand. If the dwarves hadn't been here, the Escarlish line would have crumbled long before now under the Mongavarian onslaught on this flank.

Aeroplanes from Flight A swooped down, strafing the Mongavarians, but the enemy machine gunners turned their guns skyward to rake the aeroplanes as they swept past.

Mak began stomping his feet on the ground, calling up his own plant magic. But there wasn't much for wood around, much less live plants here on a battlefield churned up by the Mongavarians' long encampment on this side of the river. A few sprouts poked from the ground and whipped at the feet of attacking soldiers, but it did little to hamper the tide threatening to overwhelm the defenders.

Still holding her main shield above their heads, Pip created smaller shields, shoving knots of Mongavarian soldiers back. But with the Escarlish soldiers so chaotically tangled with the Mongavarians, she couldn't clear more than a small section at a time. As soon as she released one shield, the Mongavarians simply surged back into the space.

"Mak..." Pip shoved more soldiers back with a shield, providing a small respite for the Escarlish soldiers to regroup. "What are we going to do?"

"Fight our way out." Mak gripped the horse's lead with one hand, green magic building over his other palm.

Pip swallowed and hefted her wrench, trying to pretend her hands weren't shaking. If she wanted to live, she had no choice but to do this.

Uncle Thortrad shouted orders, Draenelynn at his right hand. The dwarves took one step, then two, fighting their way back toward the Escarlish border.

Yet more Mongavarians poured in, as if their commanders sensed the weakness of this part of the Alliance line. Machine guns pounded the dwarven shield while larger artillery pounded into the shield Pip held over their heads.

She flinched as three large shells struck at the same time, exploding with such force that her knees nearly buckled beneath her. How much longer could she hold under this bombardment?

To one side of the circle, the dwarves lost their rhythm, their section of the shield falling away. One dwarf cried out, going down, as the enemy machine guns trained on the opening. The dwarves raised their iron shields, bracing their shoulders as the magically reinforced metal deflected most of the hailstorm.

Pip stretched her own magical shield, filling the gap. But not before two more dwarves had been wounded.

They wouldn't hold out much longer. This truly would become a fight to get out. Or perhaps simply a fight to survive.

She risked taking her gaze off the battle long enough to search the skies. But while the aeroplanes of Flight A dove and strafed, risking their own lives to attempt to hold back the Mongavarian charge, there was no familiar warbird wreathed in blue magic.

This time, Fieran wasn't coming.

She swallowed and gripped her wrench with both hands. Then she'd do what she must. Because she really, really wanted to live.

Then an iciness filled her senses a moment before crackling bolts arched over her shield. The icy magic incinerated bullets and swept over the Mongavarian soldiers, burning with intense cold rather than fiery heat.

A force of trolls pounded into the Mongavarians from the side, led by King Rharreth with his sword swinging. Prince Rhohen fought at his side, two swords swinging, his magic unleashed and crackling around them with a power that was in some ways so familiar for its similarities to Fieran's magic and yet so foreign with its undercurrent of ice.

King Rharreth and Prince Rhohen broke through the Mongavarian line to take up position next to Uncle Thortrad and Draenelynn. As they did, Rhohen stepped close to Draenelynn, closer than was really necessary. The two of them shared a look, Rhohen saying something to Draenelynn that Pip couldn't hear above the clamor of battle.

Draenelynn replied with a cheeky grin, a sparkle to her gaze that hadn't been there before.

Were they…attracted to each other? That almost looked like flirting. In the middle of battle.

Pip was going to have to survive so that she could see the look on Fieran's face when she told him she suspected her cousin and his cousin were on their way to courting.

The ground beneath her feet vibrated, a rumble growing louder and louder until it nearly drowned out even the sounds of fighting around her.

Mak had to let her go to grip the horse's lead rope in two hands as the draft horse snorted and danced.

Then a whole line of metal behemoths roared out of the haze of gun smoke, coming from the direction of the Escarlish lines. The trolls parted, giving the tanks a clear path to smash into the enemy.

As the tanks poured through, the trolls fell into the space after them, using the tanks as rolling metal shields to charge deeper into enemy territory.

One of the tanks halted before her and Mak, and the hatch at the top popped open. The head and shoulders of a dwarf, his face hidden by a helmet, came into view. His grin was revealed a moment later when he shucked the helmet. His long brown-blond beard draped down his chest, laced with warrior braids.

Cousin Da'Niel. Another Detmuk cousin, although he wasn't Draenelynn's brother.

Pip waved before she rested a hand on the quivering horse to brace herself.

She was actually going to survive.

THE PRESSURE WAVES of explosions battered Fieran's magic and shoved at his gliding aeroplane. Ahead of him, Merrik's aeroplane jerked and bobbed in the competing air currents, the elevators and ailerons flapping as Merrik fought to keep his biplane steady.

Without their engines propelling them, their momentum wasn't carrying them away fast enough, especially as they lost air speed trying to keep their aeroplanes steady in the battering. Nor could they turn quickly enough to fly at a right angle to the crash. The airship was crashing down right on top of them.

They needed power and fast. The magical power cell was drained, but Fieran had the magic to power it. Could he refill it on the fly? The magical cells didn't take that much magic.

He let a trickle of his magic flow down the control column. Finding the engine wiring, he followed it back to where the magical power cell rested.

He tried to ease his magic into it, but the various dampeners and restrictors that kept the magic of the ancient kings controlled now created a barrier between his magic and the power cell. Without being properly loaded and locked into a refilling machine, he would likely blow it up if he tried to forcibly fill it.

Did he have to actually fill the power cell? He could simply send his magic around the wires to power the engine himself, couldn't he? He'd have to be careful not to burn out the wiring, but he could keep his magic under control.

He let his magic flow the other way, along the wires to flow into the engine. The wires directed his magic around and around, creating magi-magnetism that sent the rotary engine spinning. The more the engine spun, the more it almost seemed to eagerly take in his magic. It wasn't the greedy, relentless pull of that Mongavarian machine, but it was automatic enough that he didn't have to concentrate as much on his magic once he had the process going.

With a whir, his propeller whipped the air again. The radio crackled to life, voices bursting in a cacophony in his ears.

He whooped and dove his aeroplane toward Merrik's. As his aeroplane had power, he overtook Merrik within a second.

Merrik was focused ahead as he struggled with his aeroplane. He flicked a glance at Fieran, then glanced again, his eyes widening.

Fieran swept closer until their aeroplanes were nearly wingtip to wingtip, throttling back so that he was barely more than gliding once again. He stretched out a line of his magic, clamping down on it with a familiarly tight control. Growing up, he'd used his magic in small amounts for something fiddly more often than he'd fully unleashed it.

It was a good thing this was so familiar. A strange, lingering tiredness weighed him down. *This* was what it felt like to have a significant amount of his magic depleted, even if he still had more.

If he was this drained, how much more were Merrik and Tiny? They'd had that machine drawing from them for a shorter amount of time, but they also didn't have the magical reserves that he did.

His magic latched on to the protective wiring surrounding Merrik's aeroplane, eagerly dancing over it as it was designed to do. Fieran had to grit his teeth and shove harder to force his magic to jump from the wire to the aeroplane itself.

Flaming debris clunked against his fuselage. Something larger plummeted straight through Merrik's left wings, punching holes in both the upper and lower wing. Merrik's aeroplane bobbled but he kept it from flipping.

A great shadow fell over Fieran's aeroplane, an intense heat prickling the back of his neck. He didn't dare glance up to see how close the falling body of the airship was.

His magic found one of Merrik's machine guns, and he followed the trigger system down to the solenoid, then back toward the engine.

There. He poured more of his magic into Merrik's engine until it spun, roaring back to life.

As soon as the propeller spun up, Merrik's aeroplane shot forward. Together, the two of them made a dash for clear skies. All around them, fiery debris fluttered through the air, pieces of metal stabbing downward. Dark smoke clouded the sky, choking with the stench of burning fuel, heated steel, and other things that shouldn't be burning.

Then Fieran and Merrik burst into a brighter sky, the air clearing around them. With a groan of twisting metal and the whoosh of flames, the dying airship plummeting past them, far too close behind their tails for comfort.

"Status report." Fieran gripped the control column as he powered both his and Merrik's aeroplanes farther from the wrecked airship.

"Fieran!" The chorus of voices filled the radio, drowning out anything Merrik or Tiny might have said.

"We couldn't reach you on the radio!"

"We thought you were caught by the airship!"

"What happened?"

"Is Merrik all right?"

"We're both fine." Fieran certainly hoped that was the case. When he glanced at the other aeroplane, Merrik's face was even paler than usual, his jaw tight. "That machine took the power from our engines, but it's fine. I'm powering both aeroplanes now. Tiny, Merrik, that machine got a hold of your magic too. How drained are you?"

"Tired, and I shouldn't use any more of my magic, but I can still fly." The sound of Tiny's voice filling the radio eased some of the tightness in Fieran's chest.

"Also tired." Merrik's voice held that tight strain that gave away just how exhausted he was.

"You should return to Fort Defense." Fieran wasn't going to let Merrik and Tiny risk themselves more than they already had.

"I do not think that would do any good." Merrik pointed his aeroplane's nose in that direction. "Look."

Fieran finally took a moment to scan the skies in the distance, his stomach plummeting. Without him holding the border, the Mongavarian aeroplanes had fought their way past Capt. Fleetwood's and Lt. Hadley's squadrons. Plumes of smoke rose from various parts of Fort Defense with a large concentration of the smoke coming from the railyard, dockyard, and warehouse section of the fort complex.

The sight confirmed that Dacha was still unconscious or otherwise out of action. For this battle, Fort Defense had been left without any kind of magical protection.

"Let us finish this." Despite the tiredness from having his magic partially drained, Merrik's voice rang strong and firm over the radio.

When Fieran glanced at him, their gazes met and held. There was an understanding there. The shared sense of determination and brotherhood that had carried them through everything from their first scrapes as children to basic training at Fort Linder and all the battles since.

Merrik nodded once before he flared his wings, slowing his aeroplane just enough to fall back to his usual wingman position. The thread of Fieran's magic still connected their aeroplanes as Fieran kept both of them in the sky.

The rest of Flight B gathered behind them, falling into place to form a large wing of aeroplanes roaring across the sky. Lije and Stickyfingers took up the position at the fore above Merrik and Fieran with Tiny and Murray below. Fieran cast his magic outward, forming the protective net once again.

Below, a wavering line of carnage sprawled across the marsh and mud flats, punctuated by smoke and the flashes of the big artillery guns.

Something twisted tight in Fieran's chest again. He'd sent Pip into that. Where was she? Was she all right?

The sooner he ended this, the sooner he could find out.

Flight B of the Half-Breed Squadron swept across the sky in a blaze of magic, and the aeroplanes of Flight A soared in to join the formation until they were a mighty force of roaring engines and spitting machine guns.

Together, they were Laesornysh, the winds of death that would clear the skies of the enemy.

TWENTY-NINE

As soon as Fieran stepped down from his aeroplane, Pip was there, running toward him. Mud coated her overalls all the way past her knees while something brown and red spattered her green shirt.

But she was here. She was alive. That was all that mattered.

Ignoring his own filthy state, he swept her into his arms, holding her tight to his chest and bending to press kisses to her hair. "I'm so sorry. I never should have volunteered you for that. I'm so sorry."

She clung to him, shaking, her face pressed into his shirt. "It was awful."

He rubbed a hand up and down her back, his own hand shaking. "I'm sorry." The words were so empty compared to what she must have seen and done.

When Pip pulled back, she swiped a hand over her face, the steel returning to her spine and expression. "No, you were right to send me. We got them. Two of those machines. They're already being boxed up to go out on the first train."

Based on the number of fires burning and wreckage piled

up in the trainyard, dockyard, and warehouse section of Fort Defense, who knew how soon that would be. The Mongavarians had gotten in a few good hits before they'd been chased off.

Pip reached up and traced her fingers over the back of his head. "You're hurt. You should see the healer."

Even that light pressure sent a stab of pain through his head. When he touched the same place she had, he felt a knot rising on the back of his skull. Right. He'd hit his head on the bridge in the magical explosion. At least only a few brown flakes of dried blood showed on his fingers. Any bleeding had stopped.

He wasn't seeing double nor was he dizzy. His head ached a bit, but it was nothing he couldn't ignore.

"I doubt they have healers to spare for something this mild." Fieran lowered his hand. He'd seen the line of trucks unloading both at the field hospital at the base of the bluff and the main hospital on top of it. The healers would have their magic stretched thin.

"Still, you could have a head injury. You should at least get checked by someone." Pip stepped farther out of his arms and plucked at his shirt, her fussing the frantic, frazzled kind, as if she fussed because it was that or break with the horror of the day. "And you really need to get cleaned up."

Even as he stood there, he grew all the more aware of the deep chill in his bones, the aching in his head, and the sheer exhaustion in his limbs. Dried blood—none of it his except that on his head—spattered him from head to toe from the hand-to-hand battle wielding his dacha's swords. All he wanted to do was take a scalding hot shower, then collapse into his cot to sleep.

But he had far too many people and things to see to.

"Maybe in a while. I need to check on my dacha." He rested his hands on her shoulders, not ready yet to let her go. "You should clean up and get some rest too."

She looked away, that wide-eyed, haunted look returning. "Not yet. I should see to the aeroplanes. Some of them were shot up pretty badly."

Right. He winced, then winced again when the movement sent another stab of pain through his head. "Start with Merrik's, then mine. We had the magic yanked out of our magical power cells, then I kept us flying by powering the engines directly. I'm pretty sure I fried the guts out of the engines."

"But neither of you crashed." Pip's voice was tight, going softer. "That's the important thing. Engines can be replaced."

"And I know just the mechanic for the job." He lightly cradled her chin before he bent and kissed her. He didn't linger, pulling back a moment later. "I'll be back soon."

Pip stepped all the way from his arms this time. When she met his gaze, her dark brown eyes had softened, the edge gone. "I'm sure your dacha is all right."

Fieran nodded, but he couldn't agree. He'd struggled to overpower just one of those machines. But Dacha had taken out who knew how many of them.

The two of them strode toward the hangar, and as soon as they were inside, Pip veered off, heading for her tools.

Fieran crossed the hangar to where Merrik was settling into his wheelchair, a grimace on his face. "How are you holding up?"

"Tired." Merrik massaged his leg above the prosthetic, lines of weariness etched around his eyes and mouth. He tugged up his pant leg and revealed the neat bullet hole through the wood of his prosthetic ankle. "It seems the war really has it out for my right leg."

Fieran swallowed, a shaken kind of sickness filling him. He hadn't realized that machine gun had gotten that close to Merrik before Fieran had managed to blow it up.

He'd nearly lost all of them that day. Pip. Merrik. Dacha.

If he'd had the luxury of breaking, he might have done it right then and there. Instead, he rested his hand on Merrik's shoulder, resisting the urge to prop himself up. "Get some rest."

"Your dacha…"

"Is likely in no shape to want lots of people around." Fieran sighed and scrubbed a hand over his face. "If you get some sleep now, you'll be more awake later today when both of us will need you there."

Merrik nodded, but the lines in his face didn't ease.

Fieran turned and forced his aching legs to move from a trudge to a jog. He dashed through the hangar, waving at Lije, Stickyfingers, Tiny, Lt. Rothilion, and the others as he passed without stopping to talk, and exited on the far side. After crossing the dirt road and making his way through the tents, he reached the small rise overlooking the headquarters section.

In front of the hospital, stretchers waited in haphazard rows to be taken inside to see the healers while clusters of men and women, covered in blood and dirt, sat or lay on the ground. Some cried out in pain. Others were too still, too silent.

Fieran would just have to sleep off his own aches and pains. The healers had their hands full.

Across the way, the elven officer quarters appeared to be undamaged, as was the main headquarters building. A few wisps of smoke still curled from the Escarlish officer quarters, but even that fire had been contained. The second wave of attacks while Fieran had been busy with the airship must have concentrated on the railyard rather than up here.

Fieran hurried across the open space, his breathing tight in his chest and not just from his panting. He stumbled to a halt before the door, gasping for breath, as he took in Uncle Iyrinder standing in his usual spot. "Dacha...is he..."

"He is resting." Uncle Iyrinder stepped aside, indicating the door. But he didn't fully move out of Fieran's way, his gaze searching Fieran's face. "Merrik?"

"Tired but fine. I told him to get some sleep." Fieran would leave it up to Merrik whether he wanted to tell his dacha how close it had been.

"Linshi." Uncle Iyrinder's posture eased as he briefly clasped Fieran's shoulder.

Fieran ducked past him and hurried inside, only just managing to shut the door quietly instead of accidentally slamming it.

The outer room with its table in the center, desk to one side beneath the window, and cushioned bench along the other side was empty. The table was missing both of its chairs while the door leading to the bedchamber was only open a few inches, preventing him from seeing inside. "Dacha?"

"Come in, nirshon." Uncle Weylind's voice called out just as softly as Fieran had.

Uncle Weylind was still here. Fieran's heart lurched again as he crept across the room and pushed the door. It swung without a creak.

Dacha lay on the narrow bed against the wall, his chest rising and falling in a slow, steady rhythm, his eyes closed. His face was turned away from Fieran while his hair was a cascade of silver-blond over the pillow. Someone had washed away all the mud, or perhaps Dacha had woken at some point long enough to do it himself. His swords leaned against the wall beside the small table, cleaned of blood.

Uncle Weylind sat in a chair at the foot of the bed, stacks of paperwork arranged neatly on top of the blanket over Dacha's legs. A lap desk rested on Uncle Weylind's knees, and he scrawled his signature on a piece of paper with a pen before he added the paper to one of the stacks. He glanced up long enough to indicate the empty chair beside the head of the bed.

Fieran slid into it. His memories after his crash were hazy, but this moment was all too familiar. Only a few weeks ago, that had been him on the bed with Dacha in this chair, waiting for him to wake. Uncle Weylind had been in that chair at the foot of the bed both times.

"What's wrong with him?" Fieran crossed his arms, then uncrossed them to rest his hands at his sides. But that didn't feel natural either.

Uncle Weylind sighed, set down his pen, and met Fieran's gaze. "Beyond the magical backlash, he was nearly drained of his magic."

Dacha was…what? That wasn't possible. Dacha had the highest levels of magic of any living person. He couldn't be *drained*.

But there he lay on the bed, even paler than usual, still sleeping even with Uncle Weylind and Fieran talking right next to him.

And Fieran had the evidence of his own depleted magic. One machine had drained enough for him to actually feel the loss—even if he still had plenty left. How many of those machines had Dacha faced? From the sky, there was no sign of the Wall as far as Fieran could see along the Mongavarian-Escarlish border.

"But other elves use their magic close to their limits, and

they don't end up…like this…" Fieran gestured toward Dacha. He'd seen Merrik and Uncle Iyrinder get tired a time or two when they used too much of their magic. But never Dacha.

"Your dacha has never gotten this close to the limit of his magic before." Uncle Weylind's gaze rested on Dacha, his eyes filled with a weight as if remembering other battles, others times Dacha had used great quantities of his magic. "I suspect the sudden draining was more of a shock to his system than it would have been to another elf since his body is used to an abundance of magic."

Fieran lifted a hand, letting just a hint of his magic twine around his fingers. "Is there something I can do? I have his magic."

"No, nirshon." Uncle Weylind shook his head, the grooves around his mouth and in his forehead deepening. "You have the same type of magic, but it is still your magic. It cannot be transfused into him like blood. If he needs more magic, your macha will sense it. She will see to it that the magic stored in their elishina is returned to him."

Right. That made sense. Dacha always kept a great deal of magic in the heart bond he and Mama shared, and he wouldn't have touched it during the battle—not even when trying to overwhelm those machines. Mama would look after Dacha.

Still, Fieran didn't like sitting there, helpless to do anything.

"He will be fine with rest, nirshon." Uncle Weylind picked up his pen again, although he didn't start on his paperwork right away. "His magic will replenish. He merely needs sleep."

The reassurance only helped so much while Dacha lay

there, too still, too pale. The memories of him lying limp in the mud of the battlefield still played in Fieran's head.

Dacha stirred, his breaths hitching. He didn't make noise or lurch awake. Instead, he tilted his head, his eyelids cracking open as if even that much was a great effort.

"Dacha." Fieran still wasn't sure what to do with his hands. He settled for resting a hand on Dacha's shoulder, giving a squeeze much as Dacha had done for him when he'd been the one on that bed.

Dacha's gaze swung from Uncle Weylind up to Fieran. "F...Fieran..." The name was a slurred whisper.

"I'm here, Dacha." Fieran glanced around. Should he offer him water? Fetch food? Just sit there? He didn't know.

"Heard...fought well..." Dacha's hand twitched. Perhaps he meant to indicate the swords leaning against the wall.

That answered one question. Dacha must have been awake at least once to have been told what Fieran had done.

Fieran swallowed and nodded. "You taught me well."

Dacha shifted a fraction, grimacing. When he spoke, his voice had strengthened somewhat. "I have...one last lesson to teach. But I had not...learned it myself yet. Do not...drain your magic. It is...uncomfortable."

"You mean inadvisable and something you will not do again." Uncle Weylind shot Dacha a stern look over his paperwork.

Dacha didn't do anything as immature as stick out his tongue at his older brother, but the look he gave Uncle Weylind in return was almost the same thing. "I cannot promise."

Uncle Weylind huffed and scratched a line through something on the page with more vigor than the action warranted. Once done, he added that paper to a different stack than he had the signed one.

"Are you using me as a desk?" Dacha's nose wrinkled slightly as he peered down at the papers arranged on the blanket.

"Yes." Uncle Weylind wrote something on another paper and added it to a third stack. "Do not move, otherwise you will mess up my organization."

Fieran further relaxed against the back of his chair at his dacha's and uncle's banter. Surely if Dacha was awake enough to joke, then he was going to be all right.

Dacha tilted his head toward Fieran again. "Call your macha. Tell her…" Dacha's hand twitched again as his eyes fell closed. "She knows."

"You can use the telephone in my office." Uncle Weylind spoke without looking up from his paperwork. "But take the time to wash first. The telephone lines will be busy for a while yet."

He must be a sight if his uncle was not-so-subtly nudging him toward showering.

"Yes. Shower." Dacha flapped a hand at him as well, his eyes still closed. "It will help."

Well, Fieran could tell when he'd been dismissed. He pushed to his feet, turning for the door.

"And you, shashon." Uncle Weylind's voice turned that teasingly stern tone once again. "You need to rest."

"Not tired." Dacha's voice was slurred.

"If you are not tired, then you can assist me with my paperwork."

"I will rest."

"I thought so."

Fieran couldn't help a smile as he eased the door mostly closed behind him.

After a shower that was longer than army regulations allowed—where he scrubbed and scrubbed and pretended he'd cleansed the feel of blood and death from his skin—Fieran made his way to the headquarters building. The MPs let him enter once they saw his identification.

Inside, a chaotic bustle still reigned, with aides, adjutants, secretaries, and army officers hustling to and fro, reporting to this general or that.

Another set of MPs halted him. "State your business."

"I'm Capt. Fieran Laesornysh. My uncle King Weylind of Tarenhiel told me to use the telephone in his office to call my mother, Princess Elspeth." If ever there was a time for name-dropping, this was it.

The MPs straightened at all that royalty in a single sentence. But they didn't shift aside until Uncle Julien called from somewhere just out of sight, "Let him through."

"Thanks, Uncle Julien," Fieran called back as the MPs jumped out of his way.

Uncle Julien stepped out of one of the nearby rooms, dark shadows beneath his eyes. He pointed down the hall to Fieran's right. "Weylind's office is all the way at the end and to your left."

Fieran waved to Uncle Julien before he set off down the hall. Even if elves weren't drifting between the rooms, he would've been able to tell he was now in the elven section since the noise almost instantly faded into a more subdued murmur.

At the end, he turned into the room on the left. A large desk took up most of the space, a few neat stacks of paperwork waiting on it. Windows set high in the wall brightened the room while a smaller desk sat beneath the black telephone mounted to the wall.

Fieran took a seat at the smaller desk, picked up the

earpiece, and jiggled the lever to call the operator. Within a few moments, he'd given the direction for Treehaven. The operators along the route didn't seem at all surprised. Then again, given how often Dacha had likely been calling home, they were well practiced at connecting Fort Defense with Treehaven House.

A few minutes later, Mama's worried voice filled the line beneath the static. "Weylind?"

"It's me. Fieran." Fieran rested his elbows on the desk, hunching forward as a lump clogged his throat. He didn't know how to go about telling her what had happened.

"Fieran." His name was a breath of relief, and he could picture the way her shoulders slumped.

"Dacha...he..." Fieran's throat closed. He couldn't manage to say it.

"I know." Mama's voice had steadied, her tone that comforting one he knew so well from childhood. "He's going to be all right. He just needs sleep."

Fieran nodded, even though Mama wouldn't be able to see the gesture. But for a moment, he couldn't respond.

He'd thought Dacha had been sending him to call Mama to comfort her. But perhaps this telephone call had been for Fieran's sake as much as for hers.

"What happened?" she asked quietly, a gentle prompt.

"There was this machine. Lots of them." Fieran found himself pouring the story out to her, barely checking himself before he said anything out loud that shouldn't be shared over a telephone, even a secure line like this one.

Such as the fact that Pip had retrieved two of those machines. The Mongavarians likely knew that the Alliance had gotten their hands on them, but there was always a chance that had been obscured by the chaos of battle. They certainly shouldn't be informed that the machines would soon be heading to Aldon by train to be studied by Uncle Lance, Louise, and other top mechanics, magicians, and magical engineers.

As he was finishing up, a new voice broke into the line. "My apologies, Your Highness, Captain. But there is an urgent telephone call for His Majesty that must be put through. I will need to ask you to hang up."

"Yes, of course." Mama's tone didn't waver. "Thank you for calling, Fieran."

After exchanging hurried goodbyes, Fieran hung up the earpiece. As he stood, he grew aware of the noise in the hall. Something bad was going down if Uncle Averett needed to be informed.

Jumping to his feet, Fieran hurried from the room and down the hall, dodging the various elves who were also hurrying about their duties. As he entered the central section of headquarters, the bustle and voices grew louder, although he couldn't pick out exactly what was happening.

He didn't see Uncle Julien, although he could just hear the timbre of his voice coming from behind a closed door on his right.

Fieran caught one of the aides bustling nearby. "What's happening? Has Mongavaria attacked again?"

Should Fieran rush to his aeroplane? Or rush to the front to wield his magic on the ground alongside Uncle Rharreth and Rhohen?

The aide turned to Fieran. "The king's great-grandson Lt. Myles Kinsley has been found dead in the rubble of the railyard."

Someone called a name, and the aide jumped, turning away from Fieran. "Coming, sir!"

Fieran stumbled forward and braced himself with a hand

against the wall. He squeezed his eyes shut as the words shuddered through him. Myles? Dead?

Myles. Always ready with a grin. One of the few cousins on that side of the family who actually had a good head on his shoulders. So eager to do his part for the war.

He couldn't be dead. He simply couldn't.

Yet war didn't discriminate. It didn't care how famous or well-connected a person was. It didn't care about one's last name or lineage.

Death could come for Fieran. For his dacha. For his family. As long as this war continued, it stalked them.

Even Dacha with his great power could not prevent it.

S wiping at the tears trickling down her face, Pip found Fieran sitting with his back to the wall in a tucked-away corner of the hangar.

Not giving herself time to hesitate, she curled up on his lap, tucking her head against his shoulder beneath his chin as she wrapped her arms around him. "I heard. I'm so sorry."

Fieran's arms came around her, holding her close, and he pressed his face against her hair. His voice was hoarse, choked with tears and an angry fervor. "I hate this war. I hate it. I just want it to end."

"I know. Me too." Pip tangled her fingers in the warmth of his shirt and didn't try to hold back her tears.

First Fieran and Merrik crashed. Then they'd lost Pretty Face. Fieran's dacha had come far too close to death that day.

And now Myles.

It was too much. Too much death. Too much pain. How much more would this war take before it was over?

She cried into Fieran's shirt, and if his chest shuddered

with his own sobs, she couldn't fault him. Today was a day for breaking.

She wasn't sure how much time passed before she sniffed and hiccupped her way to silence. Held by Fieran as she was, she was warm and cozy, even if her eyes were now gritty, her nose stuffed.

"I should have asked before now, but are you all right?" Fieran murmured the words into her hair as he cradled her to his chest.

Was she all right? She squeezed her eyes shut, trying not to remember the things she'd witnessed that day.

"Maybe." No, that wasn't quite right. She was shaken, yes. She now had memories she wished she could erase. But she couldn't regret it. She'd done what she'd had to do. "I think so."

The Alliance had needed those machines, and no one besides her could have gotten them from the battlefield that quickly. The dwarves might have been able to handle it on their own, but their magic would have taken more time and more tools than hers did. Some of them likely would have died in the attempt.

Those machines had knocked *Prince Farrendel Laesornysh* unconscious and forced Fieran to fight that airship instead of guarding Fort Defense. Because of that, Mongavarian aeroplanes had bombed Fort Defense, killing Myles. If fetching those two machines for study could prevent such a thing from happening again, then her churning stomach and weighted soul would be worth it.

"I'm sorry." Fieran's hand traced up her back to cradle the back of her head.

"You already said that." Her scalp tingled at his touch, the tingles spreading down her spine. That felt rather good. Her tense muscles relaxed further. "And you don't have to apologize. I was the only choice, and I don't regret going. I got the job done."

"I knew you would." His voice was rough, but the pride in his tone settled deep in her chest.

And she loved him for it. He was both capable himself and yet treated her with respect for her own capabilities.

This was what she'd been searching for when she'd left home to join the army mechanics. Not a place merely to use her skills. Not even just respect for those skills since her family already gave her that.

But this place of belonging. This home that wasn't the home of her childhood but one she created for herself.

She didn't know how long this war would last or how much it would demand of her and Fieran before it was over. But she was certain of him. She knew where her heart lay.

Sitting up, she cradled his face, taking in his damp lashes, the redness surrounding his piercing blue eyes, the bleakness in his gaze. "We're going to be okay, Fieran. No matter what happens, we are going to be okay."

Then she kissed him. The kiss was too filled with need, too desperate with the memories of that day, but she didn't care. She simply needed him, as she could tell he needed her.

When he pulled back, he leaned his forehead against hers, their breathing ragged between them. But a hint of a smile curved his lips. "Yes. We're going to be okay."

It was so tempting to remain there, held in his arms where they could ignore the war and the weight of their responsibilities.

But they couldn't.

She clambered to her feet before she held out a hand to Fieran. "Go check on your dacha again. I'll fetch supper and bring it there."

Terrifying as it would be to dine in the quarters of *Prince*

Farrendel Laesornysh, she could handle it. Her fear-awe of Fieran's dacha didn't seem so scary after what she'd been through that day.

She'd faced battle. She'd face Fieran's dacha too. Because she was going to fight for Fieran, whether that meant fighting Mongavarian soldiers or fighting her own fears of his famous family.

She would fight. For Fieran. For the flyboys and flygirls of the Half-Breed Squadron. For the Alliance.

And, together, they might stand a chance.

THIS TIME when Fieran approached his dacha's quarters, Uncle Iyrinder and a cordon of Uncle Weylind's guards were arrayed before the door, holding off the swarm of elves, humans, and even trolls who were asking to see King Weylind.

Fieran pushed past them, nodded to Uncle Iyrinder, and slipped inside. When he entered the bedchamber, Uncle Weylind was already packing up his paperwork.

Rising, Uncle Weylind tucked the paperwork into a leather bag, gripping the wooden lap desk under one arm. "Are you able to stay for a while, nirshon? I am needed elsewhere."

"Yes, I can stay." Fieran sank onto the seat by the head of the bed. Dacha lay in nearly the same position as he'd been when Fieran had left several hours ago. Yet his chest rose and fell just as steadily, and his color was better than it had been.

Even as Uncle Weylind left, Fieran reached for Dacha's swords. The cleaning cloth hung from one of the hilts and the tin of oil rested on the shelf of the table beside the bed.

As a peaceful quiet settled over the room, he set to work polishing the swords, the movements practiced and familiar, even if he'd never cleaned this particular pair of swords before.

But seeing to them was the least he could do after wielding them in battle earlier that day. He ran the polishing cloth down each side of the blade. Back and forth in steady motions, the glide of the cloth on steel strangely soothing.

As he was finishing the second sword, there was a knock on the outer door before it swung open with a stirring of the air and Pip's voice calling softly, "We brought food."

He sheathed the swords, leaned them against the wall, wiped his hands free of the oil as best he could on clean sections of the rag, and stood.

Dacha still slept, not even stirring at the noise. But he was sleeping easily and would probably enjoy being left in peace instead of Uncle Weylind or Fieran hovering.

Grabbing his chair, Fieran pushed open the door between the rooms, hauling the chair after him.

In the main room, Pip had set a tray on the table and was busy setting out the plates and silverware. In the doorway, Merrik stood, talking quietly with his dacha, another tray in his hands.

Fieran set the chair beside the table. After fetching the second chair and closing the door between the rooms, he and Pip picked up the table and moved it closer to the cushioned bench so that there would be enough seats for all of them.

Uncle Iyrinder claimed one of the bowls and spoons from Merrik's tray before he turned to face outward again, eating while standing guard. Then Merrik strode inside, his gait hitching in that way that betrayed how much his foot and ankle were hurting. Nor was he using his magic to make his prosthetic move more smoothly.

But he was walking, even after the strain of the day. His body was healing and adjusting.

After setting the tray on the table, Merrik sank onto the cushioned bench with a sigh. He turned sideways so that he could prop his feet up. "So, Pip, has Fieran told you about the time he dragged me out of a tree?"

"Yes." Pip perched on a chair, a grin helping to dispel some of the weight in her eyes. "Pointed out the exact tree and everything while we were at Treehaven."

"It wasn't my fault you tried to catch me when I fell." Fieran took the other chair, reaching a hand to Pip. She clasped it beneath the table. "Nor that you didn't let go as I was dragging you down."

"I told you not to climb that high." Merrik shook his head as he helped himself to the food.

Fieran hadn't listened to Merrik, and look where that had gotten the two of them. The broken arms when they'd been children had been bad enough. But Merrik was still paying for Fieran's recklessness.

Fieran held Merrik's gaze. "I'm sorry for that. And the broken arm you got out of the deal."

Merrik huffed and tossed one of the rolls at Fieran. "I did not tell you that to make you apologize. Now, eat."

Fieran caught the roll. As it was several days old, it was plenty hard, smacking into his palm. "The rest did you good, I see."

Pip had retrieved some of the mystery meat and was struggling to cut it with one hand, her other hand still gripping his. "Then the two of you had better come up with a funnier story than that. I'm sure you have them."

"Have I told you about our old tradition of spit handshakes?" Fieran grinned as he set the roll on his plate and reached to dish out some of the mystery meat.

"*Old* tradition? That implies it has been years since we last employed it." Merrik grimaced, nose wrinkling, before he took a bite.

"Hey, you were the last one to initiate it. I was the very mature one who said we should make that the last one." Fieran waggled his fork in Merrik's direction.

"I was the first one to say we were too old for such things." Merrik shook his head, his long chestnut hair flowing over his shoulders.

Pip glanced between the two of them, her fork paused halfway to her mouth. "Spit handshakes? Do I want to know?" She gave a little tug on the hand clasping his under the table, as if reconsidering whether she dared hold his hand if he went about performing such unsanitary handshakes all the time.

"It was inspired by a book we read about an elf and a human pledging eternal brotherhood during a time of war." Fieran leaned forward, trying to sound dramatic.

"The spit seemed like the safer option than stealing knives from our parents and slicing our palms to seal our pledge with blood." Merrik pointed his knife at Fieran before he used it to saw at the mystery meat. "One time you actually did listen to sense."

"I'd had the same *knives and swords are weapons, not toys* speech I'm sure you had." Fieran gave an exaggerated shudder. "I didn't want to find out what my parents would have done if I disobeyed their orders not to touch without permission."

Pip nudged him with her elbow. "What did I tell you? Little rebellions, not big ones."

Merrik tilted his head back and laughed. A genuine, full-on laugh like Fieran hadn't heard since the crash. "I would call it accidentally rebellious, at least when we were children."

"Yes! That's it exactly." Pip gestured to Merrik, grinning.

"So glad you're ganging up on me," Fieran grumbled, though there wasn't any heat to the words.

He hadn't known how much he'd needed this. But perhaps Pip had guessed, if she'd been the one to round up Merrik and bring him along.

It was a glimpse of what things might be like, someday when the war was over. When Fieran was married to Pip.

Except Adry might be there too, and as much as Fieran would like to think his sister would take his side, he had a feeling she'd join with Merrik and Pip so that all three would gang up on him.

Oh, well. He usually deserved it.

The three of them talked and laughed and ate, trying not to snort food out their noses when a particularly funny story was told at an inopportune time.

Just as Fieran was getting to the punch line of a particularly embarrassing story about the time he'd decided skinny dipping at the lake at the elven summer palace of Lethorel during the annual large family gathering was a good idea—he'd only just learned how to swim and he didn't know where Mama had packed his swim trunks—there was just the slightest noise behind him.

Dacha's voice, grumpy and sleep-befuddled, came from the doorway to the other room. "You are being loud. You woke me up."

Fieran sprang to his feet so quickly his chair toppled over. He whirled just in time to see the way his dacha winced at the sharp crack of the chair hitting the wooden floor.

"Dacha! You're awake. Here, take my seat." Hurrying to right the chair, Fieran gestured at it. "You should eat. Not the meat. It's questionable. But the beans are okay. At least, I think they're beans. It's hard to tell. The rolls are a bit stale, but they're fine if you don't mind extra chewing."

"Sason." Dacha rubbed at his temple as he sank onto the offered seat. "Just…stop talking."

"Right. Sorry." Fieran clamped his mouth shut. He wasn't sure what to do.

In the other chair, Pip had frozen, her eyes wide. Dacha's grumpiness probably wasn't helping anything.

Merrik slid off the bench. "We will leave you to eat and rest, Uncle Farrendel."

Fieran grabbed Pip's hand and tugged her from the chair. Together, the three of them beat a hasty retreat, abandoning their dirty dishes for someone else to take care of.

As they stepped outside, Uncle Iyrinder glanced from them to Dacha through the open doorway. He waved to Fieran. "I will look after him for the rest of the night. Get some sleep."

"Linshi." Fieran took the excuse to continue their retreat.

None of them spoke until they were in the clear section of land between the headquarters section and the hangar.

Then Pip covered her face with her hands. "Is your dacha actually mad at us?"

"No." Fieran shook his head, letting out his pent-up breath with a whoosh. "At least, he won't be once he has slept some more."

"Ugh. That was still embarrassing." Pip shook her head, still covering her face.

"That was hardly the first time Fieran has woken his dacha by being too loud." Merrik nudged Pip, the gesture sending her side-stepping closer to Fieran.

Fieran shook his head before a weary chuckle rose in his chest as he wrapped an arm around Pip's shoulders. "Not by a long shot. He is used to me being too loud."

Too loud. Too human. Too much.

But, no, that wasn't quite the truth. He was also too elven. Too energetic. With too much magical power.

He was Laescrnysh. More, he was simply himself. Both human and elven. Short hair and pointed ears. Loud human laugh and powerful elven magic. He would sell himself short if he tried too hard to be fully one or fully the other. He was only whole when he was both.

Merrik shook his head before he set off up the rise toward their tents. "We should follow my dacha's order and your dacha's example and rest. We will likely have another long day tomorrow."

That they would. Even now, the artillery guns boomed despite the gathering darkness, a night made all the darker because it lacked the Wall's comforting blue glow on the horizon for the first night since this war began.

He couldn't go back to a time when he didn't know what it was to take a life. When Merrik had two legs. When his cousin Myles was alive and their kingdom wasn't in a fight for its existence.

There was only going forward, growing and changing and hopefully becoming a better person by the end of it.

THIRTY-ONE

Fieran guided his aeroplane in a sweep over the series of trenchworks forming the new Mongavarian-Escarlish front lines, Merrik shadowing his movements. Puffs of smoke from the artillery guns marked the continued barrage, but the main fighting had died down as both sides sought to regroup and dig in.

The Alliance still held a toehold within Mongavaria and, unlike previous raids across the border, this time they intended to keep it. The first phase of attrition had ended. Now the long slog to battle Mongavaria into the ground had begun.

As Fieran flew farther south, the winking of sunlight on a huge, flat expanse of water spread out below. Winderdon Lake was tucked on the Mongavarian side of the Whitehurst Mountains. It had been the headwaters of the Chibo River, but now a massive landslide—most of the top of one of the mountains—blocked that end of the lake.

Instead, the lake flooded the plains to the east, inundating what had once been fertile farm fields and homesteads. Fieran could only hope the Mongavarians had moved their people out of the way before they'd purposely flooded their homes and fields.

All that effort, and Mongavaria hadn't even secured their objective. While there were a few passes through the Whitehurst Mountains and fighting was currently fierce there from what Fieran had heard, the flatland where Fort Defense stood was the best—and perhaps only—place to bring a large mechanized army into Escarland.

It had been Mongavaria's bad luck that they hadn't added Rhohen into their calculations. They'd sent machines to counter Dacha, another one to take out Fieran, but the Alliance had had a third warrior with the magic of the ancient kings to stem the invasion before it could cross the border.

Nor had the enemy counted on the strength of the magic of the ancient kings. Even with all those machines leveled against him and the Wall, Dacha hadn't been fully drained, and only the Wall between Mongavaria and Escarland had gone down. The rest of the Wall along Escarland's, Tarenhiel's, and Kostaria's other borders remained.

Turning back to the north, Fieran flew his patrol route back toward Fort Defense. He waggled his wings as he passed one of the Alliance airships also patrolling the sky over Fort Defense.

The fort itself had been mostly set to rights in the day that had passed since the battle. The trainyard was functioning again, even though piles of rubble still piled against and within the damaged structures.

Even as he flew over the trainyard, a train was parked at the station, and crates upon crates of weapons and ammunition were being loaded on trucks to be hauled to the various warehouses. A few rudimentary armored vehicles rolled off flatbeds, although they weren't as sophisticated as the dwarven-built tanks. It seemed the Alliance had also been developing such weapons for mechanized warfare, stockpiling them for the day when they took the fight to Mongavaria.

Mongavaria had moved that day up by a month or so by taking down the Wall, but that changed little in the Alliance's strategy. The time to attack was now.

Fieran passed Lije and Stickyfingers as they piloted their aeroplanes higher into the sky to take up the patrol. Waving to them, Fieran lined up on the airfield, bleeding off air speed as he came in for a landing.

Once he and Merrik had landed, both of them climbed out of their aeroplanes. As it was a short flight, Merrik wasn't limping since his leg hadn't stiffened and his stump hadn't swollen.

When they stepped into the hangar, Colonel Dentley was waiting near where Fieran's aeroplane was usually parked.

"Sir." Fieran came to attention, Merrik beside him.

"The recent battle made it clear that a more coordinated effort is needed in the sky." Colonel Dentley strode closer, a weariness in his gaze. "Capt. Fleetwood and Capt. Hadley both agree that you're the best man for the job."

Capt. Hadley. He must have been given a field promotion. Or his official promotion had finally gone through.

"Sir?" Fieran didn't shift, but he wasn't quite sure where Colonel Dentley was going with this.

"I'm giving you a field promotion and I've put in the paperwork to make it official. Congratulations, Maj. Laesornysh." With that, Colonel Dentley spun and marched away.

For a moment, all Fieran could do was stand there, blinking. That was abrupt. Perfunctory, even.

But that was the way of things now. They were at war,

fighting to keep Mongavaria from setting foot on their soil. There wasn't time for elaborate ceremonies and speeches.

Merrik clapped him on the back. And that was that.

FIERAN STOOD NEXT TO DACHA, his hand and arm raised in a solemn salute as the honor guard carried casket after flag-draped casket down the road between two lines of saluting soldiers and onto the waiting train.

Dark circles still smudged beneath Dacha's eyes, but he was out of bed, and he was standing. That was all Fieran could ask for at the moment.

Somewhere on that train, the two crates holding the machines Pip had retrieved had already been stowed and even now were under guard for their trip to Aldon. Hopefully they would have answers soon.

The very last casket had a royal red-and-white sash draped over the Escarlish flag.

Fieran's throat squeezed, but his hand didn't wobble as the soldiers carried his cousin past. He murmured so that only Dacha could hear, "We need to end this war."

"We will, sasor." Dacha's gaze remained locked on the casket. "We will."

With the final casket gone, Dacha, then Fieran lowered their hands. Dacha glanced at Uncle Weylind, who stood on the other side of him. "I should be there for him."

"Your duty is here. Averett understands that." Uncle Weylind clasped Dacha's shoulder before he stepped out of line and joined the end of the procession climbing onto the train.

Uncle Julien took Uncle Weylind's spot next to Dacha and, when he spoke, his voice was low and choked. "I know.

I wish I could go as well. He was under my command, and I...I sent him there."

Dacha rested a hand on Uncle Julien's shoulder, and Uncle Julien matched the gesture, the two of them bolstering each other with their presence.

Fieran swallowed and looked away, staring at the train as the large rolling doors were closed.

Despite the fact that a royal prince of Escarland had been killed, Dacha, Fieran, Uncle Julien, Aunt Vriska, Uncle Rharreth, and Rhohen were all staying here to continue the war. Uncle Weylind had been the only one who could be spared.

With a mournful whistle, the train chugged away from the platform, heading for Aldon. As soon as it was out of sight, the soldiers and officers forming the two lines began to disperse, everyone heading back to the demanding duties of war.

Uncle Julien released Dacha's shoulder before he, too, straightened and strode away with several adjutants and aides flocking to him. He was once again the general with a war to win rather than an uncle grieving how he'd gotten his great-grandnephew killed.

Pip appeared at Fieran's other side from where she had been waiting farther back and took his hand, leaning her head against his shoulder. A few tears tracked down her face, but she wasn't openly sobbing.

Merrik and Uncle Iyrinder joined them as well, the five of them remaining at the station even as nearly everyone else left. With every second that passed, Merrik grew more fidgety, shifting and unable to stand still in a way that was more Fieran's mode than Merrik's.

Within a few minutes, another train glided toward the platform from where it had been likely waiting on a siding for the other train to leave. This one was one of the trains modified to run on both Escarlish rails and Tarenhieli roots, and it settled into place at the station much more quietly than the other train had departed.

No sooner had the train halted than the door of the first train car opened. A tall young woman with pointed elven ears, long red-gold hair, and blue eyes the same color as Fieran's strode onto the platform, the hilts of her swords winking in the morning sunlight.

Adry.

Fieran took a step forward, but his dacha's arm shot out, holding him back. When he glanced at his dacha, Dacha gave one slight shake of his head.

Fieran felt it as an almost physical thing. The shifting as he and Dacha took a metaphorical step back, ceding the place of being the first to greet her.

Instead, Merrik was the one who dashed forward, grinning broadly, his eyes gleaming as he launched himself up the steps.

"Merrik!" Adry flung herself into his arms, and he swept her up with an abandon Fieran had never seen from Merrik before.

And then…Fieran yanked his gaze up to the sky. They were kissing. His best friend and his sister were kissing. Right in front of him. In front of everyone.

His ears were burning, and when he risked a peek at Dacha, his ears were flushed as pink as Fieran's probably were.

Pip gave a tug on Fieran's hand, and when he glanced down at her, she was grinning, eyes sparkling as she kept peeking, then looking away. At least someone found this whole situation hilarious.

When Fieran finally dared a glance again, Merrik was

picking up Adry's bag as she raced down the steps. "Dacha!"

She flung herself into Dacha's arms and hugged him. Dacha embraced her in return. "Sena. It is good to see you."

"And you." Adry stepped back, straightening her shoulders. "Practice tomorrow morning?"

"Yes." Dacha glanced around, tipped his head, and eased back to the shadows of one of the buildings, followed by Uncle Iyrinder.

Adry turned to where Fieran still held Pip's hand, although Pip was now clutching his fingers hard enough to hurt. With a grin, Adry swept to Pip and gave her a quick hug. "Pip! I'm so happy to finally meet you. Merrik, Mama, Louise, Ellie, and Tryndar told me all about you, and it really was unfair for Fieran to finally bring home a girlfriend when I was gone and couldn't meet you."

"It's…nice to meet you too." Pip stiffly returned Adry's hug with her free arm, her expression that same wide-eyed look she wore when overwhelmed around Dacha.

"I see how it is. No hello for me?" Fieran tried to give Adry an annoyed glare.

"Yes, yes, hello." Adry gave him a light punch on the arm. "Your new girlfriend is much more interesting."

"You've already stolen my best friend. You can't steal my girlfriend away for girl chats or whatever just yet." Fieran worked to hold his frown.

"If I steal Pip for girl time, you can have Merrik back for guy time." Adry made a grand wave at where Merrik stood a few feet behind her.

"The two of you had better not fight over me like one of your childhood toys." Merrik shook his head with an almost resigned shrug of his shoulders. He looked at Pip. "Fair warning. They fight like cats and dogs just as often as they get along."

Fieran exaggerated his offended look as he tugged Pip closer. "I've turned a new, more mature leaf. If I can get along with Rhohen, then surely I can avoid fighting with Adry."

After all, Fieran owed Rhohen one. Perhaps two. First for saving Pip on the battlefield, and second for saving all of Fort Defense from attack.

"You're getting along with Rhohen? Really?" Adry draped an arm over his shoulder before she reached her free hand back to Merrik. "I need to hear all about this."

Merrik took her hand, a soft smile joining the bemusement as he joined them.

With Pip's hand in his, Fieran flung his other arm over Adry's shoulders, Merrik on her other side.

They had a terrible, bloody fight ahead of them. But with the four of them together, Mongavaria didn't stand a chance.

Thanks so much for reading *Winds of Death!* Here's your virtual emotional support chocolate to help with that ending. Things will get better! I promise! If you loved the book, please consider leaving a review on Amazon or Goodreads. Reviews help your fellow readers find books that they will love.

The adventure concludes in *Storm to Victory*, book 5 in the *War of the Alliance* series! Find the book on Amazon today!

If you'd like some War of the Alliance bonus content, including a short story featuring when Farrendel decided to fly to Lt. Rothilion, sign up for my newsletter and download *Soar to Destiny* today!

Sign up for my newsletter now

A downloadable map and Fieran's family trees are available on the Extras page of my website.

If you ever find typos in my books, feel free to message me on social media or send me an email through the Contact Me page of my website.

If you want to learn about all my upcoming releases, sign up for my newsletter, and get a full list of my books, head over to www.taragrayce.com.

ACKNOWLEDGMENTS

Thank you to you readers who keep picking up the books and loving them! Thank you for making my dream of being an author possible!

A very special BIG thank you to my brother Andy for reading this book over for me! Any mistakes portraying the military side of things are my own.

Thank you to my family for all your support and encouragement!

For all my nieces and nephews, I hope you enjoy seeing your names in books!

Thank you to my friends Bri, Paula, and Jill for all the encouragement, support, and years of laughter. For my author friends, but especially Molly, Morgan, Addy, Savannah, and Sierra: Thank you so much for all the encouragement while working on this series! Thanks especially to Hannah for all the elf chats and while-you-are-reading reactions! Especially for this book and a certain kissing moment.

Thank you to Bethany for a beta read/proofread that really helped polish up this book!

Thank you once again to Deborah for a copy edit that was as filled with fangirling as it was with edits. Those copy edits always make my day! And thank you for being a founding member of the Merrik Fan Club!